WITH BLADES SHARPENED
AND SPELLS BREWING

they traverse the many realms of sorcery and adventure—women who live their lives with a blade by their sides, and those who follow the call of magic in their blood. Join these heroic women in the magical and adventurous worlds of thirty-three original stories of exotic lands, dangerous quests, and fearsome magic, including:

"Spirit Singer"—With Bera's father and only protector lost at sea and possibly dead, her family had braved the king's ban and called for a wisewoman to search for him in the spirit world. But would Bera's own ties to her father awake the magic within her and prove not only her father's salvation, but also her own?

"Rusted Blade"—As the chosen defender of his village, it was up to Darb to search out and destroy the sorceress who had bespelled his home. But finding this practitioner of evil witchcraft could prove far more complicated than anything he had bargained for....

"Poisoned Dreams"—Decades ago, Valry's grandfather the king had captured one of the fay—a magical being—and had bound her into the service of the royal family. But things had not gone as the king had planned, and the fay had injured rather than helped his reign. Now would Valry find the power to reverse the evils done both to her family and this magical creature as well?

SWORD
SORCER

SWORD AND SORCERESS XI

AN ANTHOLOGY
OF HEROIC FANTASY

Edited by

Marion Zimmer Bradley

DAW BOOKS, INC.

DONALD A. WOLLHEIM, FOUNDER

375 Hudson Street, New York, NY 10014

ELIZABETH R. WOLLHEIM
SHEILA E. GILBERT
PUBLISHERS

Introduction © 1994 by Marion Zimmer Bradley
Call the Wild Horses © 1994 by Bunnie Bessell
Keepsake © 1994 by Lynn Michals
Spirit Singer © 1994 by Diana L. Paxson
Final Exam © 1994 by Jessica R. Lerbs
The Stratmoor Bear © 1994 by Charley Pearson
Grumble Snoot © 1994 by Vaughn Heppner
Tales © 1994 by Javonna L. Anderson
Maggot's Feast © 1994 by Jo Clayton
Moonriders © 1994 by Lynne Armstrong-Jones
Thief, Thief! © 1994 by Mary Catelli
Healing © 1994 by Hannah Blair
Virgin Spring © 1994 by Cynthia McQuillin
The Haven © 1994 by Judith Kobylecky
Savior © 1994 by Tom Gallier
Bad Luck and Curses © 1994 by Jessie Eaker
The Mistress' Riddle © 1994 by Karen Luk
Rusted Blade © 1994 by Dave Smeds
Images of Love © 1994 by Larry Tritten
A Fate Worse Than Death © 1994 by Diann Partridge
Power Play © 1994 by Sandra Morrese
Fenwitch © 1994 by Sarah Evans
Green-Eyed Monster © 1994 by Vicki Kirchhoff
Snowfire © 1994 by D. Lopes Heald
Ancient Warrior © 1994 by Stephanie Shaver
Barbarian Legacy © 1994 by Lawrence Schimel
Mist © 1994 by Laura J. Underwood
Songhealer © 1994 by Tammi Labrecque
The Sow's Ear © 1994 by Kathy Ann Trueman
Poisoned Dreams © 1994 by Deborah Wheeler
Night-Beast © 1994 by Cynthia Ward
The Gift © 1994 by Rochelle Uhlenkott
The Crystal Casket © 1994 by Kristine Sprunger
Ringed In © 1994 by Mildred Perkins

First Printing, August 1994
1 2 3 4 5 6 7 8 9

CONTENTS

INTRODUCTION

On the 11th volume of this anthology, I found it very hard to get a final lineup, not because of a lack of good stories, but because, on the contrary, of an embarrassment of riches. Even after dismissing the stories by ten-year-olds who didn't own typewriters and sent in handwritten stories—which I couldn't use even if their stories were Nebula quality, which they usually, to put it as charitably as possible, aren't—and throwing out unread the single spaced efforts by people who ought to know better, and ploughing through all the stories about people who are called sorceresses but, for all the magic we ever see, might as well be plumbers or carpenters—well, I'm ranting again.

But if I can't sound off in my own editorials, where can I? A little rant relieves the mind, but even amateurs ought to know a little about the business they're trying to get into. If I had never taken voice lessons and was tone deaf, would I be singing at the Metropolitan Opera or conducting the Philharmonic? So why would a would-be writer fail to learn grammar?

But they do. Some New Age types, with more compassion than brains, insist that everyone has talent and simply needs a chance to release her creativity! Maybe so—in play therapy. But not in my anthologies, thank you.

I can't help thinking how happy I'd have been even with some of the stories I must now reject when this anthology was getting started. I found out with shock and disillusion that many—or even most—editors do not share my delight in slush piles. Where I see all that new unformed talent—

those young, original, undiscovered voices—some editors see only the yahoo who couldn't write his way out of a paper bag.

The only thing that makes me angry is people who send stories to me without having read my current guidelines. So, if you want to submit to me, *first* send a SASE (Self-Addressed Stamped Envelope) to me at PO Box 72, Berkeley, CA 94701, and get the guidelines.

A lot of slush is just that. But sometimes you do find a pearl in all these oysters. I still find plenty—and that's what makes it all worthwhile. While some editors think only of all the frogs they have to kiss, I keep my mind on the rare pearls. Or princes, depending on which metaphor you're using.

And that's what people mean by talking about their sense of wonder. The best editors never lose it—and so I go back for just one more wet smelly oyster. Maybe this one will contain the pearl. And if not this one, maybe the next. Who knows? It might be yours.

CALL THE WILD HORSES
by Bunnie Bessell

Bunnie Bessell is one of those young writers of whom I think with pride as "one of ours," since her first sale was to me, to *Marion Zimmer Bradley's Fantasy Magazine*. One of my chief delights is to discover the new writers who will turn out to have careers as writers—so I'll have something to read when the others are called—as so many of my own long-ago generation—to that great SF Convention in the afterlife. I'm looking out to see so many of my own contemporaries there.

Bunnie Bessell says of herself that she has always been a storyteller. As a child she believed that small creatures lived inside her who came out at night and told their adventures to her two sisters as they huddled under the covers. That's really how every fiction writer I know started. Despite all the New Age stuff about releasing one's own creativity, we all started with some variation of loving "Pretend" more than any other game. Another thing she says rings such a bell that it might have been my own teens. She was "the kind of adolescent who was still playing make-believe while others were discovering boys." I, for instance, was the one who hid in the library while other girls my age were being herded into the gym at noon for mandatory social adjustment—meaning dancing with boys—which may be why schools are in trouble: too much emphasis on social skills instead of reading. At the risk of being thought reactionary, I suggest schools return their emphasis to making the kids literate instead of emphasizing "social adjustment" to such a degree that girls drop out to be married while still illiterate. Bunnie adds that (like me) she wrote her first book in seventh grade and that it was a science fiction thriller. "It now resides in the darkest recess under my bed. Don't we all have one under our beds?"

Well, no; sometimes we drag them out when we're in our forties and rewrite them, and they get nominated for Hugos! Mine did! Maybe yours will. If it's as interesting as this tale of a horse-clan sorceress, it just might.

Bunnie also adds that she collects wind-up toys and, having no children, has decided "to become the world's greatest aunt." She now has the honor of adoring, befriending, and frolicking with eleven marvelous nieces and nephews. One great thing about aunthood, Bunnie: nieces and nephews never—or very seldom—wake you up for a diaper change or a bottle at 3 a.m. You get a lot more sleep—and time to dream up plots—that way.

She's female, 40 something, lives in Arlington, Texas, and is a "dedicated hugger." Long may she hug—and keep on writing.

It took all of Marlee's courage to walk into the circle of the campfire. She didn't look to either side, not wanting to meet the stares of the Clan women, but kept her gaze fixed straight ahead. The chatter of conversation fell silent as she entered.

On the other side of the fire, Hesta stood up and Marlee came to a halt in front of her. Her heart ached at the sight of the older woman. Hesta had been second mother to Marlee since her own mother died many years back. Once, she would have stepped forward to hug Hesta, but she had lost that right twelve months ago.

Sabrine came from behind Marlee, shoved her aside, and stood next to Hesta. "Tell her to leave," she demanded, pointing at Marlee. "She's done enough harm."

Fearing Hesta would send her away, Marlee quickly tossed off her outer cloak and sank to her knees in front of the fire. Underneath she wore only a plain, short tunic of untanned hide.

"I, Marlee, daughter of Quebacc, granddaughter of Iris, great-granddaughter of Leemay, ask to serve the Horse

Clan." She heard grumbled surprise at her words but carefully kept reciting the ritual plea of a novice to join the Callers. "On this the Night of Calling, I will touch the minds of fillies and colts, of mares and of stallions. I will share their thoughts and bring them forth in p–peace," she stumbled over the word.

"I will bid them to live among the People, to serve the Clan and to be one with the Clan. I do this so that the People and the Herd might grow and prosper. I will Call the Wild Horses from the Great Herd and make them gentle."

Then she bowed her head. "I will Call for the Horse Clan if This Leader wills it." She waited, knowing she should not look up until Hesta pronounced her decision.

She had knelt like this five years ago, truly a novice then. Juliane had been by her side. They had been young and full of excitement. Neither doubted that they would be allowed to join the Callers. Both girls came from families strong with the Caller magic. Their acceptance had been quick and their first Calling celebrated happily.

Tonight, though, Marlee knew she gambled desperately. By reverting to a novice, she changed the way Hesta must consider her petition. Hesta couldn't take into account Marlee's experience, not even last year's, but could only weigh her possible benefit to the Clan.

Her ploy forced Hesta to put her personal feelings aside and consider the needs of the People as a whole.

And the Clan's needs were great. The last few years had not gone well for her people. And last year, because of the stampede—the stampede Marlee had caused—no horses had been Called from the Herd. Without horses, they had nothing to trade for supplies or shelter through the winter. They had spent the long, bitter months in tents on the open plains. Many of the youngest and oldest died of starvation or illness.

No one was foolish enough to think they could survive another winter like that. Horses had to be Called from the Herd, and lots of them. And, therefore, every Caller was needed.

"You can't consider her," Sabrine complained. "Not after what she did."

"Leader," Jamine spoke up. "The stampede was an accident. Will we punish Marlee's whole life for an accident?"

Jamine had been one of the few who tried to comfort Marlee after the stampede. Yet Marlee had spurned the woman's attention, as she had turned away from everyone. She lived among the Clan but let no one touch her heart. She could not forgive herself for what had happened; she certainly would not accept anyone else's forgiveness.

"She panicked," Sabrine reminded Hesta. "She lost control and scattered the herd. Fourteen people died."

Marlee flinched at the words. Fourteen lives lost. All because of her. Fourteen gone forever. And a dozen others injured, some crippled for life. For a moment, the guilt overwhelmed her. She had no right to be here.

Then she caught herself and straightened her shoulders. Yes, she had made a mistake. She had lost control and she accepted responsibility for that. But she had not been the only one. Someone else had played a part in the stampede, though only Marlee knew about her. Marlee had to go with the Clan tonight. She had to locate the other woman and stop her before this happened again.

Against all custom, Marlee raised her head and met Hesta's gaze across the fire. She could read no emotions in the Leader's eyes.

"Marlee is an experienced Caller," Jamine continued to argue. "She brought many horses from the Great Herd."

To Marlee's surprise there were murmurs of agreement from the women surrounding her. She saw Hesta's gaze flicker around the camp as if gauging each woman. Her gaze stopped on Sabrine.

Sabrine was among the oldest and most experienced Callers. She consistently Called horses from the Herd, a fact she seldom let anyone forget. Although she could be abrasive, Marlee knew her opinions held weight.

"Look what she did to my daughter," Sabrine said harshly. "And yours. She killed Juliane. Will you let her kill again?"

Marlee saw Hesta flinch at the words and knew she had lost. Hesta would not give her another chance. A part of Marlee knew she did not deserve one.

Thoughts of Juliane clouded her mind, and Marlee fought against the pain that welled within her.

They had been best friends since childhood. Juliane, who had been so funny and vivacious, was a complete contrast to the slower and more thoughtful Marlee. Marlee could not have imagined a life without Juliane. And now the strongest memory she had of her friend was Juliane's crumpled body after the stampede.

Nothing she could do would ever make that image go away.

"And who would be her guide?" Sabrine continued, her voice tight with anger. "No one would be Sight for the likes of her."

Marlee saw a flicker of concern cross Hesta's face. A Caller and her Sight worked very closely. The safety of both women depended on how quickly a Caller and Sight could respond.

Juliane had been Marlee's Sight. Marlee knew Hesta was reluctant to ask someone else to step into the position.

"I don't need a Sight," Marlee said. "I will Call one animal and lay him down at the edge of the Herd."

More timid Callers would occasionally slip into the mind of a horse and lay the animal down to sleep until the Herd had moved on. Normally, Marlee would never have agreed to laying a horse down. She would have been insulted if anyone suggested she did not have the talent to gentle and Call a horse quietly to her side.

But for what she planned to do, she did not need or want anyone to serve as her guide.

"I will be her Sight." A girl a few summers older than Marlee stepped out from among the women. Marlee caught her breath when she saw who it was.

An uncomfortable silence settled over the Clan as the girl came toward Marlee. She walked slowly, dragging her right foot in an awkward gait, a foot crippled in last year's stampede. When she stopped in front of Marlee she held her hands out palms up. "I, Dana, daughter of Sabrine, granddaughter of Lilla, great-granddaughter of Camarre, will be Sight for Marlee. If she will accept me."

Marlee hesitated. She found it difficult even to look at Dana. She was not sure she could walk side by side with her across the plains, much less share what a Caller and Sight must share.

Dana's gaze did not waver from Marlee's. "My hands are not crippled," she said softly for only Marlee to hear. When Marlee winced, she added more gently. "Nor my mind."

Marlee saw something in the other girl's eyes. An anguish she recognized. Marlee might have suffered the

Clan's contempt this last year, but Dana had suffered its pity.

She looked toward Dana's mother. Sabrine's face was tight. It took a second for Marlee to realize that the older woman was glaring at Dana, not Marlee. Sabrine obviously saw Dana as a cripple, useless. How could a mother be so callous toward her own child?

Glancing back at Dana, Marlee knew immediately that the girl was aware of her mother's feelings. Dana was not a strong Caller, and Marlee had heard Sabrine berate her daughter more than once when she came back, empty-handed from a Calling.

Status in the Clan was determined by how many horses one Called from the Herd. A woman who brought a single horse from the Herd each year was considered worthy of the Clan. Those who brought two or more earned high esteem.

Those who brought in none had no honor. Eventually, they were sent to live among the tents of the men.

Now, lamed, Dana's chances of ever bringing back a horse were minimal. And Marlee saw that Sabrine's pride could not accept this failure from her daughter.

As she watched the older girl, another realization dawned on Marlee. Dana would never go to the Herd again unless she went with Marlee. No one else would take a cripple. "I accept Dana as my Sight," she agreed.

"This is ridiculous," Sabrine growled. "Dana will only get hurt again. What good is she?"

Hesta frowned at Sabrine's words. She remained silent for several moments, and Marlee was convinced the decision would go against her.

"Marlee, daughter of Quebacc," Hesta finally said, "Dana, daughter of Sabrine, This Leader accepts your services as Caller and Sight for the Horse Clan."

Marlee stumbled to her feet, hardly believing that Hesta had given her approval. She look hopefully into the older woman's eyes, praying for forgiveness, too.

But Hesta only seemed stern. "You are a novice," she warned. "You will Call one horse from the outer edge of the Herd, where it will be less likely to affect the entire Herd. If the horse you Call gives you difficulty, you will release it."

Marlee nodded numbly, knowing even as she agreed that these were not rules she could obey.

The entire Clan began talking, but Marlee could not tell if most approved or disapproved of Hesta's decision.

Waving them all to silence, Hesta announced, "We must go."

Immediately, the Clan was in motion. A group of young women hurried forward with baskets full of dried horse dung. The Callers and their Sights handed their warm cloaks to the girls and then dusted their bodies and tunics with the powdered manure.

As Marlee waited her turn, she counted the Callers. Only twenty-five. Last year there had been almost forty. Misgivings overwhelmed her. Should she really approach the Herd? What if it happened again? What if she caused another stampede? She had already done so much damage. Did she truly deserve another chance?

Dana touched her shoulder and held out a basket. She took a handful of the manure and rubbed it across Marlee's shoulder and arm. "You are a good Caller," she said reassuringly.

Marlee shook her head, unsure if that was true anymore.

"The Clan needs you," Dana added more firmly. She peered into Marlee's eyes. "We will be a good team, you and I. You'll see."

As Marlee looked at the other girl, she realized that Dana was probably just as frightened as she was. She wondered for a moment at Dana's strength and wondered, too, why she and Dana had never been friends. But she instantly knew the answer. Until last year, Juliane had been her friend. She had needed no other.

She picked up a handful of the manure and, wrinkling her nose at its musty smell, helped dust Dana.

When they were done, the two fell in place behind Hesta, Jamine and the other Callers. In silence, the women left the campfire and headed out across the grasslands.

A full moon cast the plains in crisp white light. Marlee felt her senses heighten as she moved through the tall grass. This was the first new moon of the Growing Season, and the one night of the year when the Great Herd would gather. The only night of the year when horses could be Called.

Memories of Juliane crowded in on her with every step.

A year ago, they had walked here, hand in hand, whispering to each other, stifling giggles of excitement. Could it have only been a year?

They'd had a plan. They intended to Call in three horses that year. It would be quite a feat for a pair so young. If they could do it.

And they almost did.

The first two horses had been located and bound easily. The third horse, a yearling colt, had been frisky and full of mischief.

Marlee was close to exhaustion when she finally had him gentle enough to begin the bonding. Juliane squeezed her hand in encouragement and with a deep breath Marlee began the spell.

Just as she started, another Caller's mind touched hers.

The contact did not concern Marlee. Callers drifting through the Herd occasionally crossed one another.

Withdraw, she warned gently so as not to frighten the colt. *This horse is claimed.*

To her surprise, the other Caller did not pull back. Instead, the other mind began to cast a binding spell on the colt.

This one is mine, she said more firmly, pushing her own mind against the other. The other mind was fresher than hers, obviously not tired by the grueling time it took to gentle a horse.

Whoever this was, she was either a weak Caller or just lazy. She was trying to steal Marlee's horse after all the hard work had been done. Marlee knew she could not give in. Once a horse was bound, the feel of his mind changed completely. Even though Marlee had spent enormous energy gentling this animal, she would never be able to recognize him if the other woman bound him.

She tried to identify the woman. But she could not recognize anything in the other Caller's essence. *Go away,* she snapped.

Still the other Caller persisted.

This was hard to believe. Of course, Marlee had heard stories of Callers snatching a horse from another Caller. But that had been when different Clans fought over the same herd. A Caller did not steal from her own Clan.

The other Caller was still weaving her spell, and Marlee

felt the colt being drawn away from her. Desperately, she cast her own magic, fighting to pull the colt back. He snorted at the strife within his mind. Marlee could feel his fear building. Still, she refused to give in. This horse was hers. She pushed harder, trying to force the other woman out of the horse's head.

Suddenly, the young horse jerked away from both of them. He reared, pawing the air.

Then, Marlee did the very worst thing a Caller could do. She opened her eyes.

Instantly, not just the colt, but the other two horses bound to Marlee saw through her human eyes as well as their own. The result was complete terror. They whinnied with fright and bolted, and with them the entire herd, hundreds of horses, stampeded into flight.

Marlee threw herself to the ground, rolling into a low spot and covered her head with her arms. Horses ran right over her. They pelted her with sod and turf. It took forever before the thunder of the hoofs faded.

When it was safe, Marlee scrambled up. Juliane lay a few feet away, her body twisted and broken.

Crying out, Marlee dropped to the ground and cradled her friend. "No, Juliane, no. Please no." Rocking the body, she wept uncontrollably. All around her others were crying out in pain and loss.

Finally she looked up to find Hesta kneeling beside her. "I opened my eyes," she confessed. "It is my fault. I killed Juliane."

She saw Hesta's look shift from disbelief to anger and then to hatred. The older woman gathered Juliane up and carried her away, never looking back.

Marlee stumbled as the memory of that night overcame her.

Dana touched her arm to steady her and Marlee jerked away. She glanced toward the other girl and Dana caught her hand, forcing her to stop.

"Last year," Dana said softly, "before the stampede, someone tried to steal your horse, didn't she?"

"You?"

"No. Not me." Dana shook her head quickly. "But the year before last, someone stole my horse. And the year before that, too."

"What?"

"Another Caller came and took the horses I had gentled before I could bind them."

"Twice?" Marlee asked.

Dana nodded.

"Why didn't you tell someone? Hesta ..."

"No one would have believed me," Dana replied.

Marlee started to disagree with her. Of course, someone would have believed. Then she paused, considering. Would Marlee have believed? After all, Dana had never been a strong Caller. If she had suddenly said someone was stealing her horses, would she have been believed? No. It would not have been accepted.

"Why didn't *you* tell someone?" Dana asked Marlee.

She looked away from the other girl. Why hadn't she? At first, it had been her grief. For several weeks she'd hardly spoken to anyone. She'd been so numb with guilt and the loss of Juliane that she could think of nothing else.

Then, too, she hoped the other Caller would come forward and admit her part in the tragedy. By the time Marlee realized the other woman was not going to confess, it was too late. Too much time had passed. "They wouldn't have believed me either."

"I would have," Dana said. She looked away her face flushed with embarrassment. "I—I didn't have the strength to stop her from stealing my horses. I didn't know how to fight."

"I fought," Marlee replied a knot forming in her throat. "And Juliane died."

They stood side by side, neither knowing how to ease the other's pain. Then Dana nodded toward the Callers who were leaving them behind, and they started walking again.

"What are you going to do?" Dana asked.

"Find the other Caller."

"How?"

"I'm not sure," Marlee said. "Do you know who it was? Did you recognize her?"

Dana shook her head.

"I think if I can touch her mind again, I can learn who she is," Marlee told her.

"And stop her?" Dana asked.

"Yes." At least, she hoped she could.

Dana said nothing for several minutes. Then she whispered, "So you won't Call any horses this year?"

"No," Marlee replied, and she saw the regret in the other girl's eyes. She turned away from her.

Eventually, the Callers came to a stop on a ridge.

Below them, the Great Herd grazed in a shallow valley.

Marlee looked down on them and caught her breath at the sight. Hundreds of horses: bays and duns, grays and paints, mares with their foals by their side and young colts flirting with quick-hoofed fillies. So many horses that the Herd stretched as far as the eye could see. They grazed peacefully, chopping at the green grass, their coats gleaming in the moonlight, totally unconcerned by the silent, still women standing on the ridge.

Instantly, she yearned to be among the horses. To stroke their soft muzzles and comb her fingers through thick manes. She wanted to slide her hands around a strong neck, pull herself onto a broad back and run. Run with the sound of hoofs pounding in her ears and her heart pounding to the same cadence.

She felt Dana move closer to her, and when she glanced sideways, she saw the same yearning in the other girl's face. They smiled at each other and then looked toward Hesta.

The Leader lifted her hand and signaled the Calling to begin.

Slipping her hand within Marlee's, Dana tapped onto her palm in the code the Callers used, "How will you look for her?"

Marlee shrugged. "I'll just drift into as many horses as I can, hoping to find her," she tapped back.

They stared at each other a moment, both aware that it wasn't much of a plan.

"You can do it," Dana signed encouragement.

With a nod, Marlee closed her eyes and deepened her breathing. She dropped herself gradually into the trance. As darkness settled around her, she lost touch with who she was, where she was. Her feet no longer touched the ground, her hand no longer curled around Dana's.

When nothing existed, she beckoned the magic. She drew essence from the moist, loamy earth, from the green stems of grass, the cool breeze and delicate touch of moonlight on her face. She pulled it all together and became a part of it. For a moment, she was everything and nothing. She drifted.

The power gathered within her, and the vibrant life-force of the Herd drew her. She moved forward, melding with the first horse she met.

A young stallion. She felt the muscles in his shoulders ripple beneath her skin. He paced with power and grace. Neck arched and tail flung high, he circled the edge of the herd, desiring the mares, but not quite courageous enough to challenge the herd leader. Marlee shared his frustration. He kicked up his heels and loped across the valley, running in an absolute need just to be in motion.

When Dana stroked Marlee's palm, calling her back to herself, she found it hard to let go of the stallion.

Reluctantly, she began her search. She drifted into the mind of an older mare. Another Caller was already there, binding the horse to herself. *Withdraw,* the Caller said instantly, and Marlee withdrew. This was not the mind she had met before.

She drifted on, slipping through the minds of one horse after another, making no attempt to gentle them or Call them, only to touch and move on.

Unexpectedly, she slipped into the mind of a horse she knew. She and Juliane had Called this mare four years ago. She had been young then, barely past weaning. The two of them had trained her, and kept her for two years. When it finally came time, they could not find it in their hearts to trade her. Instead, they turned the young horse back to the Herd as a breeder.

Marlee could hardly believe she'd found the mare again. *Windsong?* The mare reacted instantly; her head came up and she looked around, as if expecting to see Marlee. *No, I'm not here. At least, not physically.* She could sense Windsong's delight at meeting her again. She blended with the horse's mind. Something nudged her side and Marlee extended her consciousness to touch a filly. *You have a baby.* The little horse snorted at Marlee's touch, her small ears perked forward.

Marlee soothed her. *She's a jewel. That's what we'll call her, Jewel.*

She stopped herself. What was she doing? Naming this filly. She couldn't Call Windsong or her filly. She'd probably never see them again. She needed to get back to doing what she had come to do.

Take care of yourself, pretty ones. As she withdrew, she could still sense Windsong looking around for her.

Marlee's legs and back ached. She felt as if she'd been standing in the same position for hours, yet had no way of knowing how long it had really been.

Drifting, she slipped in and out of one mind after another, finding no Callers as she went.

She paused once, when she touched the mind of an older mare. The horse's personality was so very pleasant that Marlee could not pass her by. When she finally moved on, she regretted her indulgence.

Her head throbbed, and her knees were beginning to shake. She was close to the end of her energy.

Dana's arm slipped around her waist, offering her support. Marlee immediately jerked straight, not wanting to burden the crippled girl.

"Lean on me," Dana signaled.

But Marlee couldn't bring herself to rely on the other girl. Standing as straight as possible, she sent her consciousness out again, touching a dozen minds with no results. Time seemed to be stretching, and Marlee began to fear that her search would be futile.

The mind of another horse attracted her, a young colt, so full of playfulness that he made Marlee smile. She melded with the horse momentarily, tasting his essence. The horse snorted as Marlee joined her.

This one would be a handful to train, Marlee told herself, but in the end he'd be worth the trouble. For an instant, Marlee was tempted to bind the colt to her.

Then she felt Dana's quick tapping on her hand. "What are you doing?"

"What do you mean?"

"I thought you weren't Calling," Dana signaled. "Two mares have walked up. They are sniffing you and—"

"What?" Marlee demanded.

"Two mares have—" Dana began to sign again.

"Does one of them have a filly?" Marlee asked.

"Yes."

Marlee didn't understand. She had not Called. At least, not intentionally. Yet somehow she had done so. This had to be Windsong and the older mare she had stopped to stroke. She felt a flush of excitement. She had Called and bound, without even planning to. Marlee had to force herself not to laugh out loud, and somehow she sensed Dana stifling happy laughter, too.

Another mind pressed on Marlee's and she froze. The colt she had just touched was frightened. Almost frantic. Marlee had tasted this panic before. Two Callers were struggling over the mind of the young horse.

Her heart thumped with fear. Windsong, her filly, and the older mare were bound to her. If she tried to stop the struggle, these horses would become frightened, too.

Even worse, she was near exhaustion. She barely had the energy to stand. What could she do? She needed to break the bonds with the horses she'd Called. Or weaken it.

An idea came to her and she acted without pausing to think. She drew in the minds of the horses she'd Called. She collected them, stroked and petted them, binding them even more tightly.

Then in her mind's eye, she pictured Dana. She showed the horses a thin girl, with short-cropped hair and a crippled foot. She showed them Dana as a place of safety, a giver of food and shelter. Someone who would scratch their itchy spots and offer treats of carrots and alfalfa. She presented Dana as everything that was good and comforting and secure, and as surely as she had bound them to herself she bound them to Dana.

"What?" Dana tapped on her hand. "They're nuzzling me now?"

"I can't explain," Marlee told her. "I've bound them to you. Take care of them."

"Marlee?"

"Just do it."

Marlee sensed Dana responding automatically. She knew the older girl could not use a full trance to hold the horses. She would have to employ the light trance that was used later in training. Marlee hoped that she had smoothed the way for Dana by introducing the horses to her. She hoped it was enough, but she couldn't wait to be sure. As she felt Dana reaching out, enfolding the horses, she pulled away.

Once she put distance between herself and the horses she had Called, she reached toward the frantic colt.

She slipped into the horse's mind and chaos surrounded

her. For a moment she shared the terror. She wanted to run. Run fast and far.

She shook herself. The animal was almost blind with fright. Two minds battled angrily to possess him. Marlee could barely sort the Callers from within the fear of the horse.

Withdraw! she ordered forcefully.

No! they both replied.

Marlee was at a moment's loss. *The Herd will stampede,* she warned, hoping the threat would get them to retreat. For an instant, she didn't think it had worked. Then suddenly, one mind was gone.

She was left with the other Caller.

This was the mind she had met last year.

Who are you? Marlee demanded.

The other made no reply. Instead, almost casually, the Caller began to bind the still agitated horse.

How dare you! Marlee shouted.

The Caller ignored her.

Unless Marlee got the woman to speak, she realized she had no chance of identifying her. She wasn't going to be able to stop this woman. Coming tonight had been useless. As hard as she tried, she was going to fail.

Frustration and anger flared within Marlee. Instantly, her feelings washed over into the mind of the horse.

Suddenly the colt was struggling again, close to frantic.

Marlee froze. Not again! Another panic. Another stampede. The Tribe would be caught unaware. Marlee's fears flooded her. She was unable to think. Unable to move. She clung desperately to Dana's hand.

You must be calm.

Dana's unruffled tone as she gentled their horses drifted through to Marlee. The other girl's tranquil strength gave Marlee the encouragement she needed.

Yes, calm, she agreed. She took a deep breath. She had told Hesta she would lay a horse down and now she would. She focused her energy. *Calm,* she told the colt now. *Be quiet, young one. No one will hurt you.* The horse's fear ebbed slightly.

She brought all her power to play. She paid no attention to the other Caller, concentrating entirely on the horse. *Be still. You are safe.* Marlee envisioned a wide pasture with gently rolling hills. She called up warm sunshine and a soft, pleasant breeze.

The colt began to breathe easier.

It was working. Marlee added sweet green grass to the picture and told the colt his stomach was full. His head began to droop.

On the edge of her mind, Marlee realized with surprise that the other Caller was tiring, too, becoming as sleepy as the horse. It had never occurred to Marlee that she could reach past a horse into the mind of a person. Now she doubled her effort, expanding her range, deliberately including the Caller. *You're sleepy. It's been a long day. Lie down. Lie down in the grass and rest.*

The horse sagged to his knees and then rolled with a grunt to his side. The Caller's mind went with him, trapped within the horse's, sound asleep.

For a brief second, Marlee stood dazed by what she had achieved.

"We have to leave the Herd," Dana signaled. "Right now! A Caller is on the ground."

"Who?" Marlee demanded.

"Sabrine." Dana hurried on. "Yvonne will stay with her. Hesta will send help later."

Suddenly, Marlee felt Dana stiffen.

"Sabrine is the one, isn't she?" Without waiting for Marlee's reply, Dana began trying to tug her hand free. "She's been the one all of these years."

Marlee refused to let go. She couldn't think of what to say to Dana, how to comfort her, but she wasn't going to let her run away.

"I should have known," Dana tapped harshly against Marlee's palm. "Sabrine always needed to be better than everyone else. But she was getting old. She was losing her ability to Call. So she stole someone else's strength!"

Marlee sensed a confusion of emotions sweeping through Dana—disbelief, anger, grief.

"Sabrine didn't care who she hurt." Dana clenched Marlee hand. "She didn't care who."

Not even her own daughter. Dana did not say it, but Marlee knew she was thinking the words.

"She didn't know it was you," she tapped gently.

For a moment, Dana remained tense, her hand tight within Marlee's. Then she eased a little. "I won't cry. Not for Sabrine." She took a deep breath. "What will happen to her?"

Hesitantly, Marlee replied, "I will tell Hesta now. And if she believes me ..."

"She will."

"Then Sabrine will go before the Clan Council for judgment. She will probably be banished from the Clan. She will never Call again."

Dana was silent for a while and then she tapped, "That's just." She took another deep breath and gave Marlee a gentle squeeze. "Take back control of our horses, Marlee. We need to lead them away from the Herd."

At first Marlee wasn't sure she could. Her feet felt leaden and her mind foggy. It took enormous effort just to locate the minds of the horses. Somehow she collected them, then soothed each and bid them follow her. To her surprise, she found Dana's mind still linked lightly with hers.

"We're going," Dana told her and then began to guide Marlee forward.

Dana led her forward slowly, measuring her pace to Marlee's faltering gait. Still exhaustion betrayed her. Marlee tripped and then stumbled almost to her knees on the uneven ground.

Instantly, Dana caught her, sliding under her arm to keep Marlee on her feet. Marlee tried to pull away, tried to regain her balance.

"Trust me," Dana whispered fiercely. "I am your Sight."

For a second, Marlee resisted, then she gave in; perhaps, finally, she could let someone help her.

Dana was stronger than Marlee expected. She had no trouble supporting Marlee's weight. And, to her surprise, Marlee found it easy to match the other girl's limping gait.

As they moved away from the Herd, Marlee felt the horses following without hesitation.

After all, she reminded herself, they were bound not only to her but to Dana. And this bonding would never be broken.

KEEPSAKE
by Lynn Michals

Lynn Michals says that she is female and lives in Baltimore with two bright blue parakeets and a significant other who is about to move to Washington, DC, while she is moving to North Carolina to teach at Wake Forest University—which, as modern commuting relationships go, is "practically next door."

She has spent her last six years doing grad work in Baltimore and because of the current recession has spent a lot of time job-hunting and even went so far as to consider moving to Australia. She says the best thing about imaginary worlds is the ease with which they can be carried around with one; whatever she had to leave behind, she could still pack all her imaginary universes and not pay any extra weight charges. I don't know if she or her two parakeets, to say nothing of the significant other, would like Australia—don't parakeets come from there?—but it's pretty far to pay mail charges on manuscripts, and she seems to have plenty of them, too.

What I wrote on this, after choosing it, for a mnemonic for the introduction, was "very emotional." She says she's spending this summer in a windowless cubicle finishing her dissertation. I sometimes feel as if I'm the only person around without an advanced degree—even my secretary has a Master's degree in computers, which comes in very handy when my computer goes down or I do something stupid and lose half a day's work.

"I t'll never work," said Fel, with the cold certainty of a licensed seer. "First, you're not properly trained, and second, you'd never go through with it. What's Ori to you, that you'd risk your lives and your sanity to save her?"

"Listen, witch, if you don't know the Warden better than *that* after three months in her household—" Armsmaster Per began, then swallowed her fury and started again. "Child, you belong to the holding of Ash now, whether any of us like it or not. You're family. So Warden Ismail won't let your friend die—and if the Warden's going to hell and back, I'm going with her."

"I will try your plan, Armsmaster Per," Fel said, a shadow of hope stirring behind her cold eyes.

That hope nearly died when Fel met the half-grown boy who was to guard her body while she was out of it. Per and Sa Ismail seemed to trust Nil, but then Per and Sa Ismail had spent the past year howling battle cries, lopping raiders to pieces to defend the people of Ash whenever peace negotiations with the borderers broke down. Fresh from the coolly arcane discipline of Para House, Fel had considerably less practice than they at letting her life hang by a shoestring.

Thirteen-year-old Nil frowned with concentration, making contact with the three bodies that would be left behind with him in the dusty records room while their inhabitants fled to the shadow lands. Sa Ismail took the Weaver's position; Fel was surprised and reassured by her skill. Sa had eyes like night, skin like gold, and an effortless strength that defied all simile. She spun out a thread of trust between herself and Per, then reached for Fel's bright, disciplined mind, weaving it into her web.

And the thing was done.

The three stood hand in hand in the shadow lands, the shape of their souls free of their bodies' disguises.

Armsmaster Per was a gaunt young refugee with eyes like a prowling cat's—the desperate, dangerous child she still became in her nightmares. Sa Ismail was herself, as she would look in ten or twenty years, scarred by battle and by the labor of carrying her people through famine and fire. And Fel was a white-robed novice, shining and eager.

Without a word, the three set off through the gray spaces, walking toward the first of the walls that circled the heart of the shadow lands where a young woman lay dying. The shadows were always hungry; to steal a soul away from that world's greedy heart they would have to risk being devoured themselves, risk being held there forever by what they most feared.

They walked through fire and flood, across rivers of shattered glass and over mountains of burning rock, until they reached a perfectly ordinary wooden door, set in a gray stone wall that stretched away to infinity.

"Whatever happens to me, keep going. Remember that you have to save Ori, so she can save us all," Sa ordered, stepping up to that door like a fighter determined to get an unequal battle over and done with.

"Idiot," Per said, shoving Sa aside and knocking on the door herself. "Did you really think I could watch the dead go at you? Have the decency to let them take me first."

The door opened, revealing a well-dressed gentleman with a black hole where his face should have been. Per had forgotten the face, but she remembered those smooth hands, hands that had held her down and forced her child's body to bear a world of pain.

"How dare you call yourself an Armsmaster?" a cool voice asked. "The Warden took your oath as a joke, gutterbrat."

Sa's protest rang out like a battle cry, but Per had already stabbed the gentleman through the heart—they were locked together, pale as shades and still as death.

Fel tackled Sa and held her back from her friend, knowing that any one who touched Per would be caught in the shadow of her grief.

Sa ran on with Fel to the second wall, weeping, charging the leviathans and sphinxes that blocked their way, the griffins and basilisks that crawled toward them, hissing of despair and death. In the distance, over the wall, they could see shadowy towers and battlements—the top of a gray ghost of Para.

Sa Ismail drew her sword and slashed her way through the monstrosities that crowded round the door in that second wall, then pounded on it with the hilt of her knife.

"Damn you—take me this time, and me alone!" she yelled.

And a middle-aged woman stood before them, unarmed, blood soaking through a gash in her plain linen shirt.

"Daughter, have you betrayed my trust—are you trying to make peace with the border filth that murdered me?" she asked.

Sa gave a wordless cry of pain and dropped her weapons; she threw herself into her dead mother's arms, freezing into a shadow in that shadow's embrace.

Fel ran on, into the ghost of the massive house she had known so well. She flew through stone hallways that were both familiar and unfamiliar, empty of the novices and mages and seers who brought them to life in the other world. On the topmost floor she found Ori—not Ori as Fel had last known her, a wide-eyed seventeen-year-old, but Ori as she would be in future years, if she lived to become what she had been born to be: Archmage. She was like a sword blade, or the fire at the heart of a star, tall, proud, and perfectly still.

"This is what you could not face—what you would not let me become," Ori said.

"But I couldn't stop you," Fel protested. "When our Weaver said I was holding you back, I left Para. I went all the way to the other end of Imlay, I contracted out to the god-forsaken Eastern Provinces! I started a whole new life for myself."

"You left in anger—and you left your heart behind," Ori accused. "I carried the weight of your keepsake, too young to free myself. And when it grew too heavy to bear, I lay down and died at the crossroads of my life."

"No, I'll take it back, I'll let you go on!" Fel shouted. "There must still be time. Listen, Or, I didn't want you to forget me, but I never meant to hurt you. I've been an idiot, and I'm sorry."

Ori smiled. She stretched out hands that Fel could not touch, holding a gift she could not see.

"Take back your heart, love. I set you free to love your new life—as you've freed me to be what I must," she said. "But who are those others, in pain outside?"

"My family," Fel said, finding the right word without thinking. "They brought me here to find you; now we need your help to get back."

Ori smiled again, and the staff she held glowed like a streak of blue fire, the one solid, real thing in that shadowy world.

Thirteen-year-old Nil burst into tears as the three bodies

that had sat perfectly still as the sun set and the moon rose finally stirred, life coming back into their eyes.

"I did my best—I kept everyone breathing. But then you were freezing to death, Aunt Sa, and the Armsmaster was fading, too, and I couldn't find you at all," Nil cried, exhausted and unstrung. "I couldn't get you back till the lady helped me, the lady all on fire. She was right here—where'd she go?"

"Back home to Para House, where she belongs," said Fel.

She turned to face Sa and Per, her eyes alive with recovered warmth.

"Ori's found her way home," Fel repeated. "And if you two will still have me, I've come home as well."

SPIRIT SINGER
by Diana L. Paxson

Diana Paxson lives about a mile away from me in Berkeley—which makes it easy for her to drop off manuscripts
for these anthologies. She says modestly of her own writing that she "married into the job." She married my brother
Don, and after finding out that my two brothers Don and
Paul, not to mention me, had all sold commercial fiction,
she probably decided that if we could do it, anyone could.

But it's not quite that simple. About ninety per cent of
the manuscripts I get from strangers are one-timers; which
means after one rejection they disappear into the wood-
work and are never heard from again. (I wonder: If they
can't stand the heat, what are they doing in the kitchen?)
The first experience of every writer is rejection, and if they
don't want to stick it out, they'd do better to take up knitting
if they want a hobby.

After displaying the necessary blend of sensitivity and
rhinoceros hide, which is probably the one indispensable
characteristic for surviving those early rejections everybody
gets, Diana became one of the very few writers whose
work I personally find very readable. Her "Shanna" stories
have appeared in almost every one of the ten previous
volumes of this anthology; and I'm far from alone in liking
them. One of her novels, *The White Raven,* has achieved
hardcover publication—it is about the Arthurian mythos—
and was one of the few books for which I was willing to
write a cover quote. (Have you any idea how many books
on that subject I receive in the mail every year asking for
cover quotes?) More recently, she has been working on

two trilogies: *Wodan's Children (The Wolf and the Raven, Dragons of The Rhine),* and the chronicles of Fionn Mac-Cumhal (with Adrienne Martine-Barnes). If you haven't read Diana's other books, look them up in *Books in Print:* they're good.

So good, in fact, that when I decided to write the story mentioned at the end of *Mists of Avalon*—about Roman Britain and the Druid priestess Eilan—it was Diana I chose to collaborate with me on it. Because of marketing decisions, Viking decided my name alone would sell better— I'm not sure why—but here among friends, so to speak, I'm happy to acknowledge Diana's very knowledgeable help and input. It should be out in April 1994; look for *The Forest House.*

Diana has done teaching of English as a second language and is the mother of two grown sons—who were, like mine, very young when she started writing. The older, Ian, is now in college, and the younger, Robin, somewhat disabled, lives away from home in a residential facility. Time, as I become more aware every year, flies. It still seems so many of these little people should be just toddling, and they're in college. I guess that's how one knows one's growing old—or at least that time continues to pass.

The cows had gotten up onto the north slope of the hill above the farmstead, where a little snow still clung and the juiciest grasses grew. From the meadow above the barley field, Bera could hear the lead cow's bell. She tore her gaze from the longship that was slowly beating across the chill waters of the fjord and stared at the granite slopes it reflected. But her thoughts were still with the ship. It must be the one they were expecting, the one that was bringing the seeress to Bjornhall to tell them if its master still lived.

But whatever else was happening, Bera had to get the cows home. She let her spirit flow outward on the sigh as she gazed at the pine-studded heights. Time slowed around her, and in the stillness it became easy to see the tip of a horn and dark, coarse-haired shapes moving against the trees. For a moment she was aware of herself and the cattle and the earth and sky as one unity, then with a jerk she came back to ordinary awareness. It would be a hard climb to come to the herd, and she had trudged from garth to hill too many times already. But the only skill for which folk had ever praised her was her singing. Bera took a deep breath, tipped back her head, and let her throat open to the harsh wordless harmonies of the ancient cattle call.

The sound, pitched to carry across fjords and mountains, rose hauntingly in the still blue air, and her soul went with it. *"Come to me,"* came the message, *"and you will have clear water to drink. Come home and I will release the milk from your aching udders. Come to me, come to me—"* The cows heard her. Bera paused, listening, as they lowed in harmony.

Why don't you get moving, then? she thought impatiently, glancing back down at the thickly thatched buildings of the farmstead that nestled on a shelf of level ground above the fjord. The ship had almost reached the landing; its striped sail shivered a little as it turned. *Don't make me come after you!* The milk cows that were kept at the garth even in summer had been Bera's charge almost since she could toddle, but at times they were as obstinate as if the trolls had bewitched them. Certainly it seemed so today!

Then the lowing began again, louder, and old Red-ears, the bell-cow, pushed through the stunted pines and began to make her deliberate way down the path. Bera could hear shouts from below. The ship had grounded and they would be bringing the wisewoman and her companions ashore. She was called Groa the Vœlva, and she traveled about the countryside, seeing past and future for the people with *seidh* magic. Once, there had been many of her kind, attended by companies of youths and maidens, but since the kings had begun to force folk to follow the White Christ, they grew few. Yet when folk were sorely troubled, they still braved the kings' ban to summon them. But Bjornhall was only a small place; there had never been any reason for a seeress to come there.

It does not matter if I am there to welcome the Vœlva, Bera told herself, blinking back tears. *I would not get near enough to really see her anyway. Arin will greet her as if he were master here already, and Thorhild will conduct her to the hall. They have no need for me.*

If her father had been there, it might have been different. He had always been kind to the dark-haired child his Irish captive had borne to him. But Thorhild had made it abundantly clear just how unneccessary to the household she felt her husband's bastard daughter to be.

If my father does not return, will they marry me off to the first man who offers a few cows or declare me unfree and sell me as a thrall? Her stepmother, Thorhild, could do it. A year and a half had passed since Steinbjorn Sweinsson and his oldest boy had sailed down the fjord to go a-viking, and there had been no word of them, no one who could say whether they were captives in some foreign land or feasting with Ran at the bottom of the sea. *Oh, my father, where are you now?* her spirit cried. *Have you abandoned me?*

But if his family had known where Steinbjorn was now, they would not have summoned the Vœlva to the farm.

By the time Bera got the cows down from the mountain and finished milking them, the long dusk of spring was beginning to fade. She came up from the byre with the pannikins of milk suspended from a yoke across her shoulders and found the garth buzzing like a hive.

"Where is the wisewoman?" she asked Finn the thrall.

"In by the hearth, with the woman who sings the sacred songs for her journeying." He added another stick of wood to his load and lifted it.

"Will they be doing the Seidh-seeing tonight?"

"Oh, no," he replied. "The Vœlva says she must stay a night here first, to make herself known to the spirits. And she must have a meal of the hearts of every kind of beast we have—the Lady was not best pleased to hear that." He grinned sourly, and Bera nodded. Without Steinbjorn's generosity to balance her, Thorhild was one who would have hoarded the sunlight, as the saying was, could she have found a coffer to put it in.

"But Arin said she must have whatever she asks for!" he went on, and Bera nodded once more. Her half brother had been lording it over the household as if he were certain of his inheritance already. But he dared not appear too eager to assume that his father and older brother would never return.

"There you are, you lazy slut!" Thorhild's voice rasped across her thoughts. "Get that milk to the dairy before it sours!"

Bera began to move, but not quickly enough to avoid the flick of a rope's end across the back of her legs. *It's your tongue that will sour it, old woman,* she thought as she maneuvered through the tumult. She could still hear Thorhild berating Finn as she entered the cool darkness of the dairy and set down her load.

By the time Bera finished her work and went inside, their visitor was already hidden behind the curtains of the boxbed at the head of the hall. Haki, the spakona's ginger-haired manservant, was still awake, laughing with some of the other men beside the hearth, but what could she ask him?

"Is it true that the Vœlva can call storms?" *"Is it true that she can take the shape of a mare, or a seal, or an owl?"* He was bound to say it was so. If they had not believed the woman could do wonders, she would not be here. Bera would have to wait until the next day to see her, that was all.

But as it happened, it was not quite the morrow when they met. Bera had risen in the still hour just before the dawning to go to the privies. She was returning when she saw that the horse trough had grown a humped shadow and stopped short, her fingers flickering in a sign of warding. Still as the figure was, she sensed power in it, like the force she felt in the troll-rock by the stream.

"Do you think to banish me? Your master would not thank you, after all the trouble he has been at to fetch me here...." The voice was not loud, but it carried like the sighing of a distant wind.

Bera blinked. "Arin is my brother—my half brother—" she said stupidly, understanding that what she had sensed was the wisewoman's magic. It reminded her of the atmosphere that sometimes clung around Thorhild, but in this woman it was a clear glow. It was the Vœlva's *hamr,* her spirit shape. She blinked again, glimpsing for a moment not a woman but a great gray owl sitting there.

"Forgive me for disturbing you." Bera knew she should go back inside, but her heart was thumping too furiously. An opportunity like this would not come again. "Could you not sleep? I could warm a little milk for you—"

"In a new place I never sleep more than a few hours

at a time. I came out on purpose to chart the daymark of dawn."

"The sun rises there." Bera pointed across the fjord. "Just beside the crag where the troll—" She stopped abruptly.

"Where the troll-kin are dwelling?" The wisewoman's voice held laughter. "I do not doubt it. But how did you know?"

"I don't—" Bera whispered, "No one else sees them. But when I was little, I glimpsed lights there sometimes. Do not tell Thorhild I said so, please!"

"Why, do you fear she would not believe you?" asked the seeress.

No, thought Bera, *I am afraid she would.* She had learned early that her father's wife, with her herblore and her little witcheries, wanted no rivals in power. Her own mother had been a woman of Ireland, and very beautiful. The folk of the farm had credited her with mighty magic. Bera had often wondered if it were true, or whether folk simply assumed that a fair woman who sang in a strange tongue as she combed her hair by the fire must be skilled in sorcery. If so, neither magic nor Steinbjorn's love had saved her from the wasting sickness that took her life away. If it *had* been a sickness. Folk told stories about Thorhild, too. . . .

Bera shuddered, remembering, and looked up at the crag, and her breath caught, for the sky behind it had brightened, and suddenly the rocks were edged with gold. And for a moment, then, it seemed to her that a veining of brightness spread through the cliff face, and she could see a doorway outlined there. Then the sun lifted above the ridge, and dazzled, she looked away.

But somewhere close by she heard a soft singing. The Vœlva was praying, bending in homage to the rising sun. By the time she stood up again, Bera could hear folk stirring inside the hall, and a mournful lowing came from the byre. She sighed and started to turn away.

"Wait!" The older woman held out one hand. Her face was still shadowed by the shawl, but Bera had the impression of features whose beauty had been worn away by time as water smoothes stone. "What is your name?"

"They call me Bera," she answered. "But I must go now. The cows—"

"Was it you, then, bear-child, whose calling I heard from the fjord? You have a lovely voice, child."

"My father thought so—" Bera pulled her own shawl over her head to hide her tears, and ran for the byre.

That day was a strange one. Even the wind had dropped as if the world were holding its breath, waiting for what the night would bring. Down by the stand of birches that overlooked the water, the men were lashing a seidh platform together out of saplings. The sound of their axes came clearly on the still air. The Vœlva wandered about the farmstead, wrapped in her blue cloak and leaning on a staff that was carved with runes and set with jet and amber and rock crystal that glimmered in the sun. When noon came, she went to the mound where Steinbjorn's parents had been buried and lay down upon it as if she were listening.

That day Bera kept the cattle in the home meadow, astonished that Thorhild did not order her away. But as the day wore on, it became clear that the mistress of Bjornhall had other concerns. Working in the cheese shed, Bera heard raised voices outside and realized that her stepmother and half brother were arguing.

"You fool, cannot you see that this is a woman of power? You were mad to bring her here!"

"We have to know," came Arin's reply.

"Do we? It seemed to me that we were doing well enough before. With each moon that passes, folk grow more used to the idea that you are master here."

"But if my father should suddenly return?"

"He will not—" Thorhild's voice sank and Bera strained to hear.

"Then why do you fear what the wisewoman may say?" There was a murmur from the woman, and when Arin spoke again, it seemed to Bera that his voice held fear. "Do what you will, then. I cannot stop you. . . ."

She heard gravel crunch as he strode away and crouched down behind the churn lest Thorhild should look in and see her there.

Only a little time had passed when her stepmother summoned her to carry a beaker of ale to the wisewoman, but the manservant Haki laughed and told her to save herself the trouble, for Groa would take nothing but spring water until after she had done her magic. It seemed to Bera that

Thorhild's face, always florid, flushed even redder when she heard this, but after a moment her anger seemed to pass and she told Bera to take the food instead to the Vœlva's singing-woman, who was telling tales of her journeys with the seeress to the other women of the household as they worked at their spinning in the shade of the overhang outside the hall.

After that, Thorhild had other tasks for her. It was not until the sun was sinking that Bera began to understand that Arin had not won his argument with his mother after all. For when she returned after the evening milking, she learned that the singing-woman had spent the afternoon retching until she could hardly speak. She would sing no spirit songs this evening, that was certain, if, indeed, she ever sang again.

"A dreadful thing," said Thorhild, tucking a stray wisp of gray hair beneath her headwrap, "and after you have come all this way! But clearly wyrd has spoken, and we will have to wait to learn the will of the gods." She shook her head sadly, and her women murmured in sympathy. But Arin was frowning, and Bera, remembering what she had overheard, realized suddenly that Thorhild was not sorry at all.

Had she poisoned the woman? It was quite possible, and it seemed to Bera that Arin knew it.

"No—" Groa's low voice brought them all to silence. Now, the features that had seemed kindly looked hewn from stone. "The spirits wish to speak. Already they are gathering. There is another here with the power to sing the song if she will help me. Bera, will you consent to learn the chant that enables me to fly?"

Bera felt Thorhild's venomous stare as if the older woman had struck her, and she flinched away.

"The girl is a fool," said Thorhild loudly. "She will be no use to you."

"I think not. I think she is afraid. Bera, daughter of the Stone Bear, listen to me." The wisewoman lifted Bera's chin so that she had no choice but to look into those clear eyes. It was like falling into a well. "You are a warrior's daughter. Will you betray your breeding and admit yourself a thrall?"

"I am a free woman!" Bera straightened.

"Then prove it—help your father by helping me!"

"Cannot we wait until your woman recovers?" she asked, painfully aware of Thorhild's glare. Groa was still looking at her, and as the silence deepened, it came to Bera that if they waited, Thorhild would find some way to complete her work and the singing-woman would die.

"It is today that the omens are propitious ..." Groa said softly.

"Very well. But it is cows, not spirits, that will come to her singing," Thorhild laughed suddenly, "and it is you who will be made ridiculous if you insist on using her. I will not forbid her to try."

Bera felt her belly grow cold, and though Thorhild was all smiles thereafter, she was not reassured, and when they brought her some soup just before they were to begin, she contrived to dump it into the straw where no one could see.

They went down to the birch grove just as the late spring dusk was falling, in that strange time that was neither darkness nor day. Torches flared pale against the dimming sky, and Bera, her head still filled by the odd harmonies of the spirit song, found it hard to focus on the men who carried them. All the folk of the farmstead were there, and as many of their neighbors as had been able to make the journey. Perhaps it was the torchlight, but their shapes seemed distorted. At one moment she thought the thrall, Finn, was moving with the shy grace of a deer; at another it seemed to her that Arin had become an ox, driven by a she-goat who wore Thorhild's crimson gown.

Haki walked before the spakona, quick and cautious as a fox, but Groa no longer looked like an owl to her, but something nobler. She was wearing a hood of black horsehide, and it seemed to Bera that there was something of a mare's power in her movements. *And what,* she wondered then, *am I?* But the answer to that was obvious. With her thick, curling dark hair and sturdy body, she was a small brown bear.

The seidh platform stood before a line of white birches, its stripped poles gleaming faintly in the torchlight. They had put a cushion stuffed with goose feathers on the seat and draped the back with hides, and there was a bench before it. To one side they had even built an altar of heaped stones. The seat creaked as Haki helped his mistress climb up; otherwise everyone had fallen silent. Bera could see the faces of those in the first row, intent and curious, but the others were only shadows. Anything could have been out there. Bera wondered if they felt the pressure that was building around them, too.

Groa's eyes glinted from beneath the shadow of the hood; the bone and silver ornaments that adorned it gleamed and shivered in the torchlight as she turned her head to look around the circle.

"We are outside the garth now," she said in a low voice. "In the home of more ancient powers. We ask for their help, and the favor of the holy gods. We ask the blessing of the Odin All Father, who wanders between the worlds, of the Lady Freyja, who brought the art of seidh to the Aesir, and of the Nornir who know the fates of men. Pour out the blood upon the stones, that they may give us free passage between the worlds."

Silent, Arin plodded forward and poured the blood that had seen saved from the animals they killed the night before over the stones. It looked black in the half-light, but as it sank into the earth, Bera could feel a change around her. She looked up at the Vœlva in surprise, and the older woman smiled.

"Indeed, they will come," she said softly. "They are more eager to touch the world of men than you can know."

"The spirits of the land, or the dead?" asked Bera.

"It does not matter—after a time, they become the same." She drew breath and pulled her veil over her face. "I have a journey to go. Sing for me, my daughter. Sing me on my way!"

Dry-mouthed, Bera swallowed, wishing suddenly that she had brought with her a skin of water from the stream. But the calling the wisewoman had taught her was not so different from the cattle calls. If she could pretend to herself that she was on the high fell, seeking a lost heifer . . . Yes—now she could hear the music. Bera got to her feet, closed her eyes, and let it rise through her, rising and falling in bitter harmonies to end with the characteristic catch of the breath that left its echo hanging in the darkening air. And just as she could sense the cattle coming, sometimes, even when she could not see them, she knew that something was listening, its presence growing ever stronger. Above her own singing she could hear the wisewoman's breathing grow uneven, and the sound of a yawn.

And then she heard, in the silence between one breath and another, the Vœlva's voice murmuring a hero-list of strange names. Bera fell silent, then sank down at the foot of the high seat.

"Haki I hight," said the manservant, "the seeress I summon. Margerd, Margerd—" His voice dropped to a whisper so that only Bera heard the spakona's secret name. "Can you hear me? In what depths of darkness do you wander? Say now what you see?"

"The gate swings wide, the spirits gather." The wisewoman's voice came harsh and hollow, as if from a long way away. "Swiftly fare they hither, for strong was the singing. Why have you called me from my sleep?"

Haki gestured Arin to come forward. "Speak, son of Steinbjorn. What is it you would know?"

"I would know of my father," said Arin. "Two seasons ago he took his ship *Waveserpent* down the fjord with my older brother and twenty good warriors to man the oars. When he did not return after harvest we thought he must be wintering with some king. But a second winter has gone by with no word. Tell us, Wise One, can you see him? Dwells he in Hella's kingdom or in living lands?"

The spakona sagged back. Bera felt the poles tremble as she twitched, muttering. Then words became clear.

"Blackmane, Blackmane, from Hella's meadows come running. Mousebane glide hither on silent wing ... Seasinger, up from the waters I call thee." The framework creaked as she swayed and Bera looked up anxiously, fearing she would fall. Haki reached out to anchor the back of the high seat, but he did not touch the woman who sat there. Then she stilled, and in the next moment Bera looked up again in surprise, certain she had heard the snort of a pony. The veil fluttered to Groa's breathing. Had she made that sound?

Once more came the whickering, and then, very distinctly, Bera heard hoofbeats and the hoot of an owl. From farther away, it seemed to her, she heard the cry of a seal. Finn the thrall jerked and looked around and one or two others stared, but Arin and Thorhild were watching the spakona, frowning.

They do not hear it! thought Bera. *It is a spirit steed she is calling!* The hoofbeats slowed as the Vœlva's voice became a croon.

"There now, Blackmane, my thanks to thee for coming. Let me up now, far-farer, for we have a long road to travel. Thou must bear me as swiftly as ever Sleipnir carried the High One until we reach our goal!"

Once more, Bera heard the horse whinny; then the seeress seemed to relax.

"Sing!" said Haki, "Sing the journey song now, as strongly as you can!"

Bera drew breath, afraid for a moment that she had forgotten the tune. Then music came to her.

> *"Alvar, vattar, tomtar, send the seeress soaring!*
> *Nissen, duergar, troll, send the seeress sight!"*

Bera sang lustily, and the momentum of her singing sent her soaring as well. Groa had said that she was not to follow, but she could not help it. She could feel the muscles of the mare working beneath her, the rush of wind in her hair.

"From Bjornhall I rise, through the sky I am flying!" half-chanted the seeress, "from Halogaland and the Norse king's realm I fare across the sea. Now I can see the great island of the Angles—I seek Jorvik where Jarl Erik rules, but Steinbjorn is not among his warriors. I fare to the Orkneys, where men are dragging out longships, caulking and readying them to go to sea. But I do not see *Waveserpent*," her voice dropped to a mumble.

"Over sea I must travel, where ice floes graze in Aegir's pastures—" As she spoke Bera seemed to feel sea spray on her cheeks, and her hair tangled in an icy wind. "I see whales sporting below the glaciers. I see the windy fells of Iceland and the folk who live there. But I do not see Steinbjorn." Now her voice was a whisper. From time to time Bera caught names of places, but she did not know them. At last the seeress straightened and sighed.

"Nowhere in Midgard can I find Steinbjorn or Griot his son." For a moment there was no sound but her breathing. It was full dark now, and the torches cast the folds of the wisewoman's cloak into sharp relief against the black shadows.

"Is he dead, then?" asked Arin, flushing.

Abruptly Bera's exhilaration faded. *Dead!* Even now, she

realized, she had been hoping. But if the Vœlva had not been able to find her father in all Middle Earth, then he must be.

"Blackmane, Blackmane," whispered Groa. "Now we must take the road that leads beneath the roots of the World Tree to the land where the green hemlock grows. . . . Carry me across the river of blood, and the lead-colored waters where broken swords and spearheads clash, through Myrkwood and Ironwood where the wild wargs roam."

Bera gasped, for as the wisewoman spoke she was seeing everything. If soaring over Midgard was dangerous, to make the journey to Hel unguarded was precisely what the seeress had forbidden her to do. Haki and the singing-woman had been trained to withstand the lure, but Bera could not stop herself, and she dared not distract Groa.

"Help me!" Silently, she called the spirits she could feel swirling around them. *"I call to the spirit that guards my soul!"* For a moment the confusion was overwhelming. Then she heard, very distinctly, the grunt of a bear behind her. Soft warmth enfolded her, and she relaxed like a cub in its mother's arms.

For the first time since they had started, Bera was able to do something more than respond to the need of the moment. She was aware of the wisewoman's swift journey toward the depths, and at the same time she felt the spirits of wood and water who hovered around them, and less clearly, the jumbled emotions of the people who were waiting for her words. Haki was a steady strength beside her. A little farther away, she could feel Arin, indecisive as a bull-calf trying to pick his way through a marsh.

And next to him—she recoiled, and felt the power that held her strengthen—Thorhild was no she-goat now, but something rough-furred and sharp-tusked from the sea. But it was the hostility that radiated from that grotesque figure that made Bera flinch. Thorhild did not want the seeress to succeed!

"Downward, ever downward I must travel, spiraling deep beneath the Tree," came the wisewoman's harsh whisper. "The Etin-maid stands to bar my way, but I have the word of power to pass her. The last and greatest river roars below me. Blackmane, bear me over the glittering bridge— swiftly, my steed, stride forward without fear!"

With each word the seeress uttered, Bera felt her step-mother's malevolence increasing.

"The Gate swings open—within, I see darkness. It draws me, draws me ... the spirits are gathering. Call now the names of those you are seeking—" Groa cried.

"Steinbjorn Sweinsson and Griot my brother," Arin's voice trembled.

"Ugga and Ulf," called a woman. Most of Steinbjorn's crew had been drawn from the neighborhood.

"Thorvald the Stout!" "Hildir Haraldsson!" they continued. Bera clung to the bear-strength behind her as the darkness thickened. The names seemed to come from a great distance now, but shapes were emerging from those shadows. She could see them now, those good men who had pulled at *Waveserpent*'s oars, gathering at the Gateway to Hella's home.

Suddenly a shudder shook the high seat. A harsh sound came from the lips of the seeress, as if she were trying to speak, but when it turned to words they were in the voice of a young man.

"High is that hall where I sit with Swein and my fathers. Who calls me from my feasting there?"

Arin gasped, and Bera fought to make out the face of the figure who stood before her.

"It is a trick—" said Thorhild in a low voice, but her son ignored her.

"Griot! Is it you? Are you dead, then, my brother?"

"Wrecked on the rocks of an unknown shore ..." came the reply. "Long was the way and dark the faring to this safe harbor. My comrades are with me. They bid their loved ones to cease their weeping, for your grief torments them."

Bera felt suddenly cold. That was certainly Griot's voice, and the features she glimpsed through the gloom familiar.

"How did you come there?" a woman cried. Bera thought it was the wife of Thorvald. "Was it mischance, or did you fall to some enemy?"

"We battled a storm," through Groa's lips, Griot's voice continued, "through the tossing waves a fetch in the form of a she-walrus came swimming. Straight toward the ship it came, and when it touched us, the wind swept us suddenly upon the rocks, and the sea rushed in!"

"This is madness," Thorhild said again. "A clever invention!"

"Who was the sorceress?" Ulf's father called. "Give us her name!"

"This has gone far enough!" cried Thorhild. She stepped in front of her son and lifted her arms, chanting. Bera as she cowered felt a wave of hate. From the seat above her came a cry.

"Mousebane, defend me!"

Bera could not tell if she heard that call with the ears of the body or the soul. She saw with doubled vision a great gray owl sweeping from the dark gateway and Thorhild, dodging as something invisible swept past. Then she straightened, yelling, and Bera saw the shape of a walrus expanding like a mist around her, swinging its long yellow tusks to strike the high seat. The owl dove again with its own war cry. No one else could see the battle, but by now most of them were hearing the screeching. They stared wildly around into the darkness, making frantic signs of warding.

The walrus attacked once more, its shape distorting into something monstrous, and as that dark power surged toward the high seat, Bera felt her own awareness merging into that of the Bear behind her. She rose, arms extended and fingers curving into claws, shaken by a deep growling that did not seem to be her own. For a moment she faced down the walrus, but the evil blasting toward her was beyond anything she had ever imagined, and without the training to use it, her connection with the Bear began to fray.

But she had held for long enough. In the next moment another shape loomed up beside her, a face of terror with fangs that gleamed from gaping jaws, poised on a limber neck armored with glittering scales. *Waveserpent*'s dragonhead swayed toward Thorhild, given hideous life by the spirits of the men who had died when the ship went down.

In the next moment the walrus winked out of existence. It was Thorhild who stared up at the apparition with bulging eyes, Thorhild who screamed.

"it is you who killed me, my mother—" came the voice of Griot from Groa's mouth. "It is upon you that my curse will fall!"

"It cannot be true!" cried Arin. "If they all died, where

is my father? This is some troll who wishes to deceive us.
Call Steinbjorn's spirit, seeress, and let us see if he will
confirm the tale!"

Slowly the image of the dragon began to fade. Bera fell
back into her own body again with a start and saw that the
seeress had slumped sideways in the high seat. Thorhild
was crouched on the ground with her son standing over
her, while the others stared.

"Mousebane, Mousebane, can your sharp eyes find
him?" whispered the Vœlva. She twitched, turning her head
from side to side, then sighed. "Through all of Hel the
owl's sight tracks the spirits, but Steinbjorn is not among
them."

"Then you are a deceiver," said Thorhild, sitting back
on her haunches. Her kerchief had come off and her gray
locks stood out in tangles, nearly as frightening as the fetch
Bera had seen. "You have not found him in Middle Earth
and you have not found him among the dead. Your sight
is flawed, seeress, and you will pay for the accusations you
have made against me!"

"Blackmane, Mousebane, why have you failed me?"
whispered the Vœlva. She straightened a little, turning her
head as if she were listening, and then, astonishingly, began
to laugh.

"I come forth from the darkness and Helgate clangs shut
behind me," she muttered. "Blackmane bears me swiftly
from world to world. From the roots of the Worldtree I
emerge, to Middle Earth she bears me. She carries me ..."
her voice slurred and suddenly she jerked violently, "...
home!"

This time Haki grabbed her, patting her shoulder and
murmuring her name. He lifted his drinking horn and set
it to her lips, and after a few moments she sighed and
pushed back her veil.

"So, then," said Thorhild nastily, "will you admit yourself beaten now?"

Groa turned to look at her, and Bera could see that she
was smiling. "Through the depths I sought, o'er the green
fields of men and the salty waves," she said tiredly. "One
place only did I fail to search for the lost one, and from
thence I now summon him. Stand forth, Steinbjorn Sweinsson, and confound those who would destroy you!"

For a moment, no one moved. Then there was a stirring

at the edge of the crowd and a tattered figure limped into the firelight. Arin's eyes widened, and the last of Thorhild's high color drained away.

"You are the evil one," he rasped, gazing down at Thorhild. "You are the deceiver. You raised the storm, and sent your fetch to drag us down. My son died, and all my good men. Only I came alive to land, surviving for the sake of vengeance."

"What is he saying?" ran the whispers. "Her own son and husband? Even if she is a sorceress, as they say, why would she do it?"

"Did you hate Griot because he set his will against your scheming?" asked Steinbjorn. "Did you work against me so that you would be left to rule here, with this viper whom you can bend to your will?"

"Nay—" Arin was shaking his head, eyes huge with horror. "She could not ... I would not ... I did not know!"

His father ignored him. He grabbed his wife by the shoulder and hauled her upright, shaking her. "Is it not true, woman? Tell me and I may show mercy! Is it not true?"

Thorhild shuddered suddenly and broke free, facing him. "I warned you!" she spat, "When you took that Irish witch to your bed, you made me your enemy. Two living children I had borne you, and the little boy who died, and after she came, you never touched me again. Kill me if you dare, old man, and my brothers will finish what my sorcery began."

He turned from her in disgust. "Get out—I divorce you. Wander the roads or go to your family if you think your kinfolk will still want you when the tale of this night's work is known."

Thorhild spat at his feet and turned to the folk who had been her servants and her neighbors, but they, too, drew back. When she saw that none of them would take her part, she began to curse, a high, shrill mumble that set the hair to bristling, until at last two of the thralls dragged her away.

"You, too—" Steinbjorn rounded on his younger son, who still stood shaking his head in silent protest. "The sight of you sickens me!"

"Father—" Bera pulled herself to her feet, hanging onto the poles.

"My little one!" He turned to her, and now his face was that of the father she remembered. "My treasure! Come to me." He held out his arms and she went into them, hugging him with all her strength as if he were a ghost that would at any moment wisp away. He was only a shadow of the solid strength she remembered; she could feel his bones.

"Ah, my little bear, my sweetling," he said brokenly. "You are my only true child. I will find you a fine husband to be my heir and we will be done with all these witcheries."

Bera looked from him to the Vœlva. Too much had happened too quickly. She was sure of neither herself nor him.

"Do you think so?" asked Groa, looking down at them with pity in her gaze. "Old man, have you learned nothing from this night's work but how your wife betrayed you? Your bear cub has more magic in her finger's end than Thorhild in all her body. Let her come with me."

He shook his head. "What kind of a life would that be, fleeing the king's disfavor? Let her stay here, and forget what she has seen."

Bera closed her eyes. Could she forget that battle, and the soaring flight of the spirit? Could she forget the music?

"If she is not trained, the power will poison her spirit as it did Thorhild's, but Bera will be a Vœlva, and a great one, I promise you, if she stays with me!"

"Well, daughter?" asked Steinbjorn. "You have heard the offers—the life of a wanderer, or wealth and position with me!"

Bera looked from her father to Groa and back again. There had been a time—perhaps even yesterday morning, when she could have dreamed nothing better than to remain forever safe and loved in the curve of her father's arm. But beneath the rustling of the birch trees Bera could hear something else, almost like singing, and she knew that from now on that music would never go away.

"Grant Arin your forgiveness," she said in a low voice. "He only did what that woman told him. As for me—" she swallowed and forced herself to meet his eyes. "The wisewoman spoke truly. No more than Thorhild can I stay here after what has happened this day. Forgive me."

"My bearling," he whispered, drawing her close, and she knew that he was weeping. "It is you who must forgive me!"

She held him tight, but already she could feel her spirit moving away from him. The singing of the spirits was growing louder. As her own song had drawn the cattle from the mountain, it tugged at her awareness, calling her home.

FINAL EXAM
by Jessica R. Lerbs

This is an amusing variation on a djinn—not a word about
three wishes. This is another theme that we get at least
one variation on every year, so I'm very picky about accepting them.

Jessica is eighteen, a senior in high school who takes
classes at a community college. She lives in Brooklyn Center, Minnesota, and works at Burger King, but will soon be
going away to college at Bryn Mawr, where she plans to
major in French and International Relations. She enjoys
reading, writing, tennis, archery, and riding, and is working
on a novel. She says that this story was not her first submission, "nor even my tenth; still, I now believe with all my
heart that perseverance does pay off." Very true.

Strange that it should all come down to the flickering
of a single candleflame.

I am quite average for my race: black-haired,
brown-eyed, golden-skinned. My name is Djil. I am a djinn.
Almost.

You see, as with any other trade, we djinn must study
and take tests to be declared ready to go out granting
wishes to whoever knows our personal secrets. (I am not
so foolish as to put mine in writing. One of my esteemed
kinsmen was unfortunate enough to have his spread around
the world by an irresponsible master named Aladdin and
was forced into early retirement.)

Our traditional responsibility is to seek out those mortals considered "good" by popular consensus and see if, first, they are clever enough to become our masters, and, second, if they are wise enough to phrase their wishes in such a way as to get what they truly want. It is our job to make this as difficult as possible.

I reported to my testing-teacher at the appropriate time, the end of my three hundred years of schooling. He began with an encouraging smile to show off his gold tooth and announced, "For the purposes of this examination, I am your master. It is your duty to give me three wishes. Are you prepared?"

I nodded, staring nervously at the gold hoop in his left ear.

He stated with proper arrogance, "I wish to rule the world!"

That was an easy one! I smiled, clapped my hands together, and shouted, "Granted!" I made a short piece of yellow wood appear in his hand, marked with regularly-spaced black lines along one edge.

His lips twitched; I knew the other two would not be so simple. This time he said, "I wish to know how a raven is like a writing desk."

That was a tough one. I carefully kept the frown from my face. It looked as though I would have to answer him directly. Ah, well, that would happen, especially with scholars, or so my instructors told me.

Again I clapped my hands and shouted, "Granted! A raven is like a writing desk in that they both have quills."

His mouth made a moue of acknowledgment. Then he waved a hand, causing a lighted candle to appear between us. He told me, "I wish you to get rid of this flame without tools, without blowing on it, and without touching it."

Hard, huh? So, here I float, wishing I had knees to rest my elbows on. Instead, I fold my arms, assuming my best savant expression, and stare at the candle.

What if I just use magic? No, that is a tool of sorts. How about flying back and forth to create a wind? But that is still blowing. I stare at the wax forming lines that mar the smooth outside of the candle, feeling my teacher's disapproval. It does not do to take too long; bad for the image.

Like a sandstorm it comes to me, striking a blow that makes me smile. He had said only not to touch the flame!

Delicately, I cause the wax from the top of the candle-bowl to melt in from the edges. The pool of hot wax rises slowly to cover the wick entirely. The flame goes out.

For the third time I perform the required clap and shout and bow humbly, saying, "The flame is out, Master."

His smile is the sweetest sight I have ever seen. I am a full djinn at last! You who read this had best start working on your wishes, my friends, I may be seeing *you* soon . . .

THE STRATMOOR BEAR
by Charley Pearson

Charley Pearson has sold to these anthologies before this, but reminded me that we had met briefly, with a "gazillion" other people at the East Coast Darkover convention. He did find it amusing that I thought his name was female because of the spelling while the spelling of my own name has been known to give people the impression that I'm male. Once in a bookstore someone told the owner, "I happen to know that Marion Bradley is a man." Whereupon the bookstore owner replied, "I must tell her that; her children will be interested to know it."

Charley previously sold a story to *Towers of Darkover* and has been working on short stories and "silly doggerel." He firmly stated that he doesn't write poetry: "My stuff has solid meter, strict rhyme, and it's fun, which I think 'disqualifies' it."

Not for me, Charley. I prefer poetry with both—and I feel that one of the best writers of poetry is W.S. Gilbert, whom snobs don't regard as a poet at all. Considering what's called poetry these days, I would consider that a compliment rather than otherwise.

This is a story about a swordswoman turned storyteller to children—and I wrote something else on the manuscript which I cannot now decipher. Was it "remembers mutation?" Oh, no—it says "initiation," which makes more sense.

In the mundane world, Charley has been a Navy man for about 20 years, working as a nuclear engineer—sounds as if there might be a hard science novel in the making some day. After all, Hal Clement did it, and it was very much worth reading. So did the late, lamented Mr. Asimov, but he wrote some of everything—and I like much of his other work better than his hard science, as I do also with Poul Anderson. No accounting for tastes. I don't dislike hard science fiction—I just haven't the skill to write much of it myself. (And I write none of it now that I have the luxury of choosing what to write.)

"... **A**nd thus the reign of the Stratmoor Bear came to an end. No longer would it shatter barns and homes or steal livestock and children. Elrork became Elrork the Bold, married the Duke's niece, and they still live up in that mansion."

Tyrensis pointed toward the hill just beyond the village of Stratmoor. Her young audience turned and gaped in awe, though they must have heard the story countless times from local Tellers or travelers like herself. Tyrensis smiled. A happy audience was a gift. And always such a change from the shock she first met at her colorful eye patch and missing left hand. The young had no understanding of the hazards of life.

One little girl looked back. "But who fought the bear first?"

Tyrensis raised an eyebrow. "What do you mean?"

"You said the bear was injured. It limped, and could hardly use one claw. It couldn't have done all those things they said if it was hurt. Someone must have fought it before Elrork showed up."

Tyrensis blinked and sat back. All the children stared at her, eyes begging for another tale.

"Why, I don't rightly know what to tell you! No one ever asked before. You're right, of course. Yet nothing is said in the tales." Tyrensis rubbed her cheek, gazing up at the mansion.

"There wasn't anyone else!" said a boy in better clothes than the other children. He stood and brushed his knees. "Elrork killed the bear, and that's all there is to it." He turned and stalked off.

Tyrensis frowned and looked back at the other children. "His best friend is Elrork's grandson," said the same lit-

tle girl. "And his father goes to Council. He's always tongu-
ing it."

"His father is?"

"No," laughed the girl. "Bartron. He thinks he's better
than us."

Tyrensis smiled. "I see. And what's your name?"

The girl stood and curtsied as best she could in a dirty
brown shift. "Annaria, if it please you, Teller." She
plunked herself back down.

Tyrensis grinned. "And you may call me Tyrensis," she
said to all the children, "if your parents will permit such
familiarity."

"They won't mind," said Annaria. "We won't tell them."
Two of the others giggled. "But what happened to the
bear?"

Tyrensis glanced at the trees where Barton had disappeared. "Perhaps I could make a few inquiries, or do a
scrying," she said after a moment. She looked back at Annaria. "Yes, that might do. Come back tomorrow. No, the
day after."

The children groaned.

"Oh, all right. Tomorrow, then. I'll just send you off if I
don't have an answer yet. Agreed?"

The children nodded, hopped to their feet, and scattered
back to the village. Tyrensis chuckled. She scooped up the
vegetables and bread their parents had given them to take
her, in payment for her entertainment. She would eat well
tonight, and perhaps tomorrow as well. But she owed the
children a story.

Her smile evaporated. A story. One never before told.
She glanced once more at Elrork's mansion, then went up
the two steps into her dusty wagon and shut the battered
wooden door.

An hour before dusk Tyrensis left the wagon, wearing
her best linen gown. She grimaced; she might impress the
poorest cleaning wench at the mansion, but no one else.
She stared at the pillars in the distance, wondering how
many years it had been. The evening breeze brought the
scent of burning leaves; a gust sent long gray hair tumbling
over her shoulder. She rubbed one rough lock, then fingered the scar on her cheek. No, he wouldn't remember
her. A foolish thought. But it had been so long, perhaps

Elrork would be glad to tell what he knew. Perhaps he would be glad to let the world know how he beat the bear. She took a breath, walked through the village, and trudged up the hill.

When she knocked on Elrork's door, the servant who answered wouldn't let her in. She had no reason to bother the master. A beggarly traveling Teller, come to ask about a tale 40 years old? Don't be absurd. The servant slammed the door, and she turned away.

A gruff voice bellowed around the side of the house, and a child laughed. Tyrensis bit her lip, then followed the sounds. And there he stood, playing with his grandchild. At least, she presumed, such a fancy outfit would make the child his relative, and Annaria said he had a grandson. And Elrork . . . he'd aged well, and still looked fit.

"Good evening," she said.

Elrork swung the boy to the ground and spun to face her. He relaxed after a moment. "What do you want?"

Tyrensis relaxed as well. Not a glimmer of recognition touched his eyes. Good enough. She'd only met him once, after all, and she'd hardly been the kind to catch his eye. But she'd had her dreams, back then, fool that she was.

It didn't take long to draw him out. He had a child to impress and seemed happy to talk about his long-gone exploit with the Stratmoor Bear. But his account was more sparse than the written version in her wagon. He hardly seemed to remember the bear being injured at all. He had done it all himself, through prowess and courage. The little boy lapped it up, and perhaps the child's presence warped Elrork's memory of the event. Tyrensis could understand that.

She tried to pry it from him anyway. "But didn't the bear limp when you found it? Wasn't there someone—"

"No! Certainly not! Where did you hear such slander?!"

"I—"

"Get out!" He raised his fist and stepped toward her. "I won't have such lies on my own land!"

Tyrensis picked up her skirt with her one hand and raced down the hill. He looked as though he'd have taken a horsewhip to her if he hadn't had the child there. She got back to her wagon and looked behind; at least he hadn't sent anyone after her to chase her from the town.

She stayed up late, sitting by her fire and thinking. He

couldn't have forgotten what really happened. He'd never have reacted so violently if he had. But that meant he had thrown his honor, lied for a greater glory. Why? He had killed the bear. He'd earned what he had. Why deny someone else had helped him?

She tried to remember his younger self, so many years before. So gloriously self-confident ... well, no; more like cocky. But a superior man ... or perhaps merely arrogant. And handsome. Oh, so very handsome. She'd have done whatever he wanted.

She shook her head. Had she carried that memory since she was nineteen? She couldn't believe it. But nothing else made sense. She'd believed in nothing but glory, and her own immortality, and perfect endings. And now she told stories. And some who listened got inspired and went off and got themselves killed. Maybe she wasn't any better than Elrork.

And what could she tell the children? They must have heard before how badly injured the bear was when Elrork first chanced upon it. She knew the truth well enough; she was likely the only one who did. But did she want to tell them, after guarding a secret so long?

She got up to feed her tired old horse and almost hitched it to the wagon to leave. She wouldn't make anything up, just to please her youthful listeners. That would violate the Teller's Code. She'd tell them the truth or nothing at all. Yet how could she claim to know the tale? Why should they believe her?

She sighed and went inside the wagon. Maybe she would refuse to tell them anything. But she knew that wasn't true. Elrork had had 40 years of fame, and it was time to set the record straight. She stood in the center of the wagon and looked at her bed. Then she sat on the floor and leaned against a hard wall. But she fell asleep despite her strongest intent.

She woke feeling fey. Today she could do no wrong. Come what may, a tale would be told. And this time, maybe her audience wouldn't be filled with senseless dreams of adventure. She stretched out the kinks from her foolish sleeping position and tripped through her chores like a woman a third her age. Before she let herself think about it any more, a knock came on the door.

The children were already here. Her heart fluttered, and she told them to wait outside. She clutched the door frame, her eyes wandering around the wagon. Suddenly she saw the wooden bowl on the cook-table in the corner.

She sighed in relief. Of course. A scrying. How could she be so absentminded? She grabbed the bowl, dumped out a few carrot stubs, and smeared it with her apron. She held it before her and proudly stepped outside.

She saw the girl who'd asked for the story the day before. "Run fill this from the well, Annaria," she said, handing her the bowl. "Water must be fresh from the ground to work."

The child looked honored and ran off with the bowl. Tyrensis had to suppress a chuckle when she saw Annaria surreptitiously trying to clean it before she filled it. But Tyrensis managed to sit in calm dignity, ignoring the other children, until the bowl was set before her.

"No pushing," she said. The children kept jostling for a view of the bowl as Tyrensis bowed her head over it. "I must have silence."

They finally settled down, all nine of them finding some vantage from which they could glimpse the water. The rich boy, Bartron, was not among them; hardly surprising. Tyrensis watched the shimmering surface and said nothing, until feuds erupted amongst the bored children. "The water must be completely still," she said, rising and stretching.

The children took her cue and moved away a bit. But the water finally grew calm, and Tyrensis knelt over it once more. She could not have asked for a more eager group. They gathered around her. She pulled a few dry leaves from her belt pouch and crumbled them around the bowl, twice, three times, in larger circles. That would keep them back. They would not dare to disturb her pattern.

She took a breath and stared into the bowl. Clouds and the half-nude trees of autumn wove a slowly changing pattern in the mirror surface.

"It forms!" Tyrensis leaned closer, waving her right hand through an intricate dance; she steadied herself on the stub of her left. "Do any of you see it?"

"I . . ."

Tyrensis looked up. One of the boys; but the child looked down, shook his head, and flushed. None of the others claimed anything but reflections. Good enough; she hated liars. She stared at the bowl and blocked everything from her mind. The silence stretched a moment longer. Then she began.

"I see a warrior. Or rather, I see leather boots, and the sheath of a sword, and a—

"Great goddess, it's a woman! She's got a bow and an arrow nocked, and she's searching, following ... ah, yes. Bear dung. It's still steaming. And now a print. A huge one. Her hands can't be that small, but she can't stretch enough to cover the track.

"She's moving again. What a fool! She can't hope to stop that bear, even if she's poisoned her arrowheads. And alone, unless ... no. Alone. What a—

"Look out! What am I saying, she can't ... the branches are moving ahead, across a creek she hasn't seen, she's looking upstream, she's out of the trees, slipping in the muddy bank, she catches herself and looks downhill, she—

"—heard it! She spins back and the bear leaps into the stream straight at her and she fires the bow and ... she hits it, but only in the thigh, and it screams and races up the bank at her and she pulls her sword and swings and jumps away and slips and it bashes her into the stream and she's up again and swinging and—she hits it! She wrenches the blade and the beast whips around and she loses her grip and it—oh, goddess, it's got her arm, it's chewing—it slashes her face, but she's still fighting, she's got a dagger in her other hand and she's stabbing it over and over and one paw hangs limp and it lets her go and pulls away and bashes her sword and it breaks and she turns and reels, no, it comes after her again and reaches, but it falls and rips her calf and ... she's gone, staggering through the brush, and the bear's had enough and limps away, licking its wounds, and she. . . ."

Tyrensis shivered and closed her eye.

"She what?" asked Annaria. "Does she go after it again?"

Tyrensis' eye snapped open. "Are you crazy?!" She looked back at the bowl, then knocked it away, spraying the children with water. She clenched a fist and stood, facing the mansion on the hill. "The scry tells nothing more. I presume she died of her wounds. There is certainly no record she was ever heard from again."

The silence lasted but a moment. Two of the boys began

wrestling. "I'm the bear," said one. And the other, "I'm Elrork!"

Then that same damned Annaria jumped into the fray. "I'm the warrior lady!" she cried. "And I'll take you both on!"

"Stop it!" Tyrensis clutched her head, staring at the children. "Don't you listen?" she screamed. "Can't you understand!"

They looked at her blankly. She shook her head. "Oh, go home."

They scurried away, off to games and chores.

Tyrensis took a breath. What did she expect? They were children. She picked up the bowl and went inside the wagon.

She sat for a long time, pondering the tale she had told. Then she went over to a chest in the corner, threw open the lid, and reached past layers of clothing to the bottom. She lifted out a sheath, and gently slid free the broken blade. The hilt was made for two hands, and she held it up against the stump where her left should be. Then she set it down, and slid her fingers along the scar below her missing eye.

It was too late for glory. And there was none in losing a battle. If Elrork chose to believe his hired huntress had deserted with her pay and done nothing to weaken the bear before he took his shot, so be it. But it would have been nice to cool off some of those young hotheads before they grew up, went out, and got themselves killed.

Tyrensis snorted. She couldn't change the young. But then again . . . maybe she could try. She slipped the sword back into its sheath and shoved it to the bottom of the trunk, then went to her cook-table, grabbed a head of lettuce, held it with her stub, and started chopping. When it was done, she scooped it into her bowl.

She smiled as she thought of the children's faces, staring at the simple wooden bowl. It really was more useful for salad than for scrying.

GRUMBLE SNOOT
by Vaughn Heppner

If I'm fonder of anything than Tolkien-ish fantasy, it's humor. The right kind of humor, that is; I must admit I prefer George Bernard Shaw to the average sitcom—but I've been known to roll in the aisles at something really funny. There is a story in *Adventures in Time and Space,* called "Alamagoosa," which I can't think about without losing my breath giggling. When I tried to read it aloud to my writing class at Urban School, I shamefully dissolved in giggles. (Eric Frank Russell? John Taine? I told my sf class once about writing—"that's what you're busting your brains for, guys; for people to say 'I remember a wonderful story, but I can't remember who wrote it.' Ah, immortality!") If there's anyone out there who remembers, let me know. Somebody ripped off my copy—which should be a capital offense. ("Who steals my purse steals trash; but he who taketh from me my best books . . ." yeah, Shakespeare said it; only the thing he didn't want to lose was his good name—"Taketh from me what doth enrich him not, and makes me poor indeed."

Anyway, when I read this story, I literally giggled myself hoarse, and that's the best way to sell to me.

But my sense of humor is chancy at best; some supposedly humorous stories I send back with a rejection slip which asks, "Was this supposed to be funny?" But that's just one of the risks of this business. (Remember; if you can't stand the heat, why stay in the kitchen?)

The first swing smashed aside her sword. The second clanked the heavy troll blade against her helm. Razoress, a knightrix of the first rank, dropped the Queen's banner with a groan and slumped to the cold, grassy sward. Raindrops splattered across her face as she flickered in and out of consciousness. The noise of battle grew dim. Suddenly, a clawed troll's foot stamped down only inches from her eyes. She heard a croaking, heavy chuckle. But the foot rose and disappeared from view before she could stir.

Then, just before she lost the struggle to stay aware, she felt the tendrils of an arctic chill and saw that a fog was rolling onto the battlefield. The strange fog was the last thing she saw as she slipped into a state of slumber. . . .

". . . Aha, stripling! Trumpet your eagle-sight to me no more. Look! A knightrix."

After an unknown span of time, Razoress was vaguely aware of a voice, a high-pitched, pompous voice. She heard something clack, and then she felt small objects thump down near her head.

"Ho ho ho! And what's this?" When no reply was forthcoming, there came a rustling-garment sound. Then, "Come closer, you lazy fool. She's down. Can't you see that, you good-for-nothing laggard?"

"What is it?" The new voice was higher-pitched than the first and sounded bored.

"The Queen's banner, stripling. I imagine that it's worth its weight in gold."

The banner, they were talking about the Queen's banner. That was her responsibility. Razoress fought to open her eyes but only succeeded in bringing on a terrible headache instead. It seemed then that her hand moved, though she was unsure.

Somebody squeaked. There was more wooden clacking. Razoress felt something clunk onto her chest and heard a thump from farther away.

"She's still holding it, wise one."

"What?"

"The banner, wise one. The human is still holding it."

"Pry it loose, you silly laggard! Must I think out each separate step for you?"

"You mean touch her flesh?"

A rude, explosive sound was made, as if somebody was

blowing out his cheeks. "Of course not. Unless you wish to risk corruption."

Corruption? What where they talking about? Why would touching her fingers risk corruption? She wasn't a plague carrier. Perhaps as a young knightrix-in-training she'd had the mumps, but that hadn't even lasted the year. A pox doctor had cured her of that. Besides, wasn't she wearing gauntlets?

No, she'd taken the gauntlets off moments before the fight. Battle-magic had caused everything made of metal to suddenly become too hot to touch. They had all been forced to strip off their armor unless it was made of leather, and wrap any metal pommels in heavy sheep's wool. Razoress recalled wrapping her head with padding so she could still wear her thick helm. Then the trolls had attacked.

She tried to get up or at least to open her eyes. The headache still hammered mightily within her head. Once more, she failed in her endeavors. They were speaking again, so she listened.

"What are you doing, fool?"

"You said not to touch her."

"Yes, yes, I said that. That's true. But now I see that you've wrapped your hands with temple cloth. Where are your pilfering gloves?"

A muttered reply was made.

"Speak up, laggard. I can't hear you."

"I said I forgot them."

"Broomsticks and witch's cauldrons! You *forgot* them?"

"I'm sorry, your honor."

"Aaaa, so it's 'your honor' now, is it?" The sound of spitting was made. "Oh, go on and put away your temple cloth. I'll have to do this myself." He began to mutter and make rummaging sounds.

The banner, Razoress told herself, *they would take away the Queen's banner.* No doubt to flourish it inside some lodge or stronghold. But why hadn't the trolls taken it? The trolls knew the significance of the banner. It would be a gross blight on the Queen's reign if the banner were lost.

"Stand back now, and watch a master pilferer at work."

The headache raged within Razoress' head. Her tongue was swollen, while the inside of her mouth felt like shark's skin. She heard the soft approach, the velvety feel of cloth against her fingers. A whispering grunt was made as one of her fingers was pried away from the wooden shaft. The pilferer's breath smelled like pine trees.

"Fingers are as stiff as waddle reeds," the high-pitched voice complained softly. "Well, no matter. The lad's awaiting."

Razoress concentrated. A surge of pride, of responsibility, welled up within her. Her eyes flew open, and by gritting her teeth she swung up her other arm and grabbed a squealing ... She raised her head to see what she had caught and almost let go of the potbellied, green-suited snoot. He had fat rosy cheeks, a long nose that was red at the tip and a funny-looking, tallish sort of elf hat. The snoot was no taller than her knee.

Razoress' grip tightened around the snoot's thin arm. She sat up with a groan and almost slumped back down as the world spun before her eyes. The clouds were gone and the stars were out, and it was cold. She began to shiver, although the dark landscape stopped spinning and the dizziness left her. She was left with, however, a dragon of a headache.

"Let go," the snoot said primly, "or I shall be forced to practice a most foul sort of magic."

Razoress regarded him. A leather pouch overlaid with strips of colored wood was at his side, and he wore bark-made shoes. And, yes, he did indeed wear a pair of velvety gloves. His pilfering gloves, no doubt. She looked around, scanning the grassy knoll. The other snoot was nowhere to be seen.

"I said: Let go. My patience is near its end."

She concentrated on him, fighting the nausea that had suddenly gripped her.

The snoot's black eyes narrowed. He studied her carefully. "You're not well," he said at last. "Please, allow me to give you a dose of snoot medicine. You'll feel so much better after that."

She squeezed his arm. "You were trying to steal the Queen's banner."

He laughed lightly and waved his other arm in dismissal. "You misjudge me. I saw rather that you were cold and hoped to build a fire around you and nurse you back to health. I merely wanted to move the banner so it wouldn't be harmed by the warmth. One never knows with a thing like a banner. Strange forces surely reside within it."

She fought the headache, wondering if his medicine might not help. No, no, never trust a snoot. Everyone knew that. "A fire?" she said.

He nodded vigorously, his dark eyes never leaving her face.

"Snoots aren't known for their generosity," she said, "or for their spirit of helpfulness."

"Ah, you judge us by the words of evil people. A misfortune, to be sure. But I'm afraid that since you've made such a crude social blunder, I'll be forced to take my leave. I therefore must insist that you release my arm."

"So you may better build that fire to warm me?"

He nodded, his face wreathed by what she was sure he took for an honest smile. Instead, it made him seem even more like a crafty old fox and a liar of the first degree.

"Where's the other one," she asked.

He looked around. "The other what?" he asked.

"The other snoot. I heard him."

"The laggard?"

She nodded, surprised that he admitted to the fact that there had been another snoot.

Her snoot spat at his bark-shod feet. "No doubt he's scampered home, gleefully having taken my pickings with him."

"Your pickings?"

He shrugged, eyeing the hand with which she held him.

She frowned as her grip grew weaker. Her chin sagged to her chest. Snoots were looters, like magpies and jackals. They scoured battlefields after the battle, searching for coins and trinkets and other such valuables. They were said to have private hoards, the size of which determined their status.

She drew a deep breath and suddenly recalled that snoots were slipperier than eels. She looked up and saw that the snoot had drawn a long needle. She squeezed his arm harder than before. "Drop it," she said.

He licked his lips.

"Now!"

"Ow!" he complained, dropping the needle. "Gently, gently. I'm old, brittle of bone."

Razoress looked around again, scanning the battlefield. She sat on a rolling hill. A mile to the east was the beginning of the great pine forest. They had never expected the trolls to be this far west.

"Snoot," she said, "did you watch the battle?"

He pursed his lips and twitched his long red nose. "Indeed I did," he finally admitted.

"Who won?" she asked hurriedly.

He spat at his feet and shrugged, scowling.

"Tell me," she said, shaking him, "or it will go ill for you."

"Yes, yes, abuse the harmless little snoot," he grumbled. "Snort and threaten and squint your eyes. Tall folk are all the same."

Razoress felt bad. He was right, in a way. "Who won? That's all I ask."

He stroked his nose, studying her.

"The truth, please. Don't try and decide what it is that I want to hear."

"Ha! The idea never crossed my mind. Why, I—"

"What happened?" she said, shaking him yet again.

He threw up his other arm and made a strangled sound. "We were cheated, that's what."

"Cheated?"

"Indeed, indeed. The sorcerer threw his spell, and you and your ilk doffed your armor. Quite strange, quite strange. The snoots were gleeful, though, eyeing your pretty armor. Then the trolls struck. The fight was hot. Cold rain fell, and the sorcerer spoke garbled words and produced a black jug, unstopping it. A black fog issued out of the jug and rolled over the battlefield. When the fog retreated back into the jug, all were gone: trolls, knightrixes and loot."

Razoress blinked several times at the snoot. A sorcerer? A black jug? And a black fog? She shook her head, which only caused it to explode with pain. She winced, but she was careful to keep her grip on the snoot. Finally, she opened her eyes and asked, "You said they were gone. By that—"

"Yes!" he interrupted. "Vanished, their pretty armor and all." He spat at his bark shoes once again. "A gross injustice had occurred. The sorcerer had despoiled the snoots."

"What?" Oh, then she understood. The greedy snoots had only been thinking about themselves and their private hoards. Clearly, though, dark magic had been afoot. First the spell that had made metal hot, then the dark fog that came from this magic jug. Had something been in the fog that had *eaten* everyone? She shivered. No, no, the trolls were gone, too. It seemed clear that the trolls had made an alliance with a sorcerer. She frowned. Or perhaps it was the sorcerer who had persuaded the trolls to march west.

"Tell me, snoot, what did this sorcerer look like?"

"Nothing for nothing," he said.

"What?"

He drew him himself to his full height, doffed his tall elf hat, and bowed as low as he could with her holding him. "Grumble Snoot, at your service, knightrix," he said, putting his hat back on.

"What was that for?"

He jerked his head back, his face filled with surprise. "Excuse me? You asked for my service, did you not?"

"Huh?"

"You desire information about the sorcerer who defeated the Queen's knightrixes. For a small fee I shall be happy to be of service. Surely this is the *Queen's* business."

Razoress laughed. She'd heard how quick-witted snoots were. It was true. "Listen, snoot . . ." She paused, eyeing him. Perhaps it would be better to play the game by his rules. Maybe he wouldn't lie as quickly that way.

"You said that the black fog took everything," she said.

"Indeed I did not. I said that once the fog was gone, so were the trolls, knightrixes, and loot."

"But not the banner and I, right?"

He shrugged and muttered, "Perhaps, perhaps."

"Why wasn't I taken?"

"The intricacies of magic are varied and imprecise. Mayhap because of your slumbering state. But we advance too quickly. First we must discuss my fee."

"No fee, Grumble Snoot. You tried to rob me. Now—"

"Untrue, untrue. I've said as much."

"—Now, you must pay me your purchase price."

From a grassy knoll forty feet away a high-pitched laugh trilled in glee.

Grumble turned and shook his fist in the direction of the laugh. "I'll box your ears for this!"

Razoress shook his arm. "This is important. Listen to me."

He turned around and waved his free arm at her. "Speak. Speak. Say what you must."

"Do you agree to my deal?"

"Ha! Do you take me for a stripling? First, what are the terms?"

She blinked at him, trying to concentrate. The nausea had returned. "Terms, terms? Yes, these are the terms. Describe the sorcerer to me, his name, his place of residence, and where he may now be found."

Grumble was stroking his chin and nodding. "And when these factors are listed?"

"Then, I'll let go of your arm."

"Done. The sorcerer is shaped like a bent old human male and wears a black robe and cowl. None have seen his face. His name is Nine Fingers, for such did a troll call him and nine are the number of his fingers. You may be assured that his *true* name is well hidden. Nine Fingers lives near the Cave of Listening. Tomorrow night he may be found at the stone glen. Now, release my arm, I've met your terms."

Razoress stared at him. "The Listening Caves," she asked, "where's that?"

"That isn't part of the terms."

"At least tell me where the stone glen is."

He lifted his chin and looked away.

"Will you tell me if I give you a coin?"

A light seemed to appear in his eyes as he regarded her. "Gold or silver?" he asked.

"Neither. Copper."

He side-glanced at her hand, then shrugged and nodded. "The stone glen is two leagues into the forest, south of the brook that flows beneath skull bridge."

Razoress had a vague knowledge of the great pine forest. She knew where the skull bridge was, having fought there during the Wurm Wars. "Can't you be more specific?" she asked.

"Take up the wolf run once you're past the skull bridge. It will lead you to the stone glen."

"The wolf run?"

"It's the trail that the local pack uses."

She wondered how wise it was, in her present condition, to use a wolf run. But she had no choice, did she? No, she didn't. With a shrug, Razoress rummaged through her pouch and took out a copper coin, handing it to Grumble. He snatched it up, tested it with his teeth, and slipped it into his own pouch. The colored pieces of wood rattled as he did.

"I'll give you a silver coin if you lead me to the stone glen," she said.

"My arm, if you please."

Oath-bound, she finally let go of his arm.

He laughed with glee and skipped back out of her reach. "Better," he said.

"Well, how about it, snoot?"

He shook his head.

Despair welled up within her. If she was to find out what had happened to her companions, she *had* to catch up with Nine Fingers. No one else had heard about this sorcerer. She needed Grumble's help.

"I'll pay well," she said.

"How well?" The fire was back in his eyes.

"A gold coin."

He snorted. "A single coin? To lead you to the mighty sorcerer? To perhaps my very death? No, a single gold coin is much too little."

"Two coins, then. That's my final offer."

"Let me see them. Too many folk offer without the resources."

Razoress dug out two gold coins, rubbing them together.

Suddenly, another snoot was standing a foot behind Grumble. "I'll do it," the smaller snoot said. "Throw me the coins."

Grumble whirled around, gave a cry of rage, and jumped at the smaller snoot. The smaller snoot dashed out of sight. Slowly, Grumble turned back around, nodding to himself. "Very well. I shall do it. Toss the coins here, if you please."

Razoress tossed him one coin.

Grumble snatched it out of the air, bit it, and slipped it into his pouch. "The next, please." He held out his hand. The smaller snoot had reappeared behind Grumble.

"No," Razoress said. "Only once I'm at the stone glen."

Grumble frowned. "I work best when trust is freely given."

"I said no."

The smaller snoot hooted with laughter. Grumble chose to ignore him. "Very well, when are you ready to travel?"

She wondered that herself. Slowly, she drew up her legs

and picked up the banner. Then, using the banner, she worked her way to her feet. She swayed, feeling light-headed.

"You're ill," Grumble said. "Perhaps you should rest."

"Later," Razoress whispered. "Once I'm in the woods. Lead on." She began to twist the pole, wrapping the banner around it. Then, following Grumble, using the banner like a giant cane, she headed toward the forest.

The trek was hard. Razoress barely managed to stumble one foot ahead of the other, her head bent, her fingers clutched around the banner. She knew several weeks of rest was the best medicine for a bad head blow, but first she had to find out what had happened to her companions. She frowned. How did Grumble know what Nine Fingers planned? But she was too tired to ask. Later, when they had stopped somewhere inside the fringes of the forest because she'd nearly fainted once too many times, she shivered around a small fire, a heavy cloak thrown across her shoulders. She finally stirred and forced herself to eat some hardtack.

Grumble watched her, feeding small sticks into the fire.

"I must sleep," she muttered. "My head feels too heavy to go on."

"Wise, wise," he agreed. "Lie down. I shall guard your possessions."

She moved her cracked lips, barely smiling. "You must wake me in time for tomorrow night, say, tomorrow at noon. And, Grumble, know that I've cursed my goods in case any should lay hands on them while I sleep."

His eyes widened. "A curse? No, no, trust them to me."

She lay back, wrapped her arms around her pouch and the banner, pulled the heavy cloak across her chest, and fell into a deep sleep. Her eyes opened when drops of water were flicked onto her face. Grumble stood beside her, his hand wet.

"It is noon," he said.

She sat up slowly, regarding him, then checked her pouch. Everything was there. "You did well, Grumble. I'm therefore adding a silver coin to your pay."

"Ply no more curses, rather," he said. "I felt the curse the whole night through. It sang from your pouch, enticing me to snatch coins. You did not say that you were an enchantress."

She wasn't, but maybe in her delirium and extremity she had tapped a power that she didn't know she had. Or maybe snoots were more gullible than the storytellers said. At any rate, although she felt only marginally better, she ate more hardtack and resumed the trek.

The half-day fled into dusk, and dusk soon turned into night. Crickets chirped, wolves howled at the moon, and an eerie wind moaned through the pines. By starlight Grumble walked jauntily down the wolf run, while Razoress used the banner like a cane and dragged one foot after the other. Thanks to Grumble's cunning and alert senses, they'd already slipped past a troll patrol and moved off the trail to watch a snorting behemoth lumber by.

"Hold," Razoress whispered. Sweat sat heavily on her lean face while her long dark hair was plastered against her scalp. Her head felt leaden and her thoughts were slow.

Grumble strolled back toward her. "Why pause? The stone glen lies a mere half-mile beyond yonder turn."

"Is Nine Fingers there?"

"Of course."

Her brown eyes narrowed. "How do you know?"

He used both hands to tug on his green suit. "Because the snoots told me. The forest is filled with snoots, you know. We know all the comings and goings of the forest."

"I didn't hear any snoots."

"Of course not. But you heard crickets chirp and wolves howl and the wind moan through the trees. By such deceptions and tricks do we speak to one another."

"He's lying," another snoot, who had suddenly stepped out of the forest, said. "I scouted up ahead and whispered it to him when your head was down." The young snoot shot a scowl at Grumble. "Give credit where credit is due."

Grumble bent down and inspected his shoes.

Razoress wondered suddenly if Grumble had made a deal with Nine Fingers. She put her hand on her knife hilt. "You practice too much deceit, snoot. Have you sold me to the sorcerer?"

The young snoot gasped. Grumble gave her a look of pure surprise; then his round, fatty face twisted into disgust. "A snoot trust a sorcerer? Bah! You must think me a simpleton. Snoots are not such fools as that. None gain in such deals but the powers that the sorcerer thinks to wield."

Razoress marveled at his passion. "I did not know. Please, forgive me."

Grumble turned on the younger snoot and boxed his ears. "Why are you here, stripling? I gave you orders to watch for the troll king."

"He's come. He's come."

"The troll king?" Razoress asked.

The young snoot stepped forward. He, too, wore a green suit and a tallish sort of elf hat, although he was thinner than Grumble. "Yes, yes. They speak of the exchange, of the deal and the jug. Nine Fingers claims that the knightrixes are well within the jug."

Razoress frowned. The troll king, and here she was no better than an old hag, weary of mind and limb.

"How many trolls?" Grumble asked.

The younger snoot held up three fingers.

"Tell me," Razoress said slowly to Grumble, "why do you fear sorcerers so?"

Grumble spat at his bark-shod feet. "Like gargoyle bladders, snoots are rare. Sorcerers are said to prize the foot of a snoot for stealth potions."

Razoress shook her head in disbelief, then looked around for something to sit on. She spied an old stump. Sitting down, she used a handkerchief to wipe the sweat off her face and then regarded Grumble. "You're filled with surprises, snoot. Now I have a surprise for you."

"Yes?"

"I need your help in order to gain the black jug."

He gave a hoot of laughter, as did the younger snoot.

"No, no, hear me, out," she said. "You just said that you hate sorcerers. And now I understand why. They hunt your kind for the ingredients that your bodily parts can bring. A disgusting practice. This is your chance for revenge."

"Vengeance is fine in principle," Grumble said after a moment, "but where lies the profit in it?"

Razoress put away her handkerchief, and with her hands on her knees she studied Grumble. She needed him; that was beyond doubt. The lives of her companions were at stake. How to sway him?

Grumble glanced at the stripling, nodded, then turned to Razoress and said, "I have fulfilled my commission. Please be so good as to hand over my fee."

"Stripling," Razoress said, ignoring Grumble, "you said

that the troll king and Nine Fingers spoke of an exchange, did you not?"

"I did."

"What does the troll king plan to use for exchange?"

"One of his warriors clutches a heavy coin-sack."

Razoress gestured at Grumble. "There you have it: your profit. *Gold* coins, no doubt."

Grumble snorted. "Please, I'm not a greedy dwarf whose eyes shine with lust at the mere mention of gold. A snoot, above all, is a realist of the first order. You spoke of needing my help in gaining the jug. I fail to see how that relates to the troll king's coin-sack."

She was asking a jackal to play the lion's part. That was foolish. She saw that now. Yet how to gain the jug and thereby release her companions? She rubbed her chin in thought. Slowly, a sly smile stole over her face. The snoot's essential nature was that of a crafty looter. She must appeal to his sense of easily gained loot.

"Very well, Grumble Snoot," she said, "I have another offer."

He shrugged, appearing to be indifferent.

"We first met because you wished to gain the Queen's banner. If you help me in this endeavor and I cannot clink into yours and the stripling's arms as many of the troll king's coins as you can possibly carry, then I will take my knife and slice the banner from this pole and give the banner to you."

"No tricks?" he asked, his foxy eyes alert at once.

"No tricks. I will give you a knightrix's oath instead."

Grumble narrowed his eyes and stroked his fat chin. "First, tell me your plan."

Razoress leaned forward and whispered it to him.

"Risky, risky," he kept muttering. The stripling paled when he heard his part.

"Are you two skilled enough to do it?" she asked.

Grumble blew out his cheeks. "Of course we are *skilled* enough. That's not the issue. Your plan has so many ifs, however. I know not, I know not . . ." He took to shaking his head.

"Listen, Grumble Snoot," she said, "I suspect that most snoot hoards don't contain masses of gold coins. After tonight, you'll surely be the highest ranked in your clan."

He gave a reluctant nod.

"But high rank means risks," she said.

"That," he said, "is a strange philosophy."

"Come, come," she said crossly, "the danger lies with the part I play. You must merely expose yourself for a few, fleeting moments. Quit your haggling tactics for once. You're already going to gain tremendous wealth and status as it is."

He grinned at last. "Very well. I agree."

"Me, too," the stripling squeaked.

She nodded. "Good. Then let's get started."

Her head throbbing, with her naked dagger clutched in her fist, Razoress eased herself toward the stone glen. She brushed aside a twig and slithered across brittle pine needles. Finally, she drew back a pine branch and peered into the ancient glen.

Moonlight filled the circle of stone, and each stone had a worn and age-smoothed symbol chiseled upon it. The area that the glen encompassed was that of a castle turret. The stone glen, Razoress knew, was said to have been built during the reign of the wizard-kings of Dan.

At present, a small, cowled man stood in the middle of the glen. Three trolls stood beside him. The trolls were shorter than Razoress, about as tall as her shoulders. But they were incredibly wide-shouldered and had thick, ugly skin and small, tusked heads. Belted at their sides were wide-bladed swords, although one troll held a heavy coin-sack. The troll nearest the sorcerer had a blue cape thrown over his shoulders—the troll king, no doubt.

As she blinked cold sweat out of her eyes, she saw Grumble Snoot suddenly appear at the far side of the glen. He dragged the banner pole, which was minus the banner, however. Razoress absently touched the folded banner that was thrust through her belt.

Grumble dropped the end of the pole from his hands. It clattered against the stone glen.

Nine Fingers turned, although his face was hidden by the folds of his black cowl. The trolls turned also, their coarse, stupid features never changing.

"Look what I've brought," Grumble shouted. He was about ten paces from the nearest troll.

The troll king grunted something to the sorcerer.

Nine Fingers told the king, "It's a snoot." The sorcerer

spoke in a harsh whisper, as if afraid to be heard. Shifting the jug in his arms, he called out, "What do you want, snoot?"

From her hiding spot Razoress saw that the sorcerer did indeed have only nine fingers. She squeezed her eyes shut, willing herself to be ready. Although she still felt light-headed and queasy, she eagerly opened her eyes and watched.

"I have come to haggle," Grumble said.

Nine Fingers cawed harshly. "Haggle? For a pole? Be-gone, snoot, before I track you down and cut off your feet."

Grumble took off his hat and held it in his hands, bowing his head. "Great Sir, I believe that you would first wish to inspect the pole before you dismiss me out of hand."

The troll king grunted something again. One of the trolls advanced upon Grumble. Grumble nimbly danced back out of reach. The troll bent low and picked up the pole in his widely splayed hand and brought it to the king. The troll king inspected it as Grumble took up his former position.

"Notice the intricate carvings," Grumble shouted. "See how the battle designs curve ever so beautifully and boast of the Queen's many conquests. Then I ask you: Do you know what was attached to that pole?"

Nine Fingers suddenly hissed, "The banner!"

"Indeed, indeed," Grumble said. He put his hat back on.

The troll king grunted quickly at Nine Fingers. Nine Fingers nodded absently, his cowl turned toward Grumble.

"Now, I believe," Grumble said, "that we can begin the haggling."

"You have the banner?" Nine Fingers said.

"Indeed I do."

"Produce it," Nine Fingers said.

"Ho ho, great Sir, please, I am not so foolish."

The troll king grunted a few syllables at his guards. The two guards drew their wide-bladed swords.

"No," Nine Fingers said, "put up your blades."

"Yes, yes, that's right!" Grumble said. "Otherwise I must promptly leave."

The two guard trolls stepped toward Grumble, while the troll king grunted at Nine Fingers. Nine Fingers began to shake his head.

"Sorcerer," Grumble called, "please call them back."

The two guard trolls advanced another step. The troll king grunted again.

Shifting the black jug to the crook of his left arm, Nine Fingers suddenly held up a gnarled arm with the fingers outspread.

Razoress whistled and worked herself up to a crouch. Even through her head continued to throb, she readied herself to rush forward.

"Halt!" Nine Fingers cried at Grumble, "or I will be forced to release a spell."

From a pine branch high above the glen a thin loop suddenly fell. The loop expertly snaked over the jug's neck and tightened with a flick. As the branch shook and the stripling hooted like an owl, Razoress threw herself up and into the glen. The line jerked tight and the black jug was lifted up out of the crook of Nine Finger's arm and swung toward the rushing knightrix.

Nine Fingers shouted in alarm, clutching after the jug. The trolls croaked in dismay at the jug that seemed to fly.

Razoress reached for the jug as it swung toward her. She grabbed it by its long neck and slashed down with her knife.

"No!" Nine Fingers howled.

A black smoke began to issue out of the jug.

"Flee!" Nine Fingers shouted.

The smoke was icy cold and soon the stars were blotted out. Razoress felt an instant of dread. Would the spell be reversed? She didn't know, but she hoped. Sheathing her dagger, taking the banner from her belt, she lifted it and waited. Slowly, the smoke began to fade. As it did, Razoress saw that the glen was now filled with dazed knightrixes and trolls.

"The banner!" Razoress shouted, lifting it as high as she could. "Rally round the banner and then drive the trolls away!"

The knightrixes, hearing Razoress' familiar cry and seeing the banner surrounded by enemies, rallied more quickly than the slower-witted trolls. It was a brief contest, and soon the demoralized, croaking trolls were in full flight.

After they had gone and the knightrixes rallied again around Razoress, Grumble shouted and worked his way among them. The stripling was at his side.

"Knightrixes," Razoress shouted, "here is the bold snoot who served the Queen's cause this night."

The combined host looked upon the small snoot as Razoress bent on one knee before him.

"Tell me, Grumble Snoot," she said, "did you see what happened to Nine Fingers?"

"He disappeared when the fog did."

Razoress nodded and asked for the troll king's coin-sack. It had been dropped when the trolls fled. A tall knightrix handed it to Razoress. She opened the sack. It contained gold coins of double-weight.

"Tell me, Grumble Snoot," she said, "would you claim your fee?"

"Indeed, indeed." For a snoot Grumble produced a very large leather sack.

Carefully, in full sight of the Queen's knightrixes, Razoress filled Grumble's sack with as many double-weight gold coins as he could carry, and then did the same for the stripling.

"Go, then, Grumble Snoot," Razoress said when she was finished, "and tell the other snoots about the generosity of the Queen. For tonight you did indeed do her a service."

And then all the knightrixes cheered.

TALES
by Javonna L. Anderson

Javonna Anderson says, "In case my name doesn't make it immediately obvious, I am female." I'm as sorry about it as you are, but in a day when girls are named "Scott" and "Paige" there's probably no such thing as a gender-specific name any more. Not only have I received many letters addressed to Mr. Marion Bradley, but an acquaintance at a picnic some years ago refused to tell me the gender of her overalled toddler, saying I'd probably relate differently to her if I knew.

Be that as it may, Javonna Anderson lives in Wichita Falls, Texas, having been born in Springfield, Illinois, and lived near there on a farm for eighteen years. Like most would-be writers, she can list a number of odd jobs, some very odd, such as nursemaiding newly hatched pheasants, pruning tons of fruit trees, and helping raise Doberman pinscher pups. Jobs she was paid to do include ticket sales for grandstand shows at the State Fair, ground water protection education intern (there's a job I'd never have dared to invent—who says truth isn't stranger than fiction?), and student law clerk. She attended Washington University in Saint Louis for seven years, earning a B.A. in Biology, a Master's in Engineering and Policy, and a J.D. She is married and resides in Texas. The Air Force brought them there for Euro-NATO Joint Jet Pilot Training for her husband. At the end of the year he hopes to be assigned to a fighter plane, and she hopes for a new computer and an address that won't change for at least three years.

This is her first sale. She plans to continue writing—

between taking the Texas bar exam, jobhunting, and quizzing her husband on things like engine temperatures for T-37s. She wants to thank "Mike, Nancy, Dagvin, Erik, Tom, Anne, and my family."

"Tell us a story, Mommy."

"Yes, tell us one, just one. Tell us, tell us, please? Please?"

The Queen sighed gently. "Very well. But only one."

"Will it have monsters? Nurse's stories always have lots of monsters."

"Shh. Let me think, Antieri."

"Make it a really long one, Mommy. Really long."

She smiled at them. "All right. Not so long ago there lived a Princess."

"Like me!" said Midi.

"Yes, dear, like you, only older."

"Was she very pretty?" asked Midi, snuggling deeper in her bed.

"Yes, dearling, she was very pretty."

"Ewh," said Antieri. "I want to hear about monsters and knights."

"The Princess grew up in a lovely place where people stay young. She learned to sing, and she learned to hunt with falcons. She learned to read all manner of books and she learned to write—"

"Lessons. Ewh," whispered Midi. Antieri nodded grave agreement.

"—and she learned how to be a very proper Princess."

"Was she happy, Mommy?"

"Ah. So you see, already? You're right, Midi; despite all she saw and did, the Princess was not very happy. Do you know why?"

"Why?"

" 'Cause it was boring there?" ventured Antieri.

The Queen straightened the boy's blankets. "She was unhappy because she was lonely."

"Didn't she have a Prince?" yawned Midi.

"Well, no, not then."

"Didn't anybody want her?"

The Queen laughed. "Oh, yes, several people wanted her. She just didn't want any of them."

"Why?"

"Because ... because they all thought she had silly dreams."

The children thought about this for a moment, then Antieri spoke. "That's a stupid reason. Everybody has silly dreams."

"No, not really dreams, then. Silly ideas, I suppose."

"Like what?"

"Well, several things. She wanted to be able to do as she wished. She wanted to share the power of her Prince absolutely equally. And she had several magical gifts that had been given to her when she was born, and she did not want to have to give them away."

"Was she spoiled?"

The Queen winked at him. "Oh, maybe just a little."

"What magic gifts, Mommy?" asked Midi, tugging at her sleeve.

"They were the very best kind. She had a little necklace that let her speak to some animals. She had a little box which played music on command. And she had two hawk feathers, which were the very best treasure of all, since they permitted her to become a real hawk herself."

"Oh!" said Midi.

"Can I have something like that?" asked the boy.

"No, sweetheart, I am afraid they were very special gifts that only worked in certain places."

"Not here?"

"No. Not here."

"Nothing fun ever works here."

She held his hand gently and did not speak for a moment.

"What happened to the Princess, Mommy?" Midi asked.

"Well," she began, with a glance at the boy, "great knights came from everywhere to try to win her hand in marriage, for she was very lovely and very wealthy. They brought treasures to her father and hired bards to sing about their adventures for her, so that she would know how brave they were. They fought each other to prove which one was stronger. Her father was kept very busy thinking up new tests and riddles for them."

"How many were there? Hundreds?"

"Not quite so many as that, but quite a few."

"Did they fight monsters? I'm going to fight monsters."

"Oh, yes! They fought and killed every monster for miles around."

"What kinds of monsters?" Antieri asked, skeptical.

"Well ... there were gryphons, and serpents, and minotaurs. I think a few of them might have brought in giants, and even a couple of trolls."

"No dragons?"

"Dragons of every color in the world, Antieri. Big ones and little ones, with wings and without, and even some with more than one head."

"Oh ..." whispered the boy, eyes wide.

"Did any of them get hurt?"

"Yes, Midi, some of them did. Some of them gave up and went home, saying, 'This Princess is not worth all of this effort. There are many other Princesses to be found.' "

"What next, Mommy?"

"Well, next her father came to her and said that she must pick one of the many knights and marry him."

"Did she? Did she, Mommy?"

"Shh, now, I am getting to that. First she spoke with all the knights that had stayed. Then she went to her father and told him that none of them made her happy."

"Surprise," said Antieri. The Queen frowned at him.

"Some were mean and some were shy and some were very handsome, but not one of them was just what she wanted."

"So what did she do?"

"She tried to send them all home."

" 'Tried?' "

"Yes. You see, one of them wouldn't go. He said that the Princess was being unfair and he had traveled too far to be dismissed so quickly, and so he stayed."

"Hmm. Then what happened?"

"Then the Princess fell in love with the knight from another land."

"Just because he stayed?" asked Antieri, incredulous.

"Well, that was part of the reason," the Queen admitted.

"Why else?"

"Well, the longer he stayed, the more she learned about him. The more she learned about him, the more she liked him. He showed her that loneliness is often something a person does to herself."

"Then what?"

"Then he asked her to marry him."

"And everybody was happy?"

"No, because the knight said he would not stay in the Princess' kingdom, but would return to the other land, and he would take his wife with him."

"So?"

" 'So?' So, if she agreed to go, she would have to leave her home, her family, and all of her people forever."

"Why forever?"

"Because that was the condition."

"Did she go, Mommy?"

"Yes, yes she did."

"Did she have to leave all her special stuff, too?"

"Yes she did, Antieri. But before she left, her mother and father promised her three great wishes."

"Did she use them?"

"Some of them."

"For what?"

The Queen turned away from the children. "For good things," she whispered.

Midi tried to keep her eyes open. "Then what?"

"Well, after the Princess went away with the knight, who happened to be a Prince, they raised a family."

"Were they happy?"

"Oh, yes. The Princess forgot how to be lonely, because she was so busy being a mother to her children. She didn't even notice the day she became a Queen."

"Was she a good Queen?"

"Some people said so."

"What did she do then?"

"Well, then she stayed for as long as she was needed."

"How long was that?"

"Long enough to see all of her wishes filled."

"But, she didn't use them all."

The Queen winked. "That's right."

"Oh," said Antieri.

"What are you children doing awake at this hour? We won't have much time for a story tonight, darlings— Oh, my," Nurse cried, nearly tripping on the Queen in the dim light. "Oh, well, Your Highness! I really didn't expect you here! I was just coming to put them to bed, you know, and tell them their story." She laughed nervously, waiting, then backed out of the room.

The Queen kissed them both and stood up to leave. "You need to do as Nurse says, dears. You have early lessons tomorrow. Tutor will be upset if you can't stay awake." She went to the door.

"Mommy, you forgot," Midi said, yawning.

"Forgot what, dear?"

The girl smiled. "You didn't tell it right. Nurse always says everyone lives happily ever after at the end of a story."

The Queen smiled back carefully, hoping her voice would not shake. "Of course, honey. I forgot all about that part."

The Queen hurried alone through the dim halls of the keep. She paused momentarily at a large ornate door with the royal crest. The noises she heard within convinced her that her husband was not alone, again. She hurried by to reach her own quarters.

For this, I became human.

Standing at her high window in the dim moonlight, she held out her hands.

"I have a fine strong son," she whispered to the stars.

The wind murmured through her hair. After a moment, she said, "I have a lovely little girl."

She looked at the tattered feathers in her hands.

Then she used her last wish, and flew away.

MAGGOT'S FEAST
by Jo Clayton

I've met Jo Clayton several times now at conventions, and she looks a little like the late Leigh Brackett—that is, not altogether unlike my second grade teacher; anything less like the author of such exciting and adventurous tales of science fantasy would be hard to imagine. On the other hand, the one thing writers have in common is that none of them "look like writers." What should a writer look like anyway?

She is a thoroughly amiable woman, who now lives in Oregon and writes where she can hear "Oregon's rain on her balcony and her cats chasing each other over, around and through a dozen bookcases." And people think I make these things up?

Jo Clayton appeared or burst onto the writing scene many years ago with a novel called *Diadem of the Stars;* she followed it up with other books, including the well-known *Moongather,* and has recently published a trilogy set in the same world as *Moongather: The Dancer's Rise, Serpent Waltz,* and *Dance Down the Stars*. Sounds like fun.

It goes to show how individual my guidelines are that I very nearly rejected this as "too gruesome." I have never cared for the theory that Stephen King once stated as "if you can't scare em, gross 'em out!" I don't much mind being scared by a book, but I don't want to lose my lunch. Some editors feel just the other way—they don't mind gross; but they don't want to be scared. It winds up as "know your editor and her prejudices."

A faint brushing sound, a tiny click, a crunnnch.

Hallah's eyes opened. She kept her breathing slow and steady as if she were still asleep, then exploded from the bed, bringing the knife up to meet the darkness which leaped from the doorway.

Blood. Sticky on her arms and across the old scars where her breasts had been.

Scrape of buskins on the floor. Wordless gargle that faded almost before it began.

Silence thick as the stink of the blood.

Hallah stood taut, alert, waiting.

Silence.

And still silence.

She let out the breath she was holding and padded to the door, her bare feet grating on the bits of stale bread she'd laid out as a cheap alarm. After listening a moment, she dropped to her stomach; keeping her head low, near the floor, she eased it around the jamb.

In the faint light trickling up from the taproom she saw that the hall was empty. *Breathing room. Good.*

On her feet again, she eased the door shut, engaged the latch and moved swiftly back to the bed, caught up the quilt and hurried to the window. The shutters were closed and barred, but the wood was filled with rot and cracks and would leak like a rusty bucket. After she'd hung the quilt and poked it into the cracks, she crossed to the rickety table that was one of the amenities the Host charged her for, groped for the plate with its leaning candlestub, and set it on the floor. She lit the candle, then hurried back to the body and knelt beside it, her mouth tightening as she saw the Aspirant's iron ring on an outflung hand. *Guild baby.*

The dead man's face was round with small delicate features; he probably was older than he looked, but he couldn't be much over twenty. No one she knew. *Maytre! I'm a farkin' graduation exercise. Hmm. He won't be alone.*

She pulled on her clothes, frowning as she considered her next move. *Roof? No. Even more a trap than this room.* She wrapped a spare set of underwear about her pouch of poison phials and the box that held her chess set, shoved the packet into the belt pouch with her supply of coin, then began slipping her knives, needles, picks, and darts into their concealed slots.

Not the front door. Not the stairs either. Likely someone in the taproom watching.

She scooped up the candle, blew it out, sat on the bed, and reached for her boots. When her fingers slid over the slight stiffness of the ivory poison knife in the left one, her mouth tightened. That was one of the things she would have preferred to dump with her Guild oath, but prudence said no. She folded the ends of her trousers, pushed her feet into the boots, and left the room.

At the end of the hall was the room the Host had tried to foist on her four months ago, when she was new off the boat. It was the one over the stable and the kitchen midden, the room that got all the noise and stink.

She listened at the door, heard the buzz of loud snores, and wrinkled her nose. *That's going to be one unhappy soul when the cook starts emptying slops come morning.* A tiny pry eased the tongue of the latch from its seat, and she slid inside; she sniffed, grimacing at the stench of rotten apples. *Gahh, he must've drained the town of mosht.*

She crossed the room and unbarred the shutters, glancing at the sleeper as the moonlight poured in. He was a big man, face and arms webbed with scars. The snores blowing past his mustache were loud enough to drown out a marching band. *Just as well he's got that monumental load. Tough-looking ratj.* She eased her shoulders through the small square window, twisted round and pulled herself through it, lowered herself to the stable roof. She crouched in the pool of shadow next to the wall, scanning the malodorous alley that rambled past the barracks of the Customs House, then along behind the line of warehouses and taverns that hugged the curve of the harbor.

She saw a slight movement near the corner of the barracks and turned her head so she was looking from the edges of her eyes. *One. Good. I can deal with that.* She crawled to the roof's edge, rolled over it, and hung from the eaves until one of the horses inside the stable snorted and banged a hoof against a wall, then dropped to the dried ruts of the enclosure.

She ran to the gate in the back wall, unbarred it, and eased it toward her, stopping at intervals to let the night go quiet, moving it slowly, warily inward, as if she actually meant to go out that way as soon as the opening was wide enough.

He came over the wall and should have landed behind her—but she wasn't there—he started to swing round—a flick of her hand and the poison knife slid between his ribs—her knee in his back, her hand over his mouth, he shuddered and died.

That's two who've failed their finals. Wonder how many in this class? Mmp. Now for a horse. She glanced at the window she'd dropped from. *His, for choice. Nothing else worth stealing in there. Joke. Hung for a horse thief or hung for the corpses left lying around. Doesn't look like I'd better come back here any time soon. No loss, that's sure. Gorjo Xil. Boil on the butt of the world.*

As soon as they were out of the stableyard, she kicked the horse into a gallop and went clattering down the alley, heading for the edge of town as fast as she dared.

She took the road north, the one that led to the Forest, the notorious Forest of Xil, where exiles from a thousand lands for a thousand years had gone to ground and turned as strange as solitude and the silences demanded. Her best chance to shake the remnant of the kill-team was making it across the mountains into the plains country beyond. It was rich land and well-settled, a crazy quilt of small realms with fluid alliances. Fifteen years ago one of her first jobs took her to the plains. Flat failure. Her target was warned and vanished in the seethe of peoples. Easy to get lost there. Especially from fledglings not yet fit to solo.

The horse was a tall, rangy beast, white-eyed and dun-colored with brown and white blotches on his hindquarters. Odd looking creature but well made, with a good reach to his stride. His saddle was an old one, worn and scarred like the man that owned him. She wondered a moment who he was and what mix of disasters had brought him to Gorjo Xil. *Something I'll probably never know. Unless he decides to come after me. Hmp. Just what I need, another pissed-off tracker wanting my head loose from my body.*

"Hah-hey, whoa boy, let's sloooow down a while. Don't want to run you off your feet. Yes, yes, he's got you well trained, hasn't he. Wonder what your name is. Hmm. I'll call you Spurge because you're spotted. That's good, smooothh. That's it, a nice long reaching walk."

She turned her head, listening for followers, wondering if the would-bes had mounts ready or had to find them on the run as she had. *I'm getting sloppy. Wouldn't have gotten caught like this if I were still Guild-sworn.*

The Forest closed in around her; only a few stray glints of moonlight reached the ground.

When her life changed, when she rode into Atwarina with the Shiza'hey Kihyayti'an, one of the two Guild Assassins he hired to display his wealth and power, the leaves were green, the early summer days hot and dusty.

It was late fall now, the leaves that clung to the trees and blew across the road were red and gold and burnt orange, and Atwarina was across a sea and a hundred miles south.

Atwarina. Where she'd found her daughter, where she'd renounced the Assassins Guild.

She shivered, remembering the anger and the anguish of that day twenty years ago when she thought Traccoar and his Wild Ride had killed her baby. That day, ah that day, when Traccoar hacked off her breasts and left her to die. That day when somebody said: *Shut the brat up, knock her head against a tree.* The brat. Her daughter, her Rowanny, two years old with hair brighter than any fire, frightened and screaming. *Shut the brat up, knock her head against a tree.*

Twenty years. It was long enough to grow calluses on the wound but not long enough to keep them from ripping open when she saw her daughter's face in the Alayjiyah's court.

She thought about the bargain she'd made in the upper room of Thonsane's tavern—*if you get my daughter out of there, and my daughter's daughter, if you swear to keep them safe and in comfort, I swear by Stone I will serve you till my life's end*—the bargain that left her vegetating in Gorjo Xil, waiting for her employers to tell her what they wanted from her.

And waiting for the Guild to come after her.

Only the dead left the Guild once the Master Oath was sworn.

She shivered again, halted Spurge, and listened.

Nothing. Not even the cry of a bird or the bark of a fox.

Wind stirred the dry leaves over her head.

Wind whispered among the leaves but didn't touch her or lift the red dust round Spurge's hoofs.

She started the horse walking again. "Right. We keep

moving, Spurge. That heavy thing on the back of the saddle isn't me, it's a sack of grain. Keep that in mind, ol' horse. One foot in front of the other and hope nobody skewers us. And you get water and a scoop of grain when I see a place I can defend if I have to. I'd set up an ambush, Spurge, but they'll be wary now. Any fool can pay his money and start the training; to last through to oath time takes a bit more doing." She grinned. "In case you're wondering, ol' horse."

Spurge snorted, danced a few steps to the left, then to the right. Then he stopped, stood trembling, head jerking, whites showing more than ever around his eyes.

A band clamped around Hallah's head and something was pulling at her. Pulling at Spurge, compelling him to a fast canter.

The wind was suddenly louder.

She smiled, a grim twitch of the mouth, when she heard yells behind her. The would-bes were caught, too. *Walked into a trap we did, as if we were blind and deaf and idiots besides. Maytre!*

Spurge turned off the road onto a track like a game trail, moving into darkness thick enough to cut. The trees closed in, hanging heavy over the track; the air under them had a burnt, acrid smell with something unfamiliar in the mix, an odor that started Spurge snorting and jerking his head. *Worse than a snake pit.* It set her teeth on edge.

The ground changed. Stone underfoot. Spurge's shoes rang on it and she could hear the other horses now. They were only minutes behind her.

A wall. An open arch marginally lighter than the wall. She rode through it.

It was a ludicrous room, frightening in its monomaniacal lack of taste, a small and intimate chamber for a pair of domesticated ghouls to sip their cups of blood and chat about their latest excavations.

A mosaic assembled from bits of polished bone, shades of white and ivory with touches of gray and brown, old bone and new, the walls had a slow slippery sheen in the light of the single lamp.

In the middle of the room the bone and glass lamp sat on a table with tibias for legs and teeth embedded in pale yellow amber for the top. Beside the table, there was a settee wide enough for two.

Hallah could move her fingers and turn her head, but her feet were stuck to the floor as if they were glued there, and her shoulders and upper arms wouldn't come away from the wall. She bent her elbows, slid her hands into her sleeves; her fingertips touched the knives she wore strapped to her forearms. Anyone who wanted to add her bones to the decor was going to have to work for them.

The door opened again and two figures in Assassin gray came in, moving stiffly, resisting the pull of their tethers—a man and a woman, both of them small and wiry.

The man glanced at her, looked away; his face was wet with sweat from his struggles with the tether, and his yellow eyes had a fixed fanatical gleam. Hawk's eyes. High-bridged nose. Bony cheekbones. *Czerwon*, she thought. *Tough as old oak and about as rigid. I don't mind fighting Czerwon. No surprises. Hmm. One surprise. That it wasn't him in my room; they must've drawn lots and he lost.*

The woman was more relaxed. Dark eyes, brown almost black. Dark skin, full lips, a few wisps of black hair escaping from her work hood. Reminds me of me, Hallah thought. *Wonder if she's a chess player. She has the stone look.* "Do you play stone chess?" she said.

The woman turned her head. "Yes. I'm mid-bronze, not a beginner but not up to your weight, silver Hallah."

"You know my name. May I know yours?"

The woman ignored the hiss of disapproval from her companion. "He's Widlow, I'm Tanút."

"And I'm your Masterwork, hmm?"

"You got it."

Before Hallah could say anything more, a door in the opposite wall slid open.

Identical, expressionless, gliding with a curious formality, bringing with them the acrid odor that had spooked Hallah outside the Hold, two figures, male and female, moved into the room, shoulder to shoulder, swaying together, right hands in right hands, left hands in lefts, arms in a figure eight across the front of their bodies. They were bone white with black hair, gray eyes pale as winter ice, lips more gray than pink.

The male wore tight white trousers and a tunic embroidered with silver thread—acorns and oak leaves and paired serpents twisted about each other. His hair was long, plaited into a loose braid that was bound by a silver cord with silver acorns on the ends.

The female wore a long dress that snugged tightly across her upper body and belled into a wide skirt—white silk, embroidered with the same designs, acorns, leaves and twining serpents. Her black hair hung loose about her shoulders, held in place with a headband that crossed her brow just above her eyes and tied over her left ear, a strip of cloth embroidered in the same acorn motif with the ends caught in the same silver acorns.

They moved together as if they were one being, as if they were not merely holding hands, but each hand had grown into the other; they circled round the wide seat and settled into it. Heads turning in identical arcs, they stared at the three captives.

Demons? No. More like Wraiths given flesh. Magic, phah! She hated it when her jobs involved magic; its rules were arbitrary—a construct of the one who wielded the power—interior, abstract. Hard to defend against. You had to know the magician to understand his magic. Her magic. Theirs, in this case. *Knowing the player is better than knowing the board, that's what Tarammen said, and he said: It doesn't only apply to chess.*

Tanút brought her head forward and spoke sharply. "Who are you? Why'd you bring us here?"

Hallah took up the protest. "I've done you no harm. Why do you attack me, force me from my path, from the public road which any freeman has a right to use?"

Widlow joined them. "We are travelers bound about our private business. That woman is a stranger, we don't know her. We're merely on the same road. But I tell you this, my companion and I have colleagues who will be angry should anything delay us. They are not people whose anger is a good thing to face."

Not a muscle moved in those ivory faces, nor was there a flicker of comprehension in those pale eyes.

The female turned to the male and spoke. Her voice came to Hallah like the twittering of distant birds. She had the feeling that there were words embedded in that flow of sound, ordinary words that she might even understand if only they were spoken more slowly and clearly.

The Wraiths came to their feet and glided off, vanishing

through the door that opened for them though no hand touched it.

The tether tugged Hallah from the wall and sent her after them. As she went through the door, she managed to turn her head and saw Tanút and Widlow coming after her. "How'd you know where to find me?"

Widlow's mouth set; he clamped his hand around Tanút's arm.

Tanút pulled free; when she spoke, her voice had a dry edge to it. "Widlow's good, you know. Just because he's got an iron rod rammed up his ass doesn't mean he can't operate."

"Czerwon, isn't he? They can argue honor while a house is burning round them."

The barrel-vaulted hall on the far side of the door was lit by a few lamps in bone brackets high up on the walls. It was filled with veils of shadow that swayed and shifted as the flames flickered in the drafts that bit at Hallah's ankles and teased at the wisps of hair that escaped from her travel-knot.

Tanút laughed, a brittle sound. "True. So true. I've read your life, you know. Your reports, at least. Your teachers weren't talking. You don't waste words."

"No point in it."

"And safer. Keep your tricks to yourself."

"There is that. Going to answer the question?"

"Information laid," Tanút said. "Don't know more than that. It's all Groensacker let out when he charged us. Made something else real clear, silver Hallah. Kill you or join you."

"I imagine that's still on."

"Oh, yes."

Hallah walked through the door at the end of the hall and found herself in a long narrow pit with walls at least twenty feet high. There were three doors in the east wall of the pit, three in the western one. In the middle of the cobbled pavement there was a thin stone column with two iron rings about ten feet up, dangling rings like those on a hitching post. Lanterns hung from the rings and three torches were thrust in holes at the top of the column. Like the grand hall, the pit was filled with flickering shadow. Hallah's breath smoked in air colder than she remembered as the tether pulled her to the nearest door in the east wall. It opened and she saw a narrow stairway.

When she reached the top, she was jerked along a bench and slammed down on it when she was opposite the stone column. Tanút grunted as she was forced down beside Hallah.

No Widlow? Hallah leaned toward the iron rail that ran along the top of the wall and looked down into the pit.

He was pressed up against the west wall, writhing and grunting as he fought his tether.

Still holding hands, the Wraiths appeared at the top of that wall and seated themselves in a broad thronelike chair, the stone shining around them.

Head tilted against head, they whispered to each other.

In the pit Widlow was suddenly free. He moved quickly about the walls, inspecting the doors. There were no latches on them and they fitted so tightly it would be hard to ease a knifepoint between door and jamb. He circled again, inspecting the walls. *Looking for a place to climb,* Hallah thought. In his gray clothes he was nearly invisible.

One of the doors opened and a pardal came out, yowling and spitting and shaking its head, a medium-sized cat, its fur a pale tan with dark brown rosettes that diminished to dots on its hindquarters. It saw Widlow and went bounding toward him.

Widlow wheeled and leaped for the stone column.

"Look at them," Tanút spat. "Look at those srakas. It's like they're licking the sweat off him."

The Wraiths were leaning over their linked hands, pale eyes fixed on Widlow as he caught hold of the column and swung around it, turning his momentum into a kick.

The beast swerved a moment too soon; his boot caught its shoulder but glanced off without doing the damage he'd hoped for. Keeping the column between him and the beast, Widlow slid a knife from his sleeve and did another sudden shift of direction. Because of the pardal's quickness, he missed his target again and had to be satisfied with a shallow cut along its thigh instead of slicing through the tendon. He dodged back around the column, shaking the hand the pardal's claws had scored, drops of blood flying, the tattered sleeve whipping about his wrist.

Hallah felt the tether loosen slightly; she tried easing lower on the bench. The band came with her, but it did

shift position, tilting backward the width of her forefinger.
If she chose her time well, just maybe she could jerk loose.
She leaned forward, eyes on the pair on the far side of
the pit.

Both mouths were open a little; pale pink tongues slid
back and forth across lower lips.

Widlow was bleeding from his leg now, claw marks high
up on his thigh, the cloth of his trousers shredded. He drew
a wire garrotte from his waistband, swung round on his
uninjured leg and whipped the wire over the pardal's head.
Using the column as a partial protection from its claws, he
strangled the beast.

—vortex—blackness whirling—sucking—the Hold
whirling—Hallah whirling—round and round—sucking—
breath gone—chaos—wind and nothing—nothing—
sucking—

Hallah's mind went dark, she couldn't breathe. She
thought she was going to die.

Then it was gone and there was stone under her again
and a chill wind blowing in her face. When her eyes
cleared, she lifted her head and stared across at the
Wraiths.

They'd gained solidity; there was even a touch of color
in the pale cheeks.

Maggots, she thought, appalled. *Maggot Wraiths. Eaters
of death. And pain is the appetizer.* Fear was cold in her
stomach. *Widlow's pain. And ours. Tanút's more than mine,
because she has ties to him. Ah, girl, despite your experiences, you haven't learned the assassin's last and most important lesson. Never care. In the Guild there are no them
and us, only me and me and me.*

Beside her Tanút stirred, groaned. She sat up, clutching
at her head. "Wha . . ." she moaned, then cursed in a low
monotone as the door in the wall opened again and a
brown bear waddled out, roaring, maddened, snapping his
teeth to the right, to the left.

Widlow glanced from the bear to the Maggots, left the
wire where it was, and began running.

"What's he doing? He can't outrun the bear. His leg . . ."
Hallah closed her hand on the girl's arm and squeezed.

"No. It's not panic. He's got a plan. Be ready to move, if you can."

Tanút shuddered, tore her eyes from Widlow's intent face to stare at Hallah. "How?"

"When the Maggots—yes, listen, didn't you feel what they are? When they're distracted the tether gets a little looser and it's slow to tighten after. Watch Widlow. When he moves, be ready to follow. We'll go over the rail, get across the pit. I'll toss you up the other wall. While you and Widlow are going at the Maggots, I'll use my climbing line to follow."

In the pit Widlow stumbled as his wounded leg gave way for an instant. He yelled, the sound exploding out as he gathered himself and changed direction, circling round the bear to run close to the wall.

"How do we kill Wraiths? Do you know? How?"

Hallah flattened her palm across her mouth, contemplated the intent faces of the Maggots. "Bone," she said finally. "It's all I can think of. Your poison knife, Tanút, the ivory blade. If it doesn't work—well, we're dead anyway, so we might as well try it."

Having maneuvered the bear into the position he wanted, Widlow whipped round, leaped at it, hit its back, then its shoulder. As the bear surged to its full height, he used the movement and the muscles of his own legs to propel him upward, his hands reaching for the rail.

His wounded leg betrayed him again; his fingers scrabbled at the stone at the lip of the wall but couldn't quite hook over it. He slid back into the claws of the bear.

Sucking—whirling—roaring—

Hallah noticed something interesting as she struggled to stay aware. The Maggots hadn't moved when Widlow came within inches of getting at them. They might be powerful and dangerous, but they were slow to react—as if they didn't quite comprehend the mortal world. She tucked the observation away, hope rising higher than horror for the first time since she rode through the arch.

She saw swirls of black mist rising from Widlow's body, gray mist draining from Tanút who was sprawled beside her, unconscious. There were wisps coming from her, too, fragments of her anger. *I know you now, I know you, I know you,* she cried silently. *Know the Player, the Board doesn't matter.*

The female Maggot stared at her.

The sucking grew stronger.

She fought it—and surprised herself when she won respite and the Maggot looked away.

In the pit the bear backed from the tattered body, ran whimpering from it and out a silently opening door.

Swarms of beetles bubbled from the cobbles. Between one breath and the next—or so it seemed to Hallah—these scavenger kin of the Maggot Wraiths cleaned the bones of the dead and vanished into their burrows.

A flicker like a fold in the air and the bones, too, were gone.

Only the bloodstains were left. And the stink from the Wraiths, stronger than ever.

The Maggots were smiling, their faces flushed and plumper, their bodies straining against clothing gone tight. They turned as one and stared at Tanút.

She got stiffly to her feet and shuffled off, terror in her eyes, hands tearing at her hair, pushing and pushing at her head, trying to get the tether off her.

"Tanút!" Hallah cracked her hands together, saw the girl start, then turn her head. "Kill what they send against you. Don't think about anything else. You have to kill it before I can do anything."

The beast that came out this time was one Hallah had not seen before, a giant weasel, long and fast and extraordinarily limber. Tanút ran.

Hallah kept her eyes on the Maggots.

Tanút threw a sleeve knife. The beast yowled as it chunked home in his left hind leg. He coiled round and bit at it until he got it out of him, then went slinking toward Tanút, a disturbing intelligence in the gleam of his white-ringed eyes.

The tether band softened. The Maggots were caught in the action below, starting to forget Hallah. She slid off the bench and knelt in the space between it and the rail. Eyes on the Maggots, waiting for the moment, she eased her fingers into the slit of her waistband and began drawing out the knotted climbing cord with the folded grapple on the end.

Tanút stayed close to the beast, running in tight curves

that put a strain on his wounded leg. Round and round they went, locked in an eerie, feral dance.

The female Maggot's bosom heaved, she gripped the male Maggot's hands so tightly that the joints whitened in the plump, pink fingers. Hallah slipped the coils of the line over her hand, then got slowly slowly slowly to her feet, shifting so gradually the Maggots missed the move.

Tanút let the beast get too close and he struck at her, ripping her trousers but not breaking the skin. Panting, whimpering, she forced more speed from her body. A quick swipe of her sleeve to get the sweat from her eyes, a shrug, and her second knife was in her hand.

Hallah stood with her thighs pressed against the rail, waiting.

The beast yowled and sprang.

Tanút flung herself to one side, rolled up, ran flat out for the column, caught hold of it, and let her momentum flip her around in a tight circle, slamming the knife into the throat of the beast.

Hallah jerked loose from the band, swung over the rail, dropped to the cobbles and ran for the west wall. "Tanút! To me!"

She stooped, hands laced; Tanút ran at her, stepped onto them. Straightening her legs with a powerful thrust, Hallah sent the girl flying upward; she shook out the coils of the cord, locked the flukes of the grapple open, swung it around a few times, and loosed it.

As she climbed the wall, she could hear the high-pitched yammering of the female Maggot, a roar of rage from the male.

She got her hands on the rail, swung over it, and brought the poison knife up with her when she straightened. She was in time to see the male Maggot slam Tanút's wrist against the iron rail; the ivory knife went spinning away. He caught her by the throat and shook her.

Hallah leaped at him, drove the knife into his side—and felt a force like black water flowing from her, burning water, power channeling through her body into the ivory.

He screamed. Hallah's hands flew apart, exploding off the knife's hilt.

The female Maggot screamed. Hallah was flung backward, slamming into the rail, bouncing off to crash into the bench.

Dazed, she scrambled to her feet, sleeve knife in her hand. She took a step, stopped and stood staring.

The Maggots were burning, consumed by the force she'd fed into them, corpse fires, carrion candles, bonefires.

She took another step. Her foot caught on something. Tanút. Skin blackened, neck broken, head skewed so her cheek rested on her shoulder. "At least I was spared having to kill you," she said. She tried to feel something for the girl, but she could not. There was nothing in her but a deep sadness that was more for herself than for the dead.

There was a rumble from the building, a *sound* she couldn't identify, high-pitched and shrill, as if the stone shrieked in pain. Then a groan and a rumble as a fragment of the wall larger than she was fell into the pit. "Maytre! I've got to get out of here. Horse, get the horse, my gear . . ."

She snatched the grapple, reeling in the cord as she ran. At the end of the pit she jumped onto the bench, jumped again, caught the top of the outside wall, and pulled herself up.

The guttering gleams from the torches on the column were strong enough to show her the thorny vines that grew profusely at the base, canes as thick as her thumb looping up and over. Impossible to get down there. She swore, running along the top of the wall, feeling it crack and sway under her feet.

The squeal of a horse brought her to a stumbling stop.

She drew her sleeve across her face and looked down.

Spurge was pulling at reins tied in a half-hitch to a low limb. A glimmering translucent shape stood beside him— Thonsane in her power aspect, long black hair blowing about her body, wide curving horns spreading from her temples, alabaster horns glowing like the crescent moon. "Hurry," Thonsane called, her voice a braiding of echoes.

Hallah set the grapple against one of the crumbling merlons and used the cord as a brake to her fall. When she was down, she shook the grapple loose, caught it and ran.

She stopped beside the horse, glanced at the gear, then at the shadowy insubstantial form of the horned woman. "Information laid. It was you."

"Yes."

"Why?"

"The Eulé—the ones you called Maggots. A good name, that. They would have smelled danger if you knew too much. You carried the seed, that was sufficient."

Another crash. Hallah glanced nervously back. The roof had fallen in. Spurge tried to rear, but Thonsane set a hand on his shoulder and he calmed.

Hallah grimaced. "Poor ol' Spurge, he's going to be a nervous wreck by the time we're out of here. Carried the seed, Maytre! What if I hadn't managed it? Never mind. I know. You'd just try someone else." She coughed at the plume of dust that blew around her as a portion of the wall collapsed, then swung into the saddle. "Unknot the reins, will you? We'd better get out of here before something falls on us. Might not hurt you, Thonsane, but Spurge and I wouldn't like it." She took the reins and sat looking down at the horned woman. "Where now?"

"Tarakan."

"Will you show me Rowanny and Briony?"

"Someone will." The words were a whisper like wind through leaves as Thonsane faded.

Hallah turned Spurge, urging him into his long-striding walk. *Tarakan. One of the realms on the plain. Wonder what mess waits me there.*

MOONRIDERS
by Lynne Armstrong-Jones

Lynne Armstrong-Jones is one of my major success stories. When I first started *Marion Zimmer Bradley's Fantasy Magazine,* she must have sent me a story or two a week for a while; and now, when I find a story of hers in the mail, I know that even if I can't use it right then, it will be worth reading. Which, of course, makes me eager to find something of hers I *can* use, and often I do. She lives in Canada and says she's been married for twenty-one years to the same man and has "two terrific kids, Mike and Megan." Most kids are terrific; mine are, too. It's rare for me to see a kid I don't like. (It does happen, but usually it means I can't stand the associated adult, and it rubs off on the innocent.) Almost all of my favorite writers have great kids.

Galaan sighed, her fingers massaging the aching muscles of her back. *I'm getting too old for all this fuss!* Still, though, what else *could* she be? After all, she'd been selling her skills as a warrior and escort for—for . . . could it really be over twenty years now?

She sighed again, reaching for her tunic. *I should be grateful really,* she thought. *After all, it's a simple undertaking. If these sorcerers knew the forest at all, they'd have no need of my guidance.*

She straightened, arching her back, urging the stiffness to leave. A grimace pulled at her lips. It didn't seem all that long ago that she'd bounded forth each morning as eagerly as a young deer. Well, that couldn't be helped. She adjusted her single braid and reached out a hand.

"Come, Jewel," she murmured, finger outstretched toward the little scarlet bird. "It's unlikely that I'll have need of your skill in sensing magic on *this* little trek—but I've no doubt that your songs will soothe my spirit."

She turned toward the doorway but paused. A soft touch upon her hand caught her attention. Galaan turned her eyes toward the bird once more, a smile beginning to lighten her face. Her gaze caressed her companion, who was rubbing his feathered head lovingly against his mistress.

Uneasily, Galaan eyed the three cloaked and hooded figures. If magicians were forthright people, why did they strive to conceal themselves? She dropped her hand to touch her sword reassuringly. Her "magic."

"So, warrior," came a voice as whispery as the breeze through the leaves, "you can deliver us safely to the other side of the forest?"

"Yes," she answered. "For four silver pieces ... as we agreed upon before."

The hood moved as its owner nodded.

"I wish my payment *now*," continued the warrior.

The hood fell back a bit as the head inside moved its gaze upward, deep-set eyes seeking contact with Galaan's.

There was something about the sorceress' gaze; something about *power* that sent a quick, icy shiver along Galaan's spine. She licked her dry lips, grateful for the nearness of the bird companion upon her shoulder.

"I wish my payment now," she repeated.

The sorceress moved as though to oblige, but her closest hooded companion stopped her quickly with a touch.

"Cadera," said the low voice. "We must not—what if she should—"

The one called Cadera shook her head, but it was Galaan who spoke.

"What if she ... ? Please finish your question, Master Sorcerer! Surely we can speak honestly here!"

The sorcerer sighed, turning his bearded face in the warrior's direction. "You have only to show us the way to the forest's edge, madam. That is all that should concern you."

"My companion speaks truth, Galaan," said the sorceress. "Once we've found the way through, your deed is done."

"Yet *that* one seems to think I'll flee before my task is complete."

Cadera considered a moment, exchanging looks with the other two hooded ones. The moon was rising, and its golden glow caught a glimmer of pale blue as the sorceress once more turned her gaze toward Galaan.

"Galaan, once we're through the forest, you may turn back. But we—but we have a task to complete. We shall venture onward to the ridge."

"The *ridge*!" Galaan blinked, a twitch seizing control of her body, then releasing it. Scarlet wings flashed as Jewel sought some other perch. "The ridge? Do you know ... You *know* the danger—"

Cadera smiled slightly. "Yes," she said softly. "My companions and I shall confront the Moonriders. *Our* magic is the stronger: The people of the village shall live in fear no longer."

Still Galaan's heart *thump-thumped* in her chest. Surely not! The Moonriders were rumored to be powerful wizards, savage beyond belief; their faces were like the glowing moon, casting light back at the people until they were blinded.

Galaan considered all she'd heard. No, she had no desire to venture beyond the forest's edge! But four silver pieces would make life much easier. *Much* easier.

"I wish my payment in advance," she repeated softly. "Who else will show the way?"

The jingle of Cadera's money pouch set Galaan's heart more at ease.

Galaan tightened her long silver-black braid, and sought the familiar feel of her belongings where they hung from the saddle. She took a moment to reach forward, stroking the neck of the gray gelding.

She felt as well as heard the gentle flutter, turning her face toward the scarlet one as he alighted upon her shoulder.

"Well, my friend," murmured the warrior, "perhaps we'll have need of your skill after all! You'd best be alert for any spells. It may be, after all, that the Moonriders can sense our presence as we draw near!"

The thought sent that little shiver along her spine once more ... but, almost as though he'd sensed the mistress' need, Jewel was giving voice to melodious tones.

"I *say,* Galaan! We'd best be on own way!"

Galaan looked up. It was the bearded sorcerer who was calling her.

She nodded, urging the gelding forward and into the shadows. Galaan did not mind the cool darkness of the forest. She'd knew that lack of light did not have to mean danger or evil. And the glimmers of moonlight which managed to penetrate the growth were quite sufficient for recognition of landmarks.

But she paused from time to time, knowing that the nightbeasts would be up and about. She waited until the horses behind her had come to a halt, then she searched with her ears, her nose, for any sign of danger.

And yet I wonder. After all, if these be great magicians, could they not simply SPIRIT any dangers away?

A sudden sound had her drawing her sword—but it was only a hoofed creature which was hastily skirting their path. ...

The sight of the full moon drew her gaze upward. Could the Moonriders really have faces like that? Could they really do *anything* with their magic? She shivered. There was nothing—*nothing*—which could draw her from the safety of the forest this night! She'd take these three to the forest edge, yes. But she would not go any closer to that ridge.

She clucked at Gray to proceed.

"There," she whispered to the sorceress beside her. There, indeed. Just beyond the few trees ahead of them lay the ridge. It was not all that high, yet in these parts it was as close as one could come to the moon itself.

And the moon was huge in the sky, almost as though it *could* bestow power. It gleamed wonderfully, the darker patterns forming an ominous face.

Galaan suddenly remembered the sorcerers' mission. She licked her lips, swallowing the lump in her throat.

"You have served us well, Galaan," came Cadera's silken voice.

And with that, they were gone. The warrior watched as the last horse's tail swished through the bush.

What would happen when they'd gotten to the ridge-top?

Would they . . . *could* they really destroy the Moonriders? Set the villages free of the evil? Galaan found herself tucking her necklace inside her tunic. It was said that the Moonriders craved items which caught the reflection of the moon's glow. Anything bright and beautiful would be taken, and men and women slaughtered should they resist.

Well, enough of this! She pulled on Gray's rein, happy to turn back to the shelter of the forest.

A shrill *bree-eet* suddenly had her heart thumping. *Jewel*! He'd sensed magic! And just as suddenly, he was gone— then Cadera's hoarse cry echoed from the ridge.

The ridge! The Moonriders—and their *magic*! Jewel shrieked again. Cadera and her companions must be facing strong enchantment. Perhaps it was *too* strong.

Galaan hesitated only a moment. Sword in hand, she urged Gray forward. They plunged through the growth and into the open space—and she *saw* them—

Great, round, bright faces they had—if one could call the things "faces." The bodies were humanlike, with mounts beneath them—But those great, gleaming faces . . .

Galaan could see the magic now: shards of silver lightning . . . but it was from *Cadera* and her companions. It was *their* magic which Jewel had sensed.

The magicians sent another spell. Yet there was no change in the Moonriders. Could it be that they *were* stronger than any other magic?

Even now, the first Moonrider moved in closer toward Cadera, blade catching moonglow. Galaan's response was immediate. "*MY* magic," she proclaimed, her sword slicing through the air as Gray leaped up the embankment.

Instead of attacking that glowing face, she struck at the more human-looking parts. And the moan which emanated from the "face" area was very human-*sounding*.

Galaan had no opportunity for speculation, though, as she was quickly forced to defend herself against the next one, who had produced a sword of his own. From the corner of her eye she saw the bearded sorcerer preparing a spell.

"No!" She leaped from Gray's back, in her true element now. Two men: two men and nothing more. She shoved her foot into one's knee; his moon-face clanked and split as he hit the ground.

Galaan was busy with the last one now. He was struggling with one hand to release the awkward moon-mask, so he could better concentrate on the sword in his other.

Not so easy without FEAR to bind your opponent, thought the warrior, teeth grinding as anger gave her new energy.

As the moon-man's fingers sought whatever held the mask in place, Galaan braced her weapon with both hands. The clanging sound echoed throughout the forest as her sword clashed hard with his, knocking the blade from his grasp.

The larger of the sorcerers seized the man from behind. Galaan leaned over to study the remnants of a moon-mask. It was fashioned of shiny metal. And it *did* resemble the moon, somewhat. Galaan chuckled. Then she laughed outright.

She was still smiling when she turned to face Cadera. The sorceress' fingers toyed with a gold amulet which rested upon her breast. The hood had fallen back, and the moon's glow caught reddish glints amid the short, brown locks. Her face was serious, with pale lips set in a frown which seemed somehow permanent.

"Tell me, Madam Cadera," Galaan grinned, "how is it that your 'magic' failed to stop these plunderers—plunderers who are only mortal men and not 'magic' at all?"

A long sigh escaped the sorceress. "We issued a spell to counteract any enchantment used by the Moonriders. Had they truly *been* magicians, our spell would have been effective. We'd *assumed*, you see . . ." The voice trailed off, until it was nothing more than the whisper of wind through the leaves.

Galaan said nothing, climbing to Gray's broad back and urging him back toward home. But her heart was pounding. There was something about this sorceress which had reached inside Galaan. Impulsively, she turned. "Cadera."

The sorceress raised her azure eyes to meet the warm brown ones of the warrior. Quickly, before the words could hide inside, the warrior spoke: "Perhaps—perhaps it *was* your spell, Cadera. It must have been your *spell* that enabled me to discover the Moonriders' secret so easily. Yes! Don't you see? Your magic must have weakened them."

Cadera's face had visibly relaxed, her lips curling upward a bit. She nodded, though Galaan had a sense that Cadera, too, did not really believe all that had been said.

The warrior turned the gelding once more into the pleasant familiarity of the forest, slowly enough that the others could follow easily. She sighed once more. But then the strange dark cloud around her spirit cleared somewhat in response to the cheery twitter beside her.

"Ah, Jewel." She reached a finger to touch the soft feathers as the bird settled comfortably upon her shoulder. "It must be wonderful to be a *creature,* free of the confusions of *human* life. Free of concerns, living only for pleasures. And there you are, listening to my natter and understanding naught. Ah, well. You may give us a song, now, my friend . . . Jewel?"

But for once the little bird kept his silence.

THIEF, THIEF!
by Mary Catelli

Mary Catelli started to write when she was twelve and had to "return books to the library without getting more out and was running out of things to read." This was another story I almost rejected because it deals with two of my pet hates: thieves and dragons; I've simply read too many bad examples of both. But here is proof that I'll still buy a good one—which means a really compelling new twist.

The nests looked vaguely like the nests of several eagles clustered around a cave, only much bigger. Though of course they would be larger. No dragon could fit in an eagle's nest.

Sylvie contemplated the pale dried brushwood of the nest as she walked up the road. These dragons did not keep the enormous piles of treasure a wyrm would demand, but she could see things through the brush now: a sapphire necklace hung from one branch; a broken chest spilled not gold pieces, but pure white pearls; a tapestry of a dragon in flight hung between two boughs.

Sylvie walked right by. The dragons were not the lords of the land for nothing. She couldn't sell these things within the dragons' lands. They might be benevolent, held by their subjects and by travelers through the land to be the most benevolent lords in many days' journey, but they were definitely dragons, with a dragon's memory. One of those pearls would bring unending pursuit, and no one would buy that pursuit from her.

"But if they only have some *books*," she muttered. Most potent magicians, the dragons were, and if Sylvie could find their books of magic, she could sell them. Any magician would give his right arm for those books, and could handle the pursuit as well. And Sylvie would be set for life.

She hurried quickly through the first nest. The wand with silver patterns might be magical, but it was human-sized and would be human magic. Only dragon magic would do. Besides, the dragons were seen flying off, but they would be flying back soon enough.

It was in the next nest that Sylvie found the first of the spheres: pale pink, perfectly spherical, warm to the touch, almost as large as Sylvie was. "An egg? But it's not egg-shaped." She glanced over the cloths and jewelry and went on to the next nest. Odd spheres buttered no parsnips.

There were half a dozen of the spheres in this nest and that one, but no books. Sylvie even looked through all the chests of gold and gems, disturbing them so that the dragons could see she had been there. She sat with a sigh in the largest of the nests, half looking at the sky blue sphere resting in it.

"Well, it might be an egg, egg-shaped or not. But it might be a secret hiding place. I'll just tap it (she picked up a stick) and see if it's hollow. If it is, I'd best be off and seek my fortune elsewhere." Sylvie scrambled over the brambles and up to the sphere. Though she knocked softly at it, she could clearly hear the solid sound. Sylvie sighed and dropped the stick, then her practicality asserted itself and she began to leave the nest.

"Dragon eggs are round all over," she noted, climbing down. "That fact might be worth a few coins to some scholars—enough for a dinner at any rate."

Tap, tap. Sylvie looked behind herself. The blue egg shifted a little, and another tap shifted away a piece of the egg. A large bronze eye peeked out the hole, looking directly at Sylvie, and an indistinct noise came from within the shell. Bits of shell flew in an explosion. A baby dragon, pale blue with enormous bronze eyes, leaped from the shell to run to Sylvie. "Mommy, Mommy!" Half opened wings flapped widely as it tossed its arms around her waist and looked up at her adoringly. "Mommy!"

Sylvie gasped for breath. After a minute, she managed to persuade the baby to let go, but it curled up at her feet, closing only one eye.

Well, the dragons would not be pleased at this outcome. She could only flee and hope that they never figured out who had snuck into their nest. Sylvie started down the road. The baby dragon eagerly scrambled after her.

She turned to scold it when some thing moved over the sun. It might have been a cloud. Somehow, Sylvie knew it was not. She slowly turned to face the descending dragons. Her teeth worried her lower lip. There were seven of them; the leader was a pale golden dragon with silver and copper patterns running through its scales.

"WHAT?!? My love, my own, my darling Azurine has hatched! Where is he? What could have befallen him? Oh, I should have known to not trust that spell the Eglatinor gave me! My darling chick has hatched without me, for all his promises! Where can he be?"

The pale green dragon who landed nearest to the road stretched a long claw. "There he is," it said slowly, and blinked.

The distraught dragon looked at the road. "A human? What are you doing here, human? And what have you done to my darling Azurine?" demanded the dragon, looming over Sylvie and Azurine.

"Help! Mommy! Save me!" Azurine dived behind Sylvie, his tail whipping around her feet, his arms around her waist, and one fearful eye peeking from behind her back.

"He *imprinted*," hissed a large black-bronze dragon. A murmur of hisses echoed through the nest. At least, Sylvie thought it was a murmur; still, had it been any louder, it would have deafened her. Azurine's arms tightened about her.

A smaller dragon, deep heart's-blood red, looked Sylvie over. "Well, she'll have to raise him now. It's going to be a bother, arranging for shelter and all—but you know as well as I, Auream, that we have no choice."

Sylvie stiffened. How long did it take a dragon to grow up? She glanced back at Azurine, trying to guess; he looked back at her with guileless eyes.

Auream gave a long sigh, smoke flowing from her mouth like fog. "There's no help for it, then. We will have to arrange matters for this human." She settled down in her nest.

"But, Great Ones, I can not remain here," Sylvie began pitifully.

Twenty eyes looked at her.

"I make my living seeking out new magic, and selling it to magicians—I would surely starve, after."

Auream drew herself up on to her hind legs. "New Magic! Why, we have magics older than any civilization! We will give you new magic to sell to these magicians."

Sylvie smiled.

"Why, I will teach you alongside Azurine! He shall learn nothing that you shall not; I shall even test you as Azurine will be tested! . . . Dear cousin Gillias, are humans *supposed* to turn green?"

HEALING
by Hannah Blair

When I accepted this story and asked for a biography, I was very surprised to find out that the writer was only fifteen. As far as I'm concerned, that's when I like to find out about the writer's youth: after I've bought something. All too many beginners, of course, make their youth and incompetence all too obvious, and I never make allowances for a writer's youth; if they're good enough to be in print, I don't have to. But that one of my greatest delights is finding really young writers can be proved by Micole Sudberg, Stephanie Shaver, Vera Nazarian, and both David and Margaret Heydt—all of whom made their first sales to me before I knew how old—or how young—they were. Who now remembers how young Mozart was—or anything about him but the excellence of his music?

In the letter she wrote after acceptance, Hannah writes that she thinks about being a chef, but the prospects aren't very bright for an underage vegetarian. Well, at least being young is something you'll grow out of. And some young people do grow out of being vegetarians, though there's George Bernard Shaw, who, being told that vegetarianism was not healthy, said that, being ninety-odd, he was too old to change and must resign himself to an early death.

On the other hand, an early start doesn't mean all that much either; no one would have known from reading the first stories of Ray Bradbury, Harlan Ellison, Bob Silverberg, or Marion Zimmer Bradley that they'd ever write anything really worth reading or remembering.

111

P relude: Sunderings.

"Why?" Malia asked for the third time, not really expecting an answer.

"We don't know why," her aunt Eirian replied wearily, shaking her head. "We just don't know."

"Malia?" her little cousin Iphis ventured. "They said your mama's with the gods now."

"Why can't she be with us?" Malia cried.

Eirian looked reprovingly at her as Iphis scurried away. "Everyone has her time to go, Mal. I miss Ketrina as much as you do."

"That's easy for *you* to say. *Your* mother is still alive," Malia muttered, with an edge of resentment and bitterness to her unhappy voice. "And for all the healing powers they say I have ..." she added, half to herself and with deep regret.

"Stop it, Malia," Eirian said warningly from across the room.

"All my talent ..."

"*Stop it*, Malia."

"Why couldn't I save her?" It was plaintive and childlike. She felt like a little girl again, with no control over her world. "Why?" She sat silent and trembling for a moment, red and blotchy cheeks gleaming with tear tracks, and then she began to cry.

Eirian was beside her, holding her carefully and quietly until her tears quieted and she raised her head again.

"She was a good woman, your mother, and a good healer. Let her life be her memorial," Eirian said gently. "That's what she would want, I think. That's the best thing you can do for her."

Mendings

"In order to become a Masterhealer, Journeywoman Malia," said the Dean of the Healer's Academy, stopping his pacing, "you must come to terms with past failures. You cannot have faith in your abilities without putting your failures to rest, and you cannot heal without that faith." He looked anywhere but at her. Then, with as much sympathy as the Dean could ever muster: "You must put behind you your failure to save your mother."

His words hit Malia like a bucketful of cold water. She had been basking in the approval of her teacher, expecting only the usual responsibility lecture that she had gotten on each of her previous promotions. She had known from his first words that this wouldn't be quite it, but she hadn't expected *this*.

"Malia?" the Dean's voice brought her back to the painful present. He seemed to be groping for a way to express himself, then said, "I'm sorry, child, but it must be done." He spread his hands as if to say that he knew the inadequacy of his words.

Malia nodded numbly. "I'll—I'll go down to her grave."

"I think that would be best," he said, adding silently, May the gods help you, child. I certainly cannot.

The Healer's gravefield was bathed in late afternoon light and smelled deliciously of sunwarmed grass, but Malia was too distraught to appreciate it. Her mother's grave was silent and unchanged when she reached it, and she wondered again at the life that flourished amongst this death: The apple tree dropped blossoms on her mother's headstone, a sprinkling of flowers sprouted about it, and the air was alive with birdsong. Despite the glory of the day, Malia felt accusation emanating from the stone: Malia had failed. How could she? Didn't she know what was at stake? Had been, her mind pointed out cruelly. Too late now ... . Malia threw herself at the stone in an agony of self-accusation and began to weep. As her tears subsided, she found herself slipping into Healer's Trance. She tried to fight it, but in the end it won out, and she slipped into the warm, welcoming darkness.

Malia.
A touch upon her mind, a familiar voice. Malia flinched, remembering, and fled from the voice.
Do you scorn me now that I am dead? I feel no pain, I only regret that I have caused you pain.
"No!"
Do not deny it; I have caused you pain. But have you forgotten the times we had?
There was a smile in her mother's voice, and memories rose to the surface of her mind—

Her mother led her into the stables. "Here he is." The enormous gray gelding looked down at the child, small enough to walk under his belly without touching it. "Malia," her mother whispered. "Give him the apple."

Malia took a nervous step backward. "he's big. He'll bite me."

"No, he won't. He's gentle. Go on," her mother encouraged.

Malia took another step backward. "He'll *bite* me!"

Malia's mother shook her head. "No. Here, you hold it—" Ketrina cupped her hand around her daughter's small one, "—there. Now we can both feed him the apple."

Malia raised her hand up with her mother's. The gelding sniffed the apple with interest, then lipped it up from the little girl's hand with a whicker.

Eirian's voice came across a vast gulf of years. Let her life be her memorial.

"Well?" Malia asked anxiously, standing in the doorway. The room was dim, in deference to the condition of the man who lay on the bed, his face beaded with sweat.

"I don't know." Her mother checked his temperature with a hand on his forehead. "His fever's broken, but he's still unconscious." Ketrina appeared serene, but there were lines of worry at the corners of her eyes and mouth.

Malia extended the hot mug she held. "Here's the tea you wanted."

Ketrina took it gratefully and drained half of it in a gulp, despite the temperature. She shut her eyes for a moment and leaned against the wall.

"Will he recover?" Malia ventured.

Ketrina opened her eyes and sat up. "I don't know, Mal. I wish I could tell you he would. If he were conscious . . ." She shook her head and looked around for her herbs. She measured a tiny amount of dried purple flowers in a small spoon. "Open his mouth, would you? I've got to put this on his tongue, and it's like he's got his jaw wired shut . . . there. Thank you. If that doesn't bring him to . . ." She shook her head. "It doesn't bear thinking about." She was getting up to straighten her medicines when the man on the bed made a rasping sound and began to cough. He grimaced slightly, and his eyes opened.

Let her life be her memorial.

* * *

Malia sat on the blanket. "It's going to rain."

Her mother waved a hand. "Nonsense. Look at that sky! Hardly a cloud. Eat."

Malia scowled. "I hate cheese."

"Then don't eat any. We've got bread." Ketrina popped a wedge of yellow cheese into her mouth and uncorked the waterskin. After a long draught, she offered it to Malia.

"We'll have all the water we need in a minute or so," Malia said darkly, but she drank anyhow. A gust of wind whipped the leaves of the tree under which they sat. A cloud moved over the sun and darkened the landscape. Malia raised an eyebrow at her mother. "Told you."

"Ha. It's not raining yet." Ketrina replied.

"It will," Malia assured her. "Give it time."

"Nonsense."

Malia gave her mother a vindicated grin as the first drops began to hit the leaves of the tree. Ketrina muttered a curse and began to put the food back in the knapsack. "We'll have to run for it," she said, squinting at the sky through the leaves. "This looks like it's going to be a long one."

"Mm," Malia said absently. "Knew it would."

"You sound as if you've got the weather witching," Ketrina said, almost amused. "You're a Healer, remember?"

"Yes, Mama," Malia replied with almost fawning docility.

Ketrina laughed. "Shall we go?"

Malia gave her an arch smile. "Might as well. It's not going to get better any time soon, you know."

Ketrina took up the knapsack and together they ran out into the rain.

Let her life be her memorial.

There was a fleeting brush of lips against her cheek, then her mother was gone.

Her eyes opened, and she found herself leaning against her mother's still-warm gravestone. Her eyes were moist, and though tear tracks lined her face, no more spilled down her cheeks. Malia touched her fingertips to the gravestone, and then she got up, walking back to the Academy in the deepening twilight to face her future with a clear heart.

VIRGIN SPRING
by Cynthia McQuillin

I've forgotten how many unicorn stories I've read and re-jected—which just goes to show that almost all of them were forgettable or worse.

However, three in my whole lifetime were memorable; one was what I still consider the finest unicorn story ever written, Theodore Sturgeon's *The Silken-Swift*. The second was by the—regrettably—late Robert Cook, who left only a slender handful of stories and poems by which to be remembered. But for that one, at least, I'm sure he will be long remembered. The third is by Cynthia McQuillin, one of my housemates, who has sold two or three stories to the Darkover anthologies, and has many talents. She is one of the few people I've ever acknowledged as a better cook than I am myself. For another of her talents, look in almost any convention dealer's room; she makes splendid jewelry. She is also half of the musical team "Mid-Life Cri-sis" and has produced at least one excellent CD of dino-saur songs, "Fossil Fever," with her partner Dr. Jane Robinson. She appears with Jane at many local coffee-houses and conventions—where you'll also find many hu-morous and serious tapes of both folk and filk songs, as well as some of the best originals of their kind, many writ-ten by Cindy, who specializes in songs about vampires, both humorous and romantic.

One of the things I repeat almost ad nauseum is that to be a success as a writer usually means choosing among many talents—few people can stay afloat as part-time writ-

116

ers, but must choose it above all else. Cindy just might be the exception.

The sun shone brightly and the day was warm and pleasant, but Esmeralda found no joy in this. It seemed strange to be on the road by herself after all the years of tramping the highways and byways with her mother. Altura had raised her daughter to her own trade, that of herb selling; but it was never what the girl really wanted. And now that her mother was dead, she had to pursue the trade alone, without the comfort of company on her long journeys from village to village. She was alone with her thoughts, and they were always the same. . . .

Years ago, Esmeralda had lost her heart in a moment of magic, lost it so completely that nothing and no one could lay claim to it again. Even now, her longing burned as strongly as it had when she first saw the unicorn while she was bathing at the Goddess' sacred Virgin Spring. From that moment on, nothing would satisfy her but to have him. But to bind a unicorn took a bridle of gold; then, and now, she had no money to purchase such a thing.

Still, she'd worked hard in those intervening years, hoarding every penny like a treasure, spurred on by repeated glimpses of the beast. He would glide ghostlike through the trees that surrounded the glade of the spring, or stand just out of reach to watch her as she explored the ruins of the Goddess house nearby. Altura had told her that it had once housed the virgin priestesses of the spring. She'd also told her tales of how every year the maidens would come to the spring in hopes of proving themselves worthy of claiming one of the three-year positions as guardians of the shrine.

With a sigh, Esmeralda resigned herself once more to the fact that she would never see her dream fulfilled. She was seventeen, hardly a maidenly age. With her mother gone, everyone urged her to find a young man and marry, but she stubbornly insisted that she would continue her own life, as Altura had lived hers, alone in the forest she loved. After all, she had a perfectly nice stone hut hidden safely away from prying eyes. Furthermore, she would tell those who persisted, she was young and strong, and schooled in a reasonable trade. Why should she shackle herself to a man and be another's servant? And, of course, as long as she stayed in the forest, there was always a chance that she might see the unicorn.

Esmeralda paused for a moment to take a rest from pushing the cart full of herbs. She'd already made the rounds of all the nearby villages and was on her way to the Solstice Faire at Prentiss. While looking for a suitable spot to sit, she noticed a rare plant whose leaves, powdered and mixed with cream, were useful for treating Summer Rash. It grew several feet off the side of the road. As she went to collect it, she saw a gleam of gold flashing up at her through the tangled grass and weeds. It was a bit of gold chain spilling from a small chest, its wooden sides almost rotted away. Hardly believing her good fortune, she knelt to expose the rest of her find. Within the remnants of the chest lay several more chains, two plain gold rings, and a bracelet set with a discreet pattern of garnets. From its condition she judged that it must have lain there for a very long time, probably joggled from a passing cart.

Elated and anxious, she took the gold to old Rolpho, a smith she knew well and felt she could trust, asking that he make a golden bridle of the chain and rings.

"A bridle?" he asked incredulously. "But, young woman, you have no horse!"

"It's not actually for a horse; it's ... it's a magical piece, Rolpho; and one must not question the necessities of magic," she answered, but she hadn't fooled the old smith. He'd heard her prattling about the unicorn at the spring since she was fourteen years old. Still, what could he do? She was almost a grown woman.

When she returned to pick up her bridle, she offered him the bracelet for his labors. After chiding Esmeralda again for her lack of sense, he agreed to accept it.

"If your mother still lived, she'd see this put to better use," old Rolpho said kindly as he presented her with his handiwork.

"I suppose so," she said quietly, saddened at the reminder of her loss. She knew perfectly well that Altura would have wished her to use the gold for a dowry. In an odd way, though, that was exactly what she was doing.

"You know, it isn't good for a young girl to be alone." the smith said, shaking his head.

"But I'm not alone, Rolpho." she replied with a reassuring smile. "I have lots of friends in the forest. I have all I could possibly need—a good home, my trade, and my freedom."

Sensing her resolve, he let the matter drop; but her situation continued to concern him, the more so since she failed to return the following year, or any year after.

Having acquired the key to her desire, Esmeralda decided to return home immediately rather than complete her usual circuit of villages. She'd made enough already to supply herself through the lean months, and her heart bade her put her faith to the test with all speed. Upon her return, she went directly to her mother's grave. Shedding a few tears, she spread an offering of sweet herbs upon the stones that cloaked Altura's resting place, then whispered a charm for a spirit's ease.

"Forgive me, Mother," she said at least." I know this isn't the life you would have chosen for me, but while your heart wandered the world gleaning and giving, my heart runs in the forest on cloven hooves." When she was done, she returned to the hut in the clearing to make a simple meal of cheese and bread, then she laid down to rest, with thoughts of magic and unicorns chasing one another through her mind. . . .

Legend said that the magic of the unicorn's horn, dipped in the spring, purified the waters and kept the forest and the land healthy and fertile. When she was younger she'd laughed at the superstition, but that was before she'd seen the unicorn and felt his magical influence. Wonder had replaced skepticism as she often sought out the ruins of the shrine, restoring what she could. One day she came to realize that it was the unicorn himself who made the spring sacred, and that the maiden priestesses had become so by capturing him. And soon, if she proved worthy, she, too, might become the shrine's guardian priestess. . . .

Finally, Esmeralda slept. She awoke at daybreak but didn't rise, knowing she must conserve her strength. Her plans had been carefully laid; she knew that the unicorn would come to the spring at sunset, so the morning was gone before she rose to fix herself a cold meal. Then she drew on the breeches she'd purchased for today's encounter. To this she added a loose blouse, her stoutest pair of shoes, and a belt. Wearing men's clothing would give her greater freedom of movement than her own cumbersome skirts in case he bolted, as he had always done before when she tried to approach him. At last, she tied back her hair and tucked the bridle into the belt, making sure it was secure but easily grasped. Then she went to the spring to wait.

As the shadows grew long, her mind wandered, lulled by the warmth of the fading summer sun and the soft murmurs of the spring. She'd waited so long, she thought, surely by now she'd proved her devotion. A quiet sense of agreement stirred gently in the back of her mind, and she knew that he'd come. Maintaining her placid state of mind, she rose to meet the unicorn as he stepped from the nearby trees.

"Didn't expect me home so soon, did you?" she said softly, holding out her hand. Her comment was answered by a sense of amusement, but he bent his head to snuffle at her palm. Ever so slowly she reached her left hand to pet his silken neck. She hoped to catch hold of his mane while she reached for the bridle with her other hand. But just as she touched him, the chain jingled ever so slightly. His ears pricked and he was away in the beat of her heart; but she was ready.

At first she ran easily, matching him stride for stride, but as they raced through the twisted forest track she began to tire. He slowed his pace, allowing her to keep him in sight, but he was always just out of reach. Finally, he doubled back to the spring where it seemed he might surrender to her ardent pursuit. Blowing hard, he stood facing her across the glade. She was so spent that she could barely stand, and she fell to her knees sobbing,

"I'm done. You've had my best."

Then, miraculously, the beast came striding to her and lowered his head. It was all she could do to reach up and fasten the bridle, but somehow she managed.

"I love you, unicorn!" she murmured; then he, too, knelt, laying his head in her lap with a sigh. Cupping her hand, she dipped water from the pool and offered it to him. When he'd drunk his fill, she quenched her own thirst, and they both drifted into an exhausted sleep, the unicorn caught in the maiden's embrace.

Contented in each other's company, they lived happily together for many years. Daily, Esmeralda would lay in fresh grasses for him and he, in turn, taught her the ways of the wood. She no longer left the forest to seek the company of others, for she had all she needed. They might have continued so till the end of her days, but for the meddling of a human heart.

Rolpho had never forgotten her, nor the bridle he'd made. When she failed to return, he felt guilty for not having convinced her of the folly of her plan. After all, when did a young girl ever have the sense to know what was good for her? Thinking that she must have perished in pursuit of the unicorn, he grew morbid and would often speak of Esmeralda when he was in his cups.

Unfortunately, one night his tale caught the ears of three hunters in the employ of a magic worker. With cunning and guile they were upon him for every detail the old man could give them about the girl and her mother. Near dawn, they left him to sleep off his drunk on the floor of the tavern.

The trail was long cold, but these hunters were the hounds of a mage lord, finest of their kind, trained to sniff out the rare and magical creatures whose blood, bone, or hair was needful to their master's conjuring. Three cycles of the moon were all that had passed since their meeting with the old smith, but they'd already traced Esmeralda to the forest where she lived. The leader, Karl, was a tall, lean man of force and cunning; he held his fellows in check when they found the enchanted glade with its cozy little dwelling. Thrace and Grumm were more men of brute than intellect. They wanted to hunt the beast down like a deer, but Karl knew a better way. He made certain that the house was deserted, then he had them lay an ambush for Esmeralda's return.

They didn't have long to wait, for it was almost noon and she returned shortly to prepare her midday meal. As was his custom, the unicorn was roaming the forest and wouldn't return till sundown. Then he'd be drawn inexorably, by the enchantment of the bridle, to Esmeralda's side.

"Who are you?" Esmeralda demanded as she entered the house to find Karl taking his ease at her table. She seemed more irritated than alarmed, until the other two stepped out of hiding behind her, blocking her escape.

"You must be Esmeralda," Karl said coolly. "We know

a friend of yours, a metalsmith from Prentiss. He frets himself quite a lot about you."

"As you can see, there's no need," she replied warily.

"Here now," Grumm grunted, "I thought she was supposed to be a maiden, not some grown woman."

"She only has to be a *virgin* to catch a unicorn; the master's books don't say anything about bein' young," Thrace chimed in, always trying to seem knowledgeable. Esmeralda's heart sank at the mention of the unicorn.

"Well," said Grumm wiping his mouth in anticipation, "maybe we should see whether or not she's a virgin."

"But won't that release the unicorn?" Thrace asked Karl.

"Not if he's wearing the bridle. He's bound till someone removes it, or he's dead," he said, casually letting his hand stroke her chin. She realized they were after the unicorn's horn and the magic it contained, but before she could speak, he grabbed her face and squeezed it hard, saying, "We didn't find a bridle or any gold at all when we searched this place."

"I sold it," she lied.

"Then we've come all this way for nothing," he commented with mock woe. "Surely, then, you wouldn't begrudge us a little womanly comfort for our trouble." His hand was now on her breast and she found her arms pinned behind her.

They hauled her roughly to the bed. She tried to fight, but to no avail; they were too many and too strong. Karl cut her garments away with his dagger while the other two held her down. They took turns with her, finally leaving her to sob into the rumpled bedclothes. Actually, her tears were from frustration and rage, though she allowed the ruffians to think otherwise, hoping that if they thought her cowed enough, she might find a chance to escape before sunset.

At last she pulled herself to the edge of the bed. Gathering the quilt about her, she said meekly,

"Please, can I go to the trough and wash myself. I'm so filthy." She gestured with lowered eyes to the blood that streaked her legs and arms. Karl hadn't been gentle, or careful with his dagger either.

He eyed her critically, then said, "You go with her, Grumm, and look sharp." It was still some time before nightfall, which Karl knew would bring the unicorn, so he thought it would be safe enough. She certainly seemed biddable, now that she'd been properly schooled.

She stumbled and trembled as she walked, mostly for their benefit, though she really was quite sore. Her anger carried her past the worst of the shame and discomfort. Carefully, she hobbled around to the other side of the trough, pretending to be afraid of her chaperon. Then she gingerly laved her hurts with the cool water that she'd brought herself from the sacred spring. As she did so, she felt strength and resolve flowing through her. She felt certain the unicorn was near, that he'd been watching the glade all afternoon, waiting. And now she knew just what she must do.

"I need to relieve myself," she said, plaintively leaning on the trough as if for support. "Perhaps you could help me to those trees."

"God's breath, girl," he grunted. "Just squat and do your business."

"But I'm sore," she whimpered, contriving to twist and fall backward into the mud.

"Well, you're the picture of grace." He laughed as he bent to pull her up.

As he did, she reached out to grasp the fist-sized rock she'd managed to land next to, and without hesitation struck him on the side of the head. He sank heavily on top of her in a grotesque mimicry of his earlier rape. For effect, she cried out piteously,

Her plaint was met with crude laughter and calls of encouragement from inside the cottage. She grunted and whimpered as she shoved Grumm's limp body away from her. She continued to moan until she was on her feet, then bolted toward the edge of the clearing where she'd seen a telltale flash of white. She ran with desperation, heedless of the pain in her legs and belly, until at last she found him.

Frantically she threw her arms around his neck, reaching to unfasten the clasp which held the bridle in place. It wouldn't give for several heartbreaking minutes; when it finally did, she dragged it roughly from his head crying, "Run!" The unicorn just stood there looking into her eyes. Tears streamed down her face as she beat at him with closed fists. "Go! Please go. I'd rather never have seen you once than to see you die this day."

Karl cried out from somewhere nearby, then she heard

the sound of running feet and was sure that they'd have him. The unicorn started, then blinked and nodded as though making up his mind about something. He stepped back, bent his head to her one last time, and pierced her through the heart with his horn. The pain was a distant coldness in the midst of the warmth and light that seemed to be pouring through her, then his voice was in her mind urging *her* to run. She saw him turn and leaped to follow.

Too confounded by what they'd witnessed even to draw bow or blade, the three hunters watched as two unicorns bounded away into the secret depths of the forest.

THE HAVEN
by Judith Kobylecky

Judith Kobylecky is married with three children—10, 7, and 3—which shows up the women who say that kids and writing don't mix. But then I already knew that—didn't you? It's easiest when the kids are still small enough to stay where they're put and need only a few diaper changes. My own late husband languished under the delusion that it would be easier as the kids get older, but it isn't; the needs of babies are mostly physical and limited to making them comfortable, but the needs of adolescents are psychically demanding and unending; so cherish their brief infancy!

This story forces the reader to question and probably reassign the definition of monster. That's what writing—and everything else—is really all about: rearranging, as you grow, your definitions. Of everything.

Mirelle sat wrapped in shawls against the chill morning air and waited for the destroyer of her world to come.

Carefully, she smoothed the charts that lay on her lap and checked again her findings, knowing all the while that she had made no mistakes. Perhaps it would not have come to this if all the sorcerers had banded together while they still had the strength, but the opportunity passed before they had begun to realize what they had lost.

With stiff fingers she rolled her charts back up and pulled

her wraps tighter around her. The cold greatly aggravated the disease that ravaged her joints and caused her so much suffering. She looked down at her painfully twisted fingers; as a sorceress, it would have been so simple, years ago, to have cured herself of the disease, but that was before magic had all but disappeared from the world. It was the colors of sorcery, she felt, that she missed the most. From that long ago morning of her childhood when her gift had come to her, she had been able to see the enchantment around her, reflected in even the most ordinary of objects. In the beginning, the loss had been so gradual that few noticed; even later it was wondered at and commented on, but no one grasped its significance until it was too late. She fingered her charts. There was no longer any doubt of how complete the destruction was. Whole areas had been stripped of their remaining magic, the wizards who inhabited them found dead.

Faint music roused Mirelle from her thoughts. She looked up to see a tiny golden sphere hovering in the air before her. At her gesture, it landed on her opened hand as lightly as a soap bubble, threads of enchantment still swirling around it. Mirelle looked at it for a long time, certain she already knew the message it carried. Reluctantly, she breathed on the sphere; it spun and burst in the air, releasing the dying words of another sorcerer. Her eyes filled with tears as she listened to his few words, he had time only to say that what he had planned had failed. She grieved at the loss of another friend. There were so very few of her kind left.

In the distance she saw that the colors had begun to drain away; the creature was coming closer. She reached for her cane and got up slowly from her chair, her charts falling unnoticed to the ground. For years she had hoarded what little magic she had left and done nothing to ease her pain. Holding on to the doorway for support, she went into the old house that had sheltered generations of sorcerers before her; magic clung to its very stones. Many times over the years she had sought the comfort of listening to the echoes of enchantments long past, but now when she ran her hands along its smooth walls she felt only stone. Gone were the whispers of vanished sorcerers; the creature had to be very near. Working as quickly as her aching hands would allow, she assembled a small collection of materials and gathered them up in a small pile. Deep in concentration, she began to summon the magic that she had kept sealed within her for so long. The effort took all of her failing strength, but when she was finished she cradled a shimmering ball in her hands not unlike the one that had brought her the message. Larger, its gold was shot through with every color that magic had been to her, every color that she had lost. Trembling with exhaustion, she sat down in the armchair near the fire.

The door that led to the outside slowly swung open, and in the doorway stood a small figure wrapped in a blanket. Mirelle thought for a moment that her fear would paralyze her, but she forced herself to speak, "Please, come in." The quaver in her voice dismayed her. She had to bring the creature close to her and keep it there, or all of her work would be for nothing. Mirelle took a deep breath to calm herself and called to it again, "Come, join me by the fire where it is warm."

The monster walked very slowly into the circle of firelight where it could be clearly seen. Mirelle was shocked to see that the creature they all feared looked more like a starving child than a destroyer of worlds. Its skin was pulled tight over its face, its eyes frightened and staring. The colors of sorcery began to fade from the room; the skeletal figure was absorbing them before it would begin to feed on her own magic. Soon, she knew, it would pull to itself the magic that was at the core of her being and kill her in the process. Holding the sphere out to the creature, she beckoned it closer. Was it once an apprentice who had unleashed a terrible spell, Mirelle wondered, or just a child to whom the gift had come twisted, always starving and never finding enough to eat. She grieved that she would never find out what had happened, that she probably could not have saved the child even if she had known.

"Come here, little one. I have some beautiful magic for you. I know you are hungry. Come to me."

The creature turned yearning eyes on her and slowly climbed onto her lap and laid its head on her shoulder with a shuddering sigh, its eyes fixed on the enchanted sphere she held in her hand. Already Mirelle was beginning to feel cold as her magic left her, but she let it flow out of her to hold the child there. And to comfort the little boy, for that was what he was to her now, a dying child and no longer a monster. She breathed on the sphere to give forth its magic and ease the child's hunger. In her other hand she broke open a small vial; together they breathed in the sweet scent of poison gas. Mirelle held him close and sang to him the way she had sung to her own children; he smiled up at her and closed his eyes to rest. As death came to them, she felt the magic released from the child's tortured body. She kissed his cheek and eased their way with a lullaby.

SAVIOR
by Tom Gallier

Tom starts out by telling me it was a thrill to receive my letter of acceptance. It always is; that's one thrill you never grow out of—no, not even at my age, and I've probably been at it longer than most of my audience has been alive. He says "Savior" is his first professional sale, and: "Since it is quite possible for Tom to be a female name in China or Mongolia, I will tell you that I am male and have been since before I was born." He adds, "I live in Dallas with a lot of persistent characters—most carrying swords and blasters—living inside my computer and demanding my constant attention. When not slavishly attending their needs, I work as an electronic technician for a fiber optics firm. I am single and intend to stay that way until I get married. Like the other 3.4 billion writers in the world, I am currently working on a novel, and have a couple looking for homes in the publishing world . . . I guess deluging you with a story a week worked; you finally got tired of rejecting them."

It usually does, sooner or later—though there are some people out there—nameless, of course, who send me a story a week for months or years without ever learning anything. But Tom's stories kept improving to the point where rejecting them was no longer necessary for the benefit of the reader. Persistence is more important than talent; talent unappreciated is the commonest thing in the world. I'm glad your stories finally came in out of the cold.

129

The dragon bellowed, spewing flames all about the cavern. Princess Myriah cringed back against the cold, damp stone as one stream of searing fire came close. Too close. Once the dragon calmed down somewhat, she considered voicing a complaint but ruled it out immediately. That nasty overgrown lizard wouldn't pay any heed to her anyway.

The faint echo of steel grating against rock came from the tunnel again. Princess Myriah threw her hands before her face to fend off the expected heat and flames of the dragon's vented rage. The rusty steel manacles bit painfully into the tender skin of her wrists. When the expected torrents of flames didn't happen, she peeked warily between her fingers at the dragon. It had pressed itself flat against the floor, watching the entrance with those unnerving, unblinking reptilian eyes. The score of fires burning about the cavern now lit it brightly, bringing out the beautiful iridescent blue of the monster's scales.

Myriah bit her lip nervously. This was the first man to try to rescue her in nearly three months of captivity. That he was of noble blood and stout of heart, she had no doubt. Only ... *she* looked atrocious. Her once-lustrous brown hair was filthy and tangled. Her silk gown was equally dirty, and half-shredded by the sharp rocks. She feared any noble savior wouldn't find her appealing. Gods, he might even refuse her father's offer of her hand!

But then an armored head peeked out of the darkness of the tunnel. The ruddy light of the dragonfire reflected off its mirrored surface. Myriah was impressed. Such armor was expensive. Once he dispatched the dragon, she'd live life in luxury. With her savior, her prince.

The dragon and knight sprang at each other at the same time. The knight was remarkably agile and quick, avoiding the dragonfire as he raced in. Myriah watched in awe as her would-be savior attacked, sword and shield a blur. She had never seen such brilliant weapons handling, and she was a regular at the Games. She would surely be the most envied of all princesses!

"Be wary, my prince! The beast is an ancient and crafty foe!"

If the knight heard her warning, he was too busy to acknowledge her. She didn't fault him that, though.

Within minutes, the dragon was on the defensive. The

knight was fast, a deadly talent with edged steel. The dragon was nearly hysterical, spewing fire all about in its pain and fear. The fire and smoke only served to further camouflage the knight's vicious attack. Then, when the creature lowered its massive triangular head to spew fire at what it thought was the knight, the knight leaped over the flames to and plunged a yard of cold steel though its brain.

Princess Myriah squealed in delight and clapped her hands, careful not to further injure her delicate wrists. Her prince-savior had vanquished the evil dragon and rescued her. Their names would go down in romantic legend. And she would finally be married. And married well.

"My prince! My hero! I promise undying love and adoration," she cried as the knight headed her way.

The gore-splattered knight stopped a pace before her, chuckling. Myriah was slightly taken aback.

Hesitantly, she asked, "May I see the face of my savior? I would see the strong warrior whom my father will surely reward with my hand in marriage."

"Actually, I'd prefer gold instead," the knight said, removing the great helm. With a slight bow, "Karyn of Ohmsford, Paladin of Traq'el, at your service."

The knight was dark-haired, with a proud nose and strong square jaw. And clearly a woman. She stood there, arrogantly grinning at the princess.

Princess Myriah was dumbstruck.

"A woman! Gods! No, please, no!" Myriah wailed, head thrown back in despair. Turning away, she began pounding the stone walls and stomping her feet. Karyn stepped back, eyeing the princess warily as her tantrum continued. It was not the response she had expected. Then Myriah abruptly stopped and whirled around to face away from the knight. "Sarrin!"

The wall several paces before the enraged princess slid aside revealing a comfortably appointed chamber. Karyn cocked her head to get a better look inside the unexpected room. A tall gangly man in black wizards' robes was shuffling out. He stopped several paces before his princess, wringing his hands and looking sheepishly at Myriah.

Princess Myriah pointed at Karyn, "Explain this!"

"I . . . I don't understand. The spell should've . . ." he said, then turned abruptly to Karyn. "Paladin, are you of noble birth?"

Shrugging, she answered "My father is king of Parquin."

"Ha! That's it, my princess. The spell wasn't specific enough," Sarrin said. "It hadn't occurred to me that a princess would try to rescue you, otherwise I'd have taken care of that. It won't happen again, I promise."

"It better not," she snapped.

Holding up her hands, she glared at the wizard. He cringed a bit at her anger, then made a strange motion and the chains vanished. Without another word, Princess Myriah marched into the chamber behind him.

"This was all a setup," Karyn said, eyes narrowing at the wizard. Her hand fell to her hilt. "Explain yourself."

He didn't fail to notice the menace in her wide blue eyes or her actions.

"Nothing sinister, Lady Paladin," he said hastily, assuming that sheepish look again. "As a princess, you should understand, what with all the wars recently."

Realization dawned. "Which leaves too many princesses without suitable husbands. And no prince worth his salt would be able to resist coming to a princess' rescue, and winning her hand from a grateful father."

"You see, it's all harmless," Sarrin said, smiling. "The dragon is not real and is designed to lose after a close fight. And a spell in the tunnel diverted unsuitable men to a side chamber and a dragon's skeleton. They would then leave disheartened."

"Ha! I love it!" Karyn cried, slapping her thigh.

"You won't say anything, will you?" the wizard asked. "My king will surely reward your silence well."

Smiling, Karyn pulled her nearly empty purse off her sword belt. "Silence is golden, wizard. The more golden the better."

Sarrin grinned, "And I thought paladins were above such mercenary desires."

"And I thought princesses were above such deceit as this," she grinned back.

BAD LUCK AND CURSES
by Jessie Eaker

This is Jessie Eaker's fourth professional sale; his other three stories appeared in Sword and Sorceress #VI, #VII, and #IX. Despite the traditional female spelling of his name, he is male. That spelling is traditional in the Eaker family. He adds that his last name is pronounced "Acre" as in a measure of land. "Admittedly this causes gender and phonetic confusion, but it gives me great pride to wear a name so rich in family history."

He and his wife Becki are kept busy with all of their exceptionally bright and talented children. Daniel, the youngest, is entering the "terrible twos" just a little early. "He has always been active, but of late he has given the word new meaning."

Well, as for the "terrible twos"—which aren't so terrible (the only kids who never give any trouble are feeble-minded ones who are no trouble at all)—the sooner into them, the sooner they're over.

A twig snapped behind her. Jerking her dagger out of the loose soil, Geyth leaped to her feet and faced two approaching men. They were nearly upon her. Both wore rough and dirty clothing, and their hair was long and unkempt. She knew their kind well.

The nearer flinched back a step and regarded her cautiously. She took comfort in that small motion; he had not counted on the dagger. But his hesitation did not last long.

She saw his eyes flit from her well-made tunic, to the broken amulet around her neck, to the bracelet around her wrist. He grinned, revealing yellow, broken teeth.

Yellow Teeth spoke, "Working the flowers, I see."

The other man snickered and began to hit his thigh with a short club, a rhythmic *slap, slap, slap*. He stepped to one side, cutting her off from her horse grazing several paces away. Brandishing her dagger, she pointed it from one man to the other, clutching it tightly, and feeling the grit and the sweat on her hand. She took a wary step backward, brushing against the bushes whose soil she had been tending. They were *itha* bushes ... from her homeland.

Geyth cursed her foolishness. She should have known better than to have taken off her travel cloak with the symbol of her trade. *That* protection lay draped over the saddle of her horse, facedown and unseen. The delight of smelling *itha* bushes—even finding them!—had overridden her usual caution. Surely, she had told herself, there would be no harm in stopping for a moment. The clump of bushes grew concealed in the center of a large forest clearing. She had located them by scent alone! What could possibly go wrong on such a fine day. . . .

Yellow Teeth calmly pulled a long knife from his belt. Geyth tried not to show her fear as she eyed its length. It was ugly in the manner of blades without even a proper handle. But it was well honed—something a farmer might use to gut an animal. Yellow Teeth licked his lips and crept closer.

"My lady," he said. "Put the dagger aside and we will not harm you. Your silver is all we want—and we aim to take it one way or the other. Be easy on yourself."

Geyth's dagger did not waver. The man's eyes whispered his true thoughts, and his greed was plainly great. But she would *not* give up her hard earned silver without a fight.

"Thief!" she called to him. "I am not a lady of wealth. Magic is my trade. Leave now or I will curse you."

Undaunted, Yellow Teeth shook his head. "Your amulet is broken and you wear no symbols." He gestured toward her with his knife. "I think you lie."

Geyth ground her teeth and glared at him. If she could reach the cloak on her horse and the symbol it bore, she could show them what she really was. Then they would flee, running and screaming. But, for now, another tactic. . . .

She heaved a despairing sigh and dropped her arms in submission. She bowed her head.

Yellow Teeth chuckled. "Wise choice, my lady."

Suddenly, Geyth feinted toward the man with the club, then switched and leaped between Yellow Teeth and the bushes. Her speed surprised them and they reacted a moment too late. Yellow Teeth grabbed for her but only caught the edge of her tunic. It ripped, leaving a piece in his hand and spinning her around. Surprisingly, she kept her balance, and she fled toward her horse. She looked back and saw Yellow Teeth running after her, close behind, knife held ready. She tried to force her legs faster.

Unexpectedly, she felt a sharp pain in her left leg and she stumbled. She landed hard, sliding to a stop on the short grass and knocking the wind from her chest. Yellow Teeth immediately slammed on top of her. Rough hands grabbed her, turned her to her back, and held her down. Yellow Teeth leaned over her, breathing hard, his stinking breath hot in her face. He smirked in victory.

Geyth prayed that—for once in her miserable life—something good would happen. *Please, Goddess Mother, haven't I been punished enough . . . !*

Unexpectedly, a battle cry rang out from the other side of the flowering bushes. Surprised, both men looked up to see a lone, unarmed figure leap from the hedge and charge toward them. Yellow Teeth grunted in frustration and sat up. He pointed toward the interloper, and the man with the club stepped over to meet the challenge. Yellow Teeth watched for his chance to approach from behind.

Through a haze of pain and shock, Geyth stared at the approaching figure. At first, she couldn't make out anything except a blurry shadow against the bright sky. Was it the Goddess Mother herself come to save her? But Geyth knew better. She blinked and managed to make out a woman—silver-haired and in her middle years—but tall, with bare, well-muscled arms. The woman ran with incredible speed, and with the grace and agility of one accustomed to fighting.

Geyth knew from experience that her sudden change in luck would not hold. With the men's attention diverted, she tried to stand, but toppled back to the ground with her left leg burning in pain. She found the calf covered in blood—a ragged gash from yellow Teeth's knife. She tore a strip from her tunic and tried to staunch the flow. It did not want to stop. Unable to run, she kept a weary eye on the developing fight.

The man with the club had positioned himself in the woman's line of approach. He stood waiting with his weapon raised to his shoulder. The woman never hesitated.

When the woman came into reach, the man with the club swung at her head. But with uncanny speed, she ducked under the swing and drove a fist into his belly. The blow nearly lifted him off the ground, and the air went out of him with an audible whoosh. As he gasped for breath, the club slipped from his fingers and he staggered. Twice more she punched and the man toppled toward her. She staggered back under his weight. Yellow Teeth slipped behind her and raised his knife.

"Behind you!" Geyth yelled.

The woman wheeled, using the momentum of the collapsing man to throw him into Yellow Teeth ... and onto the man's knife. Spitting in anger, Yellow Teeth jerked his blade free and dove for the woman. She caught his arm and the two grappled. Then, so fast Geyth could scarcely believe she saw it, the woman sidestepped, bringing Yellow Teeth's arm quickly down and under to impale him with his own blade. With a cry, he fell to the ground and did not get up.

Feeling light-headed, Geyth watched nervously as the woman walked towards her. This woman could want her silver as much as the men. And with her leg so badly injured, she could not flee.

But the woman, breathing hard and covered with sweat, quickly knelt beside her and tore another piece from Geyth's tunic. She pushed aside Geyth's thick fingers and began to bandage the would. "Goddess mother, girl! This leg is bleeding like a palace fountain! It's going to need sewing." She leaned forward and placed a hand on Geyth's forehead. "And you're sweaty and pale. Feeling faint, too, I'd wager."

Geyth managed a weak nod. It felt as if her strength were pouring out of her. She felt so cold.

The woman rose and walked slowly to the horse. She patted it reassuringly on the shoulder and moved the travel cloak which had been thrown across the saddle. . . . But she froze at the symbol it revealed.

Geyth swallowed and waited for her to do as everyone did: make a warding sign, and then quietly slink away. *No help to one such as you.* But to Geyth's surprise and admiration, the woman only grunted and pushed the cloak aside.

Geyth must have blacked out for a moment, because the horse was suddenly standing beside her and the woman was bodily lifting her onto its back. Geyth gritted her teeth at the pain in her leg. The woman mounted behind her and held her in place.

"Don't worry, child," said the woman, covering Geyth with the travel cloak. "My old gardener's cottage is just beyond these bushes. We'll be there before you know it."

The last thing Geyth saw before she faded from consciousness was the symbol on the travel cloak. It seemed to float before her: a snake, an eye, and the moon within a silver circle. She had put it there herself, laboriously stitching the pattern into the black fabric. Many tears had gone into its making, and it symbolized not only her profession, but her own failure and disgrace. *Bad luck and curses,* it said. *Sold for silver.*

Geyth awoke slowly, noticing first the warmth of the bed, then the brightness of the room, and finally the faint smell of mustiness, mixed with spices and bread. At first, Geyth thought herself back in the temple city of Percillis—in the room she had shared with the dozen other priestesses in training. And that at any moment, old Sidra would come to wake them and take them to the tower for prayer; then later after a quick breakfast of cold bread, they would review their lessons while kneeling on their mats. It had been strict, but she had enjoyed the rigor . . . until they had expelled her.

No, she scolded herself. *You ran away. Couldn't stand to see another blessing turn sour and didn't dare go home in failure and disgrace.* In their eyes, she would be worse than dirt. So with no other way to earn her next meal, she had turned to selling curses. *I had no choice,* she told herself. *And I was very good at it.*

Opening her eyes, she found herself in a small cottage. Bright light streamed through two open windows on either side of a wooden door and she lay on a straw pallet covered with a linen sheet. A fur lay over her. Except for the pain in her leg, she hadn't been this comfortable in ages.

The latch on the cottage door lifted and the silver-haired woman entered. She smiled and her eyes seemed to twinkle. Geyth was frozen by her genuine warmth.

"Awake, I see," the woman said. "And just in time for breakfast." She set a heavy basket on the room's only table.

Geyth blinked in surprise. "Have I been out that long?" It had been afternoon when the men had attacked her. But, gradually, wisps of memory floated by: being lifted off her horse, others looking at her, being given something to drink. . . .

The woman chuckled. "You've been out for *two* days, child." She began unpacking the basket. "The healer feared the wound would go bad and gave you a potion. I've had it myself, and it puts you right to sleep."

The woman brought over a bowl of porridge and helped Geyth prop up on her pallet. Geyth tentatively took a first bite, unsure how her stomach would react. But it took it well and quickly demanded more. She looked up, embarrassed to find that she had emptied the bowl.

The woman had sat quietly on a stool while Geyth ate. "Don't be embarrassed," she said. "You've lost a lot of blood and you need to eat." She grinned. "I just wouldn't try to do it all at once." The woman reached for the empty bowl.

Geyth handed it to her. She couldn't help noticing the ring the woman wore—a warrior's band of gold.

"You have been so kind to me," said Geyth. "My lady, I thank you from the bottom of my heart."

The woman snorted. "Just call me Myrrha. I've long since abandoned the idea of becoming a lady." She grinned. "And you owe me no thanks. I would do the same for anyone on my lands."

Geyth's eyes widened. "Then this is not your house, you must have something . . . bigger."

Myrrha chuckled. "Yes, child, my keep is at the top of the hill. This cottage belonged to my gardener, who passed away during the winter. Lucky for you, I was cleaning it out when I heard the commotion. Although, I should give you a lashing for leaving the road. That was sheer foolishness girl."

Geyth blushed. "I smelled the *itha* blossoms from the road. And I . . . I *needed* to find them."

Understanding dawned on Myrrha's face. "Then you're from the southern lands?"

Geyth bowed her head. "Yes, my . . . uh . . . Myrrha. My name is Geyth and I come from Bechure." Myrrha was obviously ready to hear more, but Geyth thought it best to say no more. She could never go back anyway.

Myrrha nodded, finally understanding. She stood. "Well Geyth, you are welcome to stay here until you mend. I brought enough supplies to last you through the day. The healer will be by to see you later. Be warned that he may want to put another potion in you. And don't worry about your horse. He's being cared for at my stables."

Geyth bowed her head. "You are doing too much."

Myrrha smiled. "Not really. I owe you something for weeding those damn *itha* bushes. They certainly needed it, and if I'd touched them, they would have shriveled up and died."

Geyth couldn't help but smile in return.

Myrrha continued. "I have some business back at the keep, but I will return before night to check on you." She took a step toward the door but stopped and looked back. "I took the liberty of hanging your cloak outside. No one will bother you with that visible, although I suspect it will draw those wanting your services." She frowned and Geyth suddenly felt the world frown with her. "I would appreciate it if you did not practice your craft while you are here. I feel bad enough that I had to put you up here, but if I had put you in the keep, I fear my servants would have run off. I hope this doesn't offend you."

Geyth bowed her head. "Not at all. I am surprised you even let me stay on your lands. Most fear the bad luck I can bring."

Myrrha smiled, the twinkle returning to her eyes. "As for myself, I do not believe in bad luck. There are only opportunities. You can always turn something bad into something good, if you look at it the right way." And with that, she walked out the door.

Geyth frowned after her in disbelief. *Not believe in bad luck!* How could she possibly say that? Bad luck was all Geyth had ever known, even before she had tried to become a priestess to the Goddess Mother. Wasn't the death of her mother when she was seven seasons bad luck? Wasn't the cruelty of her father's new bride bad luck? Wasn't her own rape by a passing soldier bad luck? Geyth shook her head. Myrrha was certainly kind, but she knew nothing of bad luck.

Geyth sat up, looking for the chamber pot and wincing at the pain in her leg as she slowly stood. It did not feel as bad as she had expected. In only a hand's worth of days, she would be able to travel again. The young woman frowned. Not that she was all that anxious to move on. Living on the road was hard: sleeping on the ground, eating meals prepared over an open fire, traveling alone.... Always alone. Even when she visited a village, they would not talk to her—just spit as she walked by. They visited her only to make a request: curse this man for cheating me, bring bad luck on that woman for refusing me. To all, she said yes. But she never stayed long enough to see the fruits of her work. She had no lack of confidence in her powers.

Geyth went to the open windows and inhaled the gentle spring breeze. It was so pleasant here and her favorite flowers were only paces away. Geyth decided she would stay in the cottage as long as she could—maybe even stretch it out a little. Geyth grinned. Maybe she would even tend the *itha* bushes again. That was the one thing she took pleasure in—taking care of flowers and plants. They did not trouble her like people did—nor desire bad for those that ill treated them.

The evening of the fifth day at the cottage found Geyth brushing her long hair in preparation for bed. It was a habit she had practiced since childhood and one she had doggedly stuck to while on the road. Although at times it had been pointless, she usually enjoyed it. And this evening was no exception. She hummed to herself a melody from her childhood.

Suddenly, she froze. Outside she heard hoofs approaching. She held her breath. They drew up outside her door and a heartbeat later someone banged loudly on the door.

"Who is it?" she called.

"One seeking your services," answered a man's voice

from the other side. It was deep and commanded respect, as one used to giving commands.

She groaned inwardly. *So soon? I had hoped to stay just a little longer.*

"Go away," she called back. "Lady Myrrha has forbidden me to practice on her land." She started at the brush in her lap.

"I have silver," the voice answered. "I will pay you well. No one will know but you and I."

She hesitated. "Go away."

She heard boots shuffle on the stones before the door. "I will pay you quite well. Even in gold. . . ."

Geyth looked up in surprise. Most were willing to pay well for a curse, but not too well. And never in gold. She licked her lips. With gold she could buy a cottage just like this. Maybe even a small farm—and give up her life on the road. She opened the door.

A tall man strode into the room—broad shouldered and bearded in the fashion of the northern men—he had to duck to enter. The cottage suddenly seemed tiny in his presence. Geyth thought he would have been handsome if his mouth had not been fixed with a permanent sneer. Without hesitation, he sat down on a stool and placed his elbows on the table. She sat on the other side and waited for him to speak.

"I need you to curse someone for me," he finally said. "I want them severely crippled, but not killed. Can you do this?"

Geyth nodded. "I can."

The man leaned forward and grinned. "And can you do it tonight?"

Geyth sighed and glanced down at the brush she still held. "If you can get me a personal item—like a lock of hair or a favorite piece of clothing. . . ."

The man reached into his belt pouch and pulled out a tiny bundle wrapped in a piece of linen. He tossed it on the table along with three pieces of gold. Geyth licked her lips and tried to keep her eyes from the coins. Her hand trembled as it took the bundle. Inside was a lock of white hair.

"Who is it you want cursed?" she asked.

The man clenched his fists. The blood left his knuckles. "Do you need to know?"

Geyth suddenly understood that this man was very dangerous. All her clients were a threat to one extent or another. But this man—the slitted eyes, the tensed shoulders, the cocked jaw—all indicated he was more than dangerous. He was deadly.

"No," she stammered. "I do not need the person's name. The hair will do."

He nodded once and stood. "Then unless you require my presence, I will be leaving." He strode to the door and opened it, but paused at the threshold and turned. "Do not think to cheat me. If the person is untouched, I will seek you out and kill you. Even if you run." He walked out into the night.

Geyth began to wonder if she had just made a mistake.

The next morning, Geyth went out to work the flowers. But they brought no enjoyment. The cursing had been easy, no magical backlash as sometimes occurred. But she couldn't shake the feeling of uneasiness ... and guilt. Not for the curse itself, but for the betrayal of Myrrha's trust. She felt dirty and used. It was time to move on.

At noon, a messenger from Myrrha arrived, asking her to come to the keep. No explanation was given. She was to be "consulted" was all he would say. Geyth decided she would take this opportunity to tell Myrrha she was leaving. She owed her host at least that much courtesy.

Deciding not to pull on the cloak of her office, she went with the messenger. At mid-afternoon, she entered the keep—a large stone tower surrounded by high walls. The messenger got them quick passage inside and she was taken up several flights of stairs. Finally, they stopped before a thick wooden door guarded by a man in light armor. He examined her critically before allowing her to pass.

They entered into a bed chamber. Myrrha lay face up on a fur covered couch. She appeared to be asleep. Around her stood several servants and men she recognized as Myrrha's commanders. Expressions of concern were on every face. *What is wrong?*

One of the men snarled at her. "Whore! How could you—"

"Now, Kerrard," said Myrrha calmly from her bed, startling Geyth. "We don't know that yet."

Geyth felt her stomach tighten. "What happened?"

"You don't know?" asked Myrrha.

Geyth shook her head. But she was beginning to suspect. She looked from the men and back to Myrrha. "What is wrong?"

One of the servants answered, "My lady fell down a flight of stairs this morn. She took some nasty bumps to her head. Now, she can't move, nor can she see. The healer says she has broken something inside and will be like that till she dies."

Geyth's hand flew to her mouth. *I need you to curse someone for me,* the man had said. *I want them crippled. . . .* It had been Myrrha's hair the man had brought—the only one in this whole northern country that had shown her any kindness. And she had cursed her! A ragged sob escaped her.

The man Kerrard watched her closely. "She's shaking her head," he said for Myrrha's benefit. "And she appears confused and shocked. Your accident seems to have taken her by surprise."

Myrrha smiled sadly. "I'm afraid gentlemen, that you are going to have to admit that this just *happened,* and a curse had nothing to do with it. Besides, Geyth gave me her word."

Geyth swallowed and fought back tears. It felt like someone was squeezing her heart. She stared in horror at the prone figure. Blind *and* crippled. Geyth had done her job very well.

"Bad luck," whispered one of the servants. "Just bad luck."

Myrrha chuckled. "No, old friend. It was not bad luck, only my own clumsiness. You've been telling me to watch myself on those steps since I came here." She shook her head. "No, this is an opportunity. I just need to find the *good* that will come of it." She grinned. "Although I admit, it might take me a while to figure this one out."

Just then a tall man, broad shouldered—bearded in the fashion of the northern men—strode into the room. He paused at the threshold and surveyed those inside. Geyth bit her lip. *It's him!* It was the man who had come to her last night. *What is he doing here!*

The man coolly noted Geyth's presence but said nothing. He immediately went to Myrrha, knelt beside her, and took her hand. He pressed it reverently to his lips. "My lady, it is I, Leighton. I came as soon as I heard."

"That was kind of you," said Myrrha, a note of irritation in her voice. "I expected you would."

"How could such a thing happen?" he demanded.

Myrrha smiled. "That is exactly what we were trying to discover. My captain here thought this woman might have put a curse on me. But she is apparently as shocked as the rest."

Leighton looked over his shoulder at Geyth. He shook his head. "I believe her. It would not make sense for her to hurt you. What could she gain by it?" He signed. "But never fear. I will make sure all is well. I will personally see that no further harm comes to you."

"That is kind of you," said Myrrha. "But I am still perfectly able to command my people."

Leighton shook his head. "No, I insist." He glanced at Geyth and for just a moment she caught that flash of dangerousness in his eyes. It was a clear warning.

"And maybe later," he continued. "We can discuss my proposal. I know you've turned me down many times, but the offer is still open. Even confined to a couch, you would be the best wife a man could want. Just give me the word and I will arrange it." Myrrha stiffened as Leighton patted her hand. "Think about it. It could be advantageous to us both. Joining our lands would make us both powerful. . . ."

"No, Leighton." Myrrha shook her head. "It might be advantageous for you, since you would have complete control, but it would not benefit my lands or my servants. Besides, your many creditors might confuse my property with yours."

Leighton bowed his head. "As you wish."

But Geyth could see the issue was far from over.

Geyth sat at the small table in her cottage. The sun had long since gone down, and only a tiny lamp, resting in the center of the table, illuminated the room. She kept touching the three gold coins spread on the table before her. Combined with her meager savings, it would be enough to purchase a small cottage. Nothing fancy, of course, but it would be enough.

She turned the coins over and examined their other side. She should be happy. But thoughts of poor Myrrha, unable to see and unable to move, kept intruding. She turned the coins over again—searching. Searching for the blood that should be on them. Blood for the evil she had done.

Not since the early days had she seen the results of her curses—she was usually well away the next morning. She had pushed from her mind just how devastating they could be. *You do not believe in goodness.* That was what the old priestess had told her before she left Percillis. *You have to believe in good, before good will happen.* Her first attempt at a blessing had proven this well.

Still an apprentice, they had decided to allow her to bless the novice guardswomen after they took their oath of allegiance to the Goddess Mother. Nothing difficult, just a general wish for good luck and well-being. But as she had gazed upon their upturned faces, all she saw was strong women with weapons—weapons just like the one the soldier had held to her throat while he had raped her. And her blessing had turned sour. If the head priestess had not intervened, they would have all died.

Suddenly, there was a loud pounding on her door. It rattled the whole cottage. Geyth reached for the dagger at her belt.

"Open the door!" a man's voice commanded. It was Leighton.

"Go away!" she shouted. "I won't be tricked again."

The door shook violently. "Let me in or I will chop this door down. I have no time for your remorse."

She thought of the man, his broad shoulders, his long sword, and knew that she stood little chance against him. And the door, only meant to keep the wind out, would hold only a short time.

She lifted the latch and he strode into the room. He wasted no time on formalities. He tossed another small linen pouch onto the table. "I need another curse. This time, I want her dead."

Geyth swallowed hard and tried to muster her courage, but found little to support her. "I ... I will not do it. You tricked me into it last time. You used me to force Myrrha into marrying you. . . ."

Leighton grabbed her by the front of her gown and lifted her bodily until her face nearly touched his. "Don't whine to me about your wounded morality. You've given no thought to the harm you've already caused others. Now do it, or I will kill you!" He released her roughly.

She staggered back. With her eyes frozen on the man before her, she groped for the pouch. Something heavy was inside. She opened it and found a gold ring with tiny symbols inlaid into its band: the lion for valor, the hammer for strength, the hawk for faithfulness. Geyth slipped the ring on her finger. Those symbols were not awarded lightly. And to think that Myrrha had earned each of them. She must be truly an exceptional person. Geyth turned the ring with her thumb. Myrrha was also the one person who had accepted her as she really was. The one person who had shown her kindness. Geyth grit her teeth, a deep seated anger beginning to burn. This man had tricked her—*used* her. Just like all the others. Yes, she had brought harm to many, but she didn't have to continue. She could stop. Could stop at any time. *She* was in control of her fate. *She* could do something *right*!

"NO!" she screamed. "I will not do it!" She flung herself at him and raked his face with her nails.

On reflex, he backhanded her. She landed against the table, knocking it over and sprawling on the floor beside it.

"Damn you, woman." He dabbed at the flow and glanced at the blood on his fingers. His eyes narrowed. He leaned over, jerked her up, and punched her hard in the face. Her head snapped back with its force and pain exploded in her head. She immediately collapsed unconscious.

Geyth awoke as she was roughly tossed onto a low couch. Groaning from the agony in her skull, she slowly opened her eyes and found Leighton's sneering face hovering over her. She tried to scream and squirm away, but she had been gagged and her hands and legs were bound.

And she realized she was not alone on the couch.

"I want to make sure we are not interrupted," said Leighton. "You two be still and I promise your deaths will be quick." He stepped to the door, peered out cautiously, and quietly left the room. The door latch slipped softly into place.

"Geyth? Is that you lying beside me?" asked a familiar voice. It was Myrrha.

Geyth fought with the gag and managed to grunt assent.

"I thought so," Myrrha answered. "I was pretty sure you would join me tonight, once I understood what Leighton was doing—trying to force me into marrying him by making me a cripple." She sighed. "And you were his chosen tool."

Geyth fought tears. "I'm sorry," she tried to say.

Myrrha nodded slowly. "Do not fret, child. I forgive you. No doubt Leighton tricked or threatened you. Even I did not realize how low he would stoop to get control of my lands. And I realized it a little too late." Myrrha licked her dry lips. "Since I would not marry him, he has chosen another way. You see, among my people if one dies without an heir—and I do not have one—then their lands can be given to anyone who attempted to save their life. When he's finished, it will look like you murdered me and he caught you, no doubt claiming he had to kill you as you tried to escape." She took a deep breath. "Now, we have to get you out of here before Leighton returns. I take it you are bound hand and foot?"

"Yes," was her muffled reply.

"Quickly then, you must get to your feet and feel along the wall at the head of the couch. The third stone, waist high, on your side is loose. Behind it is a dagger. Use it to cut your ropes. But hurry. Leighton will be back in only moments."

Geyth squirmed and fought to sit up. She carefully stood and managed to back up to the area Myrrha described. By touch alone, she found the loose stone, pulled it out, and grabbed the dagger. She cut her hand on its well honed blade. It only took a few swipes to free her. "I did it!"

Myrrha chuckled. "Good! Now, you must get help. It may take a little time to find someone—I believe Leighton cleared all my servants from the building."

Geyth looked longingly at the door, but turned back to Myrrha. "How can I get you out, too? Leighton could kill you before I get back."

Myrrha nodded. "True. But you would have to carry me out, and I do not think you can. No, you must leave me behind and get away quickly, so you can prove your innocence."

Geyth looked at the dagger in her hand. "I cannot leave you."

"You must!" Myrrha sighed. "With luck, they will catch Leighton in the act. And if I do die, my death could actually be a good thing. At least this way, I will not have to live out the rest of my days in this crippled body. And I will die for a friend. In the short term this may seem bad, but in the long run, things will work out. Of that I have no doubt. Even your curses will eventually bring good."

Geyth blinked back tears. Before her, unable to move, lay a truly good woman. Even in the face of death, she saw the good in what was to come. If only she could see that herself ... believe in it. She felt something warm in her hand. She still wore Myrrha's ring! *Could it be?* She shook her head in denial. But at the same time, she couldn't help herself. Myrrha was a good woman, and Geyth honestly wished her the best the Goddess Mother would allow. Wished her life, health, and happiness. She repeated the litany over and over. Her hand grew warmer and she felt the building of magic—but of a kind she had never known. It felt different. It felt right.

The door suddenly opened and Leighton entered. Myrrha groaned unexpectedly, and Geyth's breath caught in her throat. He drew his dagger and stepped nearer. "Ah ... I see you are waiting for me. And thank you for cutting your ropes—it will make my story all the more believable."

Positioning herself between Myrrha and Leighton, Geyth brandished her dagger. "I will not let you harm her!"

Leighton laughed and took a step nearer. In a lightning blow, he knocked the dagger from her hand and shoved her backward. She sprawled across Myrrha's chest. Leighton grabbed Geyth by the throat and raised his dagger.

"Myrrha," spat Leighton. "See what you have done by not accepting my offer. I would have made you happy." He grinned. "At least you and your friend wouldn't be dead."

With a powerful downstroke, he plunged the dagger toward Geyth's chest. Geyth couldn't tear her eyes away from the descending blade. *Oh, Goddess Mother, please no!*

Suddenly, an arm shot up from behind her catching Leighton's wrist and stopping the dagger's descent. Geyth's eyes grew wide in disbelief.

It was Myrrha's arm.

"This is not possible," Leighton gasped.

Myrrha laughed. "It is when a priestess blesses you!" Still holding Geyth, Leighton tried to free his hand. But Myrrha doggedly held to it, forcing him to release Geyth to better deal with the experienced fighter. He quickly moved to grip Myrrha's throat.

This diversion was all Myrrha needed. As Geyth rolled

out of the way, Myrrha grabbed his shirt and yanked him to one side. Thrown off-balance, he went to one knee beside the couch. In a blur of motion, Myrrha leaped to her feet and turned to confront him. Leighton roared in anger and lunged for her, but Myrrha again caught his descending hand and the two grappled. Then, as she had done with the thief, Myrrha side-stepped and brought Leighton's arm quickly down and under to impale him with his own blade. With a cry, he slumped to the floor and did not get up.

Geyth immediately dropped to her knees before Myrrha. "Once again you saved my life. I am in your debt."

Myrrha took the young woman's hand and pulled her up. "Actually, I think we are about even. You showed Leighton for what he really was. For that, I am in *your* debt."

"But I placed a powerful curse on you."

Myrrha grinned. "And removed it with your blessing."

"But I cannot ... I don't have ..."

Myrrha nodded. "Oh, yes you do, priestess of the Goddess Mother."

Geyth stared at her in disbelief, then realized that Myrrha spoke the truth. She had given a true blessing. She had found some goodness. Geyth slowly nodded. "Maybe you are right. But I am not worthy to be a priestess. Not yet. First, I have to atone for the wrong I have done. If I make it that far."

Myrrha slapped her on the back. "Well, you will always be welcome here. I know the *itha* bushes would be glad to have you back." She leaned closer. "In fact, you may want to bless them before you leave. They need all the luck they can get if I'm tending them."

They both laughed.

THE MISTRESS'S RIDDLE
by Karen Luk

Karen says that she got a computer and a printer for her birthday and Christmas, which makes it easier to write up her stories and edit them. Doggone right; it takes real dedication to—as all of us did when *we* were young—bang them out on the old manual and retype every page that had more than three or four corrections or changes. I remember Damon Knight saying, even back before he founded SFWA, that with word rates what they were, nobody could afford to rewrite a story, so one should get in the habit of doing it right the first time. In other words, put brain in gear before engaging fingers. I still pause before every sentence to stop and think what I'm going to say. I especially read my dialogue over to myself and see if it sounds right—before committing it to paper.

All too many young writers, especially those with computers and printers, think that if their manuscripts look good, they are good. But no amount of nice clean printing will make a bad manuscript into a good one, so think before you write. And read what you write, out loud to yourself, and see how it "plays."

Karen Luk is sixteen now, and this is her second sale to *Sword and Sorceress*. She has been writing fantasy seriously since a friend introduced her to her first true fantasy series in seventh grade. Her plans for the moment are to finish high school and college and to keep on writing through her school career.

This story has a weird colorful feel that for some reason

150

reminds me of the early work of Tanith Lee. High praise; and may it be only the first of many.

A worshiper of the Mistress of Darkness stood upon the bloodied field of war. His dark robes fluttering in the light wind disturbed the reign of silence over the battlefield. The orange sun of dusk set in the gray fog which blanketed the earth.

"I, Dawen Stroph, worshiper of She Who Darkens, give these battle-weary souls to you," he said. "And my soul in exchange for my death." His soft voice carried across the broken bodies of the soldiers on the ground. The breeze bore Dawen's request beyond the world of man.

Without the slightest stirring of air, the Mistress of Darkness appeared next to Dawen. She wore a thick hooded cloak of the finest black velvet and silk and held herself aloof with the quiet dignity of possessing all there is to know in the world of man. With pearl-white, slender fingers, the Mistress of Darkness gently pulled away her cowl.

For a moment, Dawen thought he saw the bleached skull of a dead man with crimson-fired eyes. But within the blink of an eye, he saw the soft-chiseled features of a beautiful woman. Glorious ebony locks of hair cascaded down to gently brush her slender shoulders. Her eyes were swirls of black and crimson, but were empty of any emotion or feeling. The Mistress had thin curving lips drawn in a line of dead seriousness.

"So you offer me these souls," said her eyes to Dawen Stroph. With a pale hand she gestured to the field of rotting bodies. "Yet you give that which I already have in my domain. If you are what you claim to be, my true worship, prove it."

"I have no kin of my own," replied Dawen Stroph. "They were all taken by your hand, and I would give anything to see them. So I shall willingly yield my soul to you. There is nothing for me in this life."

He knelt before the Mistress of Darkness. His head was bowed, awaiting his death blow. She bade him rise to his feet. He quickly stood. The wind rose. Dawen could barely withstand the gusts that tore at his clothes. Soon enough, Dawen was stripped down to his bare skin. The Mistress of Darkness, however, was unmoved by the gales of air. Even her velvet cloak did not ripple.

He dropped to his knees before her once more. Dawen Stroph did not fear the Mistress; rather he loved her for the peace he might be granted in exchange for his life. She clutched his shoulders and pulled him to his feet. The Mistress of Darkness took Dawen's face in her hands. In her eyes he saw his approaching death, yet he accepted his fate without hesitation.

The Mistress of Darkness spoke to him one last time with her black-blood eyes.

"Yes, I shall accept your life and soul," said her hard eyes. "Though I think you may not find the peace you have sought."

Her soft lips barely touched Dawen Stroph's forehead. He shuddered once, then fell to the Mistress' hidden feet. Her eyes fixed on the disappearing sun as it fell over the edge of the world. The orange sphere's fiery warmth diminished as the day ended. The Mistress of Darkness waited until the full moon shone its reflected light upon the silent battlefield.

Smiling, the Mistress of Darkness began her journey to her domain. . . .

The Mistress of Darkness sat quietly on her throne of bleached-white bones and skulls. She saw all that was happening in her domain. Everything was in shades of grays and blacks. The only white was her throne. The cowl of her cloak shrouded her face from the spirits in her domain, unless the Mistress wished it otherwise. Her dark clothes hid nearly every inch of her being.

The Mistress sensed the disembodied stare of a spirit's empty eyes. She knew its identity at once and inclined her hooded head to the spirit.

"Mistress?" queried the spirit.

"Yes," said a quiet, silvery voice. The word seemed to linger in the air until the spirit spoke again.

"Is this your domain?"

"Yes, Dawen Stroph. Come, I shall show you what Death has meant to other souls."

The Mistress of Darkness rose from her throne. Her feet did not seem to touch the floor at all. The spirit silently joined her. Several moments passed as the spirit noticed that they were drifting away from the throne room. The Mistress of Darkness stopped without so much as a stirring of air.

A vast room filled with endless rows of books materialized before the Mistress of Darkness and the spirit of Dawen Stroph. Ghostly scholars, librarians, and various other highly educated people drifted in and out of the aisles of volumes.

"Why are you showing me this?" asked Dawen's spirit.

"These people had a thirst for knowledge so great that they carried that unquenched thirst to their very deaths," spoke the Mistress of Darkness. "Here," she gestured to the never-ending library, "they can attempt to quench their thirst for knowledge."

The Mistress of Darkness floated over to yet another room. The spirit quickly caught up with her and saw a huge feast laid out in a starlit dining hall. Heaps of roasted meat filled the air with their aromas. Fruits of every shape and color were piled into baskets for the eating. Many were the spirits who were indulging themselves with the prepared food.

The spirit of Dawen Stroph waited for the Mistress of Darkness to speak first about the vision before him.

"A feast of this magnitude was heaven to many people in their lives," she said. The dining hall vanished, and in its place was a kitchen with every conceivable cooking utensil in or out of use. "And to some, preparing those feasts was a way of life and an art," she continued.

Spirits in translucent white clothes were busily cooking up a staggering variety of foods. The Mistress of Darkness turned away from the images of the prepared food and the feasting. The blurred visions made Dawen's eyes foggy for a moment. Then he found himself in the throne room of the Mistress of Darkness. The Mistress sat on her throne unmoving, as if she had never shown the spirit of Dawen Stroph the images of her domain.

"The visions I have shown you are but a few out of a myriad of ideas of death," the Mistress of Darkness said. "The most chiefly believed are the Heavens of eternal peace and the Hell of eternal torture. What were your interests in your past life?"

"They were death and you," the spirit of Dawen replied. "My parents and my two siblings were taken by death—

their souls gathered by your hand. I lived until the day you would come for my soul as well."

"Then you have nothing here to die for," she said in a weary voice. "I shall have to discuss this with my husband."

The Mistress of Darkness rose, hidden within her robe. She threw her arms wide. Her ebony robes fluttered, but the spirit of Dawen detected no wind. A glistening light of pure white stars gathered around the Mistress in a small whirlpool of light.

"Who is your husband?" he asked.

"The Lord of the Living." The Mistress' voice drifted from the whirlwind of light.

The light surrounding the Mistress of Darkness lifted her higher into the grayness of her domain's sky. The spirit of Dawen Stroph watched the swirl of light diminish until he thought it was a star on the gray sky.

The spirit of Dawen Stroph waited for what seemed a long time for the Mistress of Darkness to return. Suddenly, she appeared as if she had never left her domain. The spirit hastily drifted over to the Mistress' throne.

"Well, Mistress of Darkness, what did you discuss with your husband, the Lord of the Living?" he asked.

"That is none of your concern," the Mistress coolly replied. "I have met many of your kind, but none who dwelt solely on death and me. You must understand that I have not encountered such a problem for many hundreds of years. My husband, fortunately, did remember how we dealt with the problem."

She stopped her flow of words. From the shadows of her hood, the Mistress studied the spiritual form of Dawen Stroph. The Lord of the Living had given his wife the means to enable a spirit to return to his body in the living world.

"Do you even grasp the relationship between life and death?" the Mistress asked.

"No, I don't know," answered the spirit. "All I know is my desire for death."

The Mistress of Darkness sagged on her throne. Her hooded face fell forward to rest on her black-shrouded chest. With a pearl-white hand, the Mistress beckoned the spirit closer. Dawen Stroph's spirit floated over at the Mistress bidding.

"With all life, death lurks within each and every thing," the Mistress murmured. "Death needs nothing but a moment in time to pass. If there is life, death is there always.

"If there is death, there has to be life for death to end life. Life and death go hand in hand—neither would exist without the other."

"I don't understand life," said the spirit sorrowfully.

"I know," whispered the Mistress, "and that is why I must send you back to the world of the living."

Dawen's spirit threw himself at the Mistress' unseen feet. He howled in forgotten rage for her mercy. She remained unaffected by his screams and impassioned pleas. The Mistress of Darkness moved away from the shouting soul in her throne room. She withdrew from her midnight-robes a tiny sphere of glowing chartreuse light. The Mistress threw the sphere at the spirit of Dawen Stroph.

The small ball encased the spiritual essence of Dawen Stroph. Even within the globe he continued to mouth his pleas to the Mistress of Darkness. She held the glowing ball in her two hands. Although the spirit of Dawen could not make himself heard, the Mistress secured his attention without a sound or gesture.

"I shall come for you once more—to see if you have learned anything about life," said the Mistress of Darkness. "Until then, death will never come to lead you into my domain."

With that, the Mistress of Darkness tossed the glowing sphere aloft. She guided the ball with one slender finger toward the sky. The trapped spirit of Dawen Stroph succumbed to the light in the globe ... sphere ... light ...

... Light invaded Dawen Stroph's eyelids. He shook himself awake and felt his body with unsure hands. Unfortunately, he found himself to be in the same mortal husk he inhabited before he met the Mistress of Darkness.

"No!" screamed Dawen Stroph.

But his cry of anguish fell upon the deaf ears of the living and the dead alike.

The years passed swiftly for Dawen Stroph, and he forgot about his encounter with the Mistress of Darkness. He was knighted by his King for his valorous deeds. He had killed the leviathan of the Long-Lost Sea. He had slain a dragon as large and as immovable as a mountain. He had also rid the kingdom of a band of greedy ogres invading the lands.

Despite his many accomplishments, he still found time to marry. Less than a year into his blissful marriage, his beautiful young wife bore Sir Dawen a healthy baby boy. When his son was barely old enough to take two steps at a time, Sir Dawen Stroph was summoned by the King to go on a perilous quest.

Sir Dawen Stroph kissed both son and wife farewell. He mounted his horse and left his castle, lands, and family behind him. Sir Dawen rode for the kingdom's border. A fortnight later, he saw a slender figure clad in black velvet robes.

Sir Dawen dismounted, cautiously approaching the figure with a drawn sword. When he had come within a yard of the ebony-robed person, he tried speaking to the figure.

"Who are you?" Sir Dawen queried. "In the name of the King, identify yourself." He raised his sword in a forceful manner.

"If you think back a few years, I think you shall remember who I am," a low voice said. Sir Dawen Stroph thought about it for a few moments.

"The Mistress of Darkness!" Sir Dawen breathed. He quickly sheathed his steel weapon.

"The King did not send you here—I did," continued the Mistress. "Though meeting me once more may prove to be your most challenging feat yet.

"Sir Dawen Stroph, have you changed? Yes, you have. I think you have a different view of life from when I first encountered you."

The Mistress of Darkness stepped closer to Sir Dawen. Her eyes were still swirls of crimson and black under her cloak's hood. She raised her hands to the sky above. Murmured words escaped from her blood-red lips to the four winds. Sir Dawen paled. he knew it was nearly impossible to stop Death from coming for him. Yet Sir Dawen decided to speak. He wanted to live.

"I do not want you to take my life from me! I have a wife and son. I have to live, if only for my family's sake."

The Mistress of Darkness wryly smiled in the shadows of her cowl. Sir Dawen had learned about life. She let her hands drop to her sides. Then she disappeared from Sir Dawen Stroph's sight and the world of man as well, not to return until his time to reenter her living room.

RUSTED BLADE
by Dave Smeds

If there's anyone who still thinks I am prejudiced against male authors (although how they can possibly think that after ten or eleven volumes, I'm blest if I know), Dave Smeds alone should be enough to make them reconsider; I forget just how many of these anthologies he's graced with his presence, but it's a good many by now. He also lists on his biographical update a daughter Lerina, age seven, and a newborn—May 5, 1993—son Elliott, as well as his wife Connie. He lives in Santa Rosa which, all things considered, is not very far away.

His list of publications is long and honorable: two novels, and any number of shorter pieces naming almost every surviving magazine in the sf/fantasy field as well as out of it, and more anthologies than I've appeared in myself. I've met Dave at many conventions and have a fairly clear picture of him in my mind. He's been the English-language writer of Japanese comics and teaches karate, holding a black belt in that art. He has made his living before turning to writing as a graphic artist and typesetter—much to my surprise; I thought it was all done by computers these days.

D arb found the ewe in his upper pasture. It lay on its side, convulsing. As Darb lifted its head, blood poured from its mouth, spotting his hands. The animal let out a final gurgling breath and grew still.

In the grass upon which the sheep had been grazing bloomed tiny white flowers. Darb ripped a handful from the ground, inspecting the shape of the petals. Lamb's bane. The herb should have grown only in the wake of melting snow, when alert shepherds had not yet released their flocks to open pasture—not now, after snows had closed the high pass for the year.

He let the animal lie where it was. The carrion birds could have it. He'd have his hands full rounding up the other sheep before they were poisoned, or before the taint of blood on the wind brought wolves or glacier bears. He turned away.

Climbing up through the woolthorn and granite came his daughter Oleya. His frown deepened. She would not have left the magician's cottage at this hour without grave cause.

She gestured at the dead ewe. "That's the work of a sorceress. She's driven locusts to attack Metch's grain fields, guided the fish in the lake away from the nets, and who knows what else. Her song comes from the high country on this side of the pass. I've called a gathering of the elders."

"I will get my sword," Darb said.

Here at the edge of the old empire, the mountains climbed halfway to the moon. Their peaks hid in perpetual shrouds, unclimbable and forever bound in ice and snow. It was said that they rose so high that the air around them grew thinner than a man could breathe. The lowlanders believed the folk of the alpine valleys demented to live among such giants, cut off from civilization for nine months of the year.

Perhaps his folk were demented, Darb thought as he stood staring at the granitic massif that screened him from the rising sun. And never was their madness greater than after the snows had sealed them off for the winter.

The village of High Pass lay far below the actual gap in the mountains for which it was named. Here snow would not blanket the ground for weeks yet. But no one would be coming from or going to Cold Lake or Bent Rock or Long Mine, the nearest communities on the far side. No matter how clement the weather in the vales, the ridges were covered by unstable drifts and wracked by winds that could freeze a man's eyelids shut during the course of a blink.

If a hostile sorceress shared the bowl with them, with nine long months in which to sing, that was the stuff of old legends and classic fears. True, a witch could bend only the simple things of nature to her will. No plant, insect, or fish would listen unless she learned the songs perfectly, and that took time and patience. Any one use of her powers might seem pitifully unintimidating. But a winter in which rats invaded the grain stores every night or snow ticks spread fevers among children while they slept—that would be a long season indeed.

Darb scanned the snowless timber country on this side of the looming granite wall. That was where his search would begin. Turning away from the vista, he brought the grindstone to its proper speed and set the blade of his sword against it.

Sparks danced across the pebbles at his feet, and the specks of rust on the metal fell away. Though he had wrapped the weapon in an oiled cloth, after so many years unused the wet and cold of the mountains had reached it. Call it the ghost blood of its last victims, dead these twenty-six years. Only when the steel was clear and bright did he cease his labor.

How long since he'd last tightened his fist around the hilt, even in practice? Ten years? Twelve? The weapon still felt as if it were an extension of his arm.

His wife emerged from their home as he finished the sharpening. Ilisi stared at the sword, dissatisfaction marring her features as it had the night before when the elders had declared that Darb would go after the witch.

"I wish it did not have to be you," Ilisi said.

He slid the blade into its scabbard and buckled it around his waist. "You know it has to be me."

"By yourself?" she asked in a tone that implied that when it was her turn to sit among the elders—she had one more year until she turned fifty and would join the matri-archs—policies would change.

"The heights are no place for shepherds and weavers with snow season nigh. Better that everyone stay here and harvest the fields. There will be little enough fodder this winter as it is. I don't need companions to die beside me should the sorceress prove too strong. I don't need wit-nesses should I trap her in her den and do what must be done."

Ilisi's expression clouded. Darb wasn't sure which bothered her more: the possibility of losing him, or the possibility he would succeed.

"You could have refused to go," she stated. "As old as you are, none would think less of you."

"I am old," he admitted, running a hand through his graying beard. "But I could not have refused." He took hold of the grindstone. "Here. Help me put this back inside."

Ilisi stepped back, keeping her distance from the stone wheel and from the sword around his waist.

"I had hoped," she said softly, "that twenty-six years would have changed you. Go, then. Do what you must." The last word struggled from her mouth, her lips contorting as if she'd tasted raw bitterwort.

"As will you?" he asked.

Ilisi produced a sprig of flowers and held it out to him. Meadow bonnets. They guarded the trail from the village to their house. Darb doubted they could guard his path in the heights as well, but he fastened them to his otter-fur hat. The blooms would wither by the end of the day, but for a few hours their fragrance would waft down over his face, brightening the trek.

"I packed food, bedding, a tinder box," Ilisi said. "And I sent Bren to the fletcher for three fresh arrows. Your quiver was low. Now leave that thing out here," she indicated the sword, "and come inside, my husband."

His quiver had not been all that low, but waiting for his son would delay his departure an hour. He understood what Ilisi was asking and yielded to her wish.

The desperation of Ilisi's lovemaking hung fiercely in Darb's memory as he climbed through the forest. The passion had been worthy of a wife who feared she might never see her husband again. He wished that was all it was, but he had no illusions. Should he return home with the blood of another human being on his sword, Ilisi would not soon welcome him to her bed again. This was not something she held over him by choice, as a threat. It had simply to do with the way she was. After his return from the wars, five years passed before she could avoid cringing whenever he placed his hands upon her. Neither of them had wanted

that, but there that cold reluctance had been, tainting
their love.

Darb's two companions let him brood as they struggled
to match his pacesetting strides. For the first phase of the
search, the elders had not sent him into the heights completely alone.

Bringing others with him made Darb feel as though his
feet were struggling through powdered snow. He worked
best solo. He was the wolftracker. No one knew the mountains as he did. No one could help him more than they
hindered. Yet if he had to have company, this pair would
have been his first choice. Oxfor was strong, quick, and
capable. In the two years the lad had been Darb's apprentice, he'd kept his head and learned his lessons thoroughly.
And then there was Oleya, Darb's daughter.

At thirty, Oleya had served as a sorceress for twelve
years, the first five as apprentice to her great aunt, Lakli,
the last seven alone. In a village as small as theirs, a magician manifested no more than once every other generation.
With Lakli dead, Oleya would likely remain unaccompa-
nied in her profession for another twenty years. The alter-
native was to hire a magic-worker from the foothills or
lowlands, but High Pass had little to tempt such a woman
to immigrate. That left Oleya as the supreme authority
within the valley concerning things magical.

There was little of her mother left in her. Now she was
like Darb—all hardness and purpose. In some ways he regretted that. In other ways he was glad. When the villagers
avoided her cottage in dread of the supernatural, that was
the same as when they stared wide-eyed at the new sets of
bear claws he brought back from his hunts. The people
were grateful to Oleya for her sorcery, and grateful to Darb
for keeping the bears and wolves at a distance, but they
feared them. Of all the individuals who shared his life, only
his daughter fully understood what it was to be set apart.

They covered the ground quickly. By noon Darb looked
down and saw the chimney smoke of High Pass far below
him to the west. The land descended again ahead of him,
continuing on in sawtooth fashion toward the massif, some
of the terrain cloaked in hardy conifers, some of it in
stony brush.

They stopped to eat. Meal done, Oleya entered a trance

to listen for the enemy sorceress. She brushed the ground smooth beneath her, sat cross-legged, and closed her eyes.

Automatically Darb matched her breathing, though he remained upright, scanning the forest with a hunter's eyes. At times he almost believed he could hear the sounds of nature as a sorceress did. That was not a foolish notion. He was father to a sorceress and the great-grandson of another. Though the full talent rarely manifested in males, he often knew in advance when the weather would shift, when the caterpillars would appear.

As Oleya sang, a sweetness filled the air, as if he stood on the bank of a river that carried a torrent of scents, tastes, feelings past him, barely a hand's reach away. Beside him, Oxfor inspected arrows, oblivious to the sensations. Oleya opened her mouth and inhaled until her chest threatened to burst. She opened her eyes as she exhaled.

"I hear the crooning of rock heather, and the whisper of the pied-wing butterfly," she said.

Darb nodded. The heather and the butterflies lived only at one elevation. "She is near timberline," he said aloud to show he understood.

Oxfor looked out across the slopes and ravines around, and at the barren tops of nearly every peak. "That still leaves a great many places she could be hiding."

"It is enough for now." Darb's tone caused the young man to lower his glance. The wolftracker helped his daughter to her feet. She swayed, perspiration dotting her brow. Opening herself so fully to the region's songs and picking out those associated with the witch was not a trivial task.

"We'll continue toward the pass," Darb declared, "and keep to the upper limit of the forest."

The hunt had truly begun. As they hiked onward, the small aches and pains in Darb's joints faded. His eyes peered into the shadows of firs and junipers with a hawk's clarity. He plucked the string of his bow, smiling as the vibration spoke of its readiness to serve.

Life was never so keen as when he roamed these heights, alert for his prey. And the keenest time of all was when he knew the hunt might turn against him. Just as a glacier bear could rip him open with one swipe of its claws, so could this sorceress destroy him. She would soon know he was out here, might know it already. The very gnats, the wind, the sap in the pines would tell her. Darb preferred it that way. This was the spice he could never find down in the valley, tending sheep and listening to stories at the lodge fires.

Oleya saw the vigor in his step and smiled. He need make no apologies to her for the time he spent roaming these mountains, hunting, seldom staying in the village long. In front of her, he did not have to regret the person shaped by ten years of war.

He removed his hat. The meadow bonnets Ilisi had given him were fading, their aroma almost lost in the thin, crisp air of the granite peaks.

The night's campfire, hidden in a cleft where spying eyes could not see it, barely cut the chill of the night air. Darb ignored the discomfort; he'd known far worse.

"She is somewhere near," Oleya said, coming out of her trance. "I can no longer tell which direction."

She stood up with only a little unsteadiness this time. The trance had been short, meant to confirm what they already suspected. A sorceress could not pinpoint another of her kind precisely. The very presence of a witch changed the songs of nature over an entire area, and the target might be anywhere within the zone. Oleya had fulfilled her task—to narrow the search area as much as possible. Now Darb knew that his prey waited somewhere within a day's hike.

"Oxfor will take you down the mountain in the morning," Darb said.

She frowned but did not disagree. She was too valuable to the village to risk from this point on. Her father alone would run the gauntlet of enemy magic. The elders insisted. Only if Darb failed would other options be considered.

The firelight reflected brightly in Oleya's pupils, almost a feral gleam. She wanted this rival dead very much, Darb realized. She would have conducted the hunt herself if she could.

"Where does she come from?" Oxfor wondered aloud, as he spitted the rabbit he had snared and cleaned. He placed it above the hot coals. "The lowlands? Cold Lake?"

"I believe she comes from Long Mine," Oleya said.

The young man raised an eyebrow. "I thought of that. The miners have had a bad year. But they've been without a magic-worker ever since Mihana died almost ten years ago, and if one of their girls has manifested the power, surely they wouldn't waste her harassing us."

"No," Oleya replied. "But if the girl has succumbed to witch's madness, they might deposit her on this side of the pass rather than kill her, so that we suffer the effects of her affliction. I can believe such spite of the miners."

Darb stepped away from the fire, where the smoke did not obscure his view of the gossamer net of stars above. He often stared at the night sky the year Oleya had manifested her gift, worrying. He had not relaxed until the transition period ended and the possibility of witch's madness vanished.

"I've no love of the miners," Oxfor continued. "But the truce has held for more than a generation. Would they renew the feud now?"

Darb turned and spoke. "When I find her, I will look for signs of where she is from. At the moment, where she comes from does not matter. She has attacked us, she must die. Time enough for the particulars later."

Oleya nodded with satisfaction. Oxfor dutifully pretended to be absorbed in cooking the rabbit. Only when the meat was nearly done did he venture another comment.

"Is the story true?" he asked Darb. "Did you really kill the lord of Long Mine bare-handed?"

Darb pursed his lips and did not answer. Vivid images filled his mind: his father and brother, headless on a bank of snow turned crimson from their blood, victims of the picks and spears of the miners. And a miner, pale as a grub from long workdays underground, face contorting as Darb blooded his sword for the first time. Darb had been seventeen.

Like Oleya, he could well believe evil from the folk of Long Mine. He knew the depths of the urge for revenge. He almost hoped the sorceress did come from there. Yet he spoke of none of this. His apprentice was quick with a bow and not afraid to face the dangers of cliffs and snows, but there was a high, treacherous mountain range he would have to cross to reach the spot Darb called home. Of all those now living in High Pass, Darb was the only man who had ever slain another human being. Let Oxfor cross those ridges himself if he must, but Darb would not beckon him.

"A story grows in the telling," Darb said. It had not been the lord, but his grown son. And Darb had not killed him bare-handed, but with the axe the man had used to mutilate the corpses of Darb's kin.

Oxfor did not press for further explanation. The meat cooked. They ate. As the settled down for the night—Darb taking the first watch—Oleya began to sing.

At first, the sounds emerging from her throat seemed nothing more than the noises of the forest grown slightly louder and more rhythmic: frog croaks, the rustle of an owl's wings, cricket chirps, the faint roar of a mountain stream. The noises blended into a chorus. Oleya straightened her spine, inhaled, and sang out fully, her neck quivering from the effort.

Bit by bit, the tangle of songs unwound. The melody of growing plants vanished, followed soon by the low thrum of the earth and rocks, freeing the more energetic music of the animal kingdom. Wiping the sweat from her eyes, Oleya stripped away the notes of the fishes, the worms, the spiders, until all that remained was a keening whine.

Darb's ears began to hum. The sorceress had found the song she sought. Smiling in spite of her weariness, Oleya smiled and ... changed ... the tune just slightly.

Immediately the gnats and mosquitoes that had plagued their camp all evening drew back, as if they suddenly found the taste and scent of human flesh unappealing.

"There," Oleya sighed. "That should last until morning." She crawled into her bedroll and fell immediately into a deep sleep.

By morning Oleya stood straight, eyes bright, fully recovered from her spell-casting. Once more it seemed to Darb as if she would lead the hunt if she could. Instead, she kissed her father and said, "I *know* you will succeed." She retreated to where Oxfor stood waiting to take her back to High Pass.

"Guard her well," Darb told his apprentice; then the two disappeared down into the forest as he climbed uphill.

Darb searched all that day and saw no sign of his quarry. If she was clever, she would remain in one spot, leaving no spoor he could track. But if he was lucky, she would wander about, thinking to avoid his search.

Darb was not lucky. The next morning, as he rounded a stand of brush near a stream, his quarry found him.

A glacier bear rose from the brush. Darb had time only

to see a great mass of brown fur with a streak of silver around the mouth and throat, and then it was swiping downward at him with one of its massive claws.

Darb spun away from the blow. Talons sliced deep into his thick leather cape and jerkin, tearing into the woolens below that and grazing his skin. Darb flung his bow to the side and collapsed facedown on the grassy slope.

He lay still. A heavy thump told him the silverjaw had lowered to all fours. The bear poked his side with its snout, snuffing loudly. Darb didn't move. He dared not. If he showed the slightest indication that he was capable of resistance, the animal would rend him limb from limb.

The bear reached beneath him with one of its paws and heaved, rolling Darb over as easily as if he'd been a leaf. Darb deliberately maintained the spin until he was facedown again.

As he had spun, he had glimpsed the animal through slitted lids. It was a large adult male just beginning to turn white for the winter, thick with accumulated fat. Perhaps, with all the gorging it had been doing, it was not hungry.

The bear stalked over to him, sniffed, growled, and rolled him over again. Darb made sure he ended up facedown. Twenty times the bear repeated its action, tumbling Darb downslope beside the stream, and twenty times Darb played dead.

At last the bear gave a disgusted snort and ambled away.

Darb remained where he was until he heard the silverjaw splashing through a pond fifty paces downstream. He walked quietly back to his bow and retrieved the weapon. He was not tempted to shoot. A wounded, angry glacier bear was the last thing he needed. He merely kept up his guard lest the animal wander back in his direction.

Moving upstream, Darb looked at his injuries. The bear's talons had dug shallow gashes along his chest and shoulder. Painful, but not life-threatening. He cleaned the cuts and fastened a poultice and bandage over them. He rotated his arm experimentally. His muscles would be stiff in the morning, but he would not be unduly handicapped.

Darb sat down on a boulder above the stream, where he would see the bear if it turned back his direction. How had the sorceress managed this? The appearance of the silverjaw was no random occurrence, surely, yet creatures as complex as bears would not heed a witch's songs directly any more than a man would. Perhaps she had coaxed bees to scatter honey, or caused the fruit of nearby sweetberry bushes to ripen all at once, and the scent of food had lured the bear down the trail at just the right time to encounter him.

That told him three things. First, this was a powerful sorceress to strike out so soon. Oleya could have turned sweetberry bushes to her will in such a manner, but she would have had to sing for hours. Bees would have taken even longer. Second, she knew he was hunting her. Third, she was nearby.

She had lost a gamble. Had he not known the nature of glacier bears well, he would have died. With his survival, her danger increased greatly. By tomorrow he might have journeyed far from this little valley without suspecting she was here.

Darb stood and looked out across the terrain, choosing a path that would lead him in a wide circle—the perimeter of the area within which he suspected the sorceress lurked. He smiled grimly. It had come down to a contest between her magic and his woodcraft. Whichever was stronger would determine who was hunter and who was prey.

His hand tightened around his sword hilt.

Hours later, as he faced out over the small valley from the other side, tingles began to crawl up his spine. His gaze darted to the scree-dotted slope behind him. Suddenly he broke into a stumbling run toward a hardy, thick-boled juniper.

Above and behind him, rocks suddenly shifted. An avalanche came hurtling down.

He reached the tree barely in time. Huddled behind the gnarled trunk, the rain of stones rumbled by on both sides. A boulder large enough to crush his spine landed squarely against the juniper, but the tree, veteran of a hundred snows and more than one rockslide, stood fast.

Darb rubbed his ankle, which he had twisted in his head-long flight for shelter. Angrily, he watched the last few stones trickle to a stop. He'd been careless. Even a minor sorceress could coax a sand tick or a beetle to shift a pebble, and on a slope such as this only a few moving pebbles could seed an avalanche.

Hardly was the mountain still before he rose and headed

out at a jog. The sun had dipped behind the peaks to the west, haloing them in alpenglow, but the sun's light would not fade for hours yet. To guide an avalanche, the sorceress had to look at the scree. That meant she was within a line of sight. If he could find a trace of her before dusk, she would not have the night in which to slip away.

His legs, even with a tender ankle, carried him with a sureness he had not felt in years. He nocked an arrow and scanned ahead, eager to have reason to loose it. His sword arm itched.

He knew this feeling. This was the drug he'd spent ten years as a lowland mercenary to have, once the clash with the raiders of Long Mine had whetted his appetite. Life pitted against life. It was glorious.

For all his speed, he moved quietly, alert for guards. She might not be suffering from witch's madness at all; the miners might have escorted her here and be protecting her. He avoided a copse of dense trees that held potential for ambush. He checked behind himself every few moments, to be certain no one was following.

Then he came across a trail, and there in the dirt was fresh human spoor.

Cautiously he bent down. Only one set of feet had made the tracks. They were too small to belong to an adult man. They lay all across the trail, coming and going, some new, some days old. The person had not had companions, or the latter would have left marks.

Darb rose and loped quickly and silently along the trail. The way led into a shallow ravine. Scanning right and left, he saw more signs of the same person's travel.

Suddenly the earth gave way beneath him. He scrambled forward, arms automatically clutching a small boulder. The soil swallowed him to the waist, but the rock was a sturdy anchor. He pulled himself out laboriously, as he would dig himself out of a pocket of trap snow. All the while he kept his bow beside him, ready to pick it up and wield it on a moment's notice.

As he scrambled onto solid ground, he saw how the trap had been made. Ants had honeycombed the earth, causing it to collapse as soon as anything as heavy as a human came along. The sorceress had again shown her mettle, to have coaxed the insects to do something so alien to their habits, and upon such a specific spot, within such a short time.

But it was also a desperate measure, not likely to be effective. Darb knew he was close. Clambering to his feet, he hurried down the trail.

As he neared a giant pine, he heard the crooning on the wind. The sorceress sang with a sweet, high, clear call—hauntingly beautiful in comparison with Oleya's throaty chanting.

Instinctively Darb avoided the tree, thinking that a large branch might fall upon him should he pass under. The branches remained still. In the back of his head, something told him the song he heard was not that of pines.

He broke into a full run. Whatever the song was, it was nearing completion. He wanted her in range of his arrows or sword before it was done.

Darting around a bend in the streambed, he saw a cave ahead. A firepit lay at the entrance, with gathered firewood stacked to one side. The ground surrounding the site was packed down, as if the occupant had lived there for weeks.

He scanned the area right and left. There was no place a sentry could be hiding where Darb could not see him coming. He ran to the front of the cave.

The song ended.

Darb paused. No matter. The die was cast. He set his bow down—it was too awkward for close quarters—and drew his sword. Eyes bright, breath controlled, he advanced into the cave.

A shape huddled in the rear of the shelter. She was small, fine-boned, at most sixteen or seventeen years old. She was unarmed.

He raised his sword. She reached out. There on the cave floor, where it could not have grown naturally, waved a freshly blooming spray of meadow bonnets. She plucked them and held them up to him.

Night cloaked the village of High Pass. Smoke adhered to the rafters of the great lodge as if afraid to venture into the fog beyond the vent holes. A wolf called for its pack somewhere far off in the direction of the cliffs. Villagers huddled near the hearths, stamping cold feet and frowning at the need to be abroad on a night such as this.

Darb saw confusion and worry on Oleya's face as she

entered. Her escorts led her to the center of the room, where the patriarchs and matriarchs had gathered around the great oak table. Julde, eldest of the community, raised his scepter of elkhorn and gold inlay, silencing the buzz of the crowd.

Oleya turned toward her father at the left of the table. Her eyes widened at the sight of the foreign young woman at his side.

"Why does she live?" Oleya asked the elders. If she meant it to sound bold and forceful, the quaver in her voice ruined the effort.

Matriarch Sahanna spoke. "Your father spared her. Rather than strike her down, he paused to ask a few questions of her. She told an interesting tale.

"Aya is of the folk of Long Mine. She is a sorceress. When she sensed Darb stalking her, she defended herself. But she did not come into our valley to harm us. Aya's powers manifested suddenly this spring. They were so strong she caused accidents. A child nearly died of the stings of the hornets Aya roused while trying to learn a song the insects might respond to. Her village elders feared witch's madness was beginning to claim her. For her safety as well as that of her people, she exiled herself to the high mountains for the summer to learn her skills where she would not endanger anyone. She was trapped on this side of the pass when the snows fell early."

Darb did not look at his daughter. It was hard enough to remain in the lodge. He kept his glance upon his hands. He held a withered sprig of meadow bonnets. How desperately Aya must have sung, instinctively summoning what was needed to calm her stalker's blade.

"It was not this young miner's daughter who chased off the fish, who called the locusts, and who caused lamb's bane to grow out of season," Sahanna said. "Your songs brought that evil down on us."

Oleya stepped back. "What reason would I have? You believe her story and not mine?"

"We know you, Oleya. You have always been proud and set apart. You have always belittled the stories of magicians of other times and places. You have never accepted that you are a minor sorceress."

"When Aya came," added Matriarch Eleera, "you must have heard her songs in the distance and realized her potential. Once Aya learns full control over her power, she will be the most gifted magic-worker the mountains have seen in three generations, so strong that for matters of importance, people will journey from High Pass to Long Mine to hire her services the way folk sought the aid of Temri, who lived in Bent Rock in my grandmother's youth. To save your pride, you fabricated a threat, risked renewal of a feud, and nearly turned your father into a murderer."

Oleya stiffened. For a moment, she seemed ready to call down a plague of fleas upon the elders to chastise them for their audacity. Then her shoulders drooped. A sorceress without the support—or at least the tolerance—of her community was nothing.

Oleya stared at her father. Darb knew what she was thinking: Where was his sharp sword, his warrior spirit? Why hadn't he slain Aya instantly, as the man she knew would have?

"I have never killed without cause," he said. "I helped forge the truce, thirty-six years ago."

"You have a means to rectify what you have done," Matriarch Sahanna told Oleya. "Aya needs training. She has learned a great deal on her own, but there are songs and ways of shaping songs that only another sorceress can offer. If you will help her achieve her potential, you may continue to live among us."

Oleya swallowed hard, glaring at Aya with unconcealed jealousy. Darb almost hoped she would chose exile, but in the end she lowered her head and murmured, "I will . . . help her."

"We will, of course, have you closely watched," Sahanna added. "Now you may go."

Darb excused himself from the lodge not long after his daughter's guards returned her to the magician's cottage. Oxfor and two of his sons started to accompany him.

"Let him go," said Ilisi. "Let him be alone for a time."

Darb touched his wife's cheek. She knew him better than he gave her credit for. She smiled. "You did what you had to," she said gently.

"Aye," he said hoarsely.

His wife, apprentice, and offspring went back inside, where Aya was telling the assemblage of her family, her hopes, and of the wonder of the songs of the land.

The village glowed with victory. And well it should, thought Darb. The villagers had won, for they were safe and had a new sorceress to curry favor with all winter long. Aya had won, because her life had been spared and she faced a bountiful destiny. Even the miners of Long Mine had won, for not only would they gain a trained sorceress come summer, but for the first time since the feud the two communities had a potent reason to cooperate.

Only two people had lost. Oleya, of course. And himself. The person he had thought had known him best knew him not at all, and just as he could never forgive the miners for the deaths of his father and brother in the raids, he could not forgive his child. He no longer had a daughter.

Ilisi was asleep when he ceased wandering in the starlight and returned to his home. He did not wake her. Somberly, he placed his sword in its oiled cloth and tucked it out of sight. Perhaps, with luck, it would stay there until it rusted completely.

IMAGES OF LOVE
by Larry Tritten

Judging by the curriculum vita sent to me by Larry Tritten, he's been writing for all the magazines, and anthologies past, present, and future. (He had a very amusing article published in the April 1993 issue of *Writer's Digest*; it tells how to "master the affections, nuances, and absurdities" of the genre of fiction you write.) I can't imagine how I've missed him before this; but if people don't write books or turn up at conventions, it's a matter of luck—good or bad— whether I ever locate anything they've written. This is probably as near to a romance as I've ever published—I object to romances only when they're considered the only suitable reading for women. I started out with Grace Livingston Hill myself, but outgrew romances before I was thirteen. I find it hard to imagine adults reading romances or comics when there are so many other things to read, but "each to his own taste, as the old lady said, kissing her cow."

Clarity had been the maid of a wizard in the manse where Saran had completed his most recent adventure. Walking her home now through the nearby woods, he had the odd but exhilarating feeling that he had known her for a long time. Already he treasured his first sight of her: at a glance, the short-cropped cut of her vivid orange hair had given a boyish impression, but then the soft and lovely feminine features of her face had registered—the full lips, lightly rouged, the warm blue eyes under delicate brows, and pretty ears with green gems at the lobes. His gaze had fairly danced to her body, which thrust itself to attention in voluptuous collaboration with the snug black blouse and tight black pants that gave emphasis to high full breasts and wonderfully curved legs. Her eyes had met his and each had engaged the other's gaze. In most such contacts strangers will regard each other for a moment and then look away, but in this instance each regarded the other with a catlike intensity and the mutual gaze evolved into a sort of locked stare. Those who esteem sensuality as a primary trait tend to have a natural magnetism for others like themselves, and this was a moment of such recognition—sensual chemistry moving in the vanguard of words, introductions, social niceties.

It was twilight. The day's blue sky had deepened to a soft lilac, which was darkening to a plum color as incipient darkness began to infiltrate the light. The two were alone together for the first time since leaving the manse. Clarity's employment there had ended, yet she seemed undaunted by the fact as she listened to Saran talking about his adventure, talking with leisurely deliberation but with his mind scarcely on the story. As he spoke his eyes told a story of their own as they traveled with elaborate observation, lingeringly and caressingly, over Clarity's body—a story with a specific message of desire. It was in essence a visual dalliance, so that when he finished speaking the sense of intimacy between them was resonant in the minds of both.

And then the old familiar buoyant moment was nigh and Saran stepped toward her, his face a momentary blur to her eyes before his lips unsealed hers and she yielded in his arms to an even bolder advancement as one of his hands glided appreciatively along the contour of a breast.

"Ohhh," she murmured.

"Mmmmmm," Saran said, snuffling in the fragrance of her orange hair where tufts of it stuck up awry near the front of her skull.

"I think . . ." Clarity said, between short breaths.

"We should . . ." Saran continued, his touch enlivened by the soft resilience of her breast through the material of her blouse.

Clarity substituted a libidinous smile for the final word of the collaborative sentence, whose meaning both acknowledged by gaze and touch, then exerted herself rather more graphically, using her mouth, hands, and the surging thrust of her bosom.

Saran's senses seemed vaguely out of kilter as he watched Clarity unclothe her body, whose pale tan planes and curves seemed to shine with an undertone of spectral radiance from the lines and patches of light accenting it. Her fingertips gilded him expertly with intermittently shimmering touches of warm sensation, and he was engulfed in a flow of luxurious desire that reduced his mind to exclusively sensual motivation.

"And now," came the hot-worded whisper in his ear.

Saran had the feeling that his mind was orbiting inside his brain, every erotic thought and fancy he'd ever had being distilled into some psychic locus by the whirling transit, every other thought of any kind obliterated, and when the process was complete he had become pure voluptuous resolve. He watched with wondering detachment as his hands embraced the intoxicating beauty of his lover. There was an abrupt expansive sensation of ingress as if he'd gone with a soft plunge into another medium, an experience somewhat analagous to slipping from warm air into warm deep water, but the mediums were denser and more viscid than air and water.

Asprawl and agog in a great tunnel humid with fragrant air from some distant sea grotto or tropical reef, Saran rose to his feet, tottering. Along the tunnel and into its distance the pearly illumination of an illimitable sequence of chandeliers overhead softened the dank pink gloom.

Along the tunnel, plodding toward him, came an alabaster phantasm, aglow, its arms extended. In its tenacious, viscous embrace, Saran began to dance with it, first a slow, endearing, close dance, and in moments a faster and more rhythmic one emphasizing synchronous oscillation of the hips. The darkness of Saran's mind was flamboyantly splashed with a bright effusion of opalescent flowers, and he was aware of a remote rumbling of ocean surf, the scent of brine thick in his nostrils. The phantasm all at once became an oozy melting figure in his arms, the light from the chandeliers flickered apocalyptically, and he passed with a sudden explosive plunge back into the realm of reality, the egress achieved with a sensation of pleasure so extreme that he could feel his body pyrotechnically firing thousands of neural sparks into the sifting, savoring meat of his brain.

Opening his eyes, Saran saw a bird of vivid orange plumage start from the topmost frond of a tree and sail away toward the sky.

"Did you like that?" Clarity asked, looking up at him— or was it down? He had no clear bearings in the sensory epilogue to his climax, which left him in a demulcent daze, balmy with satiation.

In lieu of an adequately glib reply, Saran nodded, but that seemed hardly adequate either, so he made a small grimace of perplexed delight. Gently, he drew apart from Clarity and sat looking at her in astonishment. She smiled at him with lurid complacency.

"Was it a good trip?" she asked.

Saran nodded again, searching her eyes with a sharp glance. "Unlike any I've known." He looked at himself and at his surroundings. "I was ... not *here* ..."

Clarity smiled at his dismay. "No, my love, you were elsewhere—in the rose and lilac lands of your deepest phallic desire, exploring the imagery of your libido. Was it pretty?"

Saran grinned with salacious emphasis.

"Where were you?" Clarity inquired. "Spelunking? Sea diving? Baking pink comfits in a sultry subterranean kitchen? Wrestling golden mermaids on a sodden beach?" She smiled knowingly.

"You are a sorceress," Saran said uncertainly.

Clarity laughed. "No, Saran. It's something I inherited from my mother. To her, sexual concert was the antithesis of exciting harmony—she detested its sensory gluttony, its effusive physicality. Yet she was a slave whose fate was bondage as a prostitute because of her beauty. She became in time a prodigy of repression, disdaining the sexual conduct of her body to the extent that her mind transcended it, carried her into a more abstract realm of symbol and imagery where all of her sexual energy was invested and expressed. In the process a psychosexual synergistic tangency transmitted the same ability into the minds of her partners, and with equivalent power. Her partners left their bodies and went on metaphoric journeys of their own creation, dreamlike yet ectosomatic journeys infinitely more vivid than normal dreams and enlivened by the neural ecstasy of their bodies' sexual endeavors and culminated always by sexual consummations of hypersensual ecstasy.

"Ironically, this avoidance technique made my mother the most popular prostitute among a select clientele of highborn men so that her every day was spent perfunctorily roaming the phallic summits and purple vales of her mind's imagery. By the age of thirty, it is said, she was a sort of mechanistic zombie who proferred her embrace with the blunt resignation of a lemming en route with another beast to a beach where she would drown while it would rollic in the surf. I was my mother's only issue, given to the world from a delirious labor that she believed was a spectacular copulation, and in the moment that she drew her last breath and I my first, I saw the white mirage of the obstetrician's lamp and fell intact into the world with her "gift" already teeming vestigially in my newborn brain."

Saran's mind grappled with the fantastic story as he sat regarding Clarity with ardent feeling.

"Your mother's revulsion of sex was not, however, passed on," he said, giving her an inquiring look.

"Just the opposite," Clarity said. "I am something of a sensualist, and have refined a world of metaphoric experience in my mind full of celestial cities, exotic continents, and extraterrestrial weathers beyond the imagination of the most impassioned poetess."

"One question," Saran said.

Clarity smiled.

"Shall we talk more now or make more love?"

"Love is such a lovely thing to make, isn't it?" Clarity said, and touched her lips to his.

Later, sprawling naked upon their shadows, Saran asked Clarity how she came to be working as Longicorn's maid. His hands were combing softly through her tufty orange hair.

"It was a job that paid well," she said, "and so I took it. I needed the work, and his ill manner seemed the price I must pay for a respectable wage. Also, I could take all sorts of things home—fine foods, cast off items . . . he was not selfish with me for all his boorishness."

"Home?" Saran asked. "You live alone?"

"Yes, a mile or so yonder. Will you come home with me now?"

"Will a storm wind propel thistledown?" Saran answered rhetorically.

Clarity kissed him.

On their way there, hand in hand, Clarity asked Saran where he was bound.

"I have no way of knowing," he said. "My life unfolds like the pages of an adventure story, a long novel, hopefully in tetralogy form. I am an errant on an aimless odyssey, whose only goal is to enjoy the journey."

"Going nowhere," Clarity mused.

"And everywhere," Saran said.

"But if you could become rich ... Then?"

"I would build a manse and settle."

"Ah."

"And I *have* been rich."

"Oh?"

"And lost it forthwith. Another story."

"Now what?" Clarity asked. "Will you look for work? *I* must—my savings are not large."

"Work," Saran said dispiritedly. "Well, I have fifty-two maxims. It seems that I must, too, before long."

"First, though, let's have a carnival of love for a day or three, no?" Clarity suggested with a warm sidelong glance.

"Yes, yes," Saran agreed and squeezed her hand tightly, walking a bit faster as they emerged through sun-dappled shrubwood to the crest of a hill that gave a view of her cottage in a floral glade cluttered with shade trees a few hundred yards away.

Clarity's cottage was to become to Saran an island of warmth, pleasure, and comfort in the choppy seas of his life. Shaped like a chocolate truffle, it was small and yet appointed with such economy and style that its three rooms seemed anything but restrictive. The darkly wooded walls of the main room gave it the ambience of chocolate, which was complemented by the thick pelts of vulpine and ursine beasts carpeting the floor and a voluptuous umber couch covered with leather-colored and antique gold pillows. The bedroom was a purple haven, the walls encanopied in purple damask to achieve a tentlike effect; the bed was a plush dais against one wall, itself canopied with plum-colored silk so that upon it one felt doubly enswathed in sensual fabric; and all about it were exquisite objects: a brightly painted golden carousel horse; a baroque dresser of dark wood on animal legs whose drawers were brimming with lacy pastel silk, satin, and velvet lingerie and whose top supported a marvelously detailed model of a palace beneath whose roof a complex array of cosmetics and perfumes were stored. The kitchen was tiny, its shelves and drawers stocked with cookbooks and equipment, but there was an ornamental sensibility overall: containers and jars were exotic rather than plain; figures and pictures deemphasized the utilitarian sense of the room: golden lions rampant bracketing the cookbooks; paintings of black cats on the walls; opulent bouquets in colorful vases. Directly off the kitchen there was a small patio hedged in by boscage and containing a single table at the base of a conifer whose umbrella-shaped branches enclosed and protected the patio even in heavy rainfall.

During their first few days together, Saran and Clarity enacted a sensual idyll. Morning, after breakfast in the patio, was occupied by walking in the nearby woods, with an occasional impromptu romp on pillowy sward; afternoon and evening were given to reading, play, talk, and concentrated virtuoso lovemaking enhanced by theatrical games and role-playing. The flames of their mutual passion rose high, banked, and in each aftermath left them pleasantly aglow in the wake of their carnal blaze. Saran, during this time, became a *pro tempore* vacationer in enthralling and alluring purlieus: on warm verdant plains caught in alabaster downpour from livid clouds; in subaqueous grottos teeming with sea flowers and leisurely iridescent sea creatures, where the water was warm as a savannah wind; in the sweating mauve glow of deep caverns whose rocks were soft as mallow and where saline springs ran deeper yet to some hidden thermal well where golden fish migrated lemminglike to ignite themselves like incandescent lights; in gourmet kitchens where epic food battles were staged with monumental bouillabaisses, noodle casseroles, and ornate desserts. And throughout each leisurely sojourn there was the continuous soft awareness of physical delectation, a deep pleasure that metamorphosed into a pure exaltation that culminated in an apocalyptic celebration of nerves, blood, and flesh.

This existence seemed timeless, but time at length became relevant with the lovers' realization that money was a need. Every other day Clarity had gone into Zeisler's

Ramps to buy special cuisine, and abruptly the finances of both were nearly exhausted.

Saran reflected on another annoyance. He had always considered himself a ladies' man—not out of vanity but on aesthetic grounds. Women were his primary pleasure, and simply because of their beauty and style, no less than their alien psychology, captivated him, delighted him, aroused him. He had been an astute gallant from his earliest years and had caroused lovingly with scores of women; he knew the monomania of true love as well as the ephemeral lust of shallow dalliance and spontaneous debauchment, and also the pangs of being lovelorn. Yet the end of romance would never leave him fatally wounded and incurably embittered as it might some, because there were so many wondrous women abounding in the world that even when totally enamored of one he was always excitedly aware of the myriad others; and he craved every sort of love—he wanted the whore as well as the virgin, the mother as well as the daughter, the lass as well as the lady. His attention could not ultimately be unfailingly and single-mindedly monopolized by even the most beautiful and fascinating of women because there was so much varied beauty and character and sexuality to be heeded. Saran regarded the tenaciously resolute monogamist who refused to even note the beauty of other women as the sort of man who might walk through a fantastic tropical garden carrying a bouquet of his own violets without showing any interest in the goldenrod, pinks, honeysuckle, moongolds, and confetti bells surrounding him; it was tantamount to an affront to beauty.

And thus, though completely tantalized by Clarity, whose erotic skill was absolutely singular, he still began to think of other women, of the infinite varieties of appeal made possible by differing permutations of face and figure and individual nature.

Moreover, Saran knew that as a self-avowed sensualist Clarity was, to some extent, of like mind and that soon or late she would exhibit polyandric twinges to match his own incipient restlessness. Still, Saran was uncertain what his course of action should be. The idyll was ending, the matter of money had reared its ugly head (as ever), and the necessity of work, probably of some tedious day-to-day or menial kind, made him morose; yet he knew that there could be many more pleasant days, or weeks, with Clarity, and the situation was extremely comfortable. What to do?

Saran wandered alone in the woods and pondered. He had become so infixed in Clarity's cottage that he had never even been into Zeisler's Ramps with her, although it could hardly be said that he was sedentary since his erotic exertions were continuingly exhaustive. Even so, he disliked the disinclination to get about that inhabited him. What to do? Clarity's lure was strong, and to set out again with only a few maxims would be like the proverbial plunge into cold water. But daily toil ... would *that* not undermine the very meaning of an idyll? In such circumstances he would become in essence a husband.

In a clearing, Saran skipped flat stones across the surfaces of a pond and swore halfheartedly under his breath, little aware that Clarity, now en route home with a basket of fruit and crullers, would also bring an answer to their mutual problem.

Later that afternoon, unpacking the basket, Saran's eye was snared by an illustration of a great-breasted siren on a page of the gazette lining the basket. He snatched it up and read the boldly lettered proclamation beside the picture: VOLUPTUA WILL TRAVEL ANYWHERE IN THE PROVINCE OF SHADEL TO FILL YOUR BOWL WITH HOT FONDANT. 14 Meadowhawk Lane, Melander.

"What is this?" Saran exclaimed, uncrumpling the paper from the basket. It was a four page gazette whose pages were emblazoned with garish advertisements showing men and women in sexually suggestive apparel (as well as none at all) and postures.

"It's *The Spectator*," Clarity said, looking over his shoulder. "Oh, haven't you seen it yet?"

"The Spectator?" Saran blinked.

"Yes. The hedonist's gazette," Clarity smiled. She stepped up beside Saran and studied an illustration of a woman in a black gown with low cleavage revealing a necklace of tattooed hearts impaled with blood-dripping arrows. "Most of the advertisements are for transactional sex," Clarity said, then as an afterthought, "Not my heart's choice ... and yet—" She smiled. "—one's heart is not the arbitress of all sexual experience. I have, of course, experimented in that direction."

Saran gave her a questioning look.

"It was very . . . interesting," Clarity said, putting crullers in the pantry. "Education in perversity."

Saran took the gazette into the bedroom and relaxed among purple pillows, glancing through it. Its pages were rife with advertisements, large and small, placed by prostitutes, libertines, pornographers, models, and the like. At one point he discovered a small printed ad, somber and inconspicuous between the brandished breasts and protuberant buttocks of two jades soliciting attention for, respectively, The Epicure's Salon and The House of Horizontal Meditation.

The ad read: CASH PAID FOR INFORMATION ON LEGITIMATE AND VERIFIABLE SEXUAL CURIOSITIES. CONFIDENTIALITY GUARANTEED. Dr. Hindermull, 42 Monopolis.

The cogs and wheels of cerebration began to move in Saran's brain. "Look at this," he said to Clarity.

She came and read the ad over Saran's shoulder.

"What do you think?" Saran asked.

"Hmmmmmmm." Clarity made a small moue while reflecting, a habitual and somewhat sexy mannerism of hers. "Well," she said, "I don't know. It's spare and academic sounding. Intriguing, I suppose."

"Cash paid," Saran said thoughtfully.

"It could be the ad of a dispassionate pervert who only likes to listen," Clarity laughed.

"Ummm." Saran's eyebrows arched.

"Or someone too timorous or circumspect to make bold overtures in print before a meeting."

"Cash paid," Saran reiterated, with a sly glance at Clarity, who suddenly looked back at him thoughtfully.

"Do you want to answer it?" she asked.

Saran shrugged. "Cash, Clarity. What do *you* think?"

She considered for a moment, then nodded. "Yes," she said decisively, "of course, we could use a bit of intrigue as well as cash, couldn't we?" She arched her head sensually and her lips curved back in a provocative smile.

Monopolis was a scattering of houses and shops hardly numerous enough to qualify as a village, located three miles beyond Zeisler's Ramps. The next morning Saran and Clarity set out to discover Dr. Hindermull's place and investigate his interests. Saran wore a loose pink shirt and gray pants that Clarity had given him (he suspected that they had belonged to a previous cohabitant of hers, but did not inquire) and had laundered for the occasion; she herself wore a broad lavender headband, a low cut black satin dress highlighted by multiple circlets of filmy black material wrapped around her bare shoulders, three inches of silver and golden bracelets on one arm, and flat black slippers; she carried a bag containing a pair of dagger-heeled black velvet boots that she intended to change into at the end of the trek.

It was a temperate day, filled with birdsong and warm breezes, and by noon they arrived at a hill overlooking Monopolis. The urban area consisted of an inn, a stable, a greengrocer's stall, and a curio and candle shop. Beyond, in a glade, three houses stood. These turned out to be numbered 12, 22, and 32. After investigating the addresses, Saran and Clarity saw, across a small stream on a wooded hill, a large and imposing stone house with stained glass windows asparkle with sunlight.

Clarity changed her footgear and they approached the house, which was numbered 42. A candidly phallic bronze knocker on the huge front door made them exchange a droll smile.

"My guest," Saran smiled, and Clarity hefted the phallus, banging it three times on the door while Saran, in a mood of ribald amusement, jabbed one of her buttocks with a forefinger.

The door was opened by a tall man with a long face dominated by a big nose and an ingratiating smile; his eyes were bright behind the octagonal lenses of his spectacles; his hair was gray, but his features and physique appeared youthful.

"Hello," he said in a deep and mellow voice.

"Dr. Hindermull?" Saran inquired.

"The same."

"Hello." Saran extended his hand. "I am Saran, this is my friend Clarity. We saw your notice in *The Spectator*."

Hindermull gave Clarity a savoring glance. "Really? Please come in." He took Clarity's hand and stepped aside, drawing her inside, and beckoning Saran to follow.

"Clarity, is it?" he said with cordial zest, leading the way through a corridor and into an elegant and neat salon whose walls were lined with volumes and framed paintings of pagan saturnalias and expressionistic sketches of figures in sexual accouplement.

"Sit here, won't you?" Hindermull said smoothly, indicating a low couch and sitting across from them in a leather armchair. "I'm eager to hear what you have to say," he enthused, his eyes steadfastly on Clarity, which provoked a fleeting sardonic grin from Saran.

"I must say, my dear, you are a lovely lovely lovely lovely woman," Hindermull said to Clarity, then gave her a quick smile to fill the momentary pause.

Lovely, Saran thought. He noted how Hindermull's fingers moved with slight impatient jumps on the arms of his chair as Clarity generously gave him a tempestuous smile.

"Can I get either of you a drink?" Hindermull asked suavely, with his gaze monopolizing Clarity.

When both deliberated, he exclaimed, "I have just the thing—have you ever had a Rumpled Sunrise?"

Silence. "Well!" Hindermull exclaimed. "Allow me. Please excuse me for the moment." He rose and hurried from the room, leaving Saran and Clarity to look at each other.

"What a gracious man," Clarity said.

"Hummph," said Saran. "His graciousness seems extended in a single direction."

"Jealous, jealous," Clarity chimed, giving him a teasing smile. "This was your idea, no?"

Saran sighed.

"Grump," Clarity tweaked.

Hindermull returned with such vigor that he seemed to have been propelled into the room. He was carrying two outsize crystal goblets filled with dense orangeness, which he handed to Clarity and Saran in turn. Then he returned to his chair, crossed his legs, smiled broadly, and said, "So, you saw my advertisement!"

Saran was about to speak when Clarity said, "Yes, Dr. Hindermull. I myself am the custodian of a sexual anomaly of *sui generis* proportions."

"*Please* call me Tomathy," Dr. Hindermull said with a casual gesture and ever greater smile. Saran fidgeted.

"Tomathy," Clarity said, enjoying the name.

Hindermull leaned forward in his chair. "Let me explain myself, my dear. I am Dr. Tomathy Hindermull, sensologist, late of the Fabulous Clinic at Hampton's Lap, where

I supervised the definitive study of sensual erubescence, soon to be published by Eyeball Press. My specialty is sexual sensations and I am currently engaged in the production of my magnum opus, *Principia Sexualis,* which is the source of my advertisement and curiosity."

"What is the theme of the book?" Saran asked.

Hindermull turned a distracted glance on him. "It is pervasive, as the title indicates. I hope to chronicle all sexual activity that is anomalous, esoteric, out of favor, or in any wise inconsonant with what is generally conceded to be the behavioral norm. It is my supposition that a coeval world of sexual reality exists beside that which we know and talk about, but that a conspiracy of silence, nourished by taboo morality, has prevented us from discerning its marvelous scope and aesthetic amplitude. In a scientific investigatory capacity I have glimpsed this world, which I maintain is to the one of our awareness as the flight of an eagle is to the boxy jerkings of a tethered kite. I would have the truth known. Where the truth lies hidden, life is a sham. Of course, the elimination of shame is necessary where sex is rampant. The dichotomy of the cerebral and the sensual in life generally characterizes the behavior of people, who tend to live separate lives above and below the waist. I hail the day when the genitalia and the cerebrum are allowed a symbiotic status in the scheme of things, when the stirrings in my lap are credited no less than the activity of my brain and the two are free to work together to create a psychosexual aesthetic oriented toward the best pleasures both have to offer."

Hindermull sat back, his eyes agleam. "This is my work," he said with fervor, scratching absently at one thigh. "And so I have uncovered sexual manners, feats, and curiosa that would make you bite your kneecaps!" His smile was mysterious, tantalizing.

Saran was fascinated and saw that Clarity's rapt expression characterized her attitude. He tasted his drink and found it exquisite.

"Tomathy, I think I can give you a special chapter in your tome," Clarity said in a somewhat hoarse, sensuous voice.

Hindermull smiled. "Something special?"

"A price was mentioned," Saran interjected, though not

failing to note that Clarity had locked gazes with the older man, whose quiet smile was indelible as he looked at her.

Saran began to perceive the inevitable.

"The price is proportionate to the lore," Hindermull said after a pause. "What is the lore, my dear?"

After a measured silence, Clarity looked at Saran and said, "This is an experiential matter. Frankly, Tomathy, it can only be discovered through making love to me."

Saran winced. "Oh, my redness!" Hindermull exclaimed in a sharp voice. His fingers scrabbled. He looked at Saran, or more precisely, through him, then back at Clarity. "My dear, my mind and body are open to your revelations," he said in warm tones.

"Shall we, then, without further awkwardness, retire to your laboratory?" Clarity asked, and looked quite complacently at Saran for compliance.

Hindermull stared at Saran hopefully. Saran puffed out his cheeks, stood, and paced across the room. "I think I will go for a walk," he said, as if to himself. He gave Clarity a strained glance, and she nodded. Hindermull started to rise, but Saran gestured him away with a flourish. "I'll let myself out," he said.

Moments later, before he shut the door behind him, he heard a thumping sound from the salon, followed shortly by Clarity's laughter.

Saran wandered somewhat ill-at-ease along a ridge. There was a tiny point of queasiness in his belly. Jealousy? He sighed. He fully knew that Clarity was a sensualist. Was he getting possessive? It irked him, he acknowledged, that Clarity found Hindermull acceptable as a lover. Ah. Women! Men!

Saran took a dish of mauve sherbet at the inn and ate it solemnly, irritably speculating on what the color of the dessert reminded him of.

Three hours later he returned to Hindermull's house. He wielded the phallic knocker with annoyance, waited long minutes impatiently until the door was opened. Clarity stood before him, her hair disheveled, her expression languourous. She was holding a vast beige towel around her nakedness. She seemed not to recognize him.

"Well?" he said.

Clarity bit her lower lip, deliberating. "Saran, darling, this investigation is arduous. Himdermull is smitten. I do need time. Could you, do you suppose, take a room in the village and come back, say, noon tomorrow?"

Saran gave her a wild look. "A room! What are you doing? Are you talking money in here?"

Unexpectedly, Clarity seized him and kissed him with passion. "My love," she said, "enjoy my pleasure. Forbear your emotions. Wait here!" Before he could speak, she turned away and left him standing, but was back momentarily, pressing ten maxims into his hand. And again before he could speak, flushed and vivid, she closed the door.

Saran stood watching a dust mote descend past his gaze, a stringent sexual fragrance wafting over him like a wave in the wake of a swift boat.

At loose ends, Saran chose to drink in the inn all afternoon and into the early evening, sitting by himself at a table and listening with no concern whatever to the regular clientele discuss the small matters of rural existence. It was a warm night, and so to save money he slept in a bower of figgle trees. In the morning he took waffles in the inn, and by eleven was at Hindermull's door again. It was answered by Clarity wearing an ivory pink two-piece pajama of lace-trimmed satin that shone like icing in the pale sunlight. She looked distraught.

"Saran, come in," she said. He followed her into the salon and she sat across from him. He sensed it from her, then knew it, and braced himself.

Their eyes engaged. "I've taken a job," she said.

"Job?"

"As Hindermull's assistant."

Saran made a face, looking away.

"Please, please don't," she said. "Our time was wonderful, and all things change."

"So an ancient philosopher asserted," Saran said. "You cannot step in the same offal twice." He scowled. "I suppose Hindermull is a legendary lover."

"Do you want to know this?" she asked.

Saran said nothing.

"He is not unskilled."

"How could he be?"

"He is a repository of cryptic lore," she said with subtle implication.

Saran felt, undeniably, terrible—yet could not manifest a

bitterness that would poison his memories of Clarity. He truly loved her, and knew it in this moment.

"I want you to have the fee, for this was your idea."

"No matter," he said.

"One hundred maxims, darling." Her use of the word darling was pert, and yet there was an undertone of deep and true affection in it, and he saw, then, that a tear had begun a journey down her cheek. A novel secretion for her, he thought, and then felt anger for the bitterness in that and felt a brimming of tears in his own eyes.

"I love you," he choked.

She held him, and in the glory of the most exciting kiss he had ever known passed the money into his hand. "Love, love," she said into his mouth, and their tears ran into their kiss, and Saran pulled away, almost running.

In the brightness of the day he felt a sudden terrible exhilaration and he seized a stone, throwing it into the sun with a stifled cry of woe and joy. He twirled and shook himself, the tears pouring, and when they were gone went along his way, wherever that might be; but it did not matter. It did not matter at all, for he was wildly alive.

A FATE WORSE THAN DEATH
by Diann Partridge

Diann Partridge has been one of "my" writers since before I was doing any editing of anything but fanzines. She sent me a biography reminding me that she's about to turn 40—you'd be surprised how young that seems from the other side of sixty, Diann.

It's all a matter of perspective. I used to be convinced that fifty was old; now, from the far side, it seems young, On the other hand, I know a lady of more than a certain age, who said she didn't believe in aging, and began counting backward when she was forty; by now, I think she's run out of time, and is getting into the minus numbers. (As for me, I just say, "I'm not getting older—I'm getting better." If age improves wine and violins, why not women? Sometimes I looked forward with pleasure to being ninety.)

Diann says that her eldest teenager moved out of the house last January; she still has one teenager and one preteen at home. (Isn't it odd how a kid who still ought to be toddling around in rompers is now driving his own car, or getting married?) Her family has a black and tan coon hound and the same two cats, Harriet and Winston. (Vane and Churchill, I presume?) She got fired from her job as a cook and is now fighting with unemployment. She still lives in Wyoming.

Diann has appeared in several of my fanzines "way back when" and in many of my anthologies. She doesn't mention other sales—but the loss of other editors is my gain.

189

The market day crowd surged around the riders as they pushed through the noisy throng. Two women, dusty and tired-looking, each led a pack horse laden with pelts. A massive lionkiller bitch trudged beside them. The bitch wore a pack harness strapped across her broad back, and three puppies rode on each side. She snarled at anyone who came too close; even the puppies snapped at curious fingers.

The group turned off into a side street and entered the stable gates of a large inn. Boys came running to take the horses, but the women waved them away, scattering a handful of coins for the boys to scrabble over. They stabled the horses themselves. The bitch was settled with her puppies in a stall lined with thick straw. She flopped down with a gusty sigh, and the puppies nuzzled at her milk-swollen teats with happy little yips and squeals. A stableboy arrived with a meaty bone and was allowed the privilege of handing it to the bitch himself. They left their serious weaponry with their saddles and the pelts.

"Where the hell ya been?" shouted Amos, as they entered the side door of the inn's large tavern room. A large hullow! went up as the other patrons recognized them. The skinny little barkeep plonked a tankard and a glass on the bar and filled them up.

"Britta whelped on the new moon. We were held up a week with that, so it's been slow going guarding both pups and pelts." answered Cozrina, the taller of the women. Her smaller companion downed the glass of the wine in one gulp.

"Well, it's about damn time ya showed up. How many pups this time?"

"Six." Cozrina downed her tankard of beer in one long swallow, sighed deeply, and wiped the foam off her lip.

"It's a good thing, too. I've a list as long as me whacker fer people who want them pups."

Jet, Cozrina's bondmate, gave a snort and motioned for him to refill the glass. "If the list's no longern that, we won't make much out of them."

Everyone in the room roared with laughter, including the barkeep. He refilled both glass and tankard. They found an empty booth and sat down. Jet had taken off her trail drape and now wore nothing more than a tight chest band, loose knee-length trousers, and laced sandals. Her hair was cropped short, but it still managed to frame her head in a halo of golden curls. Even under the coating of sweat-streaked dust and scars, there was no denying her beauty. Cozrina was equally attractive, but in a much larger way. She stood taller than the majority of the men in the room. Her black hair was wrapped in tight braids wrapped around her head. Brawny and large breasted, the muscles across her broad shoulders rippled under her tight silk shirt. Her trousers were thin, supple leather, tucked into lion-hide boots.

They finished their drinks just as Tulda, the barkeep's wife, brought them a platter of steaming meat pasties and a bowl of her famous hot sauce. She gave them each a warm, damp towel to wipe their faces and hands. Cozrina moved over so Tulda could sit beside her.

"Six puppies this time. What luck! An' the pelts! I saw those, too, in the stable. Such a color! They'll bring a tidy sum, what with this being Cer Durlina's weddin' moon an' all. O' course, ya'll have ta gift one of the pelts to her and the bridegroom as a weddin' gift, but even with that there'll be enough left o'er to set the two of you's up fer awhile yet. Won't be no need fer ya to hie out after them nasty lion-beasties fer a year or so."

Tulda rattled on aimably, relating the current gossip and allowing the two hungry women to eat without the need to answer. The third time she mentioned Cer Durlina's wedding moon, Cozrina wiped her mouth and held up her hand.

"You mean that Lord Durl finally found a husband for that old maid daughter of his?"

"Shhh!" Tulda hissed. "Not so loud. Lord Caffra brought a passle of 'is own men with him and there's a few in here. We don't want no trouble with the future Lady and her Lord husband.

"So who got the honor of joining their house with Cer Durlina?" Jet asked so politely that Cozrina grinned.

"He's Lord Caffra's second son, Sacon. With a second son there won't be no argument about who's really in charge."

"As if that dull-witted cow ever knew who was in charge to begin with," sneered Cozrina.

A large shadow darkened their table. Cozrina had to look up even farther than normal at a huge dark-haired man blocking the sunlight.

"I am Indonel, Lord Sacon's First. Woman, you owe my Lord and his chosen Lady an apology."

Tulda gave an angry squeak and scooted out of the booth. "Ya can't fight in here and ya know that duelin's forbidden until after the nuptials. I don't want no problems with either of ya!" She stood with her fists on her ample hips and glared at both Indonel and Cozrina.

"We'll not fight, Tulda, so rest easy. I apologize for my inappropriate words, First." Cozrina replied in a tone that Jet knew was not at all apologetic. But it seemed to pacify the large man. "Sit and I'll buy you a glass of Amos' best."

The tension drained out of the First, along with the rest of the patrons. He nodded and squeezed in beside Jet. She pushed back into the corner of the booth and sent a brief glare at Cozrina. Cozrina gave her a wide guileless smile in return.

The First had already downed a number of Amos' best, and it quickly became a match between him and Cozrina to see who could drink the most. Jet would have left early on, but she was trapped by the man's solid bulk. The more beer and wine that went into her bondmate the more sociable she became toward the First. And it didn't seem as though he were unappreciative. As one drink led to another, so did the stories, each becoming wilder and more outrageous than the last. Jet could see the inevitable coming. Everything, even hand knives, had been outlawed until after the wedding, so it wasn't long before her friend challenged the First to about the only thing left—hand wrestling.

Jet sighed and shook her head. The rest of the patrons had eagerly been expecting a fight and bets were quickly exchanged. Cozrina's hand was as large and hard as the First's. Their grip made everyone wince. They both grunted and gasped as first the back of one hand and then the other wavered toward the table top.

After the first minute it looked to be an even match, and the bets changed again. Sweat streamed down Cozrina's face and she blinked her eyes to clear them. The First caught her eye and grinned. He grunted hard and slowly forced Cozrina's hand down on the table. Muscles rippled along her arm as she fought back, and with a thin, skreeing sound her shirt split along the shoulders.

"The battle goes ta the First!" Amos shouted. "An' ta

loser will be buyin' a drink fer everyone!" A cheer went up before Cozrina could protest. She gave in gracefully and tossed a couple of coins at Amos. He caught them and darted behind the bar.

Indonel's gaze was on Cozrina's shoulders. Parallel ridged scars could be seen on both shoulders under the ruined shirt. She tensed, meeting him eye to eye, waiting for his next words.

"I've only seen such scars once before and the man was dead."

"Aye, First, the love scars of the Tumaleon. I was their prisoner for near four years. Everyone had long given me up for dead."

"I have heard that no one survives capitivity with them."

"No *man* does. But a woman, if she's strong enough in body and can hold the hate long enough, can survive. I did. Now I hunt the Tumaleon for their skins. It's very profitable." There was old bitterness in Cozrina's voice. Jet's sandaled foot touched her leg under the table.

"I would hear this story, lady, if you would care to tell it. I have a room upstairs where we could be more private."

Cozrina glanced at Jet, who just shrugged and grinned. Grabbing a bottle from Tulda as she waddled by, Cozrina answered the First. "The telling is as long and dry as the Tumaleon's homeland, friend. We'd best have something to keep us refreshed."

He pushed out of the booth, waiting for her. Standing, she was but a bare inch shorter than he. She grinned over her shoulder at Jet. Jet rolled her black eyes and waved her on. It wasn't often that her bondmate found a man that looked large enough to satisfy her. She didn't begrudge her the night or the obvious pleasures that would come with it. She'd caught the look that Cozrina gave her just before the First downed her hand. Sometimes you had to lose in order to win.

Two days later, on the eve of the full moon, Cozrina and Jet slipped down a small side street blocks from Tulda's tavern. No one was about; there was a festival around Lord Durl's castle to celebrate his daughter's marriage on the morrow. Cozrina stopped before a large ironwood gate decorated with the warrior Goddess Cybreta's sign—a raised eyed fist. Knocking hard, she waited for permission to enter.

"I tell you, Jet, it is him. He was just a young man, but this Lord Sacon is the same that sold me and my brothers to the Tumaleon. He's older, but I'd never forget that face. I'll go to my grave remembering it."

"I believe you, 'Rina. But I don't know what you expect to do about it. He's royalty, first off, and he's marryin' the crown princess tomorrow. He's too closely guarded for anyone to assassinate. Remember what Indonel said."

"I will have my revenge, Jet. I swore it on the screams of my brothers as the Tumaleon gelded them and put them to work in the quarries. I spent four years submitting to their lusts and I will carry their scars lifelong. I will ask Cybreta for retribution, and I will pay in whatever coin she requests."

The gate opened silently, and the two women were beckoned inside by a veiled figure. There was no doubting the figure was female, but beyond that she was invisible.

"You know the Way, sister?" the figure asked quietly.

"Aye, sister, I know the Way," answered Cozrina, holding out a bared forearm. The figure ran a fingertip down the line of small scars that striped the skin. She waved a hand and Cozrina swept by her.

She found their way in the dark to a small side room in the low sprawling building. Jet waited until Cozrina lit a candle, then she found a place to sit against the wall. The little room was bare except for the stone altar. Cybreta was not her Goddess. But she respected Cozrina's faith.

Cozrina knelt before the altar and lit the charcoal that rested in a small brazier. Flame flared up for a few minutes, then died down to hot coals. Removing her shirt and breast band, she unpinned her hair and shook it out. She picked up a bronze bowl and a small thin knife that lay beside the brazier. Raising them both, she bowed her head and began to chant. Jet could feel the power beginning to build. Cozrina began to glow, surrounded by a pale rosy aura. It pulsed and ebbed in the candlelight, then settled into rhythm with her heartbeat. Placing the bowl on the coals, she nicked her wrist and expertly directed the jetting blood into it.

For a few seconds, nothing happened. Cozrina kept chanting. The blood sizzled suddenly, smoke billowing then solidifying into the figure that Jet recognized in the warrior's armor and weapons of Cybreta.

"Daughter," spoke Cybreta lovingly. The tip of her sword touched Cozrina's wrist and the bleeding stopped.

"My Mother," answered Cozrina in a reverent tone.

"You have bared breast and blood, Daughter. The need must be great."

"Aye, my Mother. A need so great that it kept me alive through a fate worse than death."

"Revenge?"

Cozrina nodded. "When I was a captive of the Tumaleon, I called upon You and swore to be yours, body and soul, if You would bring me from them alive. You kept your promise and I have kept your faith as that of your warrior, worshiped You within my heart and out, observed your rituals, and celebrated your holy days. Now, my Mother, I come to ask another boon of You."

"And what is that, Daughter?"

"I have found the man who sold me into the lusts of the Tumaleon. I beg your help in settling my need for revenge on him. Grant me this and anything You ask is yours."

The figure on the altar wavered, faded, then brightened. Jet's eyes widened as Cybreta smiled. It was as though the sun had burst from behind dark clouds.

"Your hated has sustained you, Daughter, but has not overwhelmed you. You have nurtured your strength and waited, true child of mine. What would you have done to him?"

"A fate worse than death, Mother. An eye for an eye."

Cybreta nodded and smiled again. "A wise choice, Daughter. As you ask, so shall I give. And as payment, I ask that when your daughter is old enough, you bring her here to me."

"I have no child, Mother, daughter or son."

"You will," Cybreta answered and, with a sharp eye-searing flare, disappeared.

Cozrina sank back and sighed tiredly. Quickly Jet lit several more candles. In the little bowl on the coals was a glittery gold powder. Cybreta's gift of revenge.

"She exacts a hard payment, 'Rina."

"I belong to Her, Jet. My life is hers. Retribution will be sweet. Sacon's screams will be as water to a parched tongue."

She put her clothes back on and rebraided her hair. Then she wrapped the bowl and its contents in a scarf, and they left.

Bright sunlight splashed across the huge bed that Cozrina shared with Indonel. He had been explaining something to her, but her mind raged around the problem that Lord Sacon was still alive. She replayed the scene of the wedding festival over and over in her mind.

They could not decide how best to use Cybreta's gift. Jet thought of placing it in his food, but how could either of them get that close? Indonel was loyal to Lord Sacon, so using him was out. Cozrina had finally decided to rub the glitter into the best of the Tumaleon hides they possessed. The thick golden pelt was man-shaped, but much larger. It was worth a minor ransom, a fitting wedding present for minor royalty. Hopefully, somehow it would come into contact with Sacon.

Jet staggered up to the open dais with the pelt in her arms. Cer Dulina was a thin, homely woman well past the age or expectations of childish prettiness, but she was dressed as befitted a young maiden in a gauzy lavender silk gown. The cut of the gown revealed bony shoulders and a flat bosom. Dull, mousy brown hair was elaborately braided and twisted above a heavy crown that tilted her head backward, making her nose protrude even more noticeably over thin pursed lips. Pale, watery-blue eyes narrowed in greed at the sight of the Tumaleon hide, and she couldn't quite hide her anger as her handsome, obviously younger groom grabbed it first. Lord Sacon draped the pelt across his lap and over one shoulder, the glowing color setting off his dark, intense good looks. He never even glanced at his bride as he stroked the hide. Jet backed away, bowing gratefully, relieved that her part in this revenge was over.

In the ensuing two days, both women had expected to hear the news at any moment that Lord Sacon was dying. But so far, nothing had happened.

Indonel tweaked a strand of Cozrina's long hair.

"Are you listening to me, 'Rina? What is bothering you? I have the most important thing in my life to tell you and your mind is a hundred leagues away."

Cozrina snuggled against him. "I'm sorry, love. I just wasn't awake yet. Tell me again what's so important."

So Indonel explained again. This time Cozrina sat bolt up right in bed and let out a warrior whoop of sheer joy. It wasn't enough. She jumped up on the bed and did a war dance, breasts bobbing and hair flying, yelling at the top of her lungs. Indonel rolled off the bed, out of the way of her stomping feet. The bed groaned in protest.

The door to their room burst open and Jet charged in. Naked, she carried a long thin sword in one hand and a short stabbing knife in the other.

"What the hell is going on here!" she yelled. She relaxed slightly as she saw that her bondmate wasn't in danger. Indonel realized he was naked also and grabbed a blanket to wrap around himself. Cozrina simply dropped flat on the bed, still laughing her head off.

"What the hell is wrong with you, 'Rina? You aren't the only one who's spending the day in bed. I thought you were being strangled." A pretty red-haired girl peeped over Jet's shoulder and then ducked back out of sight.

"It has happened, Jet. I will have to make a sacrifice to atone for doubting Her, but now I see that in her wisdom She has made my revenge even better that I could have ever wanted."

"What are you talking about? Is Sacon dead?" Jet asked. Indonel looked just as puzzled.

"Tell her, Indonel. Tell her exactly what you just told me."

He wrapped the blanket more securely around his waist and cleared his throat. "I was explaining that Lord Sacon has dismissed all his guards and personal servants. He called us before him this morning and explained that he no longer needed us. He claims that he needs no protection now, that his love for the Lady Durlina shall clothe him in armor stronger than any mortal man can make. He is renouncing his title and lands, even his royal heritage for love of Durlina. And what was even worse, he made us all stand bareheaded in the morning sun while he read a ten-page love poem he had composed to his beloved wife's feet."

Jet's mouth dropped open. Cozrina stuffed a corner of the pillow in her mouth.

"He gave away all his worldy goods and money to us soldiers," Indonel continued, looking mystified at first Cozrina and then Jet. "He gave away his horses, his personal armor, even his sword. Then," and Indomel's eyes widened slightly as he remembered, "he took off all his clothes and said that he would never wear anything again unless it had been sewn by his own true love's delicate hands. Great Gods, anyone can see that the woman is as ham-handed as a cow! Stop laughing, 'Rina. It's not funny! Lord Sacon's out of his mind and I'm out of a job."

By this time Jet had joined Cozrina on the bed, and the two of them were laughing as though their minds had wandered away on moonbeams. Jet threw her arms around Cozrina who hugged her back just as hard.

"Do you realize what this means?" Cozrina asked when she finally stopped laughing.

Jet nodded. Indonel shook his head.

"I wish you'd tell me what's happening?"

Cozrina looked only at her partner. She touched Jet's cheek with one big hand. "I have my revenge, sister. I asked Her for a fate worse than death and I got it. Lord Sacon has fallen in love with his bride."

They both started giggling again. "And you know what's even worse?" she glanced up a Indonel and he shook his head, "It's known all over the realm that Cer Dulina can't sew."

The two women collapsed into helpless laughter once again.

POWER PLAY
by Sandra Morrese

Sandra Morrese starts updating her autobiography by saying she's afraid it will sound egotistical. A biography or autobiography is one place where people are not only allowed but expected to be egotistical. The only place I wish people would *not* tell me their life stories and the names of all their children and cats is in submitting a story when I don't know them from Adam's off ox—and don't particularly care. After I've bought their story, I'll call, or my secretary will. That's the time to tell me your life story. I know that one writer's magazine says to be original and try to stand out from the rest of the slush pile—but why not stand out by being brief and professional? After all, your story is your job interview, and a chatty personal letter makes you sound like an intrusive used car salesman. Wait till you're asked to tell me the names of your cats or the plots of your unwritten novels. Or better yet, wait till we're socializing in the SFWA Room at some convention.

Sandra lives in Maryland with her Air Force husband, two children, three dogs, one cat, and assorted guppies.

The spell was holding; barely, but it was holding. Calia walked past the last guard unseen and slipped into Prince Jevan's bed chamber.

Please don't let it fade now! she thought. Naked as she was (since the lotion worked only on flesh), it would be embarrassing if she became visible again anywhere in the palace, but here in *this* room ... Nothing would save her if it happened here. Knowing Jevan, he'd probably get a good laugh out of suddenly finding her this way in his chambers—that is, right before he killed her.

The *nerve* of that bastard, suggesting she'd do better as a harlot than the sorceress she was, then forcibly offering to initiate her himself! She'd barely gotten away in one piece let alone with her precious virginity, on which all her spells depended.

Well, we'll see who laughs after tonight, won't we?

She crept toward the huge bed where the prince lay sprawled on his back beside one of his concubines. The sheets were pulled to the side, her target wide open.

How lucky can I get?

Calia carefully opened the pouch she'd been hiding in her fist and sprinkled the contents lightly over Jevan's groin. The powder sparkled briefly, then disappeared.

I hope she was memorable, she thought viciously. *She'll be your last!*

Jevan stirred and Calia stepped backward. Her eyes strayed to a wall mirror and panic gripped her throat. She was materializing! And Jevan was waking up! Gods, not here!

Jevan sat up and looked straight at Calia. The sleepy confusion on his face quickly turned to anger and he bellowed for the guards.

Calia shrank back against the wall. Looking down at her rapidly appearing self, she muttered the spell again, but she only half faded. Why wasn't it working?

Gods and Goddesses! If any of you are real, you can have anything, just get me out of here!

Done, she heard, or thought she heard.

She looked up at the opening door, just as the guards burst into the room. That did it—she was as good as dead. She squeezed her eyes shut, not really wanting to see the blow she knew was coming, but they rushed right past her, as though ... She opened one eye and looked down, then quickly clamped her hand to her mouth to stifle her cry of relief. The spell was working again!

She didn't wait, afraid the spell might still falter. She ran out of the room and down the corridor as Jevan howled angry orders, trying to convince his guards that someone really *had* been in his room. She reached the top of the stairs and raced down them three and four at a time, hit the bottom floor, and bolted for the door (barely missing the guard who was entering), then ran across the courtyard and into the street, around the corner, into an alley, down another alley, and finally up the three flights of outside stairs to her own rooms. Calia slammed the door shut, slipped the bolt into place, and slid to the floor, panting.

She remembered to break the spell, then just sat there on the floor slowly regaining her wits and her breath. Her side hurt and her head pounded something awful, but she was alive—and she'd *done* it!

"Yes, you have."

Calia jerked up her head at the sound of a male voice, staring with renewed panic—and complete bewilderment—at an elegantly clad young man sitting on her bed. She swallowed hard and slowly got to her feet, sliding up against the door, then realized she was still naked and cursed under her breath. The furnishings were sparse in the best of times, and there was nothing she could conveniently grab for cover, so she clothed herself with the only thing she did have—her dignity—and refused to acknowledge any discomfiture to this intruder, who'd somehow managed to get past warding spells that were *supposed* to be unbreachable.

Unless, of course, he was a sorcerer.

Damn.

Today was really not going very well.

What next? she wondered silently.

"Paying me for getting you out of Jevan's palace would be a good start. You did say I could have anything."

Calia's mouth dropped open. *No one* could have known of her plan. "How did you ..." she started, then scowled at him. "Who are you?" she demanded.

"The god who answered your prayer, of course. Were you expecting someone else?" he asked innocently, then burst into astonished laughter. "You really *don't* believe we exist, do you? Oh, I assure you I'm quite real. Here," he said, rising and taking a step toward her, "touch me, you'll see."

Calia's eyes narrowed as she folded her arms across her chest and pointedly ignored the offered hand. He shrugged and sat back down, obviously still amused. *She* wasn't. *She* was furious. She was also more than a little unnerved by this—person—being where no one was supposed to be able to get and alluding to things *absolutely* no one but her should know.

"Okay," she said finally in very measured tones. "Let's say, just for the sake of argument, that I believe you. What, precisely, is your fee?"

Either he was a very good illusionist, or his smile actually did add light to the room. She shook herself inwardly. He was disconcertingly handsome, with gold-tinged, deep copper curls above a finely chiseled face. And he sat in a way that showed he knew exactly what effect that perfectly cut velvet jacket, highlighting that lean, muscular frame of his would have on the average woman.

But then, Calia certainly did *not* consider herself an average woman. She'd spent ten years never allowing *any* man to attract her attention, always staying carefully aloof and disinterested. Virgin Witchcraft demanded that even her thoughts be untainted by physical lust and drew its limited power from the discipline of the user's restraint. For this man to disturb that hard-won discipline so much—it was exceedingly hard to keep from staring at him—severely bothered her.

Not man, Calia, she thought to herself. He *has the unfair advantage of being a god. Or so he claims. But how else could he have known?*

"Exactly," he said and she glared at him.

"Stay out of my head!" *Damned telepathic eavesdropper.*

He was unperturbed. "In exchange for having saved your life," he said, then paused looking her straight in the eye, "I ask for the sacrifice of your virginity."

"What!" Now his eyebrows did rise. Even a seasoned mercenary might have blushed at the colorful and exceedingly personal string of curses she flung at him before he could raise his hands to stop her.

"Please!" he said, hand to his chest in feigned shock. "Such ugly words from such a lovely mouth, I don't think I can bear it. If you'll kindly let me explain?" She glared again but didn't resume the tirade.

"I've been watching you a long time, Calia; you've got a tremendous amount of talent. But you're wasting it with the lesser magics. The witch who said they were the best you could do lied. Nemet knew your potential and was jealous of it. So she lied and convinced you that you were no better than she."

Calia was suspicious but was intrigued in spite of herself. She thought back to the night she'd come to Nemet, the oldest and most feared witch in this part of the city. How she'd confided to Nemet, and no one else, the power she felt growing within her, and a twelve-year-old girl's romantic dream of sorcerous love unleashing it. It was what all the old stories said would happen. The stories whispered for centuries among the womenfolk when their men retired to their pipes and fires and the women were left alone. She'd memorized every word of every secret story and came to Nemet that night, her head filled with the promise of them. So Nemet had tested her. Calia hadn't understood the shock and anger that had shown briefly on the old woman's face before she told Calia that her feelings were false.

"You'll never have more than the powers of the Virgin Crafts, girl," she'd said. "Better satisfy yourself with that and forget the Passion Magics."

Now he said Nemet had lied? It could explain a lot of things. *If* he was telling the truth. And *if* he was what he claimed. But how else could he have known so much about her life?

"I'd like to show you what you're truly capable of, Calia," he continued and Calia listened, interest and hope edging out her suspicion and anger. "You see, I'm still a relatively young god—more of a demigod, actually—and as such, I need more than just mindless followers, though those never hurt. I also need allies. Like a powerful sorceress. I want you to be my ally, Calia. I can help you unleash the power you've craved for so long—yes, it is within you. *And* I can teach you how to use it, better than any sorcerer could." He paused and leaned forward. "But you have to *want* it, Calia."

Her chin lifted slightly at what she had a feeling was meant as an insult. He was baiting her, but she wasn't nibbling—yet.

"Do you know how many of your kind are capable of True Magic and never fulfill their potential? More than you think. Do you know why? The *real* reason why? Because *desire* is needed—an intense, passionate desire for power—and women, especially those who show magical talent, are taught to deny desire. Your menfolk fear what a powerful woman might do. They don't want to have to share their status, their control. And most of the women are reluctant to risk their comfortable niches. So they teach you *not* to want more than they hand you. They tell you that wanting more is wrong.

"The secret myth you grew up with is that a sorcerer releases the power within a mage-gifted woman. The truth is, you release the power *yourself,* when you embrace the desire for it and abandon the restraints you've been taught."

He relaxed then, reclined, and leaned on one elbow.

"It can be a long and profitable alliance for both of us; not to mention a pleasurable one." He patted a spot on the bed next to him.

Calia chewed on her lip, thinking. He sounded sincerely reasonable—or he was just damned convincing. Maybe both. It certainly was an awful lot of trouble to go to if all he wanted was a tumble in the sheets. And the part about being taught never to desire was certainly true. More powerful than the old witch had said she could be? And if he wasn't the one who'd gotten her out of Jevan's palace (she wasn't *entirely* convinced, though it seemed a logical conclusion), how could he know of her impromptu prayer?

"*Do* you want the power, Calia? Do you desire True Magic enough to free yourself of *their* restrictions?"

It was a risk, but what had playing it safe gotten her? A dingy room three stories above the blacksmith, that's what.

"Yes," she answered, looking him straight in the eye and walking resolutely over to the bed.

"Do I at least get to know your name?" she asked.

"Xander," he answered, pulling her down to kiss her.

They lay entwined on the bed as the sun broke through the night. Calia had barely slept; she was too delighted at how she felt. Amazing how years of lies could be wiped out so easily. She could feel the power tingling inside. *Her* power. Power many more like her could have if someone had the sense to tell them to take it. Enticing thought, that.

Xander stirred, waking, and reached for her. They kissed slowly, then he looked up at her.

"Disappointed?" he asked.

"Not in the least," she said. "But I do have one question. If gods in general do exist, how is it that you, and not some other god or goddess, answered me? *I* certainly wasn't being specific. Were you the only god in the vicinity or something?"

"But of course," he said, giving her a mischievous grin. "Why do you think your spell failed in the first place?"

FENWITCH
by Sarah Evans

Sarah Evans is 32 years old, was raised in the Central Valley of California, and currently lives in Austin, Texas, with her husband, son, and "one demanding tiger cat." (Actually, I don't believe I've ever met a cat that *wasn't* demanding.)

This story is her first professional sale, but hopefully she will have many more.

The two riders at the crossroads looked at one another, alike and unalike in the early morning light. Both were sword-bearing fighters on steady, seasoned mounts, wearing the housebadges of two local lords. One was trim and fit, her face unlined, blonde hair bound firmly in a braid down her back, her tunic and leather breeches still bright and firm, showing little wear. The other was heavier, hair cropped short about her ears with gray amid the plain brown, face and clothes showing a certain age and wear.

"So. What is your business in the fens, old woman?" asked the first, her very tone and attitude claiming the right to ask.

"I would guess the same as you. Someone dear to me has the wasting sickness, and I've been told the fenwitch may know a cure. And you?" returned the other rider.

"I seek a cure indeed, though not for someone dear so much as one who will dearly reward me. My lord has fallen ill and is known to pay well for service deserving of such. The fens are known to be as treacherous as the fenwitch who dwells in their heart."

"Then we may as well journey together. My name is Cara. It is my lord also who ails, but I seek to aid him for his honorable treatment of myself, and others whom he will not discard simply because they are no longer in their prime. You might say it will be his reward," laughed Cara, her eyes crinkling at the corners.

The blonde woman considered, then shrugged.

"Very well, it is all the same to me, though I warn you, you'd best keep up with me. I am Laschka."

Together they turned onto the narrow path which led into the fens. The way was difficult, but no hardship for these two, who had experience enough to keep their eyes open. Brambles, quaking sands, and sudden mists were negotiated with confidence if not ease.

After several hours, Cara spoke "Tell me, Laschka. I know by your badge that you serve Lord Mardale, and his reputation is much like m'Lord Vandon. He does not cast off those who have served him well when their years begin to slow them. Why should you wish to risk yourself if you do not truly care about his well-being?"

"I told you before, he rewards well. Even if the fenwitch cannot save him, he will order me rewarded for the risk of the attempt. Then I shall never be in the position that you are in now, of depending on another's charity when I am no longer as . . . able-bodied, shall we say?"

Cara eyed the younger woman, criticism in her face, but she shrugged and rode on without another word.

A short while later, Cara reined in, lifting a hand. A faint sound drifted to them on the thick warm air that bore the scent of the luxurious growth and decay that filled the fens.

"It sounds like a child. This way." Cara spoke with unconscious authority and turned from the path. Laschka started to protest, but Cara was already beyond sight in the thick brush, having urged her mount to a canter. With a scowl, she turned after the older woman.

She did not need to go far. In a small clearing she found Cara on her knees beside a small weeping child, his thin body dressed in little more than rags. Laschka remained astride, shifting impatiently in the saddle while Cara quieted the child and spoke with him in a low voice. After a few minutes, she stood up, lifting the boy to his feet.

"He's gone astray from the fen village where he lives. It can't be far; I doubt it will take us more than a quarter to half turn of the sand clock to get him home," said Cara.

"If it's not so far, then his people will find him. Come, we have more urgent business; the wasting sickness steals our lords' time even now, aging them beyond their years as we speak," Laschka demanded arrogantly.

"Laschka, he is only a little child. We cannot leave him to wait for searchers who may never come," the older fighter protested.

"Maybe you can't, but I certainly can. I receive nothing if Mardale dies before I return!" With that, Laschka spurred her horse back to the trail.

Cara looked down at the boy at her side; she could feel him trembling beneath her hand. She smiled at him reassuringly and swung him to the saddlebow, mounting behind him. With complete confidence, she rode out to return him home.

In even less time than she expected, she was on her way, for the frantically seeking mother met them on the path. A steady canter and sharp eyes caught her back up with Laschka in very little time, as the young woman had run into thick brambles not long after leaving them. Together they made their way through.

The fighters ate their midday meal cold in the saddle, the horses being under little pressure and so not wearying quickly. It was close to mid-afternoon when Laschka rounded a curve in the trail and nearly ran down an old woman. The rider swore and jerked the reins harshly, as the woman gasped and scrambled for the side of the path, scattering firewood and kindling hither and yon.

"Stupid old woman!" yelled Laschka angrily.

"She wasn't the one at fault! Look to yourself before you call another names," Cara rebuked her with blazing eyes. "You should have been paying more attention, as well as not riding so fast!"

The two riders glared at each other, while the fenwoman cringed in the brush. After a few moments, Laschka spurred forward without another look, continuing in the direction of the heart of the fens and the fenwitch. Cara gazed after her, then, heaving a sigh, she dismounted and held out a hand to the old woman.

"Come, I'll help you gather your wood. 'Tis not your fault, and you deserve better than the doubling of your work," she said. Together, they made short work of the task, and Cara decided that by now, a little extra time would do no harm. She tied the bundled wood to her saddle and followed the woman the rest of the way home.

"Thank 'ee for the aid. Would tha favor me by sharin' a meal?" asked the old woman. Cara shook her head.

"Nay, I need to be on my way. I seek the fenwitch, for a cure for the lord I serve."

The woman's eyes brightened.

"Ah, our Lady of th' fens, is it? Weel, Ah'll pack a 'ot meat pasty for 'ee, and point 'ee out a short path to 'er 'ome. 'Ee'll get thur soon aft' tha freend."

Pleasantly surprised, Cara laughed and agreed.

Laschka rode into the clearing before the small cottage in the heart of the fens. To one side, a woman with dark red hair cascading down her back turned from the garden patch she'd been attending. The woman waited calmly, face sober, gray eyes steady.

"Are you the fenwitch?" demanded the young rider.

"Some call me that."

Then I have need of your services. My Lord Mardale has taken the wasting sickness, where a day ages him like a year or more. I've been told you have a cure."

The woman tipped her head in acknowledgment.

"Well?" prompted Laschka.

"It will take time."

"My lord has very little of that commodity, witch."

"I realize that." The woman's voice held a sharp note now. "You cannot return through the fens at night, and I shall have it ready by the morn. And I shall make enough for your companion also."

Laschka's mouth dropped open. But it was only a moment later when she heard the sound of a horse and saw Cara approaching from a different path. Her mouth tightened in irritation.

Silently, the two women set up camp as the fenwitch gathered herbs and such from her garden and started inside to prepare them.

"Lady of the fens?"

She turned to look at Cara.

"Thank you for your help. I very much appreciate it."

The woman gave the older fighter a brilliant smile and went within.

In the morning, Cara and Laschka washed briefly, ate, and prepared to leave, all as silently as the night before.

"She promised it would be ready, damn all!" snarled Laschka, sending furious looks toward the house.

"Then it will be," replied Cara serenely. "Calm yourself. It will do no good to fret over it."

"Indeed it will not." The voice startled them both, coming from the looming fens behind them rather than the house. "Especially since it is done."

Laschka opened her mouth for an angry retort, but Cara silenced her with a look.

"Lady, I thank you," Cara nodded as she took the flask held out to her by the red-haired woman. Laschka accepted the second without a word, a set look to her face.

"There are no instructions, save for the victim to drink all the potion. It has strength to aid only one, by returning that one to his natural age and health, regardless of the ailment, be it disease or magic. I will only say that time is exceedingly crucial to the efficacy of this cure," said the fenwitch with an odd smile.

Laschka nodded brusquely and mounted, while Cara smiled and murmured thanks again before following her.

The trail was somewhat familiar today, and the two rode quickly, making good time. Again they ate on the move, seldom speaking, and only when the path required it. Suddenly, a cry for help startled them.

The blonde woman flung a furious look at Cara as the older woman reined in. Laschka whipped her horse with the reins and galloped on. Cara turned aside to seek the voice screaming for help.

She found a man with an injured leg trapped by a vicious fen-crawler, a large lizardlike thing with a gaping maw full of teeth. She drew her sword and battled the thing away from its prey, finally killing it after a messy fight in the mud and shallow water.

"I thank you for your assistance," the man said as she bandaged his leg.

" 'Twas nothing. Where is your home, or someone who can help you further?" Cara replied quickly, conscious of the passing time and the flask in her saddlebag.

"Ah, there's no need, here comes a friend now," he responded, and Cara glanced over her shoulder, to see the fenwitch approaching. The witch smiled her brilliant smile again and merely nodded Cara to her horse. Bemused, the woman obeyed. Her spirits lightened and her heart rose as she made her way out of the fens.

Laschka sighed as she left the fens behind her. Not far now, and no delays either. The two days' hard riding was catching up to her; she could feel the weariness in her bones. It would be nice to rest in the hall tonight, her reward locked safely away.

As she rode into Lord Mardale' courtyard, dusk was falling. She became aware of her filthy appearance after all the hours of fen-riding, as the keepfolk stared at her. She dismounted and flung the horse's reins to a stableboy.

"Here, care for him well, as he has carried me well these past days. I have the cure for Lord Mardale here, from the fenwitch herself!"

Leaving the surprised stableboy in her wake, she plunged into the keep, flask in hand. Kitchenmaids, guards, all the folk of the castle gazed openmouthed in her wake. She thought of the gleaming reward that would be hers for accomplishing this amazing deed as she plunged to the very door of the lord's suite.

"M'lord Mardale, I have it, the potion to return your age and health to norm—" She gasped for breath, and stopped, her eyes on her ailing lord's silvered mirror. He and his attendants stared as she caught sight of her own reflection.

Her own face looked back, lined as if a quarter of a lifetime had passed, her body thickened, her hair grayed. She licked her lips and touched her face, unbelieving. Her eyes went to the flask, to her lord as a certain limited understanding came to his face, and back to her own image. Indecision filled her as she considered: her youth returned, but unrewarded and reduced in position, or age, with reward and a grateful patron. Laschka cursed the fenwitch bitterly as the red-haired woman's laughter rang in her mind.

* * *

In another keep, a rider dismounted, smiling and greeting companions, as Cara went to also offer a cure to her lord and friend, unaware that her face and body were young once again, only an image of grey eyes and a gentle smile in her mind.

GREEN EYED MONSTER
by Vicki Kirchhoff

The whole point of *Sword and Sorceress*, as of all fiction, is to show people behaving like people; far too much of the original male form of sword and sorcery fiction showed men behaving like automatons even when they weren't. In fact, the main characters of some of Isaac Asimov's stories, who sometimes *were* robots, were more human than the average sword and sorcery hero. Jealousy is not usually a particularly admirable emotion, but it is a very human one.

One thing I can't stand is a story where the main character is a wizard or sorceress, and we never see him or her doing anything magical. Just calling your heroine a sorceress or wizard doesn't make her one; in some of the stories I get, the so-called sorceress might as well be a plumber, for all the author ever shows us to the contrary. This story, at least, shows us the heroine (a swordswoman) doing something. The late Leigh Brackett, who excelled at this sort of thing, once said "If there's a woman in my story, she'd doing something, not worrying about the price of eggs or who's in love with who." She probably should have said "whom," but you get the idea. Too much female fiction spends its time worrying about who's in love with whom. Which is all very well, but despite the *Ladies Home Journal,* there is life both before and after romance.

Vicki Kirchhoff says that her biography is nothing spectacular (whose is?), that she is 29 years old, and is looking for something to do with her English and Education degrees. She says, "I live in an apartment where the animals

213

outnumber the humans two to one, but we still outweigh them. I have two ferrets, two cats and a boyfriend to keep me busy and keep me writing even when I'm thoroughly frustrated with my job search."

Do enough of this kind of writing and you won't need a job. I hear people ask how I could keep house and write—my question was always how anyone could possibly keep house without something *real,* like writing, to do when things like dishwashing got too intrusive.

The streets of Rivertown were dark and desolate. Just a few hours earlier, the marketplace had been full of people who had come to enjoy the festival. Festivals were times when sleepy towns swarmed with merchants and anything could be bought or sold. They were times when the guards were less likely to be looking for outlaws with prices on their heads.

Kenna and her partner Dain had also come to Rivertown for the festival. They'd come to relax from the weeks on the road and on the run. Even outlaws like themselves needed a break.

Though they had come together, she wandered the now empty marketplace alone, fighting her own feelings while he and a gypsy girl named Jesarna gazed longingly at each other over an inn table.

She sighed, her steel blue eyes sweeping the shadows. It was foolish for her to be out alone so late at night. She had known that when she left the inn. Her hand rested on the hilt of her sword, a warning to any thieves that might think her easy prey.

She heard soft footfalls behind her and spun, drawing her sword as she did. A figure jumped back and then stepped out of the shadows. It took her a moment to recognize the bright red hair, blue eyes, and wide smile of her minstrel friend Galen. "What are you doing out here alone?" he asked. "With the festival going on, the streets are full of thieves looking to rob the unsuspecting."

Kenna resheathed her sword. "I don't think I'm unsuspecting."

"Very true."

He glanced around. "Where is your partner?"

"Over at the Ivory Stag."

"No doubt with a comely wench on each arm," Galen laughed.

"No," she said. "Just one."

Galen stopped. "That sounds almost like jealousy and I know you and he aren't lovers."

"That's what makes it petty," she sighed. "I'm jealous because she's a better dancer and prettier than I am."

Galen gave her a hug. "Can't be true. It takes more than a pretty face to attract men, and I doubt she can wield a sword to save her life. So, what does she look like?"

"She's a gypsy," Kenna sighed. "Not as tall as I am, thick black hair, green eyes. Her name is Jesarna."

"Poor Kenna, battling the green eyed monster."

"I don't know that I'd call her a monster."

Galen laughed. "Not the girl, my dear. Jealousy. I know a song called 'Jealousy is a Green Eyed Monster.' "

He kissed her fingers. "Dain's fancy for her will pass or it won't, and there's nothing either one of us can do about it."

Kenna sighed. "I just don't like her, and jealousy is the only way I can explain it."

"Well, m'girl. She's a gypsy. Why don't you ask Viktor about her tomorrow. You know he'd love to see you, and who knows what he might know about her."

"I think I'll do that."

Viktor was an old friend, and his gypsies had camped just outside the city walls. Their brightly painted wagons stood in a circle around a fire pit. Kenna was met with open arms by the two sentries and escorted to Viktor's wagon.

The old gypsy's eyes sparkled when he saw her. In spite of his age, his embrace was as strong as always. "So, daughter-who-is-not-mine, what brings you to see this tired old man?"

"Dain and I came to see the festival, and I knew you'd never forgive me if I didn't visit."

He smiled and said, "Vasili told me he had seen you. I had given you until tonight before I sent someone to fetch you."

He gestured to one of the cushions. "Sit and drink with me, my friend. There is something on your mind, yes?"

She laughed. "So, you really can read minds.

He laughed with her, "Since you and your friend are wanted here and need to keep your wits about you, I knew the darkness beneath your eyes was from lack of sleep and not too much drink. Since I know when you came into town, I know it is not because you were traveling late, which leads me to the fact that something else troubled your sleep."

He grinned. "Unless, of course, it was someone."

"Not someone," she assured him.

"Perhaps you should spend a few nights here, then. I'm sure there are many lads who would brave your strength. If my Marta were not so good to me and if I were but a few years younger . . ."

"Viktor, that's not why I'm here."

"I'm sorry, my friend, talk to me."

"Do you know a girl named Jesarna?"

Viktor's smile died and his jaw tightened. "Only because you're a dear friend and don't know all of our ways will I give you this warning. Do not speak that name ever again in my presence."

"But, Victor,"

"No. I'm sorry, but I will not disgrace good people with that name. Let us speak of something else."

Kenna sighed and did as he asked. She knew better than to argue with him. Still, at least she had evidence that there was more to Jesarna and that her suspicions were not unfounded.

Back in town, she waded through the crowds of people in the hope of finding Dain. Her best bet was one of the weaponers' booths, and most of those were by the stable and smithy. She had to let him know what Viktor had said.

She caught sight of a line of scarlet robes and ducked into an alley. Four men, heads shaved bald and carrying wicked looking hooked polearms, passed in front of where she'd hidden. She waited for them to be well on their way before emerging. She and Dain had an old feud with the Vulture cult, a religious group of heartless scavengers. Now she had another reason to find him.

He was in the marketplace, haggling with an armorer over a pair of throwing knives. She caught his attention and waited for him to conclude his business. He bought the knives and smiled. "Enjoying the festival?"

"Not as much as I was," she replied. "Where's Jesarna?"

He shrugged. "I'm meeting her later."

He held up the knives. "Think she'll like them?"

"Dain, about Jesarna . . ."

He sighed. "You spoke to Viktor and he wouldn't talk about her at all. In fact, he was probably very angry to hear the name. Right?"

"Well . . . yes. How did you know?"

"I told Jesarna last night that you knew him and she said that would be his response if you asked about her. They didn't part on very good terms."

He put the knives away. "I don't understand why you distrust her so much."

She sighed. "Neither do I."

"Well, if it makes you feel any better, she told me she left the gypsies because she disagreed pretty strongly with some of their beliefs. As far as Viktor's concerned, she's the worst kind of evil. I happen to disagree."

"I'm sorry."

He hugged her. "Look, I know you're just worried about me. I remember what a pig I was when you first met Galen. Jesarna really wants you to like her and so do I."

She smiled. "Guess I'm just jealous."

"Don't be," he said. "You and I have been through entirely too much for anyone to ever take your place with me. Right now, Jesarna is something to me that we already know you can't be. We tried that, remember?"

She laughed. "And what a disaster that was."

He reached into his pocket and pulled out a necklace. "I didn't forget my best friend while I was haggling either."

It was green, gold, and blue beads. "Your favorite colors."

"It's beautiful," she said as he slipped it over her head.

"Glad you like it. Want to join us for a midday meal?"

She fingered the beads, feeling even sillier for her jealousy. "Sure. Where are you meeting?"

"Central square. I saw Galen was playing there this morning. He said to let you know where he was."

"Thanks."

He turned back to the merchant. "Oh, Dain," Kenna said. "I almost forgot. I saw four Vulture priests in town earlier."

He frowned. "That's not good. Any idea what they're doing here?"

Kenna shook her head. "I can't imagine they're looking for us. No one knew we were coming."

"You check with Galen. I'll see what I can find out asking around and meet you there at midday."

She found the minstrel at the square. The bright green hat in front of him was half full of coins. He ended his song two verses early and embraced her. "So, discover anything interesting?"

"Too much," she said. "Jesarna left the gypsies because she didn't like their beliefs, reason enough for Viktor not to want to ever hear her name mentioned again. And there are Vulture priests in town."

"That's unpleasant news," Galen said. "Are they after you?"

"We're not sure. I was hoping you might be able to find out for me."

He smiled. "You women always want something."

He picked up his hat and tucked the coins in his purse. "Come, let's walk and enjoy the festival."

She and Galen had been lovers for a short time, but neither one of them had wanted to give up their lifestyle for the other. They'd settled for being friends. They were not as close as she and Dain, but Galen was a man she knew she could trust.

"So," he said. "You still don't like Jesarna."

"Do you?"

"I've never met the girl. I certainly don't see what's got you all on edge."

She sighed. "I guess it is just me, then."

He hooked his arm into hers. "Come, let me buy you a gift to take your mind off all this."

When the sun was at its zenith, they met Dain and Jesarna in the square. Galen was all smiles as he steered them toward a tavern. Kenna tried not to notice how enrapt Dain and Jesarna seemed during the meal. It was as though they had no companions but each other. She found herself gritting her teeth as she had to repeat herself twice to get Dain's attention. She finally got up and left with Galen following behind her.

"He's certainly got it bad," he said.

"I can't stand being around them," Kenna sighed.

"I remember being like that over a girl," Galen said. "I think her name was Melissa . . ."

She elbowed him. "What am I supposed to do? We can't stay here forever, and Jesarna doesn't strike me as the mercenary type."

Galen stopped and grabbed her shoulders. "Kenna, would you begrudge Dain his happiness with Jesarna? What if he decides he's tired of the road and wants to settle somewhere with a wife? Would you deny him his wishes? Would you refuse to give him your blessing?"

"I guess not," she said looking away.

"Perhaps, my friend, you're not jealous of the gypsy girl so much as what Dain has found and you have not. How long has it been since you were alone?"

"A long time."

"Then I imagine we have found the cause of your distress, haven't we?"

She sighed and leaned against him. "Now what do I do?"

He hugged her. "Wish them well or farewell. It's your decision."

"I need to think about it."

"Then find yourself a place where you can think."

She glanced around. She needed to leave the city. "Will you tell Dain for me?"

"Tell him what?"

"I'm going to Pineswood. It's not too far."

"Are you coming back?"

"Tell him to meet me there. Don't tell him until he asks, so he won't go chasing me down until he's had a chance to spend some time with Jesarna and knows what he wants."

Galen hugged her again. "What will you do if he chooses not to go with you again."

She tried to smile. "Find another partner."

"Perhaps," he said, "we could try again?"

"Not now, Galen; later, when I've had a chance to think."

"I am ever your friend, Kenna. If Dain is still mooning about, I'll come visit you in a few days."

She nodded.

He went with her to gather her horse and her things, and she left him at the town gate. It felt strange leaving the village alone, without Dain beside her. Her horse's steps seemed to echo without the second set sounding with them. It was going to be a long ride to Pineswood.

She passed the gypsy camp and decided that she should probably say good-bye to Viktor. She found his young daughter Martika first.

The dark-haired girl threw herself into Kenna's arms. "I missed you when you were here before." she said. "How are you?"

"Well," Kenna said.

"Liar," Martika replied. "You look so sad. We are like sisters, so tell me what's wrong."

Martika's remark inspired a different kind of loneliness she hadn't allowed herself to feel in years. "I can't."

"Why not? Oh, Kenna, is it something about my father? Tell me, I promise not to say anything."

"I need to ask you a question, but your father has already threatened me should I ask him about it again. Are you sure you want to hear it?"

Martika nodded. "More than ever."

Kenna sighed. Viktor would be furious if he found out. "What do you know about a girl named Jesarna?"

Martika paled. "Father said we are never to speak her name again."

"I'd heard that she left your beliefs."

"It's more than that; she joined that horrible Vulture cult."

Kenna could feel her own color draining from her face. "The Vulture cult?"

Martika nodded. "After everything they've done to our people, I couldn't believe that she'd do such a thing. There's even a rumor I heard that she's an assassin for them. I don't know for sure. Why would you want to know about her?"

Kenna only barely heard her as she jumped into her saddle and jerked the horse around. "Thank you, Martika, I owe you a big favor."

She galloped back into town, past the lazing guards, and swore as the crowds slowed her horse to a walk. She scanned the sea of faces for anyone familiar as she made her way toward the stable.

Pulling her sword free of the saddle, she wrapped it in her cloak. She didn't want to get stopped by the guard for wearing weapons openly during the day. It was always possible that one or two might recognize her.

She waded back into the crowd, glad that her height allowed her to see over most of the heads. She checked the square first and found Galen. He caught her eye and his song stopped. He excused himself from his crowd and joined her. "I thought you were leaving."

"Jesarna's an assassin for the Vulture cult," Kenna said.

He slung his lute over his back. "Let's go."

"Galen," she said. "The last time we met, you didn't know much more about fighting than which end of the sword to hold."

"I still don't," he said. "But Dain is my friend, too, and you're not going to go after Jesarna by yourself."

"So I lose two friends instead of just one?"

"I will try to stay out of the way, but they don't know I'm a novice."

"Any ideas where they might be?" she asked.

There were too many places to look and too many people to look over. Jesarna could have already killed him by now. It was a wonder she had kept him alive for so long. Of course, the possibility that the Vulture high priestess wanted them alive was always there since the cult preferred living sacrifices.

"Those priests you saw earlier, where were they?"

She sighed, "I don't remember."

He knelt down. "Get up on my shoulders. If they're still out, you should be able to find them in a crowd, and then we just follow them. They're bound to lead us to their mistress."

She climbed up onto his shoulders, and he stood shakily. High above the crowd now, she could see much further. She saw two spots in red moving through the crowd near the smithy. "That way," she said.

She jumped down and grabbed Galen's hand, dragging him through the crowd. She could just see their quarry. "Not too fast," Galen warned. "If they know we're after them, they won't lead us where we want to go."

It was hard to keep them in sight, but she was not going to let them get away. Galen ran into her as she stopped short to watch them enter a shop. "Can you go see what kind of shop that is?" she asked him. "I'd hate to burst in on them in a public place."

Galen strolled by, glanced up at the window, and then came back. "It's abandoned."

Kenna drew her sword. "Well, then, this is what we're looking for."

He followed her as she crept toward the alley beside the shop, hating the idea of going in the front door. At the back door, she pulled just enough to discover that it was locked. Before she could swear at it, Galen nudged her out of the way. He knelt beside it, pulled out a set of lock picks, and had it open almost as quickly as if it had never been locked.

He grinned as she moved past him into the doorway. "It's a talent I've often found useful."

They entered a kitchen. The hearth was cold and felt as though it had been for a while. She wondered whether or not she'd chosen right when she heard voices.

"What do you mean, she's left the city?"

Jesarna's voice was unmistakable. The replies were mumbled as Kenna crept closer to the door. "I need them both to collect the bounty. Someone must know where she's gone. Find that minstrel friend of hers and bring him here. I need to ask him questions, so make sure he's conscious."

Kenna set her hand on the door, waiting. The fewer of Jesarna's people she had around her, the better chance she had of getting Dain away.

The front slammed shut and she kicked hers open, taking only time enough to determine that there were two other red robed priests in the room with Jesarna. She dove to the side and behind the cover of a nearby table.

"So, you haven't gone," Jesarna said.

She glanced up but did not see Galen in the doorway. Jesarna stood beside Dain and the priests moved protectively to either side of her. "I'm so pleased."

Anger burned in Dain's eyes as he sat, bound and gagged, against the wall. Jesarna caressed his cheek with one of the knives he'd shown Kenna earlier. "Now, before this gets messy, just lay your weapon on the ground. I'm sure you know I'm not allowed to kill him, but I can disfigure him quite nicely if I wish."

A shadow detached itself from the wall where Kenna had come in. She stood and held her sword ready. "Word is, you're supposed to be some kind of assassin. You can't be afraid to fight me."

"Sorry," Jesarna said. "Not the game I had in mind. I'd have no chance against you in a fair fight."

She drew the knife down Dain's cheek and a line of blood followed it. Dain's lips pressed tightly together, but he said nothing. "Now, how much pain do you want to see him in?"

Kenna glanced from her weapon to Jesarna's and then to Dain. His eyes pleaded that she not give up. "You don't really think that two of your bald priests can keep me from killing you, do you?"

Jesarna drew another line of blood from Dain's face. "How much pain do you think I can inflict on him before you do? I could simply emasculate him, or cut out his eyes. You might even manage to kill me before I got both of them, but of what use would he be then? You can win, Kenna, but is it worth what it will cost Dain?"

She screamed suddenly, the hilt of a dagger protruding from her chest.

Kenna lunged for the closest opponent, grabbing his polearm with her left hand and thrusting her sword into his side. She kept him between herself and the other.

Jesarna was still screaming as Kenna pulled her blade free and dodged the oncoming polearm. She rolled to the ground and felt the Vulture priest's blade embed itself in the wood floor behind her head.

She stood and lunged, catching him in the thigh as he tried to free his weapon. She jumped over his companion's body as he doubled over and brought her sword down across his neck with both hands.

She glanced over to where Jesarna lay. The gypsy had managed to pull out the dagger and was dragging herself toward Dain.

"Kenna!"

Galen's shout made her snap around. Blood ran down his side as he backed into the room. Two more Vulture priests followed him.

"Galen, stop Jesarna!" she shouted, stepping between him and his attackers.

She ducked and rolled between them, slicing one across the side before springing back to her feet.

The close quarters favored her sword, but she was tiring. She dodged another swing and found the back corner much closer than she'd expected. She hit her right shoulder hard and nearly lost her grip on her sword. Her fingers numbed.

Another loud thunk and splinters scratched her face as a blade hit the wall. It seemed to be stuck, but it also cut off her ability to escape in that direction, and she found herself between the polearm and the other wall as one of the priests advanced on her.

She ducked between them and spun around, stepping backward as the polearm blade narrowly missed her. Her left ankle twisted on something soft and she fell, landing on her right shoulder. Fire shot down her arm and she cried out, releasing her sword.

She reached for it with her left hand and nearly lost fingers to the blade that hit the floor in front of her. She backed away, weaponless and hurting. Her attackers advanced, and she prayed that they still wanted her alive. At least then there would be a chance at escape.

A battle cry split the air and one of the priests fell to the floor in two pieces. The other arched back, clutching at something behind him.

Kenna staggered to her feet as he fell, two knives protruding from his back. Dain and Galen stood there. Dain's eyes burned with anger and Galen shook, his face pale.

Dain dropped the polearm he carried and embraced her. His arms trembled as he stammered out apology after apology into her ear. She felt Galen's arms around her as well, and they held each other in silence.

The crowd at the Ivory Stag did not seem to notice when the three of them, dark red stains on their clothing, entered and took a table near the back.

Galen collapsed in his chair. "So, this is what you do?"

Kenna and Dain had bound his wound but had needed to support him most of the way back.

"I guess this means you're no longer interested in being my partner," Kenna said.

She glanced over at Dain, who sat watching her. He'd said nothing after they'd left the shop.

"You okay?" she asked.

"I'm waiting," he said.

"Waiting for what?"

"Waiting for you to tell me how stupid I was."

The pain in his eyes made her bite back her retort. "Is that what you really want to hear?"

"You have every right to say it."

She reached over and squeezed his arm. "I don't see any reason to make you feel any worse than you're making yourself feel right now."

She paused. "Besides, part of me really hoped I was wrong."

He sighed. "I suppose it was pretty obvious what she was."

"Not at all," Galen said. "Actually, I was quite taken with her when I met her as well. She was good at what she did."

"But she's dead now, and I have my partner back," Kenna added.

"That reminds me," Dain said. "I owe you a lot, Galen. Perhaps you might have a use for these."

He slid the matched throwing knives across the table to him. "You earned them."

"You are both my friends," the minstrel said. "I'd have done it anyway, but thank you."

He glanced over Dain's shoulder. "Hey, there's a pretty blonde serving wench staring at you over her tray ..."

Dain laughed, and Galen winked at Kenna. "See, you're feeling better already."

SNOWFIRE
by D. Lopes Heald

Denise Lopes Heald says that she's Denise, not Dennis. I should imagine that with a movie just come and gone about the "Menace," that name would be wildly unpopular just now. My favorite Dennis cartoon was always the one showing Dennis in a crib asking, "Mom, why do you say 'Thank God' instead of 'Goodnight'?" Silly as it is, I once heard the cartoonist say he thought he was doing a public service by showing parents they weren't the only ones ever to think wistfully of infanticide . . . and since families are smaller these days, some parents never get to learn it by experience. It's a cosmic truth; every woman—and probably every man—reaches a point where she'd like to pitch the kid overboard, but the hypocrisy of the fifties and sixties was such that every woman felt obliged to pretend that looking after little kids is always and only thrilling and fulfilling. But every woman knows it ain't necessarily so; you can love your kids and still be driven frantic by them simultaneously—and a good laugh has often avoided infanticide or a nervous breakdown.

Denise Heald lives in Nevada with her husband and young daughter, and "Snowfire" was written with two feet of omnipresent snow ringing the house. She says it was quite a mood setter. Having lived in New England, I can imagine. She has written novels that lived only in the desk drawer—that's where they all start unless we're both savvy and obsessed. And now she has sold short fiction to *Marion Zimmer Bradley's Fantasy Magazine*, to *Aboriginal Sci-*

ence Fiction, and to *Pandora,* and her first novel, *Mistwalker,* to Del Rey Books.

Wind-whipped flames flickered in the snow, guttering gobbets of fire in a winding track—the Kizat's footprints, the Soul Eater.

Clouds hung low and leaden across the afternoon sky, and icy air shrilled, shredded by the wind. Cairn's lungs burned; he labored and struggled for oxygen where there was too little. And with each breath, his back bumped the cold stone that sheltered him.

"Half a day." Lady Stell shifted, her fur-clad body set for action, her chin up, eyes roving the snow-drifted desert hills, ever on guard.

He could only stare at the flames. *The Kizat had moved ahead of them.* Ice settled in his throat, tasting of iron and exhaustion. All the long, long days of lung-bursting effort to keep ahead of *it* lest they be taken—He'd thought that was the worst, to run, flogged to superhuman effort by his own fear. But now she asked him to run equally fast *toward* it, chasing ambush.

"Ready, Warrior?"

Secure in her pride, the Lady broke a stem of sage from a frozen bush and twirled it into the air. On her brow, the clan band of the Epah glittered, the Mother's mark. For three hundred the Epah had proven women could fight with practical lethal tenacity, cold ferocity. And yet they eschewed his male clan's championships as childish frivolity.

Warrior. She smiled, mocking him. He'd done no fighting on this trail, only waddled helpless beneath the great pack he now shouldered. But he could not complain. A saner person would not suffer him to set it down at all. Only his touch kept the ano'nuine safe. The Kizat could not take a soul while a living being held the grave cradle.

"Cairn?" The Lady's voice gentled.

He realized he'd stood, towering above her, but was not moving. His mind wandered today. He sensed the Kizat very near—sucking away his own soul with every step.

Shivering, he plunged away from the rock, spraying snow, refusing to look at Lady Stell. She bore his gaze well enough, but she had no desire for it. And *he* could not bear the constant questioning of *her* eyes, always wondering when he would break, when he would fail.

She'd trained for this one task all her life, learning things perhaps beyond his comprehension, honing her mind, body, and spirit in ways perhaps beyond his strength. That knowledge flogged him as surely as the Kizat. The Lady outstayed and out-braved him at every turn. Only size gave him advantage, and the too large ano'nuine he bore negated that, weighed him down and down, sinking him through snow crust, darkening his sight, sapping his strength until he lumbered like a woman with child.

But it wasn't life *he* bore.

"Cairn!"

He'd stopped again. Her voice goaded him on. Snow clung to his fur-bound legs, rode his boots. He drew his heavy winter veil tighter across his nose and concentrated on the fiery trail ahead. Surely if the Kizat's track led on, *it* had gone on.

This is no champion's game, Lady Stell told him when he first shouldered the ano'nuine. *There are no rules nor fouls. There are no victors—only survivors.*

"Cairn!" His head snapped up. Her shoulder hit his side, spinning him. "*The rock.* Get back to *the rock.*"

The Kizat.

He plowed into a fresh drift, staggering off their back trail, straightened, hit packed snow, and crashed on his knees next the stone.

The Lady's body swung in front of him. Her sword flashed, picking up light even beneath this sullen sky, weaving spells to stay the Kizat where the blade itself could not.

"Stay down." Her voice rasped. Tension crackled. Her muscles tensed, face drawn to bone.

He tightened the straps across his chest, heart sinking. The Soul Eater could not *take* the ano'nuine, only cause him to abandon it. He braced his knees in the snow, added knots to the straps at his shoulders lest he slip those in panic—

And his mind fled, stepped outside his body, looked down at himself cowering in the snow behind a woman's armored body.

He clutched the pommel of the sword he'd insisted on bearing, knowing it served him no use against the Kizat. His heart thundered. His pulse hammered. Spent muscles spasmed in his legs. He bit down, refusing to cry out, refusing to distract the Lady.

Lightning flashed.

Great, feathery flakes began to fall—the Lady's magic or nature's own. Batting his forehead, they snagged in his lashes. And *fear fled*, chased by chill fluttering moth wings, left him stinking of sweat and soiled furs, teeth chattering, every aching muscle knotted.

"Cairn?"

He could not respond. Hands slapped him, dislodged his veil. Let her look on an unproven warrior's face if she would. Let her be weakened if she chose. He no longer held pretensions or even hope. A man of his age never chosen for tournament battle needed more than veils to hide his shame. For this trek, he made a proper mule.

"Cairn!"

The low urgency of her entreaty roused his eyes. She should not be *beautiful,* so cold and beautiful.

"Cairn!" She shook him.

He sucked in a deep breath, realized he had been holding it since the Kizat's departure. He sucked in another.

"Ahhh, good." She *hugged* him, an act which did nothing to help his breathing. But her fists thumped his sides, reminding him to keep their rhythm, startling new breaths into him until his vision cleared to a space wider than her wind chapped face. The ringing in his ears receded.

"I failed—" His heart tore.

"No." She slapped him. "No. Can't you feel it?"

And then he could—the weight. The ever punishing weight remained. He'd failed as a warrior but not yet at this. *Waiting* proved to be a desperate battle, his only weapon defiance. He remembered his mother, her eyes. *She* understood. His sister, teeth gritted against the pain and exhaustion of childbirth, *she* understood.

But he would not look at Lady Stell.

With a tearing grunt, he lunged upward, let her steady him to his feet. The world reeled, a kaleidoscope of burning snow. He caught his breath, and she caught his arms, let him brace himself against her shoulders.

Did the Kizat ride her mind as it did his? Did— His thought blurred. Why did the snow burn? But he *knew* it did not, only the pervasive oily sage.

Of all the ano'nuines' bearers, he was the first male, because he carried the first king ever to be offered to the Stone. Some had argued against a male bearer. The Epah were trained for this task, had guided the people's queens to their rest for centuries, guarding the soul until the proper moment when the Kizat could feed upon it without devouring the people the Queen Mother served.

But Mother Nio died in *fire*. Her soul escaped on its own. Her body fell to ashes without the Kizat's fertilizing seed to see her people through another cycle. It seemed inescapable disaster—until Lord D'Nio offered up his own soul, dedicated to his royal lover's task.

For thirty years he ruled, a kind hand, strong, sometimes impatient, guided by the Mother's advisers, proving that at least *one* man could rule with sanity. Now he'd died. Now the trek was undertaken, and on the eve of departure, the Flame Priestess declared a man must carry this unfortunately bulky ano'nuine.

Yet Cairn witnessed no particular care taken in choosing that man. A priestess arrived. His Captain surveyed his hundred odd men, and chose *him*, the oldest veil. An easy loss. *You fight like a woman,* the Captain taunted him.

Cairn stumbled, chilled to the marrow, and fell on his knees next to a gobbet of flame. Let him be damned, the Kizat owed him *something*—a little heat at least.

But the fire burned without warmth.

"Cairn?" The Lady urged him up.

Quaking in every joint and muscle, he obeyed. Good boy, good donkey.

"Cairn." She pulled him to a halt, spun him about by one elbow. Her gloved fingers stroked his cheek, confusing him. "We're here."

"What?"

"We've reached the Stone."

She tore at the knots he'd worked in the straps binding the ano'nuine to his back. He fought her—lost, panicked.

Her knife flashed. A strap parted. The pack slewed, staggering him. Her weight struck from behind.

He toppled facedown in the snow. Grunting in his ear, Lady Stell sawed through the remaining pack straps. The weight *lifted*. He flopped free.

Scrabbling in slick footing, Stell dragged her father's wrapped body from the pack, skidded it across the snow and onto the great point of rock to which they had struggled.

"Come, Soul Eater!" Her voice shrilled, splitting the gloom of cloud-shrouded dusk. "*Here* may you feast. Here take your peace and rest until *my* journey brings me back again. *Eat* and spread your seed to the wind, feed your *people.*"

He should not watch. He did, lying in the snow while she danced a warrior's dance to the mountain, cried a mother's song down the wind, rained sweet tears on the earth, and lit a fire like the sun against the growing night.

The Kizat came.

Up the snow-covered track they had climbed, flames flickered and gathered. Cairn watched it rise. The Lady, lost in spell, stared outward at void, arms raised, entreating—

Shock knifed Cairn's heart. She *was not ready.* Her father, his king, lay still bound, a cube of frozen flesh, too chill yet to burn.

Slowly, he forced wooden knees beneath him, forced his shoulders up, forced his feet to stand. His sword served him at last, point down in the frozen ground, anchoring him against the wind.

Blades of chill sliced his exposed back. Fear tore his heart, his entrails— His nostrils flared.

Snow began to fall again, argent fluttering wings against the darkening sky. His vision blurred. His heart raced—

—then slowed, slowed again. Lassitude washed over him. His thoughts sank beneath mist. Terror *melted.* Ice shivered from his limbs. His lungs sucked air warm as summer's breath, scented with grass and pollen. Water trickled. Green swayed.

Through illusion and dream, he watched the Kizat advance. Snow, vaporized by pure energy, haloed it in a featureless human form, and fiery arcs bled from it in all directions.

Cairn moved, as if through a weight of water, to block the Soul Eater's path. He would *know* when it was time, when the Lady had prepared all.

Fire leaped at his feet. Tree leaves rustled, though there were none within all the scope of this highland. His legs trembled. His body swayed.

The Kizat *touched* him.

He cried out. But there was no pain, no weariness. His

body lightened. Healthy sweat ran down his sides. His heart beat strong and slow, blood coursed like fiery spume. The Kizat rose within him, drinking down his soul—

He fell. The Kizat passed, unable to encompass a living being. Snow clogged Cairn's nostrils. Fire guttered and spit next to his head.

He screamed.

And beyond the flaming hulk of the Kizat, Lady Stell, hood thrown back, turned at his cry. Tendons strained in her neck. Muscles bunched along her jaw. She raised her great ruined sword. Fire reflection ran like molten metal down its length.

"Here you feed." She taunted the Kizat, weaving between the Soul Eater and the pyre she'd built. Her father's body, ablaze in the flames, was not yet consumed. She could not let the Kizat reach him yet.

Cairn struggled to rise. She could not stop the Soul Eater, no more than he had stopped it. But he had slowed it. And dancing, she strove to distract it.

Wind gusted over the great stone headland. Flames leaped at her back.

The Kizat wavered forward. She wove the tip of her blade before the apparition's fiery visage. It followed the glowing tip. She backed. It followed. The sword danced. Flames rose. The wind howled.

Cairn staggered past the Kizat. His singed hair stood on end. His skin tingled. Hacking sage boughs, he threw them upon his King's pyre. Flames burst upward, hotter, finer, white at their heart. Flesh and bone fell.

The Kizat lunged. The Lady screamed. The Soul Eater burst upon the ano'nuine, drank deep, and exploded heavenward, raining ash into the wind and sending a king's seed outward to his people.

Cairn sagged, mired in snow. *They had not failed.*

He shuddered and cried like a woman. No wonder none ever deemed him worthy for battle.

She dragged him to the warmth of the fire and propped the pack against his back. Smoke wreathed them, smelling of sage and snow melt. She dabbed at his singed temples with his wadded veil. Neither of them had much hair left. He wanted to laugh, hid his face instead.

"It's all right." She hugged him against her armor.

"Don't look upon me. I am unproven."

"Unproven?" Her voice shook. "Unproven because you have not drawn blood with a sword?"

He would not look at her. All this trip her naked face had taunted him.

"Stop." She forced his hands down, his weary shoulders failing even the task of fending her off. "*Look* at me. *Look.*"

She clasped his bristled cheeks between her palms, allowing no escape except to close his eyes. He did not.

"This—" She shook his veil. "*This* means nothing. This—" She fought the warrior's band from her blistered temples, bent it wide, and set it on his brow. "*This* claims you. Your male clan be damned. You're stronger than any man. You've borne a king. You've survived *the Kizat.*"

Breath froze in his lungs. He stared into her glittering eyes. Something of his numbness lifted.

"*I* claim you." She shook him again. "Serve *me*. Queen Mother I may be some day. Or not. But now I gather warriors. And I am not ashamed to claim a man with your patience." Flames flickered in her eyes. "But I warn you, we guard the Mother. We carry the ano'nuine, supervise the roads, and tend the borders. Tedious tasks."

He understood. And perhaps *that* was why he'd remained unchallenged all these years, excluded by his clan's champions because he took it all so much to heart, fought with such technical precision that none would challenge his dull persistence.

"Lady—" He swallowed.

She smiled, after all these days better able to read him than he could read himself. Hard-won exhaustion flushed his body. Her hand struck his shoulder. She laughed. Sparks showered into the frozen night sky.

Women fought to a different need, saw with different eyes. But he was not afraid of what this *one* envisioned. She began to sing to the wind. If she was not ashamed to claim him, he was not ashamed to fight like a woman.

ANCIENT WARRIOR
by Stephanie Shaver

Stephanie—who is another of our youngest writers—being only about fourteen when she first sold to us—wrote that "while I still have brown hair and brown eyes and a suspiciously feline grin, I have grown an inch since I last submitted a bio to you! That's right, I'm a full *five foot three* now!" (Last time I did a bio on her, I mistakenly said her eyes were blue. Sorry, Stephanie.)

She has a novel in the works and expects "to take another two years to finish it, three years barring rewrites (between school, work, musical studies, and an active social life, I have little time to write, but I do try to make it as much as possible." All of her stories in *Sword & Sorceress* occur in the same world as this story.

She'll probably to moving to the Bay Area soon to go to San Francisco State University. "I'll be leaving minor-dom behind come the end of June, when I turn eighteen and get to graduate . . . I am currently planning on going for a B.A. in History, but, should I produce a *New York Times* Bestseller (hah-hah) will do what any sane person would do: recede from society and take up hermitage as a fantasy writer."

Well, you've made a good start, Stephanie; you'll be right across the Bay from us. The Bay Area isn't what it was thirty years ago when first I came here—among other things they've filled in over half of the Bay—but it's still the best place in the world to live, or at least it beats any other place I've ever lived, and nothing would induce me to live anywhere else!

"**S** *eir* Ario, where is your daughter?"

Ario turned her face away from the sunken eyes of old lady Grancha.

"Where she has been all this month, old woman. With her cousin down in Gyrax," Ario said smoothly in a low voice, brushing strands of her salt-and-pepper hair aside as she always did when she was nervous.

"How odd," Grancha mused. "Seems to me that the day your daughter left for the town was the day the killin' began. But your sweet li'l Helen would ne'er kill, would she now?"

Ario resolutely walked toward the blacksmith's. "Good day, old dame."

"Good day, p'raps!" Grancha called after Ario from where she sat in her chair. "But what of the night?"

Ario ignored her, passing the other houses and workshops with all their whispering occupants, and entered the home/shop of the one blacksmith Dias Village boasted.

The room was hot from forge fire and summer weather. Sitting on a beaten wooden stool and lovingly shining a copper kettle sat the blacksmith, a large man with dark hair and long mustaches, his skin a chafed tan from years of beating out his trade on a blackened anvil.

"Can I be helpin' you, *seir* Ario?" he asked, putting down the kettle and looking up at her.

Ario nodded. "Quarrels for my crossbow."

The man nodded, turned, and took two dozen handmade arrows from a box in the storeroom behind his work area. Ario paid him with the few lean silver coins she had, took the tidy bundle of quarrels, and turned to go.

"Seems to me—" the blacksmith said in an offhand manner,"—that these arrows been mighty popular in town ever since the killings began."

Ario ignored him and left the store, moving stiffly with her wooden leg. Again she passed old lady Grancha, who taunted her with questions. "And what would you be doin' with those arrows, woman?" Grancha called. "The Lady's War has been o'er a full twenty years!" And, again, the woman ignored her, making her way toward the farm where she had lived for twenty years. Ten with her husband and child, ten with her daughter only, and a month now alone.

For the first time.

It was an odd feeling for Ario to be alone.

She didn't like it all that much.

The sun was setting by the time she stumped her way up to her door. The house was cold, the ashes of the hearth colder, the emptiness that waited within looming like some unspeakable monstrosity. Even when she had been in the army, she had not felt *this* lonely. Even after her dear husband had died, she had always had Helen.

Now what did she—a used, ancient warrior—have?

Ario started a fire, prepared a meager dinner, and then went over to the mantle where her black-ash Evermist crossbow hung. She took it down gently, rubbing her hands over the oiled wood. Beautiful, as always. She would have to find the loading claw; she was not as strong or as calloused as she used to be, but that was nothing. It was firing it that would hurt—to see her undead daughter fall by her mother's quarrel—

No, no, no! Not her daughter! A ... a ... creation by that bastard Alesx, who had stolen Helen—*her* little girl, that she had held and carried and made so many dolls for—from Ario. She still remembered the night she had gone to help Farmer Zavea kill the wolves that had plagued their sheep ... and left Helen alone with that thing. She still could see the house as it had been when she had returned near dawn. Bits of broken crockery—splintered wood—the table Russo had crafted for her as a wedding-day gift split in two. And her sweet daughter—gone.

And she remembered her fool's naïvete for inviting the stranger into their house as the sun was setting. That strange, ghost-white stranger with hair so black it had blue highlights. . . .

And what a fool she had been! Despite the watch-wards she had set up against the Dark (fighting was not the only thing she had learned in the army), she had let Alesx in—invited him in, thus negating the power of the wards—because the lad with the strange Cteanian accent had looked so bedraggled, so thin. . . .

And hungry, but not a mortal hunger.

The next night, I remember that, too, Ario thought as she hunted around for the claw. *When I was tracking them down and saw those two pale figures in Dias Wood. Blood on their hands, on their faces ... Alesx and Helen's faces— my daughter!*

She reached into a closet and found the loading claw with a triumphant smile. *Well, no more. I'll kill them both tonight—or die trying!*

Her hand touched the iron of the claw, and she pulled it down. A wooden doll rolled off the shelf it had rested on, disturbed by the moving of the claw. It tumbled, impacted with the hardwood floor, and bounced. With a crackle, the handcrafted doll snapped, the faded, painted wooden face rolling away from the body.

The old soldier froze, tears rising in her eyes.

"Oh, Helen," she whispered, crouching down to pick up the poppet. "It was my fault for leaving you alone with him. My fault."

Anger made the tears fall back, made her fist tighten around the doll, crushing its dusty limbs.

"Time to finish what I started."

Her voice choked then, and she threw the doll into the fireplace. The fire crackled and swallowed the paint and wood greedily, chewing on the doll like a dog with a soup bone.

Ario walked back to her crossbow and loaded it with the first quarrel. This much she knew about creatures such as Alesx: They were malicious and cruel and hated to leave loose ends. The "game" in Dias was running lean, and if they preyed on it much longer, it might attract the attention of the Crown. Alesx might be strong enough to hold one small town of farmers and lowly artisans in terror, but he would most certainly be destroyed in the face of a greater danger such as the Royal Wizards. Whether it be tonight or tomorrow or next week, they would return to the house in search of Ario before they moved on, and either kill her or turn her into one of their own. It was the nature of the beast. Or so Ario hoped.

Behind her, the fire still glowed warmly, a few flames rising and falling as Ario opened the front door to her house. Quietly, she carried her old rocker outside, sat down, and settled the crossbow in her lap.

Moonshine lit the farmland—two of the three moons were full, insuring that there would be plenty of light tonight. Ario covered the crossbow with an afghan crocheted by her grandmother, settled back, and waited.

It was going to be a long night.

*   *   *

The old warrior woke abruptly from the trap sleep had lured her into, combat reflexes she had thought long buried beneath a soft rustic life jouncing her awake.

"Huh—wha—" She shook sleep from her eyes and looked out toward the woods, squinting with eyes that no longer functioned as well as they had twenty years ago.

There was a scatter of movement. Ario swung her head right and left, then stopped, deciding it was useless. She knew these tactics all too well: Confuse the enemy.

The floorboard creaked to her right. Slowly, she turned in that direction.

A silhouette stood against the night sky. A gentle wind ruffled the honey-gold hair on Helen's head and plucked at her tattered gown. The feral shine of Ario's daughter's eyes caught the woman's attention.

"Well," she said quietly, trying to make her voice sound stern, the way it did when she had caught Helen at something. "You've come back, daughter."

Silence. The Vampyre stood before her mother in silent tableau, shadows gathering like a host of demons around her.

"How did it feel," Ario asked with a strength she didn't feel, "to pull the life from all those folk? Did you like it, Helen? Or what do you call yourself now? Toy? Slave? You are not my daughter. My daughter wouldn't kill people for their blood!"

The words were meant to bolster her, take her to a place outside her heart where she could pull the trigger to land that quarrel in her own child's heart. The only way to kill a vampyre—short of the cleansing light of the sun—was to impale something into his or her black heart and then burn the body to ash. Ario knew very well that she only had one shot, and a chancey one at that. She would never have time to reload, for Helen, daughter though she may have been once, wouldn't give it to her. Ario was completely open after that last quarrel.

Helen stood stock-still, not moving, not breathing, her pale skin gleaming slickly under the moons.

"Where is your blood-lover, my dear girl? Where is your undead brother? Where is Alesx, the monster from the night? Perhaps standing behind me with a club? But—no—you wouldn't kill me, you'd drain me and drag me down into your nightmare. Well, these old bones won't go, dear.

I'd rather have my body quartered and burned to the winds by bandit scum before I succumb to the night."

She drew a deep breath, making the words she spoke the truth in her mind. *Not my daughter, you are not my daughter,* her mind chanted, building the illusion of a soldier's stone-dead emotion around a mother's heart, forming a glamour of cold hate. The warrior fixed her gray eyes on a set that matched her own and chose her last words carefully, a final layer on the inner barrier she was erecting.

"You are not my daughter," she repeated. "I raised my child better than this."

Helen flinched, and Ario knew that it was time she made her move.

Swiftly, she picked up the crossbow, sighting on Helen's heart, the target-peg gracing the undead's body with deadly accuracy. Sweat prickled all over her body, piercing like a thousand tiny pins. Her hand brushed the stiff trigger, her finger-muscles twitching as she started to pull it.

And Helen's voice carried to her over the night wind—
"Oh, Mother. . . ."

With those two words, her will shattered like an iced-over lake in spring's thaw, the illusions melting away. The bow fell from her numb hands, clattering on the porch, and she found herself rising and screaming, "GET OUT OF HERE! GET! DAMN YOU—leave me!"

In the light of the moons, the eyes of the undead glittered. A single tear-jewel slowly tracked its way down her cheek, slipped off, and shattered on the porch.

Then she disappeared, into the night.

Ario sat, hand over her heart, and tried to calm herself. Suddenly she felt closed in, cramped, and much, much older. Ario sat down heavily in her rocker. The moons lit the betrayed crossbow—which appeared to be scratched but none the worse for wear. The soldier sighed as she leaned over to pick up the weapon, her head bowed nearly to the porch floor.

She heard the whistling sound of something thick and heavy falling down toward her exposed back even as she was reaching for the crossbow. Ario twisted around to look and see what or who her attacker was, but the club was faster.

Darkness and stars claimed her vision.

*   *   *

Ario awoke to find herself in her rocker, her skull throbbing, a fog clouding her mind.

"Well and well again!" said a silken-sinister voice, like a midnight shadow, lilting with a Cteanien accent. "Hello, *seir* Ario." Laughter. "How are ye?"

"Alesx," Ario whispered, struggling to stand—

—only to find she couldn't, of course. The Vampyre must have established some arcane control over her body. She was held as well as if there were steel bands circling her body.

Ario stared down at the porch.

"Oh, aye, *seir* Ario, 'tis I. Ye'r personal monster. Ye'r hated shadow-lord. Ye'r—ah, but I donna need t'go on, ye can fill in the words ye'rself. Now, old woman, what shall m'bride and I do with ye?"

A foot rolled her over so that she was looking up, staring into the face of Alesx. Helen stood next to the elder Vampyre, looking away as if shamed.

"Ctean," Ario murmured. "Should've thought of it when I heard your voice the first time. Ctean—ruled by the Five Barrow Kings. Which one are you?"

Alesx laughed. "None, fool! 'Tis true, m'father is one of the Five undead Lords but I—I am bastard-born and nowhere near t'the Ctean Thrones! M'mother was a marsh-witch, and she called one of his Lordships—even I donna know m'father's name—to her abode that she might have her own-spawn." He laughed again, a hissing, strangled sound. "Can ye believe that? She seduced a corpse but never cared to research *how* a true-born Vampyre arrives out of his mother's womb." He bared his feral teeth. "That is, we donna! We rip our way out, and then we make our first meal out of our mother's still-warm body." He looked toward Helen, and his smile widened. "And, though she be not true-born, I plan for Helen to visit the same fate on her mother, old hag."

"And how do you know that you are true-born, Vampyre?" Ario said in a conversational tone. "You yourself stated you do not know your own father's name."

Alesx smiled. "I am na human, old woman. I have ways of knowing things that ye'r limited senses wouldna even dream of. All 'Pyres know where their blood flows from, and I know that the river of m'bloodline comes from one of the five original springs. I may be a bastard, but I am still a prince, just as ye'r daughter is now by law—" again he beamed maliciously, "—a Ctean princess. Did ye ever dream that ye'd be a member of a royal family, ancient warrior?"

Ario did not reply, staring instead at her daughter. Helen momentarily caught her gaze; a chill of foreboding pierced the soldier's heart as she stared into the fear and sorrow that was echoed there.

You had that fear once, something whispered in her mind. *It came when you faced a wall of men with shields and Ctean swords, intent on chopping you to bits. You know that sorrow, it was for dead friends and enemies. Your daughter knows them, too. They are what all creatures— mortal or Otherwise—feel when they face Death. You knew them only momentarily. She has known them for a full month now.*

Ario pushed away tears. *Helen,* she thought, *I raised you for better than this.*

Alesx snorted when she did not reply. "Obviously not."

Then he knelt down, until his face was directly in hers, his skin smelling faintly of the embalming juice they used to keep the worms out of corpses. He forced her eyes into his, and she saw her own image gleaming flatly in his pupils. "She shall suck ye'r bones dry, and after she is done, hag, I shall tear ye'r soul from ye'r withered frame and devour it," he hissed.

Ario smiled, a strange peacefulness in her heart. "I hope you choke, demon spawn."

Alesx's too-pretty face twisted as he lifted a fist to strike her, his bone-white knuckles gleaming like wax.

But then a club cracked down on his perfect skull and he crumpled, his head sinking against Ario's breast like that of a dreaming lover.

Helen put the club down slowly, her eyes blank as she dragged the prince from the still-paralyzed body of Ario.

"Oh, Mother . . ." she whispered sadly, an echo of the words she had spoken only hours earlier.

Her cold lips pressed against Ario's fear-hot forehead, and a chill crept into the woman's heart as premonition pulled the hairs on the back of her neck to attention.

"No—Helen—"

But the girl ignored her, instead lifting Alesx up and

dragging him to the oak tree that marked Russo's grave. She bound her demon-lover with the strong rope Ario used sometimes to tether the field-oxen. Then she sat back and faced the west.

Toward the rising sun.

Ario struggled futilely against the magic that held her, screaming incomprehensible words of mingled rage and sorrow.

Alesx awoke mere seconds before the first finger of rose-dipped dawn shafted across the hilly horizon, crystallizing the dew that waited on the heather and wildflowers. He screamed, his skin darkening and bubbling even as Helen raised one lone forearm to cover her eyes from the burning light.

Radiant sunlight exploded over them, and when it touched the barrow-prince, he combusted into a screaming pillar of broiling smoke and gas. The scent of burning pine-sap and bitter black hair wafted on the wind, overpowering Ario's senses. Her tearing eyes flickered toward her daughter in a haze of refracted sunlight, not wanting to look, but knowing she had to.

She did not want to see smoking flesh, did not want to see old wartime terrors of burning pitch splashed on screaming bodies revisited on her daughter. Perhaps the Gods of Light had finally visited a kindness on her, for when Ario looked, she saw something entirely different—a mixed blessing—being visited on her only child.

The morning dawn ran through the ancient warrior's daughter as if she was translucent, lifting her honeyed hair and refracting its light through her so that she glowed like the sun itself, or the glorious angel Ario had always known her to be—

The stasis removed itself and Ario surged up, leaping for her daughter with an agility she had not felt for nearly ten years.

Helen turned, her hair whipping around her and her thin white garment sticking to her body as though it were wet. Around them, Alesx's agonized screams reached a new pitch even as his body burned, the eerie, silent flames touching neither tree nor rope.

"Mother . . ." Helen whispered.

Their fingers touched, brushing briefly, life against death. . . .

And then it was over. The rope coiled, slack, falling to the base of the tree, leaving naught but a greasy smear behind. Ario stood still, and quite alone, her fingers trembling as she fell to her knees, staring at a pile of dust where her last and only child had been, all the energy gone from her frail form.

And in her hands, dust sifted slowly through her fingertips, trickling slowly away like the tears that trickled down her cheeks.

In Dias town, there are many legends and many tales, and amongst them all, the ancient warriors who have taken Dias for their home tell the tallest. But the best of all the yarnspinners is a farm widow, who walks with a wooden leg and lives maybe a mile from the town proper.

And when people come and beg for a night in her empty house, she lets them stay, but never for more than one day.

And for all the tales that she loves to tell, no matter how much they inquire, the widowed soldier will never explain why, up on the mantle over the fireplace, a loaded blackash Evermist crossbow sits in silent vigil next to a cup of plain, fine-grained powder.

BARBARIAN LEGACY
by Lawrence Schimel

Lawrence Schimel is another of our very own young dis-
coveries, who writes: "What a day! I graduated from Yale,
found and bought my first copy of *Sword and Sorceress X*
in the bookstore, and came home to contracts for *Sword
and Sorceress XI*. This is my seventeenth anthology sale;
my first, to *Sword and Sorceress VII*, also arrived right
before graduation, from high school. You really know how
to give a graduation present!

"In addition to my fiction writing for various anthologies
I've made recent poetry sales to various magazines and
newspapers, including the *Saturday Evening Post* and the
Wall Street Journal . . . copies of my first Polish translation
recently showed up in my mail, marking the third language
into which I've been translated (the others being Dutch
and Finnish).

". . . what shall I do with my life? Write, of course, but
the more interesting news is that I shall be moving to Bar-
celona after the summer."

Maybe I'll see you there; if the Roman Britain novel (*The
Forest House*) goes well, my next historical may have a
Spanish setting. . . .

The "Legs" of Larry's original title are of the little house
on chicken legs, associated in Russian or Polish fairy tales
with the witch Baba Yaga.

Rows of sunflowers stood at attention in front of the inn, ever-vigilant sentinels. But their guard was not enough to stop winter from settling over us, not enough to stop time from running its course. As the cold wind blew down from the north, it blew travelers with it. They came with news of a harsh winter ahead, and of barbarians being driven south by the snows. When the travelers left, Ilyana's workers went with them, scattering like leaves. They took everything they could carry, the cook nearly emptying her pantry completely. They left her just enough food for herself to last the winter. After they were gone, she battled with the birds and squirrels who attacked the sunflowers, stripping them down to mere stalks as they gorged themselves on the sun-ripened seeds. She needed them to feed the chickens, her only companions now in the vast empty inn guarded by the skeletal stalks of the sunflowers. She'd hidden the chickens during the hasty exodus, along with what clothes and money she had. What need had she to fear barbarians when her own friends had come through before them?

She went early each day to the henhouse to feed and, when luck smiled upon her, collect an egg or two. Ilyana woke them each morning, the seven small brown hens and the old rooster who glared at her for interrupting his rest until he saw the small handful of seeds. Long gone were the days when he rose before all others and crowed the morning awake.

That morning the henhouse itself was gone. It seemed normal when she first stepped out of the inn and made her way toward it along the packed dirt path; but as she drew near, it stood up on two enormous chicken legs and began to walk away from her, taking one step back for every step closer that Ilyana took. At first, she ran toward it, afraid that the morning's eggs would break, the way it rocked back and forth, but it only ran from her faster. She stopped and the henhouse did likewise. They considered each other for a long moment, and, after deciding she would not try to approach, it folded its legs under itself and sat down once more.

The henhouse looked strange sitting in the middle of the front courtyard rather than behind the inn where it normally rested. Ilyana smiled to herself. It was also strange for the henhouse to have grown a pair of legs and to run around as it had been doing a moment ago. She wondered if the chickens were still inside it, if they were still alive. She listened carefully, hoping to hear a soft clucking of the hens, agitated at being rocked around, or the old rooster, grumpy at being aroused and not given his morning seed. But the henhouse was silent, seeming almost contented or self-satisfied as it basked in the feeble warmth of the early sun.

Ilyana folded her legs under herself as well and sat down in the path, to contemplate what was going on and decide what she should do. The small dark seeds in the pocket of her skirt spilled onto the hard, packed earth, and she diverted herself with them for a moment, imagining the kernels were stars and making constellations out of their patterns. But soon she collected them all once more, safeguarding each kernel in the deepest pocket of her skirt.

While she had been playing with the seeds, the henhouse had crept closer, as if wishing to be fed. Ilyana did not know what to do. She had enough seed to last the chickens through the winter, but not if she started feeding this enormous henhouse. However, she reflected, at the moment she did not have any chickens. They had all been in the henhouse which was now . . . transformed. Perhaps they were all dead. Or perhaps they were now the henhouse itself. . . .

Suddenly she had a ridiculous thought: What would happen if the henhouse were to lay an egg. Would it hatch a tiny henhouse, complete with little chicken legs? Maybe it would be a normal chicken egg? only the size of a small hog. She couldn't be sure of anything, but she laughed out loud at the thought.

The henhouse seemed to flinch at the sound, rising a few inches off the ground as it gathered its legs beneath it, ready to sprint to safety. But then it relaxed, realizing somehow that Ilyana was not going to do anything, despite the loud noises. It leaned forward, still anticipating the seeds. Ilyana relented and tossed a handful of kernels to the ground in front of its door. She had no idea how it would eat them, since it didn't seem to have a mouth or beak, just chicken legs. It was, after all, a henhouse.

Ilyana watched in anticipation. After a moment, the door opened and the grumpy old rooster blinked in the light, gave half a crow, and then hopped down to the path to begin pecking at the kernels. Delighted to see him again,

Ilyana was standing before she had realized what she was doing. The henhouse jumped up onto its great big chicken legs and sprinted off a distance, leaving the oblivious old rooster pecking away at the sunflower seeds.

Ilyana sat down again, watching the rooster eat, and reflected that at least they were still alive inside there. If only she could figure out what had happened, and why, perhaps she could decide what to do. In a way, she almost didn't want to do anything. It was certainly interesting having a henhouse on chicken legs. Even with the chickens Ilyana was very lonely, and the henhouse seemed more like company than the chickens did, if only because it was new. It was also a ... bigger companion, to say the least. It was more companionable because there was more of it.

Maybe it was barbarian magic, Ilyana thought, brought south with the cold winter winds. But who had cast it? And *what* exactly had been cast? Did the spell make chicken legs grow out of things? Would she find other objects suddenly growing chicken legs and running away from her when she approached them? Maybe it was a spell that gave houses the feet of whatever slept inside them?

Ilyana glanced over her shoulder at the inn to make sure it hadn't grown a pair of giant human legs and was running off while she wasn't looking. When she saw it was still the same old inn—except for a shutter which must have blown off during the night and now lay on the ground beneath the window—she felt foolish for having been worried. But after glancing back at the henhouse and realizing that it had crept forward again, she didn't feel all that foolish after all. This was magic.

Suddenly the henhouse opened its door again, like a great yawning maw. Ilyana tensed, wondering what it was doing now. Would it attack, or was it releasing something new? Although she prayed it would be the rest of her chickens, she knew better.

It wasn't them. Instead, a small barbarian girl stood in the doorway, sleepy-eyed. Feathers and bits of hay clung to her clothes. The child stared at Ilyana for a long time. Finally she decided Ilyana could be trusted and jumped down to the ground. Ilyana wondered if there was anyone else still inside the henhouse. Had the child worked the magic that caused the henhouse to grow legs?

The child came toward Ilyana, mumbling something in

her foreign tongue. Ilyana held her ground, hoping it wasn't a spell being cast against her. She was a barbarian child, after all. But Ilyana didn't really hold with the rumors of the barbarians' ruthlessness. Hadn't she stayed to brave them and the winter, alone? And certainly so young a child ... She could more easily have attacked Ilyana with her magic last night when she slept.

The child held out her hand. Ilyana flinched, fearing the final component of a spell had just been cast. Then she laughed. "I'm getting as skittish as the henhouse," she said out loud.

In the child's hand was an egg.

They did not understand each other's language, but they would learn. It would be nice to have company during the long winter. "I only hope the inn doesn't grow chicken legs and run off," Ilyana said to herself as she cooked breakfast for the two of them.

MIST
by Laura J. Underwood

Laura Underwood is a freelance writer, living in Knoxville, Tennessee. She has published short fantasy fiction in *Sword and Sorceress V* and *IX*, in *Appalachian Heritage*, and in *Marion Zimmer Bradley's Fantasy Magazine*. In addition she has published nonfiction articles and is a book reviewer for a Knoxville newspaper. She is currently rewriting her first fantasy novel. Her hobbies include hiking, biking, history, Celtic lore, and music. She was for several years the Tennessee State Women's Foil Fencing champion. She has not a multitude of cats or children at present, but there "are a lot of crows in her back yard who find themselves constantly barked at by her Cairn Terrier Rowdy Lass."

In this story a mage is concerned about the fate of a young boy. Laura Underwood is certainly one of the major fantasy writers today—and I count myself lucky so far that other editors haven't discovered her yet in a big way. It probably won't be long, so I'll enjoy being her major editor as yet.

"We need a mist."

Shona cringed, not so much in fear as in repulsion for her captor's ale-drenched breath. And because he emphasized the word "mist" strongly enough to send a spray into the mageborn's face. Behind her in the shadows created by the bandit's campfire, she heard her nephew Eldon moan. Poor lad. They didn't have to hit him so hard, just because he was trying to defend her. *Sometimes, he forgets I have been taking care of myself for nearly a century.* Not that her age showed. The gift—or curse—of her mage blood. She looked, perhaps, thirty to most men. Not quite a matron, not quite a maid. Just a woman starting into her prime.

"A heavy mist," her chief captor went on, not waiting for her to respond. After all, she couldn't, gagged and bound and seated on the ground. If she had been born a more powerful mage, she could have merely thought her spell and gestured to make it work. Well, perhaps the gesture *would* be a problem now. *Someone* had taken great pains to tell these bandits how to catch mageborn off guard and keep them helpless.

She sighed, looking at the man sitting before her. His grizzled face was broken by a scar that ran from the corner of his eye to the base of his jaw. Probably earned that decoration in the Last War, when the Barbarian King sent his uncivilized hordes against Ard-Taebh. That war had left a lot of men out of honest work. Shona's own little brother died on one of those battlefields, causing his wife to die of grief and leaving Eldon in Shona's care. *Some care.* She hoped the bleeding had stopped. Mageborn were long-lived, but not immortal.

"Our master says you are a mage who can control the weather," the bandit leader said. Gronan. Wasn't that what one of the men called him when they thought her still unconscious? She worked her aching jaw a bit and nodded.

"Good. I will remove your gag if you'll swear by your mage goddess not to call magic against me." Gronan said. "If you give your word falsely, one of my men will cut the boy's throat. Agreed?"

What else could she do? There were too many questions racing hotly through her mind. Why were they here? Why had these men braved the narrow climb to her lone tower atop the crag that overlooked one of many moors dotting the kingdom of Elenthorn? Attacked her and her nephew, dragging them out of their home unconscious, just to camp in the forest and ask her to conjure a mist? Slowly, closing her eyes, Shona nodded. There was Eldon to think of, Eldon whose mageborn powers bloomed in adolescence as her own had. He was the only family she had left now.

Mageborn rarely sought mates. What use was there in loving someone she knew she was destined to outlive?

The pressure left her bruised jaw tingling when the gag was removed. Shona raised rope-clasped hands and rubbed her chin. Her eyes flickered toward the dark where mage sight revealed the huddled form of a lad who looked barely twelve. He was older, she knew, near sixteen and still looking like a child. Something about the power slowed the aging process once mage sign manifested itself. Eldon was gagged and bound as she had been, and he shook as he cringed against a fallen log, a trail of crimson streaking his pale cheek. Dark blond hair hung ragged before his brown eyes. She wished she could go to him, comfort him. He looked frightened half out of his wits.

Gronan rose from the ground to tower over Shona. She let her own dark gaze flit up at him, shaking stray chestnut locks from her face. His craggy features broke into a grin, wrinkling the scar. "Not half bad to look at," he said.

Shona narrowed her eyes, hoping he was stupid enough to believe *some* of the ridiculous tales told about magefolk. "What do you want?" she asked.

"The mist, just as I said."

"Why?"

"That's my affair," Gronan said.

"Then, *where* do you want it?" she said. "And why kidnap us to ask me to do such a simple task?"

"My master says it does no good to *ask* most magefolk for anything. That you only give help when you think there is *just* cause."

"Why not seek a blood mage, then?" she said with a scowl.

He grinned. "True. Blood mages don't care if the cause is just or not. But they're not as easy to find, and their prices are too rich for our purse. Besides, my master says they are only a little more evil than your kind."

And dangerous, she darkly mused. Their magic required the death of the fool from whom they drew energy to perform their dark spells. All creatures—all things—had some degree of essence that true mageborn could sense and use to feed their power. But magefolk used only what they needed of this essence to keep from tiring themselves without harming the owner, or even letting them know. Oh, it could be drawn more swiftly, leaving the donor breathless or even dead, but that was not the way of a true mage. Blood mages had no such scruples.

Shona sighed again. "So where am I to conjure this mist?"

"Around Dun Cloghran."

"Dun Cloghran?" she repeated with a frown. "But that's Arianrhod's temple. Its gates stay open and freely admit anyone with a need. Even the priests of the god of healers call that place blessed. Why conjure a mist there?"

"More specifically, I need this mist in and around the main tower," Gronan said.

"The tower of the Chalice?" she said, and by his sudden silence, she knew it could be no other. Shona set her shoulders and glared. "Then you are thieves, after all, and your master sends you to steal the Chalice of the Silver Wheel, does he not?"

Gronan balled a fist as though about to strike, and Shona held herself ready for the blow. Instead, the fist loosened. Fingers caught her bruised chin. She flinched as her head was forced around toward the ring of shadows where Eldon crouched.

"He is your kin by blood, is he not?" Gronan said. "He looks like you."

Like his father, Shona thought sadly. *Like my brother.*

"How much is his life worth to you?" Gronan said in a low voice. "Surely, it is more valuable to you than a simple chalice."

But the Chalice of the Silver Wheel! Sacred vessel of the moon goddess who watched over all mageborn. Legend told that it was a gift to Her from the god Diancecht, lord of all healers, and that it had wondrous powers to cure illness. The Chalice had been placed at Dun Cloghran because leys of power crossed there, and its presence helped strengthen those lines through the god and the goddess' combined powers. Those leys were a web stretching out across the world, keeping the balance of nature whole with the healing power of the Chalice. To remove the Chalice might not destroy nature, but it would serve to weaken the power of Arianrhod in this world. And in a time when her mageborn were so few ...

"Who wants the Chalice?" she asked.

"That is none of your affair ..."

"A priest or a mage?" she insisted.

"None of . . ."

"A priest, then," she said, "for a mage could conjure a mist for you so you would not need me." A priest, on the other hand, would have no reason to steal the Chalice—unless he was a priest of the dreaded temples of Dubh Cromm, the Destroyer. His order was springing up here and there in Ard-Taebh, declaring that magic was evil and all mageborn deserved to die. *Hiding under a false mask of piety, they use blood magic to their ends and call it prayer!*

Gronan was glowering now. "Will you do as I bid?"

"Why should a priest of Dubh Cromm desire the Chalice?" she demanded. She was certain she knew why. To steal an artifact of the Silver Wheel for their own ends. To defile its magic with their own. The High King of Ard-Taebh was tolerant of them because he did not know their true nature.

"By the black arse of Arawn, woman, will you do as I bid and conjure the mist?" Gronan repeated, not bothering to deny his master's calling as he motioned across the way.

She wanted to defy him, to refuse him, but Eldon's startled gasp brought her head snapping around. One of the bandits jerked her nephew off the ground, only to shove the youth against a tree. A short dagger gleamed in the firelight as it was placed against his throat. In a panic, she lurched to her feet, forgetting her bonds. The hobbles about her ankles sent her tumbling into Gronan who caught her by the shoulders to steady her. She met his angry glower.

"Please, I'll do what you ask! Just don't hurt him. Please!"

Gronan shoved her back to the ground with enough force to make her wince. "That's more like it," he said, taking up the gag. "Tomorrow, you and the boy will accompany us to the forest below Dun Cloghran. We will leave the boy there with one of my men who will have strict orders. Should anything go wrong, he will kill the lad, and I will kill you."

Some bargain, she thought miserably as the gag was tied in place. *Oh, Blessed Lady of the Silver Wheel, what shall I do?* A priest of Dubh Cromm stealing the Chalice! The Destroyer's temples were sworn to destroy all true mageborn, save the few they had perverted to their designs. In villages where their temples ruled, children were tested for mage sign and killed immediately if it was found they could see in the dark or hear the faintest of sounds.

"Take her to the far side of camp," Gronan told his men. "We don't want her using mind spells to speak with the boy."

We couldn't do that if we tried, not bound and gagged as we are, she thought as she was hauled away from the central fire and leashed to a tree, where they left her to find her own comfort. There were mages who could commune that way. But Shona had never learned those spells. Weather control was her specialty. Long ago, she resigned herself to her lesser powers, especially when the only master who would train her was little more than a hearth wizard by trade. Oh, he taught Shona what he could about controlling the elements and using the power she had been born with. "We each have our purpose, great and small, we are all part of the Silver Wheel," he would tell her if she dared complain. He was a simple, gentle man. Like her, he had been born in the far northernmost kingdom of Ard-Taebh—the kingdom ravaged hardest by the Last War. With that birthright, he could offer little more.

She had learned contentment in the years that followed his death. The locals were mostly farmers who came to her for help with their crops. Sometimes, their superstitions outweighed their common sense when they came to see the "weather woman" living in her lonely tower. Still, they came—for rain to end droughts and sunny days when the rains threatened to give rise to floods. Shona did what she could and, for the most part, was left undisturbed to study the weather portents and signs she would pass on to Eldon one day.

He was a fast learner, her nephew, if a bit innocent and unworldly. *We are all that way sometimes.* She could just as easily count herself on that list, she who had opened her door freely—trustingly—to these men. *Fool!*

Shona sighed and glanced around at the forest world revealed to her magesight. She could find nothing within range sharp enough to cut her bonds—not even a stone to wear the ropes against. The ground beneath her was full of moisture from the rains. Moisture that would make it easy to call a mist. But even if she could get free, what could she do to save herself and Eldon? Call a storm? Lightning? *Burn the forest down around my own ears!*

Arianrhod, sweet lady of the Silver Wheel that binds us all in this world, what shall I do? she thought. How could she stop these men and still keep Eldon alive?

"We need a mist . . ." A mist to veil their evil deed, like as not. A mist to hide them from the eyes of the temple guards and priests. *If only there were mageborn living in Dun Cloghran.* Her kind preferred not to live in the temples, even temples that *welcomed* mageborn, though they were known to visit and spend a few nights with the priests to make certain all was well. Dun Cloghran was isolated up on its lofty crag. Though its central tower housed the Chalice, it was a quiet, humble place. Its priests went about their circular gardens, growing herbs and vegetables, caring for the few locals who still remained in these stony mountains and lonely moors.

Yet she could recall that the place had been one of the few strongholds in these parts to successfully resist the surge of Barbarian Tribes when they swept out of their dreadful mountains to the far north. Its eyrielike site made it difficult to plunder. In those days of the Last War a few mageborn did manage to get inside its stony, steep walls. They came to protect the Chalice from the sorcerer who declared himself the Barbarian King. Her own master had gone there to help them toward the end of the war. He had called a cold, black mist to rise and obscure the narrow trail so the Barbarians climbing it fell to their deaths. And those who did not fall were drowned by the mist. . . .

Shona frowned. That had been less than seventeen years ago, during the final decade of the Last War. Her master had ordered her farther south to keep her safe. She took her brother's wife, who was heavy with child. It was Shona who helped birth the small boy, Shona who took them back north when word spread far and wide that the Barbarian King had been captured and executed on the northernmost borders of Elenthorn. That his head had been placed there in a monolith, looking toward the Mountainous Wastes, as a warning to the Barbarian Tribes of that realm.

And what had she come back to? Her master had died—too exhausted by the constant use of power and weak from an inflammation of the lungs so fierce that even a healer of Diancecht could not keep Arawn from claiming the old man's soul for Annwn. Her brother was dead as well, a Barbarian sword in the belly, they said. Shona had mourned, but not as deeply as her brother's wife, who pined to death and left Shona with the care of a small lad. She praised the Silver Wheel when mage sign manifested in the boy. At least she would not have to watch him grow quickly and die.

But if I do not give these men what they want, Eldon will surely die! And so would she. *We are so few. Life is too precious to waste.* But how could she allow an artifact of her goddess to fall into destructive hands? Oh, they would not sunder it, these priests of Dubh Cromm. Rather, they would guard it in their own treasury, abusing its power for their own ends.

Blessed Lady, what must I do?

She closed her eyes to the world, leaning against the sturdy oak, willing sleep to come and take the worries from her mind.

Yet even in sleep, there was no peace. She dreamed she was climbing a narrow trail up a sheer face of rock. Halfway up, she paused and fell to her knees, for the dark of night burst white with dazzling moonlight that bathed Shona in its glory. And from its midst, a figure she had never seen, yet knew by the flowing white tendrils of hair and by the Silver Wheel that spun above the head that this was Arianrhod, goddess of mageborn, goddess of the moon.

The goddess did not speak, but her hand stretched toward the lower end of the trail. There, Shona perceived figures of men slipping away. Their hands were clutched about a bright, silver chalice etched more beautifully than any she had ever beheld. *Stop them!* The goddess' plea rang in Shona's mind. She turned, hurrying down the path at a run, ignoring the danger of its narrow lip that pouted over the rim of the moors below. And she was nearly on them, ready to call a heavy mist to drown them, when their leader turned and glowered. "Kill him!" he ordered, and it didn't take her long to realize *who* the bandit meant. Eldon was at the head of this fleeing party, cold steel pressed to his throat.

"No!" she screamed, stretching fingers in vain . . .

. . . only to have water thrown in her face. *Mist?* she thought, sputtering out of sleep. No. There were men around her, men whose faces were grim with distrust. And light filtering through the leaves above. Morning. Shona shook herself and tried to rise.

Gronan came forward, setting a pail aside and crouching before her. "You were dreaming," he said.

She nodded. The gag had loosened, enabling her to cry out in her sleep. His fingers worked it free, and she took several deep breaths while moving her jaw.

"Come on. We wanted to break camp early—but not quite so loudly."

A joke, she supposed as he pulled her to her feet and led her toward the fire where Eldon sat. His dark eyes were made deeper by the circles that surrounded them. She tried to smile for him, tried to reassure him with her eyes alone as everyone made ready to leave.

They took the short route, straight through the forest, arriving at the base of the mountain just after midday. Here, they left Eldon with a rather surly guard. Her nephew looked so pitiful as she turned one more glance his way. What had broken his spirit so? She kept her anger under control. Anger could interfere with clear thinking, and if she were to come up with a plan, it would not do to have her head muddled by such emotions. Her bonds had been removed, and Gronan had even insisted she clean up and don fresh clothes, lest their appearance arouse suspicion.

The climb itself was not as steep as in her dream. They made it in silence. She noted that her "company" had robed themselves in such humble garb that one might mistake them for followers of Diancecht, the healer god, whose priest were known to forgo fashion for comfort. Each man openly carried a staff fashioned of oak and carved with acorns, oak leaves, and mistletoe. Only she knew that under the simple tunics and cloaks, Gronan and his men carried short swords. The bandit leader instructed her carefully. "We are followers of Diancecht from a temple to the far south of Ard-Taebh. We are here on a pilgrimage and have come to pay homage to the Chalice; we will beg solitude for our prayers. Can you call mage light to blind the guards who remain so we can subdue them?"

She nodded. A simple enough cantrip, but she did not care for the use they had implied. "Subdue them how?" she insisted.

"We will take care of that. When I kneel and bow my head to the Chalice, that is when you must strike. My men will do the rest. Once we have the Chalice, you will conjure your mist about the tower.''

She frowned. "Wouldn't it make more sense to enshroud the whole temple and the gate?'' she said. "To conceal your escape from those guards as well?''

He shook his head. "Only the tower.''

"But they will see you leave the mist!'' she said.

"We want them to see us leave,'' he said. "We shall flee it as though it were an abomination that attacked us as we were at prayer.''

She narrowed her eyes. "They will see you with the Chalice.''

"We will conceal it.''

"What if they bar the gates when they see the mist form?''

"There will be too much confusion for that. We will all be screaming that a monster attacked us in the mist. They will want to investigate our claim before they think of closing the gates.''

"But if the *priests* of Diancecht leave and they discover the Chalice is gone . . .''

Gronan grinned, and Shona's heart froze. *They will blame the priests of Diancecht for the theft.* Not thieves serving a priest of Dubh Cromm. She averted her eyes. *Madness! All madness!* They would throw chaos into the peaceful relations that most of the religious factions in this world enjoyed. Priests of Diancecht and Arianrhod had been allies since time began. That was not to say they did not have some disagreements. That was the way of all religions. But to start such chaos would cause other priests of other gods to divide. *And the followers of Dubh Cromm would rise from the chaos to rule the land!*

By the Silver Wheel, how could she allow this to happen! She glanced timidly at Gronan, who had turned his eyes forward once more. "What *will* become of my nephew and myself once you have what you came for?'' she asked.

"I shall decide that once we are away,'' he said, and the gleam in his eyes made her shiver. "Are you familiar to any of these people?'' He gestured toward the temple gates rising before them as they rounded the last turn up the mountain road.

"No,'' she said, her mind racing furiously. *He will kill us both once he has what he wants. He cannot afford to let us live, for I know the truth of what he does.*

"Cover your head anyway," he said, and reached out almost playfully to tug the hood of her borrowed cloak.

She obeyed, more to escape his lewd gaze than anything. *Madness,* she repeated in her thoughts. She could not let this happen—could not allow them to take the Chalice. *But what of Eldon?* By all the gods, how could she make such a choice?

The gates loomed like a maw as she passed beneath the ancient stones. Gronan moved forward to greet the guards who stepped out to meet his party. Shona stared at the ground as she listened to him requesting an audience with their chief priest. In no time, they were entering the central tower, welcomed warmly by an elderly woman. Gronan made his request, and though the high priestess seemed a little puzzled, she saw no reason to deny it. She insisted there were guard priests who had to remain to watch the Chalice at all times. Gronan blessed her for her kindness and assured her the guards would be welcome.

They were soon led into the center of the tower, a circular chamber where the floors had been inlaid with pale gray and blue marble to form a wagon wheel. At its center stood a round altar upon which sat a gleaming silver cup, set round with a band of black and gold and decorated with moonstones. *So beautiful,* Shona thought as the chamber was cleared of all but four guards who stood around the altar. They wore tabards marked with Arianrhod's symbols and carried halberds whose heads were shaped like quartermoons.

Trembling, Shona waited in the ranks. The bandits arrayed themselves in a circle, facing the Chalice. Each man raised his arms as though paying homage to the beautiful cup. Then Gronan stretched his hands from his sides, fell to his knees, and bowed.

That was her signal. Shona closed her eyes and sought the stillness within, dragging light from her mage core and whispering the words of a light spell. The guards heard her, turning in her direction with startled glances before she sent the white light flashing from the tips of her outstretched fingers to strike their faces.

At once, Gronan and his men attacked the four. Shona saw steel emerge from under their robes. Blades flashed, turning crimson as they entered and left the guards' throats. She turned away with a gasp, tears of pity watering her eyes. Not one man uttered a scream in his death. Behind her, a clatter arose, then Gronan was at her shoulder, catching her arm.

"The mist!" he ordered in a hiss. "Call it now!"

Her hands shook, and Shona closed her eyes again. This time, she sought the well of power within her and conjured words to draw soft moisture from the air, letting them envelop her heart before she sent the swell of power racing forth to fill the room. Mist began to rise from the floor, billowing like clouds of white smoke. The scent of fresh water filled the air as the mist grew and traveled forth. It slithered through every aperture it could find, encasing the tower like a hand closing over a small rod.

"Now!" Gronan said.

A wailing of terror arose from the throats of his men. They hid their swords, clutching each other so as not to get lost while they raced for the doors. In a group, they fled the chamber and the tower, pushing Shona with them as they flooded out into the yard with the mist.

"Monster!" some cried.

"Oh, horrid!" screamed others.

"It's an omen!" came another. "Let us flee!"

Around them, Shona heard the temple guards running toward the mist-shrouded tower. She concentrated on staying on her feet as the bandits surged toward the open gate. No one stopped them. There was no one to try. The priests of Arianrhod and their guards were too busy concentrating on the tower they could barely see. The bandits were well down the road before they even slowed their pace. Only then did they throw off their deceptive clothing, hurrying into the woods where their temporary camp waited.

Eldon looked up at Shona as she arrived. His dark eyes were wide with misery. All around, the bandits were quickly breaking camp. Ignored, she ran to her nephew, hoping to loosen his bonds—hoping the bandits would not see either of them slipping away. Yet even as she reached Eldon's side, she was snagged by powerful arms.

"Get on a horse," Gronan ordered. "They'll know something is amiss by now and be hot on the heels of those priests of Diancecht who dared to defile their temple with blood and take its precious relic!"

He shoved Shona toward the nearest mount.

"But I thought we were supposed to kill ..." Eldon's guard started to say.

Gronan turned, swiftly backhanding the man. "Get them on horses!" he said. "The master will decide their fate!"

"NO!" Shona struggled. It was as she had believed. Death was the only way he could release her and the boy. A horrible death at the hands of his master, if the tales she heard of Dubh Cromm's temples were true.

Gronan tried to clamp a hand over her mouth. She sank teeth into flesh not yet protected by a gauntlet. He howled and struck her with a fist, sending her crashing to the ground. She saw Eldon shake free and throw himself in the path of Gronan's angry kick that would have taken her in the ribs. The boy succeeded in knocking the bandit leader off balance before Eldon landed at her side.

"Kill them now!" Gronan snapped. "And damn the priest's orders!"

Swords came rushing at them from many quarters as Gronan stepped back. Shona closed her eyes, swiftly seeking her core of power. They wanted a mist—they would have a mist, but not like any mist they had ever seen.

The words of her spell crossed her lips as she reached out to seize essence from the angry men who surrounded her. So swiftly did she draw, that some of them stopped, gasping for breath. She saw Gronan's startled look as she threw the power into the ground beneath her and called forth a watery fog of doom. Black mist began to steam out of the ground, reaching out like many tentacles to seize the bandits in a cold, wet grasp and surround them in dark cocoons. Screams of terror filled the air. She heard men running about, and this time there was no pretense in their voices as they fled—or tried to flee. Some apparently ran into trees. Others stumbled about blindly, shrieking that the cold hand of Arawn was closing about them. Her rage served to strengthen her spell, as did the essence she stole. In anger, she thickened the mist, feeding it more moisture until the air was so damp and humid, it was nearly impossible to breathe. Beside her Eldon whimpered, burying his face in his arms. Around her the black mist grew into a swirling sea of murky liquid, leaving her and her nephew untouched in the center. She heard men scream and gargle as they drowned in a mist so thick they could not draw air for the water it held.

Then silence came, leaving a gentle slap, like waves on a shore. Only then did Shona release the spell. Water splashed the earth around her. The misty dark fell to the ground and disappeared, leaving a sea of muddy bodies at her feet.

Shona knelt and drew Eldon into her arms, slipped the gag from his mouth, and unknotted the ropes that bound his wrists. He took one look at the drenched carnage around them and hid his face against her.

She let her gaze trail over the dead. Nearly all of them, from what she could see. *By the Silver Wheel, what have I done?* Her glance fell across Gronan who lay close by, head thrown back and eyes wide. His hands had clutched his throat in his moment of death. A pouch lay open at his side, revealing the silver gleam of the Chalice.

Fool! she thought as she heard the thunder of hooves and knew that the priests of Arianrhod had sent their guards to follow the men who had robbed them.

At least the Chalice was safe, she told herself. She would tell the priests what had happened and hope they would believe her. They might order her imprisoned or punished in some fashion. *Better than what the priests of Dubh Cromm would have done.* Surely, the priests of Dun Clogh-ran would be pleased that a follower of their mage goddess had saved their precious artifact and stopped them from falsely blaming the followers of the healer god.

She stared at Gronan's corpse and shook her head. *You wanted a mist,* she thought with a grim smile. *I hope you're satisfied.*

SONGHEALER
by Tammi Labrecque

In submitting this story, Tammi wrote that she had sent for guidelines but that the request must have been eaten by the postal service, so she had taken the liberty of using last year's guidelines and hoped I didn't mind. Not a bit of it—the guidelines don't change that much from year to year, and at least she thought to read them. It's always a shock to me how many don't bother—and brag of it in their cover letters.

She wrote that she's a telemarketer right now and refuses to have a phone because she sees all too many of them at work. And, she adds, they always ring just when she's finally settled down to write or read.

I know how she feels; I can't believe that airlines are actually advertising that their passengers are accessible by phone. I used to think the best thing about traveling by plane is being out of reach of that phone. But then, I worked for many years as a phone counselor, and I still hate phones.

Tammi is 20 years old, 21 in August, and she says that her biography "is painfully ordinary." She's beginning college at the University of Southern Maine after two years out of high school. "I have a cat named Zoe, and I'm working on a novel, two biographical notes that I'm sure leave you less than astounded."

In this story she tried to make Tyrnill's gender completely incidental. If she were a man, it would not change the story in any way. (But how dull a world it would be without gender.)

Tammi would like to dedicate this story to Carol Farthing.

The first faint blush of dawn had barely touched the eastern horizon when Tyrnill softly closed her bedroom door and crept down the stone-floored corridor, boots in hand. In the kitchen, which bustled with early-morning activity, she stopped to pull her boots on and fill a leather bag with as much bread, cheese, and fruit as she could take without calling attention to herself. Breathing a sigh of relief that no one had noticed her, she slipped out of the side door and headed for the stables.

Liertha's curious whinny greeted her as she approached the mare's stall. "Hello, my pretty," Tyrnill murmured, her mellifluous voice far more subdued than was usual. She led the mare into the yard and saddled her quickly. She had filled the saddlebags the night before with a few changes of clothing and more food: dried meat, more bread and cheese, and some roots that the servants ate, which Tyrnill had never tried but assumed must be hearty fare. What money she'd been able to save in the several weeks since her decision to escape was in a pouch tied around her waist and concealed beneath her loose linen shirt. All that remained was to fill the three water bags hanging beside the stable door, which she did. With that, she was ready to ride. *It was surprisingly simple,* she thought as she left the stableyard in a clatter of hooves, and by the time the stable-boys came to investigate the noise, she was gone.

Tyrnill halted around midday to rest Liertha and eat a hasty meal, tethering the mare to a bush at the edge of the stream they'd been following and propping herself against a tree several feet away. She hurriedly devoured a meager lunch, determined to stretch her supplies as far as possible, then sat back to consider her course of action.

To head through the fields on their side of the stream would take them into an area too heavily populated for Tyrnill's liking, and to go back the way they'd come was plainly not an option. This left two choices: she could continue to follow the stream and be assured of enough water and enough browse to keep Liertha fed, or she could turn off into the forest that had sprung up on the other side of the stream soon after they'd joined paths with it. The decision was a difficult one; they'd be more easily followed and caught if they stayed with the stream, but better able to survive, while the chance of capture would be next to nothing in the wood, and the odds of survival not significantly higher.

She was city-bred, unfamiliar with the ways of woodsmanship, and unaccustomed to hardship of any kind. This seemed to leave no option but to avoid the forest, but the fact that her pursuers, if indeed there were any, knew of her lack of forestry skills prompted her to untether Liertha, ford the stream, and head into the thick tangle of brush that was the beginning of the forest.

Dusk came quickly among the trees, and it was full dark in the wood some time before the last rays of sunlight would have disappeared in the world beyond it. To Tyrnill's inexperienced eye, every tree looked the same, and there were no distinguishable paths through them. The fear that she was simply wandering in circles grew in her until she could barely fight off panic, and Liertha, sensing her rider's distress, began to shy and start at every sound from the underbrush.

It was in this condition that they finally stumbled upon the clearing. It was small, only large enough for the tiny cabin and tinier vegetable patch beside it, but it was lovely, well-cultivated, and somehow welcoming. As Tyrnill moved Liertha around to the front of the cabin, the door opened, and an aging woman stood on the threshold, beaming.

"Well, hello," she called cheerfully. "I thought you'd never get here!"

Tyrnill blinked in confusion but could think of nothing to say.

The woman chuckled. "Tie your horse beside the house—the side *away* from the garden, please—and have yourself a wash at the well there, then we'll see about getting you settled." She disappeared back into the cabin, shutting the door behind her.

Well, she's obviously mistaken me for someone else, Tyrnill thought, *but perhaps she can help me. If she lives here, she must know how to get out of this thrice-damned forest.* She obeyed the woman's instructions, tethering Liertha near the well, and performing a spare wash as quickly as she could. Then she headed back to the front of the house and knocked firmly on the door. It swung open immediately, and the woman peered out.

"Oh, my," she grinned. "You needn't knock, dear—this is as much your place as mine! Come right in."

Tyrnill followed her into the cabin, noting at once that it was fanatically clean. The room was fairly small, containing only a table and two chairs, with a basin on a sideboard at the side nearest the door and a fireplace on the opposite wall. There were two doors on the wall to the right of the doorway Tyrnill now stood in, both of them closed.

"Now, my dear, let me show you what's what. Those cupboards over the fireplace have a bit of food in them, just some dried things, and the herbs I use for cooking. Of course, someone will bring fresh food around every day or two, even a bit of meat once in a while, and there's always the garden, but I like to have a bite or two put by, you know." The woman looked to Tyrnill as if for confirmation, and Tyrnill nodded dumbly, caught up in this woman's vitality. The woman smiled. "Forgive me if I go on; it's been some time since I've had a chance to really talk to anyone. Well, then—over here's the washbasin. We must keep everything scrupulously clean, you understand, if we're to do any good. And under," here she stooped to push aside a curtain which had hidden several deep shelves, "we have the rest of the herbs, and some bandaging. Clean rags, of course, to wipe up any blood, or whatever." Blood? Tyrnill blinked again. The woman grinned engagingly. "We can't very well fix anything if we don't even know what the problem is, and we can't discover what the problem is if we can't see anything, right?" Tyrnill was mystified and finally said so.

"I'm sorry, but I don't understand at all. I think—that is . . ." She searched for the right words but came up blank.

"You really don't know what I'm talking about?" The woman looked confounded. "I simply hadn't thought . . . Of course, Power as strong as yours would naturally seek out other Power, but I never thought you were unaware of it." She frowned. "My dear," she began, very slowly and solemnly, "have you any idea what I am? Or what you are, for that matter?"

Tyrnill shook her head. "I'm certain this is nothing more than a misunderstanding. You see, I'm not whoever it is you've been expecting. I'm only here because I got lost in the wood."

"Lost in the wood indeed!" The woman laughed. "You

may well have become lost, my dear, but that is most decidedly not the reason you found me. And you are, without a doubt, exactly the person I've been expecting."

"I don't see how—"

"I can see that perfectly, now, and I don't mind telling you I feel a complete fool for not seeing your confusion to begin with." The woman pulled out a chair and dropped into it. "Here, sit down," she commanded, indicating the second chair, and Tyrnill obediently sat. "Now, I suppose I should start from the beginning. My name is Raelenne."

"Mine's—"

"Tyrnill; I already know that."

Tyrnill's eyes widened. "But how?" she blurted.

Among other talents, I have more than a little of what my mother always called 'Knowing.' Primarily, though, I am a Healer. A SongHealer, to be precise." Raelenne waved a hand at Tyrnill. "As, of course, are you."

Tyrnill shook her head and protested vehemently. "I'm sorry to contradict you, but I'm no such thing. I haven't a shred of Magical ability in my entire body—why, you can ask any of my teachers! They were going to force me to become a servant at the school because I haven't any relatives to speak for me, and they said I couldn't just be allowed to leave, now that I knew where the school was." She was talking rapidly now, relieved to be telling her story. "It's supposed to be a great secret, you see, and the testing for admission very rigorous. But they just admitted me, with no more than a scan to see if I had the potential, because my parents were both such powerful sorcerers." Here she faltered for a moment. "They died, you see, in some sort of fight, and the people from the school came for me the next day. And I stayed there for six months, and I tried—I really did—but I couldn't learn any of what they wanted to teach me. And they said they'd made a mistake—that I had plenty of potential, but I would never have the ability to use it. And they said—"

Raelenne broke into her tirade. "Well, they were fools. You will certainly never be a sorceress, but you will be—are—something much more valuable. Tell me, did either of your parents have musical ability?"

"Oh, yes," Tyrnill said, remembering. "Father always said Mother's singing could put the birds to shame—and he was right. And he could play any instrument he got his hands on. It was part of their Magic—I mean, part of how they made it work."

"And did these idiots at your school know that?"

"They must have; Mother and Father were both trained there."

"Fools! Now you listen to me." Raelenne's face was almost harsh in the light from the fire. "You are going to be an extremely competent Healer, much better than even myself, and I've been called 'the best' more than once. The Power you hold is so great that I am literally awestruck. Once you learn how to use it, you will be by far and away the most talented Healer I've ever seen."

Tyrnill shook her head. "I don't know anything about Healing—I wouldn't even know how to begin learning."

"That's what I'm here for! Frankly, you need someone as good as myself to teach you; I wouldn't trust anyone else to be able to manage it. Untrained, you could actually do a lot of damage. This kind of teaching can be dangerous, to tell the truth."

Tyrnill's eyes widened even further. "Oh," she breathed, "I can't learn to do anything dangerous. I don't have enough control, enough concentration—all my teachers said so—"

"I don't doubt that they did," Raelenne responded acidly. "I have yet to meet the person with enough control to learn something that they simply haven't the Talent for."

"Raelenne, I really can't—"

Raelenne took Tyrnill's hands in her own and smiled encouragingly. "I can assure you that what I am going to teach you isn't going to hurt you or frighten you, as long as you possess the will to control it. You must remember, always, that you rule your abilities; they cannot rule you unless you allow it."

"I'm not sure—" Tyrnill began.

"I know that you are uncertain; that is precisely the problem. In what you are about to learn, even a moment's wavering will destroy what you hope to accomplish." Raelenne's smile had gone, and she regarded Tyrnill solemnly. "I say these things far from lightly, for I have seen it happen. And sometimes it is not only the work which is destroyed; it is the worker."

Tyrnill shook her head. "I'm not capable of taking on that kind of responsibility, Raelenne."

"Not only are you capable, you are uniquely suited to it," Raelenne responded emphatically. "Anyone with Power as great as yours must not be allowed to let fear guide her. You will overcome your fear. You must accept the abilities you've been given, else you risk ending up like your teachers. What difference lies between their refusal to accept you and your refusal to accept a Talent you didn't expect?" She held up a hand to silence Tyrnill's objections. "None. Such a Talent as yours is rare, but not unheard of, and knowing that both of your parents were superb musicians, those who took it upon themselves to train you should have looked for it. But they wanted a traditional sorceress and turned their backs on your real potential. You must not betray your true worth as they did, Tyrnill, lest you be guilty of worse negligence than they."

Tyrnill swallowed around a lump in her throat and asked in a small voice, "Do you really believe that? After some of the things they said, I didn't figure I'd ever be much good for anything."

Raelenne rose and came around the table to take Tyrnill into her arms. With a sigh, she rested her chin on the girl's head. "Make no mistake about it—once trained, you will be worth twice all of them put together. I can promise you that."

There followed the most satisfying period of Tyrnill's short life. By day, she tended the garden, cleaned the small cottage, took long walks, and sometimes went with Raelenne to watch the Healer tend to the other people who lived in the wood. These people, in return for Raelenne's services, brought most of the supplies, including food, that the two women needed to survive.

By night, Tyrnill studied, learning everything there was to know about the body: how it functioned, how it was put together, and how to diagnose all manner of diseases and afflictions. She learned the names of all the herbs Raelenne used in Healing, where to find them, and how to prepare them. She learned how to bind wounds and broken limbs as well as how to prevent and treat infection. Raelenne was also training her in music: she learned what timbre and pitch meant, and the array of notes and scales she needed to arrange into music to accomplish a Healing. It was the first musical training she'd had, and she blossomed; her voice grew sure and, like her father before her, she could play any instrument she was given. Raelenne often expressed amazement at how talented her charge was. "You surpass me, truthfully," she would say. "I ought to be jealous." This made Tyrnill laugh every time she heard it.

Finally, the day came when Raelenne pronounced her ready to try her own hand at Healing. "I can't teach you anything more, Tyrnill. It's past time for you to gain some experience—which is a far better teacher than I could hope to be."

It was several days before the opportunity arose. Tyrnill was weeding in the vegetable patch when the rider burst into the clearing, and she straightened to greet him. "A good day to you, sir."

"And to you, lady. Is the Healer at home " he queried anxiously.

Raelenne had already appeared at the door of the house. "What's the problem, Kiersen?"

"My girl, ma'am—she's fallen out of a tree. Her leg's broken." His face was pinched with worry.

Raelenne nodded. "Tyrnill, come inside and gather up what you'll need." Tyrnill scurried into the house to collect bandaging, pieces of wood to splint the leg if it was indeed broken, and the herbs she would need to treat a broken leg as well as those for head and internal injuries. Raelenne had explained that it was best to plan for the worst possible injury because the amateur diagnosis of those who came to fetch the Healer was not always correct or comprehensive enough. Within minutes, she was back outside, saddling Liertha. Raelenne had already clambered up behind Kiersen; as soon as Tyrnill was mounted, they left the clearing at a gallop, with her following close behind.

Raelenne spoke slowly and liltingly. "Close your eyes and do exactly what I tell you."

Tyrnill listened carefully, blocking out the sound of the girl's soft weeping.

"Remember the relaxation exercises we've been practicing—breathe deeply, recognize what's going on in your body. Be aware of *your* heartbeat, *your* breathing, *your* temperature, and then forget them, and concentrate on *hers*."

Tyrnill shifted her focus to the girl, and the harmony of her own body contrasted sharply with the discord of the child's. The music in the girl was broken, and Tyrnill saw how the music could be fixed. It was the broken leg that had caused the tear in the music. Tyrnill began to hum softly, a soothing melody that came between the child and the pain, and then to sing, as she reached for the leg, holding her hands only inches from it. She sang of broken music put once again to rights, of young girls running, of the harmony that had once lived in the child, and would again. She sang of the way blood vessels connect, and tissue closes over bones that have been put back into place almost seamlessly. She sang the song of the child's body, picking up the faltering notes and returning them to their proper place in the melody, pulling the tattered pieces of the girl's music back together with the force of her will and her voice.

It was several minutes before she became once again aware of herself. Her heart was racing, and she was drenched in sweat, but the girl's leg was straight again, the angry tear in her flesh where the end of the bone had protruded fading to a dark scab, then a reddened scar. "That should heal in a few days," Tyrnill said to the collected family. "It's going to scar; I can't help that, and I can't do bone-Healing, so I'm going to have to put a splint on her. She'll have to stay off her leg until I'm sure the bone has set properly. Anyway, it's just as well that I can't do bone-Healing—it tends to leave bones weaker than they were before. This way she'll be as good as new, even if she does have to wait a little longer." She smiled reassuringly at the relieved faces around her. "I'll get her splinted up, and then we should all give her a chance to sleep. She's using a lot of energy, healing as quickly as she is."

Raelenne nodded approvingly. "You did very well, my dear," she commended, as the others cleared out of the room. "You're a bit slow, but that will change with time, and you were actually much faster than I expected in coming out of your Healing trance. I think it won't be too long before you can Heal without having to trance at all."

Tyrnill flushed from the praise. "You think so?" she asked softly.

Raelenne laughed. "Yes, my modest little apprentice, I definitely think so."

*   *   *

That was in early fall, and Tyrnill stayed through the winter snows, continuing to learn and progressing as well and as rapidly as Raelenne had anticipated. So it came, that on a day very early in spring, when the trees had just begun to tend once again to green, Raelenne told Tyrnill that it was time for her to go.

"I've taught you everything I can," she informed her young charge, with more than a hint of regret. "There are plenty of things you still don't know, and the only way you'll learn them is to travel."

"I don't want to travel," Tyrnill protested. "I want to stay here. I like to take care of these people."

"You'll like to take care of other people just as much, dear," Raelenne said reasonably. "This is, after all, your calling. And don't think I don't expect you back, because I do. Someone will have to take over my place here someday, and I hope that it will be you. First, though, you've got places to go, girl, and a whole lot to discover. No more arguing—you're going, and that's all there is to it."

"I will come back, you know," Tyrnill said fervently. "This is the first place I've really felt I belong, and I'll be back."

"Of course you will," Raelenne said, her eyes gleaming suspiciously. "I didn't expect any differently. But don't you come hurrying back just because you miss this place. Go out, make a name for yourself, be certain that you've learned all you can—then come back, and we'll all be happy to have you again."

"When should I leave?"

"You leave at dawn tomorrow. I've been putting things away for a little while, and I think there's enough to keep you well supplied for a fortnight at least. If you haven't found a way to keep yourself alive, by then, then all my judgments about you will have been very wrong—and we both know that I'm never wrong." Raelenne flashed Tyrnill a warm grin. "And not a word of complaint about leaving so soon. The way I see it, the sooner you go, the sooner you come home."

"This is my home, isn't it?" Tyrnill mused.

"Indeed it is, my dear. And it will be waiting for you, no matter how far you go, or for how long."

SOW'S EAR
by Kathy Ann Trueman

Kathy Trueman lives in one of the kinds of tiny towns in
Texas which I know all too well. She's forty years old and
has often been described affectionately, as a "pushy
broad." If they smile when they say it, it may BE affection-
ate. But somebody said Texas was a great place for men
and horses—not so good for women and dogs (When I
lived there, most murder victims were some man's es-
tranged wife—so when I left my husband, I got away far
and fast, not wanting to be the next headlined murder.)

She has a B.A. in English which she "earned for love of
words alone, not as a career move." She says she's an
Army brat and has lived all over the world. She still gets
itchy feet now and then but mostly takes it out in rearranging the furniture. She lives with a roommate, Randi, who
has been her best friend since 1969. She tries not to count
up how long that is. They live in an old house which sags
a bit at one corner. In the "Critter's Club" are six horses,
three dogs, nine cats, three geese, and about twenty chickens. She firmly believes there are animal signs posted outside of town pointing toward the house, saying "Suckers
live here."

She "learned to write by reading"—that's the best way—
this was her first attempt to sell something and her first
sale. She feels like she hit one out of the ball park on her
first swing. "That's a compliment," she adds ... as if I
didn't know.

Janell could feel the magic building in power, resisting, tingling up her arms, almost snarling at her as she began the first unraveling of its threads of energy. This curse spell was strong and complex, astonishingly so. She pulled back slightly, not discouraged, but needing to breathe and review the task.

Across the sparsely furnished room, her customer sat sulking. She was a plain, lumpy woman, well into her middle age, but not ugly. When Janell had asked why she wanted to pay so dearly to have her curse removed, the woman had gestured down at her body with contempt. "Look at me!" she had shouted. "I was beautiful, graceful, fertile! I can't go on living in this hideous, useless body!"

Janell could understand that. She wasn't beautiful herself, but she chose to appear that way, and she knew the benefits and seductions of beauty. "Why did the mage curse you?" was her next question.

"He wanted my treasure. Now he has it, or most of it." The woman stared forlornly down at work-roughened hands. "But he's taken away the only thing I truly valued. I want that back. I want to be what I was before he cursed me." Then she pulled out a pouch and emptied its contents on the table before Janell. "Here is all I was able to come away with. I give it all to you, to remove this curse and make me beautiful again."

The pile of jewels glittered at Janell. If this was only a portion, no wonder the mage had been willing to curse her to get the rest! Further, Janell could see that one of the gems, a ruby amulet, was ensorcelled. Unable to resist, she ran her fingers through the stones, then lifted the amulet. There was no obvious clue to what kind of spell was on it.

The woman stared at her anxiously. She was no mage, and Janell began to think she didn't realize what she had here. She pretended to be bored, asking, "Where did you come by such a treasure?"

Without the least hint of shame, even with pride, the woman said, "My father was a great thief. And a great miser." Then, "Is it enough?"

The gems represented more than Janell could make with ten such spell-castings, even without the ensorcelled ruby. She couldn't wait to begin to decipher the amulet's resident magic. Still, she hadn't lost all caution. Her own spells, cast on this room, not only told her this was no rival mage seeking to attack her while she concentrated, but also whether or not the woman was telling a lie. When Janell checked, she saw the woman had spoken only the truth.

The decision was easy. Janell made the slight gesture to raise the room's protective shields which would prevent any interruption once she began. "It is enough," she said. "Barely. I will help you." And she warned the woman not to speak, not to move until the curse was broken.

Now she was deeply into it, following and picking apart the threads of energy as a tailor might pick apart seams. Even for a shapechanging spell it was complex, going off in unexpected directions, strong where it should have been weak and weak where she might have made it strong. But this was what she was best at, and she followed it all the way to its heart. When she had it, the core of light from which the rest had been born, she held it in two magical "hands," contained it, and then sent her own counterspell into its center like a knife.

The woman threw back her head and began to scream, but Janell wasn't startled. Shapechanging always involved some pain, and forced shapechanging even more. She kept her attention on the curse, fracturing it and blowing away the pieces, letting them join the energy ambient in the room. It was done.

The woman had fallen forward, hunched over herself in the chair, the scream beginning to change into another sound. Janell was already reaching for the amulet when she realized the sound wasn't the weeping that usually followed a shapechange. It was a growl, soft, but building abruptly into a roar. The roar filled Janell's ears, filled the room, until the very air vibrated with the crescendo as if unable to hold it. It wasn't a roar of pain, but of triumph. Janell flinched back, rising, stumbling backward over her chair.

In seconds, the woman's plain clothing and sallow skin melted away, and a shape unfolded that was much, much larger, richly black and shining with iridescence, as if it had feasted on colors and kept them trapped in the blackness, allowing them to play along curves as it rose and continued to rise. A long neck unfolded, arched like a swan's to keep the long reptilian head from grazing the ceiling. The body lengthened, filling the room from right to left, a tail sweeping around until it almost touched Janell. Thick muscular legs tipped with long golden claws crushed the chair beneath it, and black wings spread from the shoulders, opening on a frame of bony elongated fingers, like a bat's.

The spells! She can't have lied to me without my knowing! Janell thought in panic, and then she realized. The woman said her true form had been young and beautiful. She never said it had been *human*.

Her true form was beautiful, but it was a beauty of towering, glittering grace and raw strength, as terrible as thunderclouds rolling to fill the sky with tossed blackness and flashing lightning. Inhumanly perfect curves shuddered, stretched, shook off the last construction of its cursed form, and settled with the inevitability of the first whisper of an avalanche.

It was done. The head swung around to face Janell, the eyes red and flickering. They weren't human eyes, but Janell could still see the gleeful triumph in them. She tried desperately to cast a spell to protect herself as the mouth opened, showing rows of long teeth. But the dragon didn't bite her. It said, "Arlahalimin."

Now, horrified, Janell knew what the amulet did. *"No!"* she screamed, the protest tearing from her throat, but it was much too late. The room and the dragon seemed to rush away from her as she sank, became small, then smaller and smaller—

She saw the dragon through a red haze. She was inside the amulet.

The dragon rested its head on the table with a contented grumble that made the wood tremble, almost knocking Janell to her knees within the tiny room that was the inside of the ruby. "Now I go to take back my treasure," she said. Teeth glinted with her smile. "And you will help me. In that amulet, you have no choice but to obey me. You will fight the mage with magic, because I cannot. If you fail, you shall die," she pointed out unnecessarily. "But if you win . . ." A claw hooked the amulet's chain, and Janell was swept dizzyingly up into the air.

"If you win," the dragon said, still smiling, "you shall be the pride of my collection."

POISONED DREAMS
by Deborah Wheeler

I think Deborah has been in most, if not all, of these anthologies, since the beginning. She is a chiropractor by profession and has two daughters, whom I first met as adorable toddlers, but who are fast growing up into delightful and talented young women. Her husband, a certified Rolfer, is one of the few of that discipline who doesn't talk a lot of psychological cant, as if Rolfing could purge a lifetime's accumulated emotional problems. (Don't we all wish it could, though!) Deborah lives in Mar Vista, California, a suburb of West Los Angeles, "where you can still breathe the air some of the time."

One of her novelettes, "Madrelita," was on the 1992 Nebula preliminary ballot, and I was recently thrilled to read her first novel, *Jaydium;* her second, *Northlight,* just sold to DAW. She's currently working on a novel inspired by her experiences living in France in 1991.

Toward dawn, all conversation along the battlements trailed away into silence. The priest had made his rounds an hour earlier, shriving those who asked and silently blessing those who did not. Fighting men, archers and swordsmen and those who worked the great cauldrons of pitch and boiling oil, looked out over the darkened fields below, counted the campfires they could see, and wondered how many more remained hidden. They tightened their belts around hunger-flattened bellies and checked their weapons one more time. A few glanced nervously over their shoulders, not toward the high tower where King Reyesmond the Second met with his council of war but toward the main hall and the kitchens beneath it.

Deep within the ancient bulk of the castle, a strange, misshapen figure crouched by the scullery hearth, tracing runes in the ashes. No one drew near to hear her whispered chants. The cook and all his assistants circled wide as they rushed to prepare hot drinks and a meager breakfast for the fighting men.

At the first stirring of the single uneaten cock, the fay lifted her head and turned eyes like milky opals toward the east. The delicately pointed ears which protruded through her matted amethyst hair quivered. Ember-light reflected dully from the loop of iron around her neck, no thicker than a wire and joined by only a twist of rawhide that even a child could have pulled loose. Purplish discoloration spread across the moony skin from under the wire, leaving cracked, oozing scars. As the fay bent over the ashes once more, the movement shifted her tattered cloak to reveal the wings which hung, crippled, down her back.

With one finger, she traced over the runes, coaxing them from luck to dread and from dread to cowardice and from cowardice to mortal terror. The King had commanded her to work a charm of victory for the morning's battle and so she would, but he had not said *whose* victory.

The fay did not look up at the sound of boots on the stone stairs. She did not need to, for she could hear in those footsteps the echo of another's tread, the grandsire dead but not forgotten. The door flung open, the cook bowed and drew back as a young woman in half-armor strode it. Her dark hair had been braided tightly against her head and she carried a short sword as if she knew how to use it. Her surcoat bore the King's own arms, with a unicorn as her own insignia. As a child, she had loved unicorns; the fay had seen her watch for them by moonlight and creep out of bed to hear a traveling minstrel sing of them.

"King's-blood," the fay hissed, her purple lips drawing back to reveal needle fangs. "King's-kin, King's-daughter-who-would-be-a-son. What petty errand has he sent you on now?"

Valry King's-daughter lifted her face, pale and resolute.

The fay could sense the sadness in her and had tried many times over the years to nurture it into something more, into resentment and bitterness, a canker of malice that would poison everything the princess touched. She had tried without success, as if a unicorn truly stood guardian over the young girl's heart.

"My father bids you come to him."

The fay's knobby hands moved in a rune of Night, the sort that sent never failed to send the menials scurrying away. The princess stood firm.

"My grandfather bested you and bound you to his service by cold iron. My father's pleasure," she hesitated for only an instant, "is to keep you. And you will obey him, Old Broken Wings, if I must drag you before him on your belly."

At the mention of the old King, the open sores on the fay's wings throbbed, oozing a thick, dark liquid. She scented the grandsire's blood in the young woman's veins. Shuddering, she heaved herself to her feet and hobbled from the kitchen as quickly as she could.

In the King's Council chambers, candles cast wavering shadows across the tapestried walls. Pages darted about to replace them and cut away the night's drippings. Maps and charts lay scattered over the central table.

As the fay entered, guarded by the King's daughter, captains and councillors alike froze as they were. Some looked up. A few of them blanched. Only the King appeared undisturbed, but the fay could feel the terror gnawing deep within him. She grasped it and felt it tighten like a hangman's noose.

He resisted her, as he always did, for he was his father's son. But he had watched his father, in the fullness of his victory, ask the fay what his own future was to be. He had seen the joy bleed out of his father's life when she told him what his death was to be—a lingering nightmare of pestilence and senility. And in all the years he had been King, all the years since his father's death, all the years he had kept the fay prisoner, he had never asked her for his own future.

The King now gestured the fay to approach. She read in his eyes what she had sensed in the night, that reinforcements had arrived, strengthening the usurper Duke's position. She reached out to his heart again and tasted the twisting, dark temptation to kill her with his own hands, rather than allow her power to fall into his enemy's.

"O great king and son of my conqueror," she said in her sweetest voice. "What is your desire?"

The King hesitated for the slightest moment before replying. He must have spent hours considering the question, the exact right phrasing to obtain the answer he so desperately needed. "What must I do to win this battle?"

Oracular compulsion knotted her throat and her lips moved without her will. "You must open your gates to them."

"What!" the senior captain leapt forward. "Surrender?"

"Treachery!" someone else shouted. "The witch-demon cannot be trusted! She is too dangerous to let live!"

The fay drew herself up to her slender height, gathering her cloak around her. "By the cold iron that binds me, I have answered truly. But I can only answer what I have been asked."

"This is true, Father." Valry King's-daughter stepped to his side, her brows drawn together in thought. "But the answer does not necessarily mean your surrender. Perhaps she has seen some moment in negotiation, a truce—"

Just then the doors burst open and a grizzled sergeant rushed into the room, his face as red as if he'd run all the way from the farthest battlement.

"Your Majesty—they're gone! Every last jack of the Duke's men, gone! The whole field, empty!"

"Empty?" the King repeated.

"Aye, all but a few piles of baggage not even big enough to hide a man in. As well as we can see in the dawnlight— it's a miracle, it is!" Then, perhaps recalling his position and the august company to whom he was speaking, he broke off and bowed deeply.

"Perhaps a miracle," the King said wonderingly. His eyes flickered over the fay's impassive face. "Let us go down and make sure."

Remnants of campfires and abandoned equipment littered the field, furrowed by hastily filled latrine trenches. The marks of heavy wagons and shod hooves scored the earth. The King and his retinue strode back and forth, amazement melting into triumph as they examined what had been left. The fay, with the King's daughter watching her, followed behind them.

Scattered about, they found jugs of beautifully worked pottery, decorated with flowers and stylized bees and giving forth the enticing aroma of honey.

"Why leave them here?" one of the councillors wondered.

"As a gift," another answered, giddy with relief. "In homage to our superiority!"

Unsmiling, the King shook his head. "We might have prevailed, had it come to a fight. But it was no sure thing. They were as resolute as we, and better supplied. Why would they give up, and leave these here for us?"

He touched one finger to the smooth wax of the seal. His courtiers gathered around, waiting for him to order the jars opened. They had all been on painfully short rations, and now the sweet heavy scent of the honey made their mouths water. Someone's stomach rumbled hopefully.

The King gestured the fay forward and showed her the jars. "Our enemy has left us this, but for what reason? Is the honey poisoned?"

A ripple of compulsion set the fay's wings trembling. "It will not kill you."

"Yet there are other ways of bringing a man to harm," the King said thoughtfully. "Is the honey tainted with magic?"

Again the fay answered no. Relief spread across the King's face. The courtiers nudged each other, faces relaxing into smiles. One bent to pick up another jar.

"Father." The clear voice of Valry King's-daughter made them all pause. "Is not this honey *too* tempting? Would you risk the fate of the realm on the word of a sworn enemy . . . or the word of a fay?"

The King's brow furrowed. "She has said it is safe."

The princess shook her head. "No, she has said only that it was neither poisoned nor charmed. If it is indeed safe, let *her* taste it for you . . ."

She took the jar from her father's hands and with one swift movement stabbed her thumb through the wax seal. The smell of the honey enveloped them, cloying and beckoning. The distilled sweetness of a thousand flowers, a hundred summer days, filled their nostrils. Tension-weary muscles melted.

Unsmiling, the princess held the jar out to the fay. ". . . if she dares."

The fay narrowed her opal eyes. She had known, the moment her wings were broken, how much greater was the cruelty of humans than that of her own kind. She had known the trait would not die with the old King. Now her hands quivered as she accepted the honey jar, for although she did not know how it would come about, she was certain that her prophecy of the opened doors was true. She dipped one fingertip into the smooth thick honey and lifted it to her lips.

For a moment the world rippled around her like reflections seen on wind-kissed water. Something stirred deep within her, something long buried. Her vision swam with glittering lights, burning pale and pure like the stars above her birth. The pain in her wings eased as if they'd suddenly healed. The perfumes of asphodel and night-blooming jasmine filled the air; she drank them in, filling every pore of her being with their scent. A soothing chill shot through her; she had almost forgotten what it was like to feel pleasure.

Sound jarred her ears, grating and barely understandable, like the buzzing of insects. Reyesmond's voice: "Take the honey and the traitor inside."

Then from a far distance came the music of silvery bells and voices calling out in a familiar lilting cry. "Come! Come to us!"

I am here! she cried out from the very depths of her being. She lifted her wings, stretching wide the folds of patterned gossamer membranes. They caught the breeze; her body seemed weightless. On tiptoe, she raised her arms, poised for flight.

For a single moment, she heard the voices singing the name she had not heard since the old King had broken her wings. The name she thought she would never hear again.

"Come, oh come to us, O beautiful one, O Miranthea of the Silken Wings! Quickly, come to us!"

I am here! O my brothers and my sisters, I am here!

She came to herself again, confused and sick at heart. Pain clenched her, the old pain in her wings as fresh now as the day the old King had shattered them. Her nostrils flared, filling with the stench of human bodies, grease and filth and dried sweat.

Stay, O my sisters, stay for me!

In an instant she realized where she was, the little room which had been given to her but which she rarely used, preferring the oracular ashes of the scullery. A grim-faced guard stood just inside the doorway. His voice still echoed against the bare stone walls, and it had been his words which had woken her. For the first time in thirty years of captivity, she could not sense what was going on. All her defenses had been stripped from her, leaving her naked among her enemies.

Valry King's-daughter strode through the doorway. Her armor shone, as if catching invisible light. Or perhaps it was only the brightness of Miranthea's fading dream, she could not tell.

"Come with me, Old Broken Wings. My father is about to open the gates."

Briskly, Valry King's-daughter led the way to the battlements overlooking the central courtyard. Miranthea looked down and saw the bodies lying on the ground, their limbs contorted as if by hideous convulsions, but now motionless, yet with her fay's sight, she saw the life burning in them. The unbarred gates gaped in invitation. Everywhere she looked, she saw more men waiting, hidden behind half-opened doors and wagons, their weapons ready.

"A clever trap," she murmured. The guard had withdrawn, leaving the two of them alone on the parapet. "Worthy of the foulest treachery of men."

"If we are treacherous," said the princess, watching the fay with her cold gray eyes, "it is because we have learned it from you."

Miranthea faced the granddaughter of her conqueror. Once she would have silently cursed her, or tried to twist her words, using her hatred as both sword and shield, but now she could only stand there, defenseless against her own memories. Again she felt cold iron ripping through the delicate membranes of her wings. She heard the slender bones snap. The echoes of silvery voices faded from her ears.

The princess flinched as if she'd been physically struck. What did she see in Miranthea's eyes? Perhaps she was remembering the nights she danced in the moonlight on her balcony, singing for the unicorns. Or perhaps all the

times her father had turned away from her because she was
not a son.

"My grandfather should have slain you. My father should
have freed you."

"They were men and fools."

"But I am neither."

A shiver went through Miranthea's broken wings. Below,
the Duke's men strode into the courtyard. Their voices rang
out, as if they had no further need for stealth. Their laughter rose to the battlements. The captains lifted their pen-
nons. One of them took out a small horn and blew a fanfare
as their Duke rode past the gates on his high-bred white
stallion.

Suddenly another horn blared out from the high tower.
The portcullis, its rope cut, dropped with a thunderous
noise. The men lying on the ground leaped to their feet.
The king's archers appeared on every parapet and rained
their arrows down on the men below. Laughter turned to
screams, shouted orders, each contradicting the next. The
Duke wheeled his mount, rallying his men. But half his
army was still outside the gates and the rest in disarray,
scrambling for cover.

At a second blast from the King's horn, armed men
jumped out from behind half-closed doors, from posts and
wagons, and hurled themselves at those besiegers who had
managed to find shelter against the arrows. Three whom
Miranthea recognized as the King's best swordsmen rushed
at the attacking lord. One ran the white stallion through
the belly and the animal went down, screaming. The others
hauled the lord to his feet and held him, arms behind his
back, sword edge across his neck.

Even as the attackers surrendered and were led away,
Miranthea could not take her eyes away from the dying
stallion. It lay there, twitching, its moonshine coat befouled
and bloodied, until one of the King's men slit its throat.

Miranthea followed the princess into the great hall,
where Reyesmond sat on his father's throne. The captains
drew back from her, making ward-off signs and crossing
themselves. She stood in her allotted place while the King
heard his adversary's formal surrender. The penalties were
the usual—the Duke's firstborn son as hostage, a modest
forfeiture of lands and an oath of loyalty. The son, who'd

acted as lieutenant, was of an age that Miranthea guessed he'd be wed to Valry as a way of permanently solving the problem.

And then who will have won, King's-daughter, and who will have lost?

"And now, we come to other matters," the King said in his sternest voice. "Matters of justice, matters of vengeance for darkest betrayal. We speak now not of the ambitions of men but of the treachery of immortals. Stand forth, and hear the charges against you." He pointed at Miranthea, who hobbled forward. "But for the quick thinking of our daughter, we would have eaten the poisoned honey. We would now be on our knees, listening to our fate, instead of sitting here in judgment. You have forsworn the oaths you gave to my father and committed the most heinous crime of treason. What have you to say for yourself?"

Miranthea lifted her chin. With the slightest movement, agony surged through her crippled wings. "I told only the truth."

"Only the truth! Enough to get us all killed! The honey was gathered from dream-poppies, as well you knew! One taste and a man is lost, his body living and his mind enslaved! Yet you kept this secret from us." The King's face reddened and contorted. His courtiers drew back, murmuring. "Is there any reason I should not have your head stricken from your shoulders as you stand?"

Hope shivered through Miranthea. She could survive as she was before she tasted the honey, half-dead and the rest numbed with hatred, but she could not endure this new awareness which pierced every part of her, the knowledge of what she had been. Perhaps if she goaded him hard enough, the King would indeed cut off her head.

"You'll never be rid of me, never!"she shrieked. "Dead or alive, I'll haunt your nightmares forever!"

The King drew his sword and stepped down from his throne. His eyes burned as if his soul were on fire.

Miranthea threw her head back and cackled with joy. "I've won! I've won! You cannot escape me now! The unholy curse will be on you and yours until the end of time!"

The hall fell silent, the courtiers holding their breath. Fear rose up from them like a charnel stench. Swiftly Valry moved to her father's side. She placed one hand on his sword arm. Miranthea could feel the tenderness of that touch. The King paused and looked down at his daughter, as if seeing her for the first time.

"Have I not served you well?" the princess asked. "And may I not ask a reward for my good counsel?"

After a long moment, he bent his head in agreement.

"Then give this wretched creature to me. Let *me* be the one to pass judgment on her."

A ripple of surprise passed around the room. The King threw his head back and laughed. "My daughter! Her courage is worth twice any man's!" He pointed to the fay with his sword. "She's yours."

As Valry approached, Miranthea spread her lips in a soundless snarl, baring her needle fangs. She spat out a challenge. "Let us see what you are made of, King's-spawn. Is your courage, too, so small that you dare not strike me down, though I am unarmed?"

"I will not bandy words with you, Old Broken Wings. Only sentence you as you deserve."

With a swift, savage movement, Valry King's-daughter grasped the iron ring. The iron wire bit deep into Miranthea's flesh, causing her such agony she could hardly breathe. Somehow she managed to stumble along as the princess dragged her from the hall. The King and his courtiers followed on their heels.

They halted by the gates. The portcullis had been raised and one gate opened to permit the Duke's men to surrender. The princess released the fay and thrust her through the opening.

Miranthea staggered, momentarily overwhelmed by the bright hard light, the scent of the tramped fields and the lingering taint of blood from the courtyard. The princess slid her sword free and laid the tip against Miranthea's throat.

"Kill me now and be done with it," Miranthea hissed. "Show mercy in this, at least."

Slowly the princess smiled. With a flick of her wrist, she cut through the leather bindings and tossed away the iron wire. "You have the freedom of the road. May you live long to enjoy it."

Miranthea gasped at the sudden disappearance of the pain she had lived with for so many years. Even as she tried to straighten up, her muscles cramped, as if her spine had turned to stone. Her wings ached and she became acutely aware of her crooked limbs, the sloughing, pitted skin, the matted hair, the ash-filth calluses on her hands and feet.

Where could she go? Where in all the wide world was there a place for what she had become? Who among her own kind would welcome her now?

The princess reached into the pouch at her waist and took out a small crystal vial, sealed with wax and hanging from a loop of braided silk. She placed it around the fay's neck, saying, "A parting gift, something to remember me by."

Through crystal walls, the honey glowed like a pool of molten light. A smell, cloying and compelling, wafted upward and seeped all through the fay's senses. Visions of heart-tearing beauty clawed at her. She reached one hand up to the seal and felt the wax soft and yielding to her touch. How easy it would be to push through it, to dip a finger into the golden elixir, to hear beloved voices calling her name, to stay forever with them. . . .

Miranthea's fingers closed around the vial. A hard snap would break the cord, but she knew she would never do it. Just as she would never surrender to the dreams within. But she would live with it every moment of her immortal span, the memory of all the beauty that had ever been hers, lost to her now and forever.

The voice of Valry King's-daughter pierced the waves of longing, pitched low so that only Miranthea could hear. "You are like this honey. True and false, sweet and treacherous. I would not harm you for myself, but as long as you are here, my father will be tempted to use your powers. He will fear you, and that fear will eat away at him until there is nothing left. I love my father. No matter what the cost, I will not permit you to destroy him."

Miranthea lifted her head and her wings stretched, aching. Everything had come clear now, in the light of memory. "Think on this, O princess. Think long and hard on this. If I am evil in the eyes of men, is it not because of what men have made of me—cruel, scheming, treacherous? Did I agree to have my wings broken, my life taken from me, to live as a slave, forever cut off from my kin? Did I choose what I have become? And which one of us now is truly innocent?"

Tears glowed in the eyes of Valry King's-daughter, but she made no move to wipe them away. She might have what she desired, her father's high regard, by ridding him of the fay, but at what price? Unlike Miranthea, she had freely chosen cruelty. Out of love, perhaps, but chosen it nonetheless.

What unicorn now would come to lay his head in her lap ... except in her own poisoned dreams?

The fay nodded. "And so you have your birthright, King's-daughter, King's-heir. May you live long to enjoy it."

Without a backward glance, Miranthea of the Silken Wings turned to make her crippled way through the dust.

NIGHT-BEAST
by Cynthia Ward

I've forgotten how many of these anthologies Cynthia Ward has been in. According to her bio, this is the third; I would have thought it was more. I suspect it's just that I've gotten accustomed to seeing her name on many manuscripts.

My first husband, God rest him, used to say I should never submit anything I wasn't sure would be accepted, lest the editor start thinking of me as a writer worthy only of rejection. I knew instinctively even then that he was dead wrong, but, being young then and easily intimidated, couldn't articulate why. Now, from years on both sides of the editor's desk, I can. If the editor gets used to seeing your name on good manuscripts he hates to reject, he'll keep trying to find a good excuse to bring one of them to his readers. Which explains why I am happy to bring you one of Cynthia's stories. The note I wrote on it was "Two young sorceresses growing up." This, by nine writers out of ten in my slush pile, would be an undistinguished, even an overused theme; From Cynthia, it turned out to be good reading, and if I were an academic writer, I'd probably have things to say about its symbolism and metaphors and so on. But I hate that kind of jabber, so I'll just say, "Read it; you'll like it. I did."

In a night of blizzard it came and killed everyone it found in the street: three strong hunters, the blacksmith, and a mother and child. It was no natural beast, for it did not eat those it slew, only tore them to pieces with long claws or fangs. The men built a high palisade about the village of Habar and agreed to stand guard upon the wall, but the first night a man was slain upon the walkway, and the other guards saw a long, white-furred creature climb down the wall like a cat and run like a man. The guards pursued the creature, but it disappeared in the darkness of the village; and though Habar was tiny, a handful of cottages and shops lining a single street, the men could not find the night-beast. Now no one went abroad after nightfall, and all doors were barred, all windows tightly shuttered.

Allysa asked Nath, the neighbors' son, to teach her how to defend herself against an animal that walked like a man.

Nath's breath made a white plume in the air as he replied. "No one can defend himself against the night-beast, else the guard, an experienced hunter, would have slain it!" He shook his head, his copper-colored hair tumbling over his shoulders. "I should never have taught you the use of knife and spear to begin with; who'll want to marry a girl who think she's a warrior?"

Allysa grew angry. "Why should I want to marry, when all boys are like you?" she said and returned home.

Then Nath came to her parents' cottage, carrying two spears with their points wrapped in cloth, and she joined him in the street. The sun sank toward the forest beyond the palisade as Nath taught Allysa how to defend herself with a spear in the hindering snow. Both wore heavy wool clothing, tunics and trousers and hooded cloaks, with a raw-hide belt about the tunic and a dagger in a deerskin sheath, and they wore long-cuffed gloves and high boots of color-fully embroidered deerskin. When Nath removed his gloves, and Allysa's gloves, and placed his hands upon hers to correct her grip upon the ash-wood spear-haft, his hands were surprisingly warm. When Allysa stumbled in the knee-deep snow and fell against him, she thought she felt the warmth of his body despite the layers of winter clothing.

Nath laughed, his head thrown back, his hood fallen away, his hair spilling like impossibly fine copper wires upon the snow. Allysa glared at him and saw upon his chin soft wisps of red hair which had not been there before. She wanted to stay angry at Nath, but his laugh was so exuberant, she found herself laughing, too. But they fell silent as a shout rang in the street.

"Begone, Renor!" It was the voice of Leis, Allysa's older sister. Leis never raised her voice, yet she was yelling. "*Go! We cannot marry!*"

Leis tried to slam the door of their parents' cottage. Her betrothed held the door open.

"Leis!" he cried. "*How* have I offended you?"

"You have not offended me," Leis said. She was fifteen, a year older than Allysa; she was as fair as Allysa was dark and as gentle as Allysa was boisterous. Allysa sought to become a hunter, while Leis could not even bear to wring a chicken's neck. "It has nothing to do with you, Renor," Leis was saying. "We just cannot marry. Now *go!*"

"I have not offended you, we have always wanted to marry, we are pledged to be married in a sennight—*why* are you *doing* this? By the Gods, Leis, I'll do anything—"

Laughter rang out. Allysa looked around, and discovered a trio of neighbor-women watching her sister and her sister's betrothed. Renor also saw the laughing. His face reddened. Leis took advantage of his distraction to shut the door. His face darkened further, with anger, and he ran up the street and disappeared around a cottage.

Allysa and Nath stared at each other in astonishment.

"Nath, I must see why my sister is in distress," Allysa said. Nath nodded, and Allysa ran to her parents' house, forgetting to return the spear to Nath.

The door was barred, but she pounded upon it with her fist and called, "Leis, it is Allysa! Let me in!"

Her hands had gone numb as ice blocks before her sister opened the door. She pushed into the cottage and laid her left hand upon her sister's shoulder.

"Leis, what is wrong?"

"I cannot marry," Leis said. "I cannot have children. That is all. Do not concern yourself."

She tried to turn away. Allysa tightened her grip upon Leis's shoulder. "You've always wanted to marry him, Leis! You cannot reject him a week before the wedding! You are anxious with the ceremony so close."

"I *want* to marry him, Allysa," Leis said. "But I cannot! And you—oh, Gods, Allysa, you must encourage Nath no more. You must never marry!"

"Marry Nath?" Allysa exclaimed. "I shall not marry him, or any man! I shall live alone. I shall be a hunter, like our father, like his sister Barla. I do not want to marry."

"You may change your mind, when the changes of womanhood come upon you," Leis said. "Allysa, you are fourteen. Have the moon-times started for you? Gods, they will change you—"

Allysa flushed. "*No,* my moon-times haven't started. But they won't change me, any more than they changed our Aunt Barla. She never married—"

"That is not what I mean!" Leis cried. "Oh, Allysa, the day will come when you will know what I mean. A bitter day. You must harden your heart against that day—"

"No man will ever win *my* heart," Allysa said. "But Renor has yours. Tell me *why* you think you will not marry him!"

Leis looked at Allysa closely, her pale blue eyes moving over Allysa's face. Her colorless lips parted, and Allysa leaned closer to hear her sister's words. Then Leis jerked back her head and shouted, "*No!* I cannot!"

She ran out of the cottage, though she wore neither cloak nor boots, only the dress and slippers a woman wears in her home. The setting sun stained her yellow dress red before she disappeared from Allysa's sight.

Allysa recovered from her astonishment. "Leis, you'll *freeze!*" she cried, and ran out the door. She realized she still held Nath's spear.

Leis was running up the street toward the palisade gate, which stood open, awaiting the return of the hunters from the forest. Allysa's legs were not hindered by a long skirt, as her sister's were, yet her surprise at the older girl's flight had delayed her sufficiently that she could not catch up with Leis before she ran past the guard and through the gate.

"Leis, it's sunset!" Allysa cried as she neared the gate. "Have you forgotten the night-beast? Come *back!*"

The gate-keeper grabbed her left arm. She kept running and he didn't let go; they spun around and fell in the snow. "This is no time for girls to venture out of the village!" the man said, shaking her. She tried to pull her arm free but failed. "Where do you think you're going?"

"To get my sister, whom you did not stop!" Allysa cried, and rapped his elbow with the spear. He yelped and his hand went slack. She sprang up in a spray of snow and ran into the forest.

"Leis!" she cried as she followed her sister's deep,

shadow-filled footprints up a hunting trail. "Come back! You are not dressed for the cold!"

The heavy, snow-laden boughs of pine and fir blocked the slanting light of the sun, and Allysa found herself suddenly aware of the cold. She pulled her gloves out of her belt and drew them on and, clutching the spear in both hands, pressed onward. The shadows thickened, clotting like blood, until she could not see Leis' footprints, or her own hand in front of her face. Night had come, the time of the murderous unnatural beast. Allysa was frightened, but she pushed on, shouting for her sister.

"Leis! We must get out of the forest! *Leis!* The night-beast!"

Night had come. Her sister might be dead.

Allysa had a spear, she had a knife, but she might die, too.

She pushed forward, toward a paleness in the dark, and found herself at a clearing, before an expanse of snow that shone like silver under the waxing moon. No footprints broke the smooth surface. Had Leis left the hunting trail, pushing into the prickly fir-boughs and thick undergrowth? No, she could not have done so, wearing only her thin dress. "Leis!" Allysa shouted. Her breath was a white fog in the darkness. "Where are you? Answer me!"

A roar shivered the trees and the moon, a horrendous harsh cry that rose to an ear-shredding shriek. Allysa turned toward the sound and saw a long, white-furred beast running toward her, running on two legs like a man but howling from a gaping muzzle like a wolf. The fangs were longer than a wolf's, the hair on the body was white and shaggy, the eyes were white and wild, and the forepaws—no, hands—were upraised, and armed with claws that gleamed in the moonlight.

The night-beast leaped like a wolf, rising off the trail toward Allysa, leaping toward her as it had surely leaped upon Leis. With a hate-filled scream Allysa braced the spear against the ground so the point would pierce the monster's body. The night-beast might not die immediately; even if she pierced its heart, it might be able to tear her to pieces before its life fled. But though Allysa must die, she would make sure the winter-colored monster died, too.

One long-fingered, long-taloned hand swept out and struck the spear aside, and the sturdy ash-wood snapped like the thinnest twig. Then the hurtling body struck Allysa and bore her down into the snow. Claws sank into her shoulders like heated nails, and the air rushed out of her lungs, replaced with pain like white-hot liquid iron. She stared up into the gaping fanged jaws and burning white eyes of the night-beast.

The white-furred misshapen head and long dripping fangs drew close to Allysa's neck as she fumbled for her dagger, and she saw the eyes were not white, but a pale blue, as faintly colored as ice. Then she realized the jaws had stopped their approach; the head was no closer. The head cocked, as if the night-beast were puzzled, and the pale eyes regarded Allysa.

Then the dagger was free of its sheath, and Allysa thrust upward. Perhaps the monster's hide was too tough for spear or knife blade, but pray to the Gods its eyes were vulnerable.

The night-beast raised its head, jerking away from the dagger-point. Allysa lunged up on her left elbow, against the weight of the monster, against the talons sunk into her shoulder, to extend the thrust. The dagger pierced the pale eye. It vanished in a dark fountain, and blood splashed Allysa's face like molten copper.

The night-beast screamed in pain. The scream became a moan, and the moan a word, as the jaws shrank, seeming to recede into the monstrous face, and the fangs withdrew into the gums, and the talons withdrew from the wounds in Allysa's shoulders, and the monstrous head altered its shape as the fur vanished from the face and then from the entire body. And the word the shape-changing monster spoke as it slumped forward was "Allysa."

"Leis!" Allysa screamed. Her sister lay motionless atop her. She shook the bare white form, shook it violently, but Leis did not respond. "Leis!" Allysa groaned. "Oh, Gods forgive me! I killed my sister!"

Weeping, she raised the dagger-point to her own breast. But if she killed herself, her parents would have lost both their children, their only hope of grandchildren and the continuance of their family.

She had killed her own sister. That was greater evil than any family should know.

"Why did you not *tell* me, Leis?" Allysa asked the dead woman. "I would have helped you!"

Leis had recognized Allysa, despite the murderous madness of the monster-body; Allysa could have helped Leis. But what could she have done to help? Released sheep into the street for her sister to slaughter as she roamed the village in a monster's body? Ranged ahead of her sister to make sure no one else was in the night-dark streets?

Allysa knew now why Leis had driven Renor away, why Leis had decided she could not marry and told Allysa she must not either. Leis had believed their babies would become monsters. She would not create more monsters to slaughter her friends and neighbors.

How long had she been a shape-changer? The slaughter was a new thing, had started a month ago—Leis had not always been a shape-changer, Allysa realized, and terror cased her heart in ice. Leis had asked Allysa whether her moon-times had started; this meant the shape-changing had started when Leis had started the woman's bleeding.

"Allysa!" a voice broke the silence of the night. A man's voice; Nath's voice, deep as it had not been a month ago. "Allysa! Leis! Where *are* you? We must leave the wood!"

Nath had seen her chasing Leis, Allysa realized, and had followed them. Allysa felt a great relief and a curious joy at hearing his voice; she opened her mouth to call him, and then closed it again.

She dropped her dagger and rolled her sister's body off her own, and arranged the limbs so the dead woman lay in a peaceful repose; but she could not change the pain-distorted features. With a handful of untrampled snow she washed the blood from her sister's pale face, then, gritting her teeth against the pain and the cold, she rubbed snow over the wounds in her shoulders. She thrust her dagger-blade into the snow, removing the blood, then dried the blade on her tunic and cut strips of cloth from the bottom of her cloak. Then she sheathed the dagger and bound her shoulders with the makeshift bandages. With effort she blinked her eyes clear, and wiped away the tears; she didn't want her eyelids to freeze shut. She picked up the broken spear. Nath's spear. She saw him demonstrating the defensive stances of spear-fighting, saw him laughing with his head thrown back and his long red hair spilling in the snow. She wanted to go to Nath; she wanted to run into his arms and stay with him always. But she strode deeper into the forest.

As her sister had said, she could not marry. It was evil not to marry, not to have children, when she was the only surviving child of her family, but it would be a greater evil to give birth to monsters. Allysa could not risk it. And she could not return home. The moon-change would come upon her as suddenly as it did upon every girl, and if she shared her sister's affliction, she would shape-change and kill before she realized what had happened. Gentle Leis, who could not even kill a rat she found in the grain-bin, had killed many people, her own neighbors and friends. Allysa liked to hunt; she would never be able to stop herself from killing if she became what her sister had been. She would live alone in the forest, far from the village. She would not risk killing her family and friends. She could never see them again.

She could never see Nath again.

THE GIFT
by Rochelle Marie

Rochelle Uhlenkott writes that she'd like to say she can remember writing since she was old enough to pick up a pencil, but she can't. She's always wanted to try writing but never had the courage till she became a "Displaced Aerospace Worker." She has a Master's degree in Particle Physics and figured if she could write a Master's Thesis, she could write anything. Judging by this story, she was right; but she'd be surprised by the people with Ph.Ds who can't—or the 8th graders who can! Formal education, I'm learning every day, has nothing whatever with the ability to tell a good story—and that's all you really need; that and the skill to write a literate English sentence.

But then you'd probably be surprised how many people with a Ph.D. can't do that, either. I know I was.

A magical gift of great importance, the old tattered peddler had said. No one should be without one. Just hold it in your hand and wish upon it. Its uses were infinite. All the way from Doria it came. Forged in the depths of the fiery mountains of Valkyr. Blessed by Nissa, goddess of the sea, and Valierus, god of fire. Meant for protection. A powerful gift it surely must be. But when Lida unwrapped the small parcel, all she found was a tiny, water-worn, white-speckled pebble. River rock. What kind of gift was a rock? What good could river rock be? How

297

could this bit of stone protect her? It was too small for throwing from a sling. It wasn't even good for skipping.

She contemplated tossing it, then did. It was childish to believe that wishing on a rock could keep her safe. Besides there hadn't been any trouble in this secluded part of Teres in over a century. She continued down the path she had been walking, coming upon the stone and kicking it in front of her as she went. It landed in the center of a ring of wild flowers. She stopped to smell the flowers then continued into the ring to kick the stone again. The stone flew out of the ring, and she followed. Or attempted to. As she tried to step over the other side of the ring, she hit an invisible wall. Moving around the ring she tried to find another way out but the unseen barrier was everywhere. A fairy ring. Panic. People died in traps set with fairy rings. The walls were beginning to collapse, she could feel them pressing in on her. Quickly she reached into her pocket, desperately searching for the old peddler's gift. She realized too late her mistake as she saw it lying only a few feet away on the path, out of reach. The walls collapsed further. She couldn't breathe.

The old peddler came by in his wagon, nodded to her, and turned away. He stopped to pick up the rock, shook his head and looked sadly back at the suffocating girl. Then he went on his way.

"A magical gift of great importance," the old tattered peddler said. "No one should be without one. Just hold it in your hand and wish upon it. Its uses are infinite. All the way from Doria it comes. Forged in the depths of the fiery mountains of Valkyr. Blessed by Nissa, goddess of the sea, and Valierus, god of fire. Meant for protection. A powerful gift it surely must be." He handed it to the girl Tila. Happily, Tila unwrapped the small parcel—no one had ever given her a gift before. All she found was a tiny, water-worn, white-speckled pebble, but she thanked the peddler anyway. Carefully, she stowed the treasured bit of river rock in the only pocket she had without a hole. It mattered little to her if the gift was worthless, it was still a gift and meant to be cherished.

She made her way home down the path to the bridge. This time of year the river was swollen and fast. The rains had come late, the ground was still weak with the dampness. She was in the middle, hand in her pocket caressing the stone, when the bridge gave way, separating from the banks and plunging into the freezing rapids below. She struggled, trying wildly to reach the bank, but she couldn't swim. The pebble still tightly clutched in her hand, she took the old peddler's advice and wished as hard as she could for the protection she needed. Something grabbed her from behind just as she was about to go under, pulling her out of the waters and dragging her up onto the bank. She looked around, water streaming from her hair into her eyes, and saw no one to thank. Smiling to herself, she put the treasured pebble back in her pocket and went about wringing out her clothes.

The peddler came by in his wagon and nodded a greeting. He winked and smiled at her, then went on his way.

THE CRYSTAL CASKET
by Kristine Sprunger

Kristine is 22 and lives with her parents, a younger sister, and one cat. She is currently working on four novels—she wants to support herself by writing someday. She usually works at night so as not to be disturbed by the phone or the cat.

She says that she "bounced off the ceiling a few times after I read the acceptance letter—and picked up my sister and mother and swung them around. I think I scared the cat, too." Some people definitely have enthusiastic reactions to my acceptance letters.

She wants to dedicate this story to "mom and dad, who have always supported me; Susan for being a better friend than I deserve; for Jeffy, for being there—always; my friendly "editors"; and Jimmy—you know why."

It had been autumn when the woman had found the crystal casket. The woman had become enchanted by the man who was sleeping in the casket. She had talked with the tiny guardians of the man in the casket and asked politely if it was allowed for her to kiss him just once—she found him *that* attractive.

The tiny guardians had told her that they wouldn't stop her from kissing the man, but they advised her against it because, they said, she was very polite to them. The little guardians liked polite people. But she didn't heed their advice and kissed the handsome man anyway.

It was spring when a young man came walking through the forest, following a stream. He saw the gleaming of the casket in the sun. The man went up to investigate.

He decided the woman he saw was beautiful, and he wanted to touch her ginger-colored hair. But she also looked fairly dead.

The tiny guardians came along just then and found the young man there. "She's not dead, just sleeping very heavily."

"Wake her up. She's beautiful and I'd like to meet her."

"Can't. We don't have that power."

"Then I'll go ..." He looked down at the pretty woman, wanting even more what he couldn't have. "Is there anyone I could ask who *does* have the ability to wake her up?"

"No," one of the nymphs said.

"Could I kiss her just once, then?"

The nymphs looked at each other and smiled. With looks alone, they came to a mutual agreement that it would be ... interesting ... for the man. "Go ahead."

The young man smiled triumphantly at them and lifted the lid. He bent down and kissed her lower lip gently.

The nymphs were giggling behind him, and he turned to ask them why, when arms reached up from the casket and pulled him in. "Thank you," the woman (who had been there since the previous autumn) whispered in his ear. She then rolled out and away from him, jumped to her feet, and slammed the lid down. "And thank you again. I really didn't want to spend another minute in there. Now I can go on about my business." The woman looked down at the man and sighed, "Pity he has to stay here, he *is* handsome." She looked down at the nymphs, her guardians while she slept, "Thank you. I am glad you stayed. Will any of you come with me? I'd like your company."

"No," one of the wood nymphs said, "but we would be glad if you would come back to visit someday. *You* we like. That's why your time in the casket was so short. Most stay in it for years. Snow White did. But dwarves were guarding it then." The nympth rolled her eyes. "They have no concept of time." They giggled some more. Nymphs were quite silly.

"Perhaps." The woman looked down at the man sleeping in the casket, "What of him?"

"We won't hinder anyone from coming to his aid." She

smiled slyly. "But we won't help anyone either, like we did for you."

The woman laughed, deep belly laughs. "Thank you, and fare thee well, my friends and keepers." *At least I didn't have to deal with winter ... sleeping through winter isn't all that bad ... I don't like winter....* The woman strolled down the hill the way the man had come, never looking back.

RINGED IN
by Mildred Perkins

And now we come to the end; by tradition in these volumes, it's something very short and funny. I can't say too much about this, or the preface will be longer than the story.

Mildred says her two cats are delighted that summer's now fully in bloom, so they can roll in the dirt and get filthy and rip down lots of string. I know all about it—I have a dog like that. Signy regards coming back from the grooming parlor as her clue to roll in the dirtiest part of the garden—substituting the smell of cat dirt for that of soap. It's dog nature—why be cross?

This story isn't so much funny ha-ha as strange. So much the better—most people who think they're being funny, aren't.

And that's that for another year!

Something drew Maggie's eyes to the woman across the table. The woman seemed normal enough for this run-down, slimy excuse for a pub. She wore a loose, dark robe belted around the middle to support a short-sword scabbard. Another belt ran from right shoulder to waist, which caused her ample bosom to stand out in what would otherwise have been a bulky outfit. A hood covered her face and hair, leaving only a slender hand to be seen loosely holding a mug of ale. The hand was tanned and smooth, with short fingernails roughly trimmed and edged

303

with dark soil. A silver ring bound her index finger tightly, seeming to be sunken into the flesh. Fanciful flowers were carved into the thick metal band and, looking closer still, Maggie could see snakes and foul beasts peering out from behind the still and shining foliage. Looming over all was a dome of deep red, nearly black. It was garnet, but not garnet, for she found she could look inside. Calmness reigned, of an evil, brooding sort. Floating on nothing was an enormous throne of ebony and sitting on the throne was the woman! She was dressed the same as before, but was now large and imposing and as Maggie looked closer, seemed to finally notice her. Standing, growing ever taller and darker, the woman stood on the nothingness which supported the throne and spread wide her robed arms. Light dimmed and the world became the emptiness covered by the woman's growing shadow. Maggie felt herself falling, falling . . .

Her head thumped hard on the sticky floor of the pub. A moment later she was doused in a cascade of warm blood and she rolled away, gasping and gagging.

Someone took her arm and hauled her roughly to her feet. Someone else handed her a rag to wipe her face.

A crowd had gathered near the booth where she and the woman had been sitting and where now a headless corpse sprawled across the table. People made way for the palace guard, who left the body and walked over to Maggie, still cleaning her blade.

"What possessed you to sit at a table with a sorceress, girl," asked the guard.

Maggie thought for a moment, then shrugged weakly without answering. She went to the booth for her coat and as she bent over, grasped the ring which still tightly circled the woman's finger. It came to her easily and warmed quickly. This would bear looking into.